PENGUIN BOOKS

THE FANCY

Monica Dickens, great-granddaughter of Charles Dickens, has written over thirty novels, autobiographical books and children's books, and her works are beginning to be adapted for television and film. Her first book, *One Pair of Hands*, which arose out of her experiences as a cook-general – the only work for which her upper-class education had fitted her – made her a best seller at twenty-two, and is still in great demand.

Although her books arise out of the varied experiences of her life, she has not taken jobs in order to write about them: working in an aircraft factory and a hospital was her war work, not research. When she joined the Samaritans, it was the work of befriending distressed fellow human beings which she found compelling, although her novel *The Listeners* came from that experience.

She set up the first American branch of the Samaritans in Boston, Massachusetts, and lives nearby on Cape Cod with her husband Commander Roy Stratton, retired from the U.S. Navy, and her horses, cats and dogs. She has two daughters.

D1324307

MONICA DICKENS

THE FANCY

PENGUIN BOOKS

in association with Michael Joseph

Penguin Books Ltd, Harmondsworth, Middlesex, England
Penguin Books, 625 Madison Avenue, New York, New York 10022, U.S.A.
Penguin Books Australia Ltd, Ringwood, Victoria, Australia
Penguin Books Canada Ltd, 2801 John Street, Markham, Ontario, Canada L3R 1B4
Penguin Books (N.Z.) Ltd, 182–190 Wairau Road, Auckland 10, New Zealand

—

First published by Michael Joseph in 1943
Published in Penguin Books 1964
Reprinted 1966, 1978, 1982

—

—

Set, printed and bound in Great Britain by
Cox & Wyman Ltd, Reading
Set in Monotype Times

CHAPTER 1

His name was Edward Ledward and he was going home to his tea. He was spare and sandy, with the bony, burning look that makes people rap their chests and say: 'T.B., poor chap,' but it was nothing like that. He simply happened to have deeply sunk eyes and jutting cheekbones, and he had never had enough fresh air.

He walked briskly, but not because he was looking forward to getting home – or to his tea. Today was Thursday and Connie's family would be there playing cards. Connie's mother, Mrs Munroe, never fancied food until after the Nine o'clock News and you couldn't expect Connie to interrupt the game before that to get Edward's tea. Equally, a man who had been working since half-past seven could not be expected to wait until nine o'clock, so Edward foraged for himself on Thursdays, and ate either in the narrow, untidy kitchen or with his legs cramped under the little bamboo table in the living-room window.

He always walked home from the factory, conscientiously breathing through his nose and expanding his narrow chest to make up for having been indoors all day. All through the winter, while other people queued for steamy buses, Edward walked, in a heavy, waistless Burberry with his old football club scarf wound twice round his neck and crossed into his waistcoat.

It was mild tonight though, a late September evening, with gold on the flat spreading clouds and the air only just cool enough to feel. The road that ran through the Factory Estate was a stream of hurrying people, mostly Edward's crowd, but diluted every fifty yards or so by tributaries from the factories on either side. Canning Kyles, which serviced aero engines, was the only big factory of the Estate; the others were hardly more than glorified sheds that made ignition parts and unobtrusive bakelite fittings.

Edward with his brisk step weaved his way among groups and dawdlers, glancing at headlines on the paper of anyone who hadn't turned it over to see the greyhound results.

The concrete Estate road emerged between high wire fencing on to the main road, which used to go to Oxford and Bath and

Bristol, and now went, even more romantically, just 'To the WEST.' There were queues already at the trolley-bus stops. Most people turned right to the station, but Edward went straight on, crossing at his own particular spot where there was a foot-shaped dent in the kerb. He wondered idly about the people in cars. How did they get the petrol, he'd like to know? They couldn't all be doctors or Key Personnel. Not that he grudged it them, because he hadn't got a car, anyway, but he was interested in how other people managed their lives and what it felt like to be astute.

''Night, Wilf!' he called, as a creaking bicycle passed him half-way up the opposite side road. Old Wilf was always one of the last out because he took such a time putting away his things, haunted by the fear that the Night Shift would pinch his magnifying glass. Old Wilf's legs, spindling in bicycle clips, pedalled earnestly into the sunset, his mulberry beret butting him up the slight hill.

Edward had about twenty minutes' walk before he turned into his own road, Church Avenue, where the Lipmann's grocery stood slantwise across the corner. The blackout was up but the door was still open. David Lipmann's bicycle was lying on the edge of the pavement with its wheels spinning. Edward picked up the bicycle, propped it against the kerb and went into the shop. He was canny now about Thursdays, having foraged unsuccessfully too often in Connie's larder.

For no particular reason, there had always been a Jewish colony in the little streets that ran in and out of the legs of the railway viaduct, and since the War there were stranger accents and even wilder children. Next to the Synagogue, the Lipmann's shop was the focal point, a refugees' haven in this land of plain food and drab colours. There were usually one or two chatting on the bench under the spiced sausages, or leaning lovingly on a crate of Matzos, arguing with Ruth and Mrs Lipmann over the heads of customers. On Mr Lipmann's baking day, when he and David worked miracles underground with wartime supplies, there was always a crowd sublimating their nostalgia in the smells that came up the hatch from the bakehouse. And when the fragrant trays appeared *Apfelstrudel* and *Linzertorte* and plaited loaves sprinkled with poppy seeds – there would be smacking lips and sentimental gasps. Mrs Greening's eyes would

6

fill with tears, because poppy seeds reminded her of when she was a girl. She was there tonight, sitting on a sack of split peas, dry-eyed, because there was nothing left of Monday's abundance but a tray of broken *Honigkücher*. Edward wondered what would happen if anyone wanted split peas, because she looked as though only a crane could move her.

'Hullo, my dear!' called Ruth, over the head of the customer she was serving: a flushed woman with a cavernous shopping bag and stout shoes. 'Shan't keep you a moment.' There were two or three customers waiting, members of the colony, who were peering at the labels on pickle jars and sounding the depths of the *sauerkraut* barrel.

'David!' yelled Ruth over her shoulder.

'Oh, I can't!' came back a bellow from the parlour beyond the shop. No Lipmann ever spoke lower than the top of its voice.

'David! Come out and serve!' Through the half-open door Edward could see David sprawling at the table, supple and insolent in a white shirt and blue belted trousers, a lock of dark hair over his face. The rest of the family spent their energy in cheerfulness; his ran to the prococious passions of Mediterranean adolescence, although he was born and raised in Collis Park, w20. He was a throw-back to Mrs Lipmann's grandmother, who had kept a fruit stall at Palermo.

'I'm working!' he shouted, and Ruth roared with laughter, flashing her big white teeth. 'He – he working!' she called to Mrs Greening on the split-pea sack, and Mrs Greening's eyes disappeared as she laughed, too, shaking like a badly set blancmange.

'Momma and Pop are at the market,' laughed Ruth to the shop in general, and the woman she was serving nodded her sensible hat and said: 'You young things – don't tell me. I've got three kids of my own. Two girls and a boy, all at home, a gastric husband *and* the W.V.S. Wednesdays and Fridays. I always say only our own generation know what work really is.' She glanced round the shop for approval, passing over Edward as being too young to know what work was, but too old to be classed with her kids, but the two women came up out of the *sauerkraut* barrel to nod and smile socially and Mrs Greening became gelatinous again.

'Two pounds of prunes, was it, dear?' said Ruth unperturbed·

'*One* pound. I'm not *made* of points,' said the red-faced woman.

'They don't go far, do they?' said Ruth gaily.

'Far!' She raised her eyes to heaven. 'You ought to have my family. Talk about terrors for figs!' She settled in to tell them how she managed. Edward leaned over the barrier of biscuit tins and cereal packets that made the backcloth of the window display and picked himself out a long crusty loaf. 'May I?' He waved it in the air.

'Threepence-halfpenny,' called Ruth. 'No – not your prunes, dear, they're eightpence. Have you got a bag?'

'I'm sorry,' said the flushed woman, not looking it.

'Well, I'll let you have one this once, but please bring it back next time you're this way. We're wickedly short.'

'But of course,' said the other, although as the prunes were no bigger at the price than in her own district, she did not expect to be this way again. She combed a wide range of food shops; that was why her shoes were so stout.

With the bread, Edward bought a short length of garlic sausage and some pickled cucumber. 'I've got something for you,' whispered Ruth, leaning close to him over the counter, so that he could see the marks where she had plucked her strong eyebrows. She smelt very feminine.

'It's ever so kind of you,' said Edward as she smuggled a sack from behind the oatmeal barrel. 'Look,' she opened it a little under cover of the counter, 'not only outside leaves – there's some hearts in there. And – ssh! a bit of bran at the bottom. How are the darling rabbits?'

'Fine, thanks. Queenie, er – she should be any day now.'

'Ah, bless her,' said Ruth. 'I hope they'll all be champions.'

'They will be. Thanks awfully.' Edward tucked the sack under his arm and went out. The flushed woman was outside, reading the advertisements in the glass case. You never knew what you might not pick up these days. She shot a glance at Edward's sack. Black Market of course. All these Jew shops were in it.

The houses in Church Avenue were of brown gravel stucco, with slate roofs and a bow window to left or right of the peaked porch. They all had a little square of front garden and the same low wall, mostly topped by privet. A stretch of wall, two gaps together where gates had been and another stretch of wall, all down the road.

Edward turned up the black-and-white-tiled path running alongside the Dowlinson's, which was identical in pattern but broken and weed-grown. They had taken away the railings in between for salvage and Connie had made him put up some posts and wire netting. Old Mrs Dowlinson had watched him round the curtain while he was doing it, which was very embarrassing. It seemed unnecessary anyway, because the old couple never went out, living apparently on bread and milk and the *News of the World*, because nothing else was ever delivered. Connie said it was a waste of their ration cards.

The hall of Edward's house was narrow and lit only by a dim blue light, as the curtain over the coloured glass of the front door was thin. There was a coat rack with a tin base and a rail for umbrellas and a mirror with a clothes brush hanging below and a hook where Bob's lead had hung when they had a dog. All round the wall and up the stairs ran a green embossed dado which you could dent with your thumbnail.

Connie and her family were in the living-room. The sound of their voices made Edward feel suddenly tired. He wondered what it would be like to have enough vitality to breeze in and greet them heartily instead of having to screw himself up to go in and be polite at all. He went up to the bathroom first and, while he was washing, tried to settle the question he had been debating all day. Should he or should he not tell them about his new job? He might throw it out casually: 'Oh, by the way, I'm being switched from the Fitting Shop to the Inspection Shop tomorrow; charge hand on one of the girls' benches. Make a change anyway.' Or he might start straight in with: 'Got a rise in the world. Thirty bob a week more in the Inspection Shop', or he might say something funny, like: 'Hullo, Mrs Charge Hand!' to Connie, or 'Charge Hand to you!' when Don greeted him: 'Hiya, Ted?'

In any case, they would talk about it all evening and question him, although he knew hardly anything about the job himself yet. He could hear them already: 'What a cheek – taking you out of the Fitting Shop just when Mr Arnold was going and you might have got his job!' 'Female labour, eh? You're in for

9

some trouble there, my boy.' 'You're in charge of ten girls? Boy, what a break!' 'Don't be silly, Don. He daren't speak to one girl, let alone ten.'

Perhaps he should wait to tell Connie until they were alone. But then she would say: 'Why ever didn't you say so when Mum and the rest of them were here? Aren't you funny? Now I'll have to go round to the buildings tomorrow and tell them. They'll wonder why you didn't say. You *are* queer!'

He dried his hands carefully, pushing down the cuticles of his nails. After all, it was a rise, and it would be gratifying to be able to surprise them with something interesting for once; to be able to answer Mr Munroe's: 'How's the factory, boy?' with something more than: 'Oh, mustn't grumble.' Yes, he would tell them. They'd got to know sometime, anyway.

He left his sack in the kitchen before he opened the living-room door. There they all were, with the green baize cloth on the table. Connie, her father in his thick pepper-and-salt suit, Mrs Munroe with her salt cellars conspicuous in the V neck of the jigsaw patterned dress she had had for Dorothy's wedding, Dorothy herself, in the same condition as Queenie, but frog-like and coarsened where Queenie was soft and limpid-eyed, and Dorothy's husband, Don Derris, who used to be in Wireless, but was now in charge of a barrage balloon, conveniently near home.

'Hullo all,' said Edward casually.

Mr Munroe raised his empty, pear-shaped face. 'Ah,' he began in his quoting voice, 'the return of the wanderer. Well, my son, and how's –'

'You're late, Ted,' said Connie, playing a card briskly. Her mother clapped another on top of it. 'Nice to see you, Ted,' she said with her eyes on the game.

'Hiya,' said Don. 'Ace of hearts, my dear old souls. Looks like little Don's going to clean up again.' The wireless was play-ing unheeded in the corner and Edward crossed the room to switch it off before he made the announcement that would make them all look up with their mouths open. He had formed the sentence in his mind.

'I say, everybody. I've got a bit of news for you. I've got a better –' Connie looked up, the lines from her nose to the corners of her mouth deepening. 'Ted, those clothes simply

10

stink of machine oil. It's horrible in a room where people have got to eat.'

'Well, my son,' boomed her father, 'how's the factory?'

Edward snapped on the wireless again. 'Oh,' he said, 'mustn't grumble.'

He ate his tea in the kitchen. There were some potatoes in the Lipmann's sack and he put them on to boil while he ate. 'Ted,' called Connie, as if she knew he were just pouring milk into his cup, 'don't use too much milk. Mother wasn't able to bring any today.'

Oh, she wasn't. What had she brought? Ted took a look into the leather shopping-bag on the dresser. Two tins of salmon – funny things some people spent their points on – a beetroot, cheese in a cold sweat, sugar, a Swiss roll. Mrs Munroe's alkaline powder, and some of Pop's tomatoes. Edward didn't see why he shouldn't have a couple.

He felt quite continental as he broke up the crusty loaf, and holding the sausage in his left hand, sliced pieces on to the bread, which he put into his mouth with the hand that held the knife. That was the way the workmen used to eat in that place in Belgium. Wenduyne, where he and Connie had gone two Augusts running. He could smell now the dry electric smell of the trams that whined by the café where he used to have his Bock and Connie her *gateaux*. She had had a pink dress the first year they went and a big hat with a dip in front. That was when she still had ins and outs. She was fat now, but somehow the curves and hollows had levelled themselves out.

As he ate, his eyes devoured the paper propped against the teapot. It had been in his pocket all day, folded very small, so that he could snatch a few square inches of it whenever he got the chance. In the canteen, he had taken his plate over to a far table where there were two men he didn't know, but just as he was settling down to a good read, Mike had come along and spent the whole lunch-hour discussing the possibilities of super-charging his motor-cycle. Then again at tea-time, when he took his mug behind a cleaning tank, he had been hunted down for an argument about Mod. 317 by the foreman, who had already had his tea in peace in his office.

There was a lot to be said for Thursday. Even if it did bring his family-in-law it also brought *Backyard Breeding, the Weekly Journal for Fanciers.* Whether your fancy were rabbits, cats, chickens, guinea pigs or chocolate-coloured mice, *Backyard Breeding* was your Bible, and probably your chief medium for buying and selling. The four middle pages were devoted to rabbits and a section of this to Edward's own breed, the Flemish Giant. 'Flemish Footnotes' was compiled by a genius called 'Giganta', better-known to the Fancy as Allan Colley, the well-known judge, who knew every known thing about Flemishes and a few things that no one else knew. Edward thought that if he could ever meet Allan Colley his life would be fulfilled.

He was so absorbed on 'Let Selective Breeding be Your Motto', that his mouth was often open for seconds at a time with the bread and sausage poised in front of it. Then he read the Show Reports and Club News; he and Dick Bennet from the Final Assembly Shop thought of starting a Domestic Club in Collis Park. Finishing the pickled cucumber by itself, he had an idea. He would put a notice up about it in the Lipmann's glass case.

The cucumber was very salty and he got up to fill the teapot with hot water. The potatoes would be done by the time he'd had his second cup. He had already looked at the Readers' Letters: 'The Fancy's Forum', in case they had put in his note about Snuffles. One day they might print something of his. He would write another letter next week about damp-proof hutches. That advertisement was still in, for the dark steel doe he wanted: 'In kindle, square as a brick. Inspection a pleasure to Flemishites. No obligation.' Shocking price they wanted, but now that he had got this new job, perhaps he might.

He lit a cigarette and put his tea-things in the sink, then taking the Lipmann's sack and the potatoes in a bowl, he went out into the cooling evening.

Most people who lived in Church Avenue grew vegetables in the rectangle of back garden that ran down to 'the Ponds', the flooded gravel pits where children played in daily peril of drowning. But in the Ledward's back garden there was no room for vegetables. All round the fence stood an uneven collection of dwellings, hardly any of which had started life as hutches. Edward had made them out of packing-cases and odd bits of wood and wire netting. Queenie rested tired but confident in one of the hencoops given to Edward by the Time Clerk at the factory when all his chickens had died of Coccidiosis and he had neither the heart nor the capital to start again. On the crowded earth in the middle of the garden, two families of adolescents crowded and bounced in low wire netting runs. Edward was going to sell the eldest family next week. He had had a very good offer through *Backyard Breeding*. Now that the rabbits were beginning to pay, Connie didn't talk so much about the price of vegetables in the shops, nor about 'that ignorant Dick Bennet' who had originally roused Edward's enthusiasm and had given him his first doe.

Humming tunelessly, Edward went down the hutches. When they saw him coming all the rabbits except Queenie stood on their hind legs with their soft pale bellies against the wire. The adolescent families kicked and plunged and piled themselves up at the end of the runs. Edward felt like a God; his sack was Cornucopia. Putting the potatoes down to cool, he went from hutch to hutch, squatting down for a word with each rabbit as he pushed the cabbage through the wire. When he was a boy, he had read a book about a man who discovered how to speak the language of animals, and for years it was his dream that this would happen to him. He would growl at strange dogs and make snuffling and whinnying noises at horses in the street when no one was looking, in the hope of hitting on the secret. Half ashamed of his childishness, he still toyed occasionally with the fancy. He twitched his high-boned prominent nose at a large buck rabbit who twitched back at him, chewing sideways and staring out of hazel eyes. Sometimes in the evening when he was feeling particularly happy, Edward might have gone down on all fours to kick and whiffle and pretend he was a rabbit, but for the fear that Connie would look out of the window and think he had gone mad.

'Wonder if she has her fancies,' he said to the buck. 'When she's alone, does she pretend to be somebody else? I wonder if everybody does. Perhaps we should all think we were mad if we could see each other when we were alone. But then of course, we shouldn't be alone, should we?' He laughed and went on down the hutches. He had a long session with Queenie. Incredible to think of what was going on inside her.

He lifted the roof of the hutch and put in his hand to see if he could feel anything. 'Quickening' he believed the expression was. He had once heard Dorothy and Mrs Munroe and Connie talking about it in hissing whispers upstairs. Queenie immediately pressed herself into a corner of the cage.

'All right, my dear,' said Edward, shutting up the hutch, 'I wouldn't hurt you for the world. *Couche-toi, couche-toi.*' He often spoke bits of French to the rabbits, as they were Belgian. Connie had caught him once saying '*Comment ça va?*' to an ailing buck. Well, perhaps he was mad. He'd be talking to himself next like the old girl who zig-zagged down Church Avenue in a thick black veil and a purple cloak.

He gave all the rabbits a spoonful of potato. Yes, he would definitely get that doe in kindle. Have to think about getting some new hutches too. He was only in a small way now, but one day he was going to do big things. He might even become well known, like Allan Colley. It was almost dark by the time he was at the last hutch. Why should the little grey doe in there make him think suddenly of the factory and his new job tomorrow? He peered in at her, dealing delicately with her potato. How odd; she reminded him of the little fair girl he had noticed when the foreman was pointing out the bench he would be in charge of tomorrow. He hadn't noticed much about the girls, perching in their grey overalls round the tableful of metal, except that there seemed a terrifying lot of them. Time enough to take stock of them tomorrow, when he had to meet them. He had deliberately been trying not to think about tomorrow in case he should start thinking up unnatural, jocular remarks. Dinah would be nice to him, though; he knew her. He had seen her this afternoon looking tousled, and he had seen this other girl. It was tea-time and she was taking little nibblets out of an enormous bun, just like the little grey doe was doing with the potato.

The kitchen doorway suddenly flung an oblong of light on to the garden, 'Edward!' called Connie. 'It's blackout time. Are you coming in to do it? I've half killed myself trying to get the shutter up in here.'

'You shouldn't try, dear,' said Edward, going indoors. 'You know I always do it.'

'The doctor's dared me to lift weights,' said Connie, while

Edward fitted the wooden shutter into the glass of the door, still happy from his rabbits.

Connie had her back to him, bending over the sink to fill the kettle. She was wearing a blue skirt and a belted tunic blouse that made her waist look quite small. Edward was suddenly moved to put his arms round her from behind and squeeze her. He turned her round and kissed her, while she held the kettle awkwardly between them.

'Ted, for Heaven's sake – you're getting me all wet. What's the matter with you? Let me go, I want to turn the tap off. Oh *don't*, Ted, you're horrible.'

'Connie,' began Edward, and she saw what was coming and slid her eyes away.

'Now, Ted, you know what the doctor said after my illness.'

'But, Connie, that was months ago. It must be all right now.'

'D'you want to make me ill again?'

'Why don't you go to the doctor again and find out if it's all right?'

'I've been,' she said after a pause, turning away. He knew she was lying but he didn't challenge her. No use laying yourself open to any more humiliation. Just as well Connie had had that illness really. She had felt like this about him before that, but now they could keep the pretence of the doctor between them, for decency's sake.

Connie patted her hair. 'I'm going to put the kettle on. We're going to have one more game before the News. You going to play?'

'Might as well,' said Edward. 'I'll go and change.'

The living-room looked pleasant with the curtains drawn and the centre light on it. It was three lamps hanging from a circular wooden bracket, which in the days when lorries had gone down Church Avenue, used sometimes to revolve slowly, making the shadows travel. Pretty the way it shone on Dorothy's fair hair. She did it drawn up at the sides into curls on top, and low at the back in a silky fold. Connie's hair had only just been permed and was set in tight little curls under an invisible hair-net. Smart, but it made her face look too big, because she had had it cut, to give the perm longer to grow out. Edward preferred it when it was growing out and she could brush it at night without fear of losing the set.

Mrs Munroe's hair under the light reminded Edward of the blue-black oil that covered the engines at Kyles before they were cleaned. It was drawn down from the middle into two immense coils over each ear, studded insecurely with hairpins, with a few wisps escaping horizontally from the centre.

Mr Munroe hadn't got any hair; his head was like a billiards ball in the light – Spot, because there was a mole on it. No, he had got one hair; it grew out of the mole. Don's hair was dark red and followed backward the sloping line of his forehead.

Edward passed a hand over his own head. Funny soft stuff. It wasn't really thinning; it was just very fine hair. Connie had once said in a moment of vision that it was like the pile on her camel-hair coat.

'Your turn to play, Ted,' she said, spreading her cards into a fan and shutting them up secretively. 'For Heaven's sake, I never knew anybody take so long to decide, did you, Pop?'

'When I used to play at the Conservative Club,' began her father laying down his cards and preparing to tell a story, 'there was a chap by the name of Bayliss, who –'

'He's a dark horse is our Ted,' said Don, through a waggling cigarette, 'these slow starters always get your money in the end.'

'This chap Bayliss, I remember, always used to count twenty-five before he played a card. I wasn't a bad player in those days; used to go up there nearly every night, as your mother will tell you. Whist mostly – that was my game. I remember I asked this chap –'

'Oh, shut *up*, Pop,' said Dorothy, 'I can't hear myself think.' She played a card, took it back again, fidgeted and played another. Her father leaned across the table to Edward. 'So I asked him: "Are you aware," I said, "that out of every game, you waste, on an average, four minutes and ten seconds?" – I'd done a quick calculation in my head. "Multiply that by –"'

'It's your turn to play, Pop,' screamed Connie and Dorothy, 'do attend to the game!'

At ten to nine, Mrs Munroe began to say: 'Mustn't miss the News.' At five to, she said it again, and: 'Nearly News time, hadn't we better turn it on in case your clock's slow?' She suspected all clocks, even Big Ben.

Connie looked sharply at the green glass clock whose works

were reflected in the oval mirror that hung forward over the mantelpiece. 'That clock never loses.'

'What about the News?' said her father, looking up from his cards, with the air of one making an original suggestion.

'Might hear something about a big Bomber raid one of these days,' said Don confidentially.

'Let's finish the game then, for Heaven's sake, if we've got to hear it,' said Connie. 'It's your turn, Mum.'

'Well, turn it on, Ted. It always takes such a time to warm up. Oh, Dorothy, you're never going Rummy already? I might have known it; the only time I get a decent hand, someone else gets a better. I said to myself when I saw the cards Connie dealt me, there's a snag somewhere, I said.'

Mrs Munroe had been disappointed so often in life that she never expected anything else. Ill luck had dogged her. She had married a pleasant spoken man who looked like one day becoming manager of the Soft Furnishings at Hennessy's. He had turned out to be an unpleasing bore, who watched upstart after upstart climb through Soft Furnishings above him until he retired with a limited pension and the conviction that he had earned his right to be about the house all day. Mrs Munroe had wanted sons, and both her children had been daughters, and straight-haired at that. Connie, too, had inherited her grandmother's legs. Small wonder that Mrs Munroe, who had set her heart on marrying her to Fred Emery had been landed with a son-in-law like Edward. She had cried all through the wedding, even through the Breakfast, which was at the Crown, with wine and little sandwiches stuck with flags. A streak of pump water, she had thought when she first met Edward, and she still thought so.

She knew by now that no story that she ever read would live up to the promise of its opening, and that if she ever went to the theatre, there would be a slip in the programme to say that an understudy was replacing the star she had come to see. Everything she ordered in restaurants was 'off', shops sold out at her approach and she had only to step on a bus for it to be going to its garage – 'Next stop only.' As for her digestion, well it was no good hoping that what she sent down wouldn't turn to bile; she knew it would as soon as she saw it on her plate.

17

Big Ben boomed through the booming of Mr Munroe on Bayliss. Connie shut him up. 'We might as well listen if we are going to hear it. There might be something about rations.' Don shuffled the cards like a conjurer and flicked them round the table, while they listened to the Summary. A bombing raid on Germany was announced, so colossal that even Mrs Munroe was impressed.

'There you are,' said Don, with an air of showmanship, 'what did I tell you?'

'However did you know?' asked Dorothy, pop-eyed.

'. . . and other operations, fifty-three of our aircraft are missing,' concluded the wireless respectfully.

'Ah, I thought so.' Mrs Munroe's face would have lifted if the flexor muscles hadn't permanently atrophied. 'We shan't have any planes left if they go on like this.'

'How many d'you think we've got?' said Don. 'Funny thing about that raid, though. It seems that – but no, I'd better not tell you as they haven't announced it.'

'Oh, Don, do,' said Dorothy, and her mother said: 'They ought to tell us everything. It's not right.' Her voice had a moaning monotony. 'Hear about the National Day of Prayer, Connie? We might go to church. Dorothy and I went last year. They had two collections.'

'They make me sick,' said Connie, getting up to go to the kitchen. 'First they make the war and then they try and make us pray for it.'

'What was the News?' asked Mr Munroe, who had been out of the room washing his hands.

'Oh nothing, Pop; you wouldn't be interested.'

'I remember when wireless was first invented,' he began telling Edward.

'Oh get up. Pop, do,' said Dorothy. 'I'm trying to lay the table.' He stood in front of the sideboard to tell Edward about crystal sets, but Dorothy wanted to get at the silver drawer.

Edward sat with the paper, watching them eat an enormous meal with the distaste of one who has already eaten. Mrs Munroe brought food for Connie, but it was always understood that Edward had his own tea beforehand. He sometimes wondered if that was why she chose to eat so late, so that there should be no danger of having to provide for him. They ate a lot and took a long time over it. Connie ate slowly, picking and pushing at the food on her plate, while she chewed with her front teeth, because her back ones were unreliable. Mrs Munroe ate absorbedly, with her eyes on what she was going to eat next. Don ate with his mouth open, and Dorothy ate greedily, snatching at the food with sharp bites, her eyes bright. Mr Munroe slopped his tea into the saucer, crumbled his bread and shed tomato skins off the side of his plate on to the table. At intervals, he would put down his knife and fork, wipe his mouth, clear his throat and begin to talk, until someone jogged him and told him to get on with it, everybody else was on cheese.

Edward folded the paper, flung it on the floor and said suddenly: 'I've got a new job.'

'Whatever do you mean?' Connie stared at him, her jaws working automatically. 'You've never left Canning Kyles?'

'No, but I've been switched from the Fitting Shop into the Inspection Shop – means a bit more pay.'

'Ah,' said Mrs Munroe, helping herself to pickles and inspecting the label balefully as if she knew what they were going to do to her, 'but you can never trust 'em once they start to switch you. First it's from one shop into another. All right. Then they switch you again and once they get you on the move, they'll switch you right out before you know it. I'm not going to buy this grade two salmon again, Connie. It's not worth the points.'

'No, but this is a step up,' said Edward patiently. 'I'm to be charge hand, with a bench of ten girls under me.'

'Ten girls under you,' said Don, forgetting himself. 'Boy, oh boy, what a bedful.' Connie drew herself up with thin lips and Mrs Munroe rapped the table with the handle of a laden fork, so that a bit of beetroot fell on to the tablecloth. Connie dipped her napkin in water to rub at the stain.

'Sorry,' said Don unabashed, 'but what a break, eh?'

'Don't be silly, Don. He daren't speak to one girl, let alone ten.'

CHAPTER 2

SHEILA rolled over with her eyes shut and slapped down the alarm clock. It fell on to the floor and started to ring again. She was half out of bed by the time she had quelled it, so she let herself fall the rest of the way, and sat on the white woolly rug rubbing her eyes. The vaseline on her eyelids had made them sticky. She was very pretty, in a surprised *retroussée* way. Her mouth was always slightly open, and when she smiled, her lower lip caught under her top teeth and a dimple appeared. She smiled now, and prodded the dimple; it was one of her exercises.

If anyone had told me three years ago, she thought, that I'd be getting up at six every morning, I'd have knocked them down. And not only getting up at six, but not really minding it. To think of all the mornings I used to breakfast in bed at eleven o'clock after a party, feeling so glamorous, but really such a mess. Much too fat and my powder too white and my hair too tightly permed.

She got up, and pulling off her hair-net, lifted her hair away from her head and shook it out. On the way to the bathroom she looked in the mirror, earnestly, with parted lips. A bit puffy. If one were married, one would have to wake first and do one's face.

Beyond the bathroom window, dawn was just investigating the well of the flats; tradesmen's lifts, zig-zagging iron stair-cases, frosted windows, tall chromium taps and a tin of Vim or a milk bottle on kitchen window-sills, bedroom windows with the curtains drawn. She closed the window, shivering in her nightdress. Oh God, the winter! The gardener down at Swinley had said it would be a hard one because the berries were so thick. A morning like this made you think of the in-evitable weeks ahead when a gearwheel was an aching block of ice, when you couldn't think about inspecting, or about anything except how cold you were, and when you *knew* that whatever they said, no one else was as cold as you.

Going barefoot into the compact little kitchen, she put her coffee to heat on the electric stove and padded back into the bedroom. All her life she had wanted a flat with a fitted carpet.

All the years at Swinley, in the draughty, polished house where even breakfast was announced by a gong, she had wanted a place where you could walk in and out of rooms naked if you wanted to, where you could have a bath at midday or midnight and eat when you were hungry instead of when the servants expected you to be.

And now she had got it, thanks to Kathleen being evacuated with her office and letting Sheila have the flat at a rent which was more than covered by her wages at Canning Kyles. Thanks to the war, really. It was agony of course, but without it, she would never have got away from home, unless she had married Timothy, and Sheila had always thought she was destined for higher things than that.

The worst thing about getting up early was that you never knew what to wear. Clothes that seemed suitable at six in the morning were all wrong by six at night. She put on a jersey and a pair of linen dungarees. They were old, but they had faded to a blue that was attractive with her red jacket. She had her coffee and cereal while she was doing her face. Her hair took longer now that she was doing it this new way. She had meant to make her bed properly this morning, turning the mattress and everything, but there was no time now. She whipped the clothes on to the floor and threw the pillows into a corner. Sordid when you got in, but it was good for them to air. She was going to do some housework tonight too; she might even scrub the kitchen floor.

She put on the red jacket and changed her make-up and her factory pass from yesterday's handbag to the satchel bag that went with trousers.

Downstairs, the night porter was leaning in the doorway of the flats watching the light seep into the street.

'Hullo,' said Sheila, 'have a cigarette?'

'Thanks,' he said, still leaning as she stood by him in the doorway. 'Parky out. I hope you've got your winter woollies on.' She could feel him admiring her slimness in the blue dungarees. He was dark, with big eyes and a peevish mouth. His uniform was open at the neck and rather crumpled, as if he'd been sleeping in it in his little hutch, but he was not unattractive. He was rather fun. She had asked him up for a cup of coffee once when she got back restless from a party. She oughtn't to

21

have, because he rather fancied her, but he had behaved perfectly. He had told her things about the other occupants of the flats which she would never have believed. He have been very amusing.

'How's the boy-friend?' He asked this every morning.

'There isn't one.' She said this every morning, hoping he didn't believe her.

'Lucky swine,' he said. 'You know what I'd do, if I were your boy-friend?'

'No, what? ' She laughed up at him, daring him. She knew she ought not to encourage him, but it was nice to have a friend in this huge, impersonal building, and he was harmless. She imagined herself confiding in him if she ever did fall in love.

'What would I do?' He regarded her darkly, with his chin on his chest and his hands in his pockets. 'Get along to your work before I tell you. You're too young. 'Op it.'

She could feel him watching her back view all down the street, but when she turned round at the corner, he had gone inside.

Mrs Urry woke that morning with a hangover. That came of being paid Thursday instead of Friday like respectable folk. But that Greek did everything lop-sided. She'd washed up for many queer customers, but the proprietor of the Acropolis Dining Rooms was the fishiest yet. Fifth column, Mrs Urry knew. The things she could tell if she chose!

It wasn't right to go straight to the pub with your pay packet on Friday night; you saw shiftless men doing that, and pitied their wives, but a Thursday – that was different somehow. Her mouth felt like a dustbin. The gin these days was a scandal, but there wasn't much else to do with the money now that she and Urry were living rent free. Funny how little you needed to eat as you got older. She yawned, pushed her hair out of her eyes and stretched up a skinny arm to scratch on the wire above her. He was awake; she had heard him coughing through her doze for the last hour.

'Urry!' she called. 'Wake up. The first train'll be along in a minute.'

The wire above her tautened and sprang as her husband turned over to look down at her over the side of his bunk. He looked like a dirty apostle. It was years since he had shaved, months since he had had a haircut.

⌐ 'Don't feel like going today,' he said, and coughed aban-
donedly, whooping like a child.

'What, and have someone pinch your beat? You turn your
back on Holborn Circus for a minute and half a dozen smarts'll
dig themselves in. There's money in matches.'

'Shut up, Ada,' he said, heaving back into the middle of the
bunk. 'I'm going to have another wink.' He fumbled among his
clothes for his father's steel watch and held it in front of his
eyes. 'We got another five minutes yet, you lying hag.'

She lay still, like an old witch in a coffin, her black button
eyes considering the slight bulge of her husband's behind, which
was embossed in little lozenge shapes where it pressed on the
wire. At the far end of the platform, a woman cleaner was
swabbing with a mop, and behind her head Mrs Urry could hear
someone telephoning behind the glass door in the curved wall.
Otherwise it was quiet. Quiet and warm. A bit different from
the days when every bunk had been full and people had to step
over bodies to reach the trains. But they'd had some fun in the
Blitz. Singing or a mouth organ as often as not, and the canteen
with scalding tea at all hours of the night and that First Aid
post so hospitally smelling you hardly dared go inside for fear
of catching something. They had all gone gradually, the Daltons
and the Berrys and the one they called 'Spikey', who could
whistle like a flute, and those jolly girls who used to sit up and
paint their faces before they went off to their office, and that
funny old card who howled in his sleep, and the kind old fool
with the cake tray. They had all gone away, until only the
Urrys were left. There were no air raids now, but it made no
difference to the Urrys in their sound-proof burrow. The only
difference was that when you went out in the morning you
didn't find half the houses that ought to be standing up lying
all over the road, and have to go miles round to get to work
and that old Greek look at you sideways as if he didn't believe
the excuse.

The Urrys has stayed on because they had nowhere else to
go. Their two rooms over the tobacconist's in Red Lion Square
had been found lying in the road one morning along with the
tobacconist's shop. The kind old fool with the cake tray had
kept trying to pull strings to get them compensation and a new
home, but they were perfectly happy where they were, and no

23

rent to pay. They had never been so warm in their lives as last winter.

The first feet came clattering down the stairs on to the platform. 'Urry!' called his wife in a high, hoarse voice. 'Time to get up! Drat that footman, he ain't cleaned my shoes again.' She put her turned-over shoes out neatly every night, and every morning shuffled her feet into them with the same remark. Her toilet consisted in taking off the grey cardigan which she wore inside out at night and putting it on again the right way. She banged on the wire above. 'Time to get up, sir. Shall I run your bath?'

Mr Urry's legs appeared over the side, with a stretch of yellow skin between his hitched-up trousers and wrinkled socks. 'First train coming,' he said coughing, and pulling out the steel watch. 'Spit on time,' he said with surprise, although it was never a second late. The train came and went, taking a few sleepy people with it. The platform began to fill up for the next one, but before it came, the Urrys were up and dressed.

'Christ, my mouth's like a lavatory.' Mrs Urry rubbed her hand over it. 'Come on and let's get our tea before the Cosy fills up.

''Ullo, duck.' Strewth! That red jacket was a bit too much to see first thing on the morning after.

'Hullo,' said Sheila. 'Sleep well?'

'As a top. 'Urry up, Urry, I'm waiting to make your bed.'

Mr Urry, who was very short, hung by his hands from the top bunk, kicked feebly once or twice and then launched himself on to the platform, landing stiff-kneed and staggering a few steps with a hand in the small of his back and exaggerated groans.

''E'll be on to the lines one of these days,' said his wife, 'then we shall 'ave a fry. Talk about bacon for breakfast!'

She pulled down his two old blankets, and rolling them up with her own staggered with them towards the exit after his pottering figure. Sheila watched her back view in the drooping skirt and the green beret, worn well forward, with wild strands of hair escaping at the back. She might have offered to carry the bundle if she had not been afraid of catching something. She was sorry for the old girl; one couldn't conceive of a more ghastly existence. Someone ought to do something about people like that.

Mrs Urry had been there ever since Sheila had been catching the six forty-five. She was part of her mornings, but Sheila was haunted unreasonably by the fear that one day she would come down and find her dead in her bunk. Ever since that morning when her watch had been wrong and she had come down too early and seen Mrs Urry still asleep, with her waxy yellow nose sticking straight up and her horrible hair inert, the idea had haunted her like something she had actually seen. She had never seen anybody dead and she hoped she never would.

Her train came in and she got into the third carriage from the end, deliberately not looking at the boy with the curly hair and the limp who was there as usual and was staring at her, as usual.

'Mum,' said Kitty, 'I don't want any more to eat. No, don't cut any more bread and butter. I'm late anyway.'

'Just one more round,' said Mrs Ferguson. 'You've eaten nothing, childie. Look, you can have the last of the raspberry jam.'

'I don't *want* it.' Kitty got up from the kitchen table and put on her jacket. 'I must fly. Where's my bag?'

'I'll give it to you. I put it away in a safe place. You left it lying about when you came in last night, and I knew you'd never find it. Oh, Kitty! I don't call that a clean plate. What's the matter – don't you like tomatoes and fried bread? You always used to.'

'Yes, but you always give me so much. Honestly Mum, at this time in the morning – look, do give me my bag. It's nearly quarter past.'

Kitty went out to the shed where the bicycles lived among the abandoned impedimenta of her father's changing hobbies. Congealed paintpots, garden tools with the earth crusted on them, a stone slab covered with hardened concrete – relic of the time he had started to build an air-raid shelter. A yellow-brown miniature chest of drawers, with a painting on each drawer of what it was supposed to contain: buttons, looping tape, a lover's knot of ribbon, an enormous, predatory black hook and eye. The button drawer, stuck half open, showed nails and a lump of putty and a tangle of brass and hairy string. There was a chipped grindstone, and on the lowest shelf a vice still held a piece of metal, one edge filed to a perfect bevel and the others raw. The handle of the file, with G.F. burnt into it, lay on the shelf. The blade may have been on the pile of scrap metal in the corner that had been waiting since the beginning of the war to be taken to the Council dump.

Her father was on fretwork at the moment. Kitty had to manœuvre her bicycle past his treadle machine, standing clean and oiled by the door with the beginnings of an intricate book-end impaled on the saw. Her mother came out with her hand-bag as she went past the back door. Mrs Ferguson wore an overall over her nightdress, long black slippers with pom-poms, a net over the top of her abundant brown hair and the rest hanging down her back in a thick pigtail secured with tape.

Kitty wore trousers and a yellow polo-necked sweater that her mother had knitted last winter. Her hair was short and curly and stuck out at the sides where she had lain on it.

'That front tyre's flat, childie. Better let me pump it up.'

'No, I can do it. It doesn't matter though; it's not down much. Anyway, I've left my pump at the factory.'

'I'll get your father's. You'll ruin those good tyres, riding them on the rims like that.'

'It's nowhere near the rim.' Kitty pouted her soft underlip, grabbed her bag and put it in the basket. 'Good-bye then, I'm off.'

'Oh, wait – your sandwiches.'

'Oh, Mum, I don't – Do be quick then; I'll get in an awful row. I was late back after lunch yesterday through you making me go to the dressmakers'.'

She began to wheel her bicycle down the passage at the side of the house and Mrs Ferguson trotted after her with a paper bag, holding up her nightdress. 'Here you are; cheese, darling, and a piece of my cake. Leonard coming tonight?'

'I expect so.'

'Oh good. We're going to have fish pie. I know he likes that.'

'Well, actually, Mum, we were going to the pictures and have some food out afterwards.' Wheeling her bicycle through the front gate, Kitty would not look at her mother's falling face.

'Oh, must you go tonight, Kitty? I thought we'd have a cosy evening here. We might start a fire and there's a lovely play on the B.B.C. I know Len likes plays.'

'He likes the pictures too,' muttered Kitty, with one foot on the pedal, and then suddenly turned her chubby face round with a quick, sweet smile. 'Thanks for the breakfast, Mum. It was lovely. Good-bye, see you at lunchtime!'

'Don't be late!' Mrs Ferguson came out into the road to call after her as she rode away. 'I've got a nice bit of liver! Don't ride too fast,' she added automatically, although Kitty was well out of earshot. She watched the plump little behind disappear round the corner and went back into the house to put the kettle on for Mr Ferguson's tea. Quite a dew, there was. It struck damp through her slippers. Good thing Kitty had her feet off the ground; you could say that for bicycling. Such a baby to be going to work. How she'd manage when she was married, Mrs Ferguson didn't dare think. Thank goodness they were only going to live just round the corner. How could a child like that know how to look after a man, and Len so fanciful about his food?

'Charlie,' she called up the stairs, 'I'm going to put your egg on, so if you don't hurry up, it'll spoil.' She sang at the stove, cushiony and uncorseted, a forecast of Kitty's middle age.

It was twenty-five past seven when Dinah and Bill banged the door of their flat, fell down three flights of narrow stairs, bumped into Mrs Carley's pram, and down the front steps into the street. The tall grey house, build as a penance for Victorian servants, didn't look as if anyone could be wildly, ecstatically happy in it. Its exterior belied the existence of Dinah and Bill in the top storey, like a blank face concealing riotous thoughts.

They ran. 'Christ, we're late,' said Dinah as they turned into the main road. 'Here, don't come to the Estate with me, darling. You'll miss your train.'

'Don't be a fool.' He slowed down his long legs so that she could keep up, her coat flopping, one of her piled-up curls tumbling into her eye. She caught the comb as it fell out. 'Don't be late tonight,' she said, 'Alf's promised to keep me some kippers.' They were crossing the road and he pulled her back from under a car. 'I told you, Di, I've got to go up to Coventry tonight with those drawings.'

'Oh hell, is it tonight? I'd forgotten.'

'What'll you do?'

'Oh, I don't know – eat a pair of kippers, I suppose. I could.

27

Or I might go on the booze as it's pay-day. Perhaps I'll go to the flicks with George.' She looked up at him sideways out of enormous eyes. They had slowed down in the crowd converging on the entrance of the Estate road.

'Yes, do,' he said confidently. He grabbed her, and kissed her, knocking hard against her as someone jostled him. 'Cheerio darling. I'm flying.'

They were parted in an instant by the hurrying, preoccupied crowd. Dinah felt depressed as she ran on, her high heels clacking. 'Hi Joe!' She caught up with a man in overalls. 'Baby come yet?'

'No, duck.' His loose face hung in folds of worry. 'They sent 'er back from the 'ospital again. Another two days, they said, and not to keep on coming along for false alarms.'

'My God, can you beat it? Get a move on, Mr Cripps; you're going to lose a quarter if you don't look out.' The storekeeper, in tight trousers and pince-nez, looked at her with loathing as she ran by him. He loathed most people, especially first thing in the morning, so most people left him alone, but Dinah didn't seem to notice. 'Hullo, Wendy!' She swept a little mouse of a girl along with her as they turned off the road into the clock-house. She was at the clock about twenty people ahead of Wendy, who was always pushed out of any queue. As they came out on to the track between the sheds, the sun came out behind them and their shadows stalked ahead in a blaze of glory. At the end of the track, they turned through the double doors into the Inspection Shop and met the machinery smell; dry and acrid, the smell that permeated your clothes and skin and hair, that steamed out of you when you got home in winter and stood in front of the fire.

Madeleine Tennant hung her coat on the peg and put on her grey overall with the red collar, rolling up her sleeves.

'Morning, Mrs Tennant!' The foreman went past in a similar overall with a blue collar, blowing his nose. Why couldn't he call her by her Christian name as he did the other girls? Everyone else, even girls less than half her age called her Madeleine, but Bob Condor thought Mrs Tennant would be more correct. He was very keen on correctness. In the factory where she had worked in the last war, she had been Mad, or Maddy. Between wars she had been Miss Madeleine, coming into the fitting rooms of an Oxford Street store with a tape measure round her neck and her bosom full of pins. She went out to the bench and sat on her stool next to Paddy King, who was sheer and groomed with dark-red hair that swung in a fan on her shoulders. Madeleine was short and square with thin grey hair which had been irretrievably bobbed in nineteen-thirty, an anxious, modest face and legs that swelled when she was tired. But she felt that she and Paddy were friends because they both had a man in the Middle East – Paddy a husband and Madeleine an only son.

She raised inquiring eyebrows, a diffident, hopeful smile hovering round her mouth that was puckered from years of holding pins. She always greeted Paddy with this expression. It meant: 'Have you had a letter?'

Oh, Lord, thought Paddy, why doesn't she ask right out, and then I'd say: 'No,' instead of this circus every morning, with me supposed to shake my head and look sad and then raise my eyebrows at her so that she can shake her head and glisten at the eyes.

Feeling irritable this morning, she vented it on Madeleine by pretending not to see her questioning face. She picked up the gearwheel she had been inspecting when the bell rang last night and frowned at it closely under the light.

'Good morning, Paddy,' said Madeleine humbly and cleared her throat.

Now she's making the Face, thought Paddy, I won't look. I can't. If she puts her hand on my arm I shall scream. Why am I so foul-tempered? No wonder Dicky doesn't write to me. If Madeleine only knew what our beautiful love dream was she wouldn't talk about him in such a hushed voice.

Madeleine cleared her throat again and Paddy bent closer over the gear. The light touch of a hand on her arm made her taut nerves scream.

'Morning, Maddy!' shouted Dinah across the bench. 'Heard from your cherub?'

Madeliene dropped her hand at once and hurried round to Dinah, her eyes shining. 'Yes,' she breathed, 'yes, I have. Last night, when I got back –'

Poor old bitch, thought Paddy, looking across under her

eyelids, and I wouldn't play. I wish I had. Some day I'll be really nice to her. We'll go out to supper and the cinema and be girls together and show each other photographs. But not today. Good Lord, how can Dinah pretend to take so much interest? No, she really is interested. She really cares about people as people, likes them automatically instead of hating them all on sight and only gradually coming round to one or two.

Edward's body had arrived as punctually as usual at the factory, swinging his arms through the chilly morning, but his thoughts were with Queenie. He hated having to leave her to go through it alone, although with rabbits the only thing was to leave them to themselves. Allan Colley said that interference was the cause of nearly all the infanticide among does. If only Connie didn't go near her. Normally, she kept well away from the rabbits, but she was occasionally taken with the fancy to go slumming in the garden. With luck they would all be there by the time he got home. He set great store by this litter. He had paid a lot for Queenie's visit. She was very big, even for a Flemish Giant – and he had tried to accentuate this by mating her to an outsize buck. It might be the beginning of something really good. Size was important these days. Allan Colley had given him the idea in an article entitled: 'Pass on Your Doe's Best Points.' He was going to concentrate on size until he achieved something outstanding. 'The Ledward Strain' he thought, as he clocked in. Well, other people had done it. All the famous strains must have started like this.

Meanwhile, he had the day to get through. Up till now, his concern for Queenie had taken his mind off his new job, but as he stepped out of the fresh cold of the morning into the metallic cold of the Inspection Shop, his apprehension returned. It was all so different from the friendly Fitting Shop where one section was on top of another and the noise spread over everything. It was quieter here and more spacious. The two lines of benches stretched into perspective, strewn with the dismantled units of aeroplane engines. At the far end, the high trolleys were drawn up neatly, each stacked with an engine waiting to be spread on the benches. There were girls everywhere. There were even women labourers pushing the trolleys along the gangways. It was early yet and only a few of the girls were perching at the benches, powdering their noses or reading the paper. Others were chatting by the coats, or arriving, looking unapproachable in their outdoor clothes. Thank goodness he had only got to deal with ten of them.

That must be his bench; he recognized the sleek, red-haired girl with the sulky orange mouth. He was scared stiff of her. And there was that mannish one with the short thick legs and the bristly shingle. He couldn't see Dinah anywhere, or that funny little girl with the ash-coloured hair who had reminded him of the grey doe in the end hutch.

He didn't know where to hang his coat. He hung it tentatively on an empty peg, but a fat red-faced girl swept it off with: 'No you don't, cock, that's little Hilda's peg.' He tried another peg. 'Christ, Ted,' said Dinah, appearing under his arm, 'don't hang it there, that's her Ladyship's peg.'

'Who?' asked Ted.

'Oh, you'll find out, but that's not the way to start.' She knew Edward quite well; she had often come and talked to him in the Fitting Shop. She liked to get about the place and see people, so she made excuses of dirty bearings to be cleaned out, or a nut to be removed with a special spanner. She would go and look up drawings in the drawing office so that she could visit an old bent man in there who could whistle two notes at once, or invent some reason for going up to the Hardening Shop so that she could talk to a knotted man called Albert, in the glow from his hellish ovens. Bob Condor would sometimes go after her to chase her back to her own section and although she would come docilely enough, he was never sure that she was not laughing at him.

'Morning, Dinah.' He came up now, regretting that it was not correct to pinch her bottom. He had pinched it before now when the opportunity arose, and he had tried to kiss her once behind a stack of cylinder liners. Instead of being angry, she had laughed at him, and had walked calmly away while he was wondering how to proceed.

'Come into my office, Ledward,' he said, 'and we'll just run through the routine. Get out on the bench, Dinah, and start work.'

'I've got nothing to do. We're waiting for another engine.'

'Well, go and look as if you were working. Supposing some-

31

body came round? Come on, Ledward, let's get this over and then we can get these girls organized. They got hellishly slack under Tom Presser; they did what they liked with him. I'm counting on you to get a bit of discipline.'

Bob Condor had an unctuous face with prominent eyes and ears and an egg-shaped profile. He had a bald spot like a tonsure at the back of his head and he talked as if his tongue were too big for his mouth. Words like 'shupercharger' and 'shlipper gearshe' had difficulty in getting past it into the open air. Noticing this, Edward found it difficult to concentrate on what he was saying, just as he never could attend to Connie's mother for looking at her teeth.

In any case, the more he heard of his job, the greater his apprehension. There were certain units of the engine on which he had never worked. Bob Condor's remarks on the roller lift of the moderate shpeed gear were as Greek. He began to wonder why he had been picked for the job. Perhaps the Fitting Shop were dissatisfied with his work and had fobbed him off on the Inspection by way of a smart deal. He would have to get hold of a text-book and do a lot of swotting up at home and meanwhile rely on the help of the charge hand on the other bench. He was a decent chap, but it was the girls! How could he set himself up a supervisor of a girl who had worked for two years on a unit whose details he was hearing now for the first time?

'Well, I think that should give you a pretty good idea,' said the foreman. 'Come on out, and I'll introduce you to your bench.'

Edward was depressed as he followed the tonsure out of the office. He already saw himself passing something faulty that would pack up in mid-air and cause the death of a pilot. He would give the job a trial and then ask for a change before he did any harm. He didn't want the job. He didn't want to meet the girls. He wanted to go back to the Fitting Shop.

The girls had started on a new engine. They looked up from their work and stared and said things as he and Bob approached. At the nearest corner, the red-haired girl was brooding over the wheelcase. She sat round-shouldered on her high stool, her long back curved like a sapling.

'This is Mrs King,' said Bob. 'Paddy – your new charge hand. You'll find sulks don't have the same effect on him as they did on Tom.' Paddy looked at him from under her lashes. Owing to the lines of her mouth in repose, she had suffered all her life from being told not to sulk when she was perfectly happy, which immediately made her feel sulky.

'How do you do,' she said, hoping Edward was not as earnest as he looked. He might get interfering. If she was allowed to get on with the job in her own way, she was all right.

Madeleine sprang off her stool and beamed at Edward. 'How do you do,' she said, and laughed nervously, pushing back her hair.

'Mrs Tennant does the pumpsh,' said Bob. 'Oil, fuel and coolant. She's very good at the job.'

'It's very nice of you to say so,' said Madeleine seriously, 'but I'm afraid I make an awful lot of mistakes. What about that time I passed a cracked casing and it wasn't discovered until the whole pump was assembled? That was terrible.' The lapse had passed almost unnoticed, but the memory of it had haunted her for months. She had worked with desperate concentration ever since, convinced that it was being held against her and that she was being watched for the slightest slip. She woke sometimes in the night, thinking about what would have happened if the crack had not been discovered. She saw the whole fuel pump disintegrating in mid-air like a rotten apple, heard the engine stutter, cough and then cut out completely as the plane hurtled to earth. But most clearly of all, she saw the face of the pilot, blackened and charred sometimes, sometimes floating, flat and pale, just under the surface of the sea.

'And this is Kitty,' said Bob Condor with relish. He liked her tight young satiny skin and the unused look about her. Edward liked her too; he liked her friendly, guileless smile. He could imagine her curled up on the floor in front of the fire, prattling. She looked like a prattler. She was working on a box of oil pipes and it was with a shock that he noticed an engagement ring on her filthy left hand. He saw her then as a child bride, going sacrificially to the altar in cloudy white, without knowing what it was all about. Kitty liked him too; she liked everybody.

Sheila was working next to her on the reduction gear, an

enormous wheel and a little wheel that reduced the crankshaft speed to a suitable speed for the airscrew. Edward felt at home here. He had worked on this unit for a long time.

'This is the reduction gear,' Bob was saying, ignoring Sheila, who he knew didn't like him. 'There's a grinding scheme on the front of the shaft here you've got to watch out for.'

'R.S.C. 119,' murmured Edward casually. 'Er – how do you do, Miss, er –'

'I'm Sheila,' she said, wishing she couldn't see her nose shining out of the corner of her eye. Not that this man was attractive or anything except that the structure of his face was like Conrad Veidt, but you should never let anyone think of you as a girl who shone. You should never shine, anyway. You never knew – supposing some pilot came round. When Bob had moved on to the next girl, she turned her back and took her flapjack out of her overall pocket.

Grace Matthews was checking valves with speed and efficiency. She was homely and house-ridden. Her hands were not cracked and calloused from valves, but from cleaning behind the wardrobe and under the kitchen stove and all sorts of places that nobody would ever see. 'Mrs Matthews is one of our good, steady workers,' said Bob, as if she were a cart-horse. Edward was glad, because he didn't know much about valves.

'How do you do,' said Grace. 'I'm awfully worried because there isn't an engine number on this set of valves. Supposing they've got mixed?'

'Make a note to see about that, Ledward,' said the foreman. 'Take it up with George Dove in the Dishmantling Shop.'

'Righto,' said Edward, wondering who George Dove was and following round the end of the bench to where the rabbit-girl sat, smaller than ever, counting bolts.

'This is Wendy Holt,' said Bob. 'She's just been put on to the camshafts and rockers. She'll be all right, but she doesn't know much about it yet, do you, Wendy?'

'I'm afraid not,' she whispered shyly.

Well that was all right. Edward could teach her a lot about rockers. She wore her pale hair drawn back and tied in her neck with a ribbon. She had long, scared-looking eyes, just like the does when a cat got into the garden and pretended it could get into the hutches if it wanted to. He wondered how Queenie was

34

getting on. Wendy got back on to her stool and went on counting bolts attentively.

Bob had told Edward about the girl next to Wendy. 'Ivy Larter. You want to watch out for her; she's a trouble-maker.' Edward vaguely remembered having heard some gossip about her and one of the labourers, but he hadn't listened at the time. He looked at her now, with a sinking heart and hoped she wasn't going to make trouble with him because he would never know how to deal with it. She was a thin girl, with dry, dyed hair and a spiteful mouth, distorted by the stridence of her Cockney accent. Her eyes calculated Edward and found him contemptible.

Dinah was working just beyond the next girl and she leaned over and said: 'Hullo, this is Reenie. She's not as dumb as she looks.' She couldn't be, thought Edward.

Reenie giggled. 'Oh, Di-*ner*, you are awful!'

'How do you do,' said Edward kindly.

'How do,' said Reenie, goggling.

'Mrs Streeter does the nuts and bolts and the controlsh,' said Bob Condor, watching Dinah.

'That's right,' said Reenie. Every time she finished speaking, she let her mouth fall open, because she couldn't breathe through her nose.

'Dinah you know,' said Bob, going past her. 'She does the shlipper gearshe.' Thank goodness for that, thought Edward, because she'll know all about them. She'll be able to teach me something. Dinah winked at him. The last girl was the mannish one he had seen yesterday. She was standing up, running her eye down a line of studs on the carburettor. She put a dirty hand into Edward's and shook it frankly.

'Freda does the shuper and carburettor,' said Bob, which was obvious, Edward thought. Come to think of it, the whole round of introduction had been rather silly. He could perfectly well see for himself what units the girls were on. He could have trickled in among them, without this pompous business of having to think of something to say to each.

'Yes,' said Freda, 'I'm the blower wallah. Been on it a year now.' Edward knew quite a lot about the blower too and was prepared to assert himself on any question that cropped up. Freda looked as though she were prepared to assert herself too, but he didn't mind. He could deal with girls with moustaches and weatherbeaten skins. It was the ones who smelt like flowers who put him off.

There was a Trade Union monthly general meeting after work, but although Edward usually liked to go and listen to the talk, Jack Tanner himself could not have kept him from Queenie tonight. He always walked home briskly, shooting out his legs to give each one the maximum amount of exercise, but tonight he went like a man making the record to Brighton, heel and toe, elbows working. On the little hill that curved down to Church Avenue and the Lipmann's corner, he broke into a trot, jogging springily on the balls of his feet, head up and breathing through his nose. Behind the dominating thought of Queenie, which drove him forward, a jumble of impressions of his bewildering day surged into his head. Faces, odd remarks, isolated pictures kept coming to the surface like bubbles in a simmering pan, but he paid little heed to them, concentrating only on getting home. Time enough later on to try and sort out his confused thoughts into a clear picture of the job.

At the cross-roads, the church clock showed that he was five minutes earlier than usual. David Lipmann, coming out of the side door of the shop in a blue suit and a white polo sweater, grinned at the earnest, hurrying figure. People missed an awful lot by not relaxing. He passed a hand over his black hair which was brushed back without a parting, hitched up his belt and sauntered across the road towards Collis Park High Street.

'David!' yelled Mrs Lipmann from the shop door. 'Where are you going?' She was a finely built woman with muscled arms and a strong face under hair that was gathered up all round her head into a knob on top, like a brioche.

'To Mr Hillary's to get some books!' called David without stopping.

'You going after a girl, I'm going to tell your father!' screamed Mrs Lipmann. A customer came out of the shop behind her and stood wagging her head approvingly. David shouted something unintelligible.

'You come home late and you'll find the door locked!' yelled his mother, who would have sat up all night to let him in if necessary.

Edward heard the shouting still going on behind him as he turned in at his gate. He always thought the Lipmanns added something continental to this corner of Collis Park. It reminded him of that woman at Wenduyne who used to scream out of her top window when the vegetable man came round. Connie had said it made her sick to see the two big dogs drawing the cart, but they had seemed quite happy with their plumy tails always waving. But Connie suspected all animals of suffering. When a car had run over Bob's paw, she had taken him straight to the Vet's to have him put out of his misery without waiting until Edward came home. They had never had another dog; Connie was dead set against it.

Edward went quickly through the hall to the kitchen and out into the garden. Connie must be upstairs. His rabbits connected him with food and scrabbed at their netting, but he went straight to Queenie's hutch and squatted down a few feet away so as not to disturb her. She was lying in a corner, with her ears crushed along her shoulders, staring into space. In the other corner, the hay of her bed was mounded. Edward peered at the mound. Was it his imagination or – yes, the mound was moving! Straining his eyes, he thought he saw a little rat-like body but it was impossible to see how many babies there were; there was just that stirring, living pile of hay.

'Good old Queenie,' he whispered exultantly and got up quietly to get her some food.

Connie was in the kitchen, cutting yesterday's cold potatoes into a pan of fat on the stove. 'Some people,' she said, 'might take offence at their husband saying good evening to the rabbits before his wife. Don't think I mind, though. I'm used to it, I'm sure.'

'Connie,' Edward's deep-set eyes were shining. 'Queenie's had her litter – you know, the ones I told you about, by that champion at Ashford.'

'How many?'

'I don't know yet. I haven't looked.'

'What'll you do with them,' asked Connie, going past him to the cupboard, 'sell them?'

'I'm going to keep the best for breeding. I might sell one or two for fur when they're mature. I shan't sell any of this lot for flesh, though. I'm hoping they're all too good for that.'

37

'Why don't you find out how many there are? Some of them might be dead.'

'I mustn't disturb her yet. They don't like you touching the babies at first. They eat them sometimes if you do.'

'Well, would you believe it?' said Connie, taking the salt and pepper to the stove and seasoning the potatoes. 'How disgusting. That just shows you how awful animals are.'

Edward was washing at the sink. He felt very happy. 'Funny,' he laughed, gasping through the cool water as he splashed his face, 'Funny, if humans did that. Suppose Dorothy went and ate her baby because your mother went to see her at the hospital.'

'Don't talk like that, Ted. It's horrible,' said Connie, shaking the pan affrontedly. 'And it isn't funny,' she said as he came towards her laughing.

'Well, kiss me good evening then, Con. I didn't want to kiss you till I'd washed off the factory smell.' When he kissed her, her mouth was neither resistant nor yielding, just disinterested. He sighed and dropped his arms, letting her turn back to the stove. 'What are we eating?'

'Meat pie and chips.'

'Bought meat pie or home-made?'

'Bought, of course. What would I make meat pies out of? Take your coat off the table, Ted. I want to use it. Why don't you wash in the bathroom, anyway?'

'Oh, I don't know; more matey down here.' He had felt companionable and communicative, wanting to talk about the rabbits.

'Yes, but it would look so funny if anyone came. They'd think we hadn't got a bathroom.'

Edward laughed and went out to feed his rabbits.

She was dishing up when he came back and he carried the tray through into the living-room.

'And so I suppose,' she said, as they sat down, 'you were so anxious to get back to your rabbits that you forgot to get your pay?'

'Good Lord,' he said, 'I'd quite forgotten in the excitement of Queenie and all that. Here,' he fished in his trouser pocket and threw a little buff envelope on the table. 'Take your house-keeping money then, old girl, and give us some tea.'

Connie slit the envelope with a knife, counted the money, and put two notes into her bag, shutting it with a snap.

'Quite a good bonus then last week,' she said, pouring out the tea.

'Ah, you wait till next Friday when I get the first week's pay of my new job. You'll see a bit of difference. Any sugar? No, I'll get it. It was my fault really; I brought the tray in.' Connie was cutting carefully into her pie when he came back, nibbling at it suspiciously and then dousing it with O.K. sauce.

'Well, come on, Ted,' she said. 'I never knew anyone so cagey. Aren't you going to tell me about the new job? How d'you like it?'

'Well, you know, Con, it's hard to say at first; it's all so strange.' He stirred his tea thoughtfully, recalling the day, trying to untangle his confused impressions.

'Yes, but what's it like? Interesting, dull, important –?' Surely he must know. Edward was so maddeningly slow at putting things into words sometimes. She didn't pretend to be clever or read books like he did, but she could always put a name to anything or anyone immediately. She could label a film sloppy, or dry, or absurd right at the beginning, whereas Edward always had to see it right through and then think about it before he would give an opinion. She had known at once that that new couple who had started coming to the Marquis of Granby were ignorant and flashy, but Edward would not admit it until he had met them two or three times and had a talk to the man.

'Well, I'll be able to tell you more about it when I get into it.' He began on his pie. 'It's a bit worrying at the moment. There's such a lot to know. I only hope I'll be able to cope with it.'

'Oh, so you don't like it then? I thought you'd be sorry you left the Fitting Shop though I didn't say anything yesterday.'

'Oh no, you can't say I don't like it. It's just that –' He went on eating meditatively, searching for the right words to convey the responsibility of the job and his own inadequacy without giving her the opportunity to damp it.

Oh, well, thought Connie, cutting the pastry very small so that her front teeth could deal with it, if he doesn't want to talk about it, I'm sure I don't care. Goodness knows he's always

39

saying I don't take any interest in his work. Might as well have some music. She got up to turn on the wireless.

'Of course it makes it all the more strange them all being girls,' Edward was saying. Ah, now they were coming to what she wanted to know.

'What are they like?' she asked casually, turning the wireless off again and coming back to the table.

'Well, that girl Dinah Davies is one of them. You know her.'

'I ought to.' Everyone in Collis Park knew Bill and Dinah Davies, but Connie's aunt had a flat in the same house. For her sins, she said. They made enough noise for six, till all hours of the night sometimes, even when they hadn't got friends there. What they got up to, Connie's aunt couldn't think, although she sometimes imagined. The names they called each other made your ears burn, and once Dinah had come running downstairs to get their letters in a brassiere and knickers.

Connie folded her lips. Oh, yes, she knew all about Dinah. Mrs Davies, as she called herself. It would surprise no one to hear they were not married.

'Who else?'

'Well, there are ten of them altogether – mostly young – smart girls some of them. It's surprising how they take to engineering work. There's an older woman too; I must say I take my hat off to her. It must be very tiring.'

'How old?' Connie poured herself more tea, and Edward passed his cup across. 'Oh, she must be nearly fifty.'

'Fancy a woman that age taking a job like that,' said Connie. 'I don't think it's right.'

'I think it's very sporting. That's the spirit that's going to win this war. She's very good at her job too, and she seems to like it. You know, honestly, Connie, I wonder you don't come along. Or, if not at Kyles, there are lots of places near here that would take you. They need all the women they can get.'

'And who do you suppose would run your house? You wouldn't fancy coming home to unmade beds and dirty crockery and nothing for your tea, I'm sure.'

'I wouldn't mind. Other people do it. Look at Dinah and Bill Davies –'

'I wouldn't like to look at her flat, that's all.'

'Well, you could do part time then. Go in the afternoons

40

when you'd finished the housework. I've never said anything, Connie, because I always thought you'd probably suggest it of your own accord when you saw everybody else doing war work, but honestly, old girl, I do think everyone ought to help. We'll never win this war else.'

'I didn't ask for a war, did I? Let the people who made it get on and win it. After all, we pay income tax, don't we, and put up with the rationing, and I've registered for firewatching. I should have thought that was enough. I'll have a cigarette, Ted, when you've finished lighting your pipe.'

'Oh, sorry, I didn't know you wanted one.' He held out a packet and then lit up for her. She smoked in the middle of her mouth, in short, furious puffs, sitting up very straight.

'What'll you do then,' asked Edward, 'if they call you up? They are conscripting married women, you know. They might put you in any old job. It would be better to volunteer now and make sure of getting decent work in the neighbourhood.'

'No thank you. If they want me, they can come and get me. I'm not going to lay myself open to the sauce of those young madams at the Labour Exchange. I've heard about them. They won't believe you're married without you show your lines.' She began to pile the tea-things on the tray. Edward jumped up to carry it for her, but she had already picked it up and marched out, kicking open the door before he could get to it. He could hear her in the kitchen making a lot of noise with the crockery. He sat down with the evening paper, but couldn't settle to it. He went out to the kitchen.

'Can I help, Con?'

'I've finished.' She was whirling round the kitchen, putting things away, screwing up one eye against the smoke of the cigarette, still held between her lips.

'How about going down to the Marquis, then, as it's Friday? I could do with a drink.'

'No thank you. I don't fancy anything. Don't let me keep you though, if you want to go.'

'You come too. You know we always go on Fridays.'

'I've told you once, I don't care to. Go on, you go. I've got plenty to do. You don't seem to realize what a lot there is to do in a house.'

Dinah didn't feel like going to the Trade Union meeting either. As usual, when Bill, who made scale models for a tractor firm, had to go up to the Coventry branch, she felt lost and restless. She generally stayed in her flat, beginning, in a fever of energy, household jobs that had been overdue for weeks, sickened of them half-way through, listened inattentively to the wireless and finished up in bed with a jug of tea and a vast cheese sandwich, reading a library book or a magazine until two in the morning.

Tonight, however, she went back to spend the night with Sheila at her flat, taking with her the pair of kippers that her uncle's friend in the fish shop had palmed from under the counter at lunch-time. Sheila had been fascinated by Dinah ever since she first saw her, enormous eyes in full play, talking her way out of a telling-off from a hypnotized foreman. Sheila, who always studied attractive women for tips, could never decide what it was about Dinah. She would be screamingly out of place at Swinley, yet she was exactly right in herself. She was not really pretty, yet her face, her movements and her mouth when she was talking held your eyes so that you didn't always listen to what she said. What she did say was often unrepeatable. Sheila had never heard anyone swear like a man in such a feminine way.

Sheila had been aggressively shy when she started work at the factory. In her mind, she had visualized 'factory girls' as something very different from what she found. She was startled to find that they mostly looked the same as she and her friends – only a bit smarter. Dinah had taught her the reduction gear job in a slapdash, confident way, jostling Sheila's first diffidence into an unquestioning intimacy. Eventually she ceased to wonder all the time what the other girls were thinking of her. They became an integral part of her life. After working beside Dinah for weeks, day after day, nine hours a day, life seemed never to have held anything else. Sheila thrived on liking and Dinah seemed to like her. They were friends. She was the first girl-friend Sheila had had whom she had not secretly rather disliked.

'Lovely to live up West,' said Dinah, as they walked from Russell Square station, 'but my God, what a trek! Some flats; you're lucky,' she said without envy. She would much rather climb two flights of worn carpet and one of linoleum with Bill than rise in a gilt lift without him. She poked round the flat while Sheila went into the kitchen to get their supper.

'Who's this?' She came in without her shoes, holding a photograph.

'Let's see. Oh, that's Mummy and Daddy in the garden at home. That's our house behind.'

'Not bad. What do they think of you working in a factory?'

'They hate it. It's awful when I go home, because they keep on at me about it and explain me away to people as a curiosity. They hardly know there's a war on down there, you know. Thank goodness I'm over twenty-one, or I'd have had to stay and work down there. Daddy was going to pull strings to get me into the local food office as a seccy; so much kinder on the hands, you know.' She laughed and spread her fingers on the edge of the stove, looking at the chipped scarlet varnish which failed to conceal the line of dirt under each nail. 'What do you do about your nails, Di? Mine are agony; I can't keep the polish on.'

'I never try. I think they look better without if you can't keep them nice.'

'Oh, I couldn't not varnish them.' Sheila looked at her in round-eyed horror. 'I'd feel naked.'

'You ought to have stayed at home and been a "seccy",' said Dinah. 'I think you're soft. Tell me more about your home. It intrigues me. Is it all kind of like Mrs Miniver and people cutting roses and having China tea, and cucumber sandwiches with the crusts off?'

'Oh, I don't know. Don't be silly. Look, how much coffee d'you think I ought to put in?' Frowning at the saucepan she was stirring, she said: 'Where did you live before you were married, Di?'

'In bloody Paddington Green, darling. But I want to know about your place – Swinley, or whatever you call it.' Sheila didn't want to talk about her home. She suddenly wished she had been brought up in Paddington Green.

Dinah, who had been out to get a cigarette, wandered back into the kitchen with a yell: 'Here, what the hell are you doing with those kippers? They're shrivelled enough already without you go and grill them. Got a frying-pan? You want to poach them, see, and then they swell up all juicy.'

43

'What else shall we have?' asked Sheila, doing as she was told. 'Get something out of the cupboard. Mummy gave me lots of her preserves.'

'I'll say she did,' said Dinah, opening the cupboard and recoiling. 'Talk about not knowing there's a War on!'

'I know,' said Sheila, embarrassed, 'she always thinks I'll starve.'

'Wow!' said Dinah, pushing the bottles about, 'peaches! Can we have these, darling? I say, grown on the estate?'

'Yes,' Sheila stared at the white enamel back of the stove, seeing instead the peach trees, crucified docilely on the wall at the back of the stables. She could almost feel a peach in her hand, warm and furry. She was picking them for tea and there would be thick yellow cream and the table laid on the loggia and the wasps trying to get at the jam. She never allowed herself to feel homesick. Anyway there was now this vague uncomfortable feeling that it was all wrong. But there wouldn't be peaches and cream in Paddington Green. A lock of hair fell over her face and she immediately forgot about Swinley and social equality. 'Oh, damn my hair,' she said. 'Di, do you think it's worth the trouble of doing it this way? Does it suit me? It's good from the front but I don't know that it's so hot from the side.' They talked about hair for a long time.

After supper, Dinah said: 'I could do with a drink. How about going round to the local. Is it a decent one?'

'Yes, not bad.' Sheila had never been there. Timothy's doctrine that girls went into country pubs but not London pubs was deeply rooted.

They each had a gin-and-mixed in the Lord Nelson, and Dinah chatted to the landlord, who gave them their second gin on the house. It tasted just the same as at the Mayfair. When they got back to the Flats, the night porter was on duty, with circles under his eyes.

'I've got day starvation,' he told them, sizing up Dinah. The three of them chatted pertly for a while, Dinah giving him back as good as he gave. Sheila thought they were all very amusing people and asked him to come up and have some coffee.

'Not safe,' he said, looking at the neck of her red dress, 'for me – or for you.' Sheila giggled.

'You don't want to get too fresh with that guy,' said Dinah in the lift.

'Why not? I thought you liked him. I think he's rather fun.'

'Fun's all right for people who can look after themselves,' said Dinah, making a noise with the lift gates that would undoubtedly bring a note in the morning from Colonel and Mrs Satterthwaite, 'but I don't suppose you can. Poor pet, you never had a chance.'

CHAPTER 3

BY folding up and stacking the trestle tables and rearranging the chairs, the canteen at Canning Kyles could be transformed into a concert or lecture hall. It has been a judging ring once in the competition for practical, hygienic and becoming hats for female machine operators. Those walls had witnessed many amateur variety turns, but nothing so strange as the parade of abashed and giggling models in all sorts of unpractical, unhygienic and unbecoming headgear from poke bonnets to boudoir caps.

This evening, however, the canteen was transformed for more solemn business. On the platform at the far end, away from the serving hatches, was a trestle table bearing a jug of water and a glass, five chairs behind it and in front the microphone that usually worked *fortissimo* or not at all. The rows of chairs in the body of the canteen were rapidly filling up. Smoke and chatter increased every moment as employees pressed in from outside, pushing for a seat, calling to friends or making for the side wall which was the traditional leaning place for hecklers and wits. Although it was after six o'clock, not many people had gone home. Most people wanted to attend the Trade Union general meetings, to see what they were getting for their threepence a week.

The noise in the canteen did not lessen appreciably as five men filed through the door at the back of the platform and sat down behind the table in attitudes of unnatural ease. The fattest of them, who was very fat, kept saluting and making comradely gestures towards acquaintances in the audience. Next to him a pugnacious young man who needed a haircut sat avidly waiting for the talk to begin. In the centre was the Chairman, square and bespectacled, beyond him a modest man of high integrity but no influence, and at the end a twinkling little man who thought the whole thing a bit of a farce and was surprised at himself for having a hand in it.

The pugnacious young man rose, and people began to hush each other and even those who were not attending noticed that something was happening and stopped their conversations at last to listen.

Disdaining the microphone and gripping the edge of the table, the young man pitched his voice as if he were in the open air.

'Brothers and sisters!' he shouted, restraining himself with difficulty from calling them Comrades. 'Brothers and sisters all, I declare this meeting open!' A few scattered murmurs of 'Hear, hear,' from incorrigible yes-men.

'And I now call,' continued the young man, searing them with his gaze, 'I call upon our Chairman, Mr Charles Wheelwright, to read the Minutes of our last General Meeting and report progress!'

A spatter of polite applause ran through the audience as the Chairman rose to his feet, smiling benevolently. The modest man on his right reached over the table and placed the microphone more directly in front of him.

'Brothers and sisters,' began Mr Wheelwright in his normal voice, which was instantly drowned by cries from the side wall of: 'Turn the bloody thing on!'

'Isn't it on?' The Chairman looked inquiringly at the modest man, who looked worried and glanced behind him as if trying to pass the blame on to someone else.

'Yes it's on!' said a voice from behind the scenes. The Chairman nodded and went on speaking confidently in a quiet microphone voice, unaware that he appeared to his audience like a character in a silent film.

His audience did not leave him unaware for long. 'Turn it *on*, George!' yelled the side wall.

'Shut up!' said someone from the centre seats, 'and give our Brother Chairman a chance!'

'Try another station,' shouted a hoarse man in a white scarf and bicycle clips, 'you might get Sandy Macpherson!' Everyone laughed and the voice behind the scenes shouted something back. The Chairman waited patiently for the backchat between George and the side wall to subside, and when George said: 'Try it again now, Mr Wheelwright,' he tried again and was unperturbed by the bellow and squeak which he produced. The twinkling man and the fat man at opposite ends of the table were both enjoying themselves hugely, one to himself and the other in collaboration with his friends, who received many waves and salutes and raised handclaps. These two were quite prepared to sit here all night and enjoy the fun, but some of the audience were beginning to think of their trains and buses and teas, and were telling each other it wasn't good enough. Feet began to stamp and the heckling was not confined to the side wall.

Mr Wheelwright, still bland, spoke to the modest man, who came round the table and removed the microphone to the side of the platform.

'All right, brothers and sisters,' he called in a voice which needed no amplifying anyway, 'we'll get on without the – bloody thing as you call it.' This happy flash of wit restored humour at once and the audience settled down to listen when he read the minutes. His spectacles dropped forward as he read and he paused every now and then to look up over them at his audience when he wanted to make a point.

Mr Wheelwright had come to an intricate and rather dull question about income tax and was explaining how the Committee and the Management had settled it. The Committee had done this, the Committee had done that. Most of the women yawned and fidgeted. Wendy looked at her watch and hoped the meeting would not last too long. It would be awkward going out before the end with all these people between her and the door, but she must not be home more than three-quarters of an hour late at the most. She moistened her lips, cocked her head on one side and fixed a bright, dutiful gaze on the platform, trying to be interested.

Whenever the Chairman looked like winding up the subject of income tax, the pale man with the goitrous neck, who had raised the question at the last meeting, quickly resuscitated it with a further quibble. He and Mr Wheelwright stood and talked at each other boringly across the rows of heads. There

47

seemed no reason why either of them should ever stop. The modest man, who was the Union Secretary, was paying close attention, like a pupil in the front row under the teacher's eye, the twinkling man was thinking his own thoughts, the fat man, who was the Union Treasurer and should have been attending, was half asleep, and the pugnacious young man was getting impatient at having to keep quiet for so long.

However, when Mr Wheelwright and the income tax fiend stopped talking at last and sat down rather sour with each other, he was on his feet in a moment, combing back his hair with knobbly fingers.

'Brothers and sisters all!' He had a good platform voice. 'Just a few minutes of your time, *if* you please! I've got something to say to you. You may not like it, but you're going to get it.' He threw back his head and breathed round at them through distended nostrils.

Freda leaned forward. This was what she had come for. This young man was the mouthpiece of all her convictions; it stirred her to hear him talk. If she had not sublimated her sex long ago in movements and enthusiasm, she might have been in love with him. Perhaps she was. She had once had a very alarming dream about going swimming with him: most disquieting in view of what Havelock Ellis said about water in dreams.

'I'm speaking to you today,' her god was saying, 'as a member of the Production Committee of Canning Kyles. Now you all know what this Production Committee is, don't you? It's a Committee formed as a common meeting ground between the workers and the Management to give every one of you –' he paused to rake them with his eyes – 'every one of you the chance to speed up Production. If you have any ideas about how you could do your job quicker, or more efficiently, how metal could be saved or a bottleneck cleared up – anything like that – all you have to do is to tell the representative of your shop, and that idea of yours will get as much consideration from the Management – we've got 'em where we want 'em this time; I'm telling you that – as if it came from the Managing Director himself.' People fidgeted. They knew all this. They had been sated with speeches and notices and pamphlets at the time when the Production Committee was being formed.

'But you know all that,' said the young man impatiently, as if he had read their thoughts. '"Don't come at us with all this pep talk," you say. "We know." That's just the point. I might have forgiven you if you didn't know, but you do know. You've grumbled enough, God knows, about the way this factory's run, and now you've got the chance to have a say in the running of it, and you know you've got that chance –' His voice was rising – 'You know you've got that chance, I say, and what have you done about it?' His voice was so accusing that even those who didn't know what he was talking about tried to look innocent. 'What have you done about it?' He shot out a pointing finger on the end of a long arm. 'You, and you, and you?' He swung his arm round his audience, who cleared their throats and looked righteously at their neighbours. 'Yes, and you, sir!' The arm spotlighted a heavy man in creaking shoes, who was sneaking out to catch his train. 'You who are so keen to get back to your bloody tea!' Laughter, dying away uneasily as the young man swung back on them with that great knuckled forefinger. 'I'll tell you what you've done!' he roared, and even the creaking man, who had been pretending not to hear, was held in the doorway by that dramatic pause.

'I'll tell you what you've done, you fine patriots – oh, you great-hearted British workers. You've done absolutely, God – damn – all – bloody nothing.' He dropped the words on to them with nods of his untidy head. 'Three months this Committee's been going and so far we've not had a single suggestion or hint of co-operation from any one of you. We've had complaints of course – you'll always get those – that's the only way we know you're still alive.'

A spotty youth, with lips that looked as if they were turned inside out, jumped up and said: 'All right, then, but what's the Production Committee done? We elected you to – what d'you call it? – to whatsitsname Production and l-l-look what's happened.' He was not a very fluent speaker. 'The output last week was lower than it's been for months. We know that by our pay packets.'

'Thanks, Brother Collister,' said the man on the platform smiling triumphantly. 'You've asked my question for me. What's the Production Committee done? You're the Production Committee! We're only your mouthpieces. If there's been a drop in Production, it's your fault.'

'Here, 'alf a mo,' said Brother Collister. 'I don't see what it's got to do with me. I'm only in the Main*tai*nance Department. I've got nothing to do with Production – fixing the plumbing and doing the lights and such. It's higher you've got to look. We're doing our jobs and we're being let down, that's what I say. I've said that all along. We're doing our jobs, I've said ... can't do more ... fixing the plumbing ... fifty-seven fuse boxes ...' He became incoherent. His saliva glands seemed to work in conjunction with his vocal chords, so that the more he talked, the wetter and more unintelligible he became.

'What's your worry then?' asked the young man on the platform. 'If you're satisfied you can't do more at your own job, what's the trouble?'

'I'll tell you what the trouble is,' said Brother Collister, wiping his mouth on the back of his hand and swallowing. 'We know Production's gone down because of our pay packets. Ever since this what-d'you-call-it – P-Production Committee started, we've been taking less money, that's what.'

'Ah, I thought so!' The speaker put his hands in his overalls pockets and added triumphantly: 'That's the only thing that brings some of you up here, isn't it? Your pay packets!' He pronounced the words as if he wouldn't be found dead with such a thing on him. 'You haven't got the guts or the courage of your own convictions to try and get this factory going all out, but as soon as your miserable little wages are affected, up you come running with: "It's all the fault of the Committee."' He squealed it in his nose. 'I tell you we've done our best. We've had meeting after meeting with the Management, but every time they've had the laugh on us because they know we haven't any backing from the workers.'

'Well, how about electing a new Committee and see what they could do?' suggested a diffident voice which had not even the confidence to get to its feet.

'I'd like to see them do any better without co-operation,' said the young man on the platform, his hair all over the place. 'I don't care who you elect. I don't care if you put Jesus Christ on the Committee. He couldn't do anything without co-operation.' He passed his hand over his face and gave a tug at his collar. The spotty youth, who had been crouching, half sitting and half on his feet ready to protest at he knew not quite

50

what, wiped his mouth and prepared to speak again. He knew something was wrong somewhere but he couldn't put his finger on it, nor find the words to say what he wanted to say. That was the trouble, arguing against these fellows; they got you down every time by the gift of the gab.

'And look here, all of you,' the other was saying. 'I'll resign with pleasure if you like. The sooner the better. I'm just about sick of toadying round the Management, and sweating my guts out for a lousy lot of bastards like you.' He sat down amid general and comfortable laughter. His audience enjoyed being abused. It always got a laugh, and as for him resigning, well, everyone knew old Jack Spiller would never resign. That was only his joke. Good old Jack; he certainly put some life into the meetings. Pretty good speech on the whole. He's quite right about production. Someone should see about it, but what can *I* do? I'm a craftsman, that's me; I like to work with my hands. In any case, everyone knows this is the worst-run aircraft factory in England.

Men and women were saying this in every factory in the country. It is the creed of the factory worker – or rather, his motto. A truism in which nobody believes can hardly be called a creed.

The Chairman had thanked Brother Spiller for his oratory and said that although he himself was not a member of the Production Committee, he was sure, etc., etc., everyone would do his utmost, etc., etc., these things took time, but where the cause was just and the heart was right, no matter how great the difficulties, like David over Goliath we should prevail. He had lifted this last sentence from a speech he had recently made at a Lodge dinner and it evoked a certain amount of applause. A few people stamped their feet soberly and the modest man clapped his hands softly as if he had gloves on and made a judicial little purse of his mouth.

Freda had relaxed now and was making mental notes to tell the girls when she got home. She shared a flat with two friends, one of whom was a Council School teacher and the other an industrial chemist. They were all confirmed meeting-goers, and went to the kind of lectures advertised in the *New Statesman and Nation* as other people go to the cinema – for pleasure.

Reenie, who had been listening slow-eyed and wondering, turned to Paddy. 'Good, isn't it?' she said.

'What is?' said Paddy.

'Well, I don't know – Production and that. It's just what my hubby always says, "We could win the war if we had more planes than the Jerries," he says.'

'Well, fancy that,' said Paddy. 'Cigarette?' She lit one for Reenie, who smoked it hanging on her lower lip as her mouth would never stay shut, and offered one to Wendy on her other side.

'Oh, no, thank you,' whispered Wendy. 'I don't smoke. D'you know what the time is?'

'Must be getting on for a quarter to.'

'Oh dear.' Wendy fidgeted with her bag and gloves and looked along the barrier of knees between her and the gangway. 'I shall have to go in a minute.'

'I'll come with you,' said Paddy. 'Let's just hear this next bit though; it's sometimes quite amusing.'

The meeting had now reached the time for miscellaneous questions. 'I now invite any Brother or Sister who has a question to ask, to submit same to the Chair,' said Mr Wheelwright, and sitting down with a bounce, spread his knees, leaned his elbows on the table and smiled encouragingly.

At least six people had popped up like celluloid dolls in different parts of the Canteen. One was an elderly female labourer from the Inspection Shop. She wore a pot hat and a long dirty coat of enormous checks over her black overall and she was waving a cracked and bulging patent-leather handbag to attract attention. Mr Wheelwright nodded at her.

'I think our Sister there was the first up,' he said. 'Yes?'

'Well, it's like this, Mr Chairman,' she said, suddenly defiant at finding so many people listening to her. 'What I want to know is when are you going to start a Day Nursery a bit nearer the factory, that's what I'd like to know.' A lot of people appeared to want to know too and agreed audibly with this request.

The Chairman raised his hand. 'Quiet please, and give our Sister a chance to finish. You're not satisfied, then, with the existing arrangements?'

'That I'm bloody well not.' The pot hat shook and the face

below it grew red. 'Look here, Mr Chairman, how would you like to get up before five and get breakfast for your man and three kids and then go two miles out of your way to take two of them to the Day Nursery and then as like as not with the buses what they are be late in here into the bargain?'

'Yes, yes,' the Chairman nodded understandingly, like a priest in the confessional.

'Not to mention,' continued the agitated pot hat, 'having to do them same two miles out of your way on top of a day's work, to fetch the kids and they so tired by that time they can't hardly keep awake, let alone walk.' Some of the women made the cooing sounds that they made at the cinema when a dog came on to the screen.

'Excuse me, Mr Chairman.' The fat man behind the table leant forward. 'What's your suggestion then, Sister?'

'Well, what I say is, and there's a lot of others say it with me, *I* know –' She paused for murmurs of corroboration which came even before what she said was made plain. 'What I say is, there ought to be a Nursery right here in the factory, and so I hope to see before we're all in our graves, what with one thing and another.' The pot hat disappeared suddenly as she sat down and tried to recover from the shock of finding that she had actually said what she had been boiling up to say for weeks.

All this time, the modest man had been taking notes like mad, hunched in his chair with his scribbling block on his knee. Each winter he promised himself to learn shorthand by correspondence in the long evenings, but each spring came round without his having done a thing about it.

'Thank you, Sister,' said the Chairman, addressing the spot where the pot hat had disappeared.

'Regardin' the question of the smell of drains in the Redundant Stores –' A little bald man with a big nose and sad eyes, darted from his seat into the gangway.

'Half a minute, Brother.' The Chairman flapped him down with his hand. 'We haven't yet finished with the question in vogue. I think we're all aware of the difficulties our Sister has spoken of. I can assure all you ladies' – he distributed a debonair smile over his audience – 'we all appreciate how hard it is for some of you to manage in these days. As a matter of fact, we've been looking into this question of Day Nurseries for some time, and I think now, that the time has come –' A hefty girl from the Machine Shop with untidy flaxen hair and a North Country voice jumped up.

'The time 'as come, Mr Chairman, for less talk and more do! We don't want any more promises. We want to know what you're going to do about it!' she shouted, edged on by her mates, who tugged at her coat and said: 'Give it 'im, Win,' and 'That's right, tell 'im straight.'

'Sit down, Sister Bellamy, you're out of order,' said the Chairman unruffled. 'I was just going to say,' he went on, 'that the time has come to negotiate for a definite decision.'

'I'll say the time has come,' said Sister Bellamy, standing her ground challengingly.

'That being the case, Brothers and Sisters, I suggest that a resolution be moved. If our Sister – where is she?' He searched for the pot hat, who was pushed to her feet, tongue-tied now that she had had her say. 'Do you formally propose this motion, Sister, eh –'

'Billings,' said someone for her. He repeated his question and she nodded and sank out of sight again.

'I second that,' said the North Country girl and a man in a plum-coloured overcoat together. Mr Wheelwright nodded towards the man. 'Thank you. What's the name?'

'Brother Vernon,' he said, and lifting the skirts of the plum-coloured coat sat down again, satisfied with his bid for notoriety.

'Regardin' the bad smell in the Redundant Stores –' It was the little bald man again, but five others were on their feet, thrusting up their arms like schoolchildren. One of them was waving something on the end of his arm, a brown paper bag, which caught the Chairman's eye. He nodded at the sour-looking man who was waving it. 'Go ahead, Brother.'

'It isn't 'ealthy, Mr Chairman, it isn't right,' said the bald man, who was short-sighted, and thought he meant him.

'Excuse me, Brother, I'm on my feet,' said the sour man, but the other, who was also slightly deaf, was still piping away about typhoid. The Chairman played them both with his hands like a cricket captain arranging his field and also subdued an importunate woman who was trying to hark back to Day Nurseries.

'I shan't keep you long, Mr Chairman,' growled the man with the paper bag, as soon as he had the floor. 'I'm a plain-speaking man and I say what I mean without wasting time, unlike some I could mention. What I want to know is, are the Shop Stewards aware that the food in the canteen is disgusting, inadequate and not fit for 'uman consumption and that the price charged for it may be called, in plain words, profiteering?' Murmurs broke out. This was interesting. Some of the murmurs were approving and Wendy wondered whether perhaps she was wrong in thinking the canteen lunches good.

The little twinkling man at the end of the platform spoke for the first time. 'Any special complaint, Brother?'

'Yes. The meat last Friday was almost raw and I wouldn't have given the jam tarts to my pigs.'

'Just a minute. There was jam in the tart, wasn't there?'

The sour man grunted.

'And the meat was meat? Both rationed food, I may remind you, that you were getting apart from your home ration. That's a point to consider, Brother.'

'It's *not* the point. The point is that the canteen is making a profit out of selling inferior food. Look 'ere!' He waved the paper bag. 'What about this cheese roll? Threepence it cost me off the trolley this morning and what's inside it?' He had pulled out the roll and holding it above his head in both hands, he opened it dramatically: 'Look!'

'What at?' asked the twinkling man, peering.

'What at? Ah, there you are. You can't even see the bloody bit of cheese, let alone taste it.' A roar of laughter broke out and split up into arguments and promiscuous comment. Someone from the side wall told the sour man where he could put the roll if he didn't like it, and was sternly reminded from the platform that there were ladies present.

'Twenty years,' a hot red man was saying, 'twenty years before I come here I been in the catering trade and I want to say that I agree with Brother Williams. I could sell those rolls at a penny each and still make a profit.'

'Blimey,' said the side wall, 'you must have been pretty canny with the cheese, mate.'

'Now look here,' said the caterer, 'I've not come here to be spoken to like that –'

'If you don't like it,' chanted the side wall, 'you know what –'

'Order, order.' Mr Wheelwright was slapping the table with the flat of his hand. 'You're all out of order. All remarks must be addressed to the Chair, *please*.'

'About the bad smell in the Redundant Stores,' shrilled the bald man, but the caterer's voice was louder.

'Mr Chairman, I protest against the remark made by our Brother over by the wall. As a Union Member, I'm entitled to an apology.'

'Sit down,' people told him, 'you make us tired.'

'I shall not sit down,' he said, crimson in the face, 'until I get an –'

'And in the meantime,' said the sour man, who was still holding the roll before him like a sceptre, 'what about these bloody cheese rolls? Are we or aren't we to go on being robbed? What are the Shop Stewards going to do about it?'

'I'm going,' said Paddy, getting up. 'I can't stand any more of this. Coming, Wendy?'

Mr and Mrs Holt had had Wendy very late in life. The doctor had taken a pessimistic view of Mrs Holt expecting her first baby at the age of forty-three. 'A great pity,' he had said, tut-tutting through his stained moustache at the prospective mother's worn frailty. 'You should never have taken the risk. I wonder your husband –'

Mrs Holt did not tell him that it would have been as much as her or anyone else's life was worth to dictate to Mr Holt in these or any other matters, and in any case, her heart was singing with joy at the fulfilment of her twenty-year-old dream.

The doctor, who prepared Mrs Holt for the ordeal of her confinement by making no bones about his doubts that she would come through it, was only partially justified. The baby was little and colourless and ran the gamut of every childhood disease on its way to adolescence. Mrs Holt was left with a heart that occasionally seemed to tip over and beat double quick time, leaving her gasping and speechless until she could get at her pills, and sometimes long after that. As for Mr Holt, his nerves, which had always jangled at noises and disturbances, were red-hot wires every time the baby cried.

Mrs Holt's life became a struggle to keep the noises of childhood from him, but it was impossible in such a tiny house, although she, and eventually Wendy, were turned into mice on tenterhooks 'not to disturb your father'. By the time Wendy had crept into her teens, his nerves were screaming, and he with them, every time a car backfired or he read something upsetting in the newspaper.

He was screaming now, and banging something, as Wendy hurried into the house. She closed the door softly behind her, wiped her shoes, put her umbrella in the stand and hung up her hat and coat before she went into the sitting-room to see what was wrong. No sense in going in with her outdoors things on, it only made him worse. He thought you were going to die of pneumonia if you didn't put on a coat every time you went out and take it off immediately you came in. Even if you only just popped out without a coat to post a letter, he would yell at you from a window, and although the neighbours must be used to him by now, it wasn't very pleasant.

Her mother came out into the hall, her little monkey face screwed up to say Hush. At sixty-five she was an old lady. She wore shawls and long black old-fashioned dresses, with a locket on a chain hanging right down her front and tucked through her belt. In the street she wore button boots and a high archaic hat balanced on her puffed grey hair. For reading and sewing, she had gold-rimmed spectacles with half-lenses which she wore either right at the end of her nose, which still didn't make them very far away from her eyes, or hanging in a little leather bag from her waist.

'Is he upset because I'm late?' asked Wendy. 'I did say I would be.'

'He was at first,' said her mother, 'but it's his potatoes now. He says they're waxy.'

'But they always are this time of year, aren't they?'

'Yes, but he says the shops sell nice ones to everyone but me. Oh dear, I wish I'd baked them, but I didn't like to use the oven just for that.'

'What about – you know – what we planned this morning?'

'Oh, I don't know, dear. I haven't asked him yet. We'd better wait and see how he goes on. Perhaps it would be better to leave it for tonight and go another evening when he's not upset.'

'But the picture will be off then.'

'Oh, dear – well, I don't know –'

They were talking in whispers, with one ear on the measured thumping that came from behind the sitting-room door.

Wendy gave her mother a quick kiss and went in. Her father was leaning back in his chair, banging on the table with a spoon. At sight of her, his untidy eyebrows shot to the top of his long narrow head and he rocked his chair forward with a crash. 'Aha!' The eyebrows came down again; the left one grew forward and the right one hung down at the corner, almost into his eye. 'So you're home at last? If you'd stay home instead of rushing about with this ridiculous nonsense about work, I might get some comfort in my own house. The Lord God knows your mother has as much idea of housekeeping as a – as a –' He clawed the air for words.

'It's all right, father.' Wendy bustled round him, straightening the tablecloth, patting his shoulder. 'Look, I'll make you some toast, shall I, instead of the potatoes? It's much nicer, really.'

He liked toast. He smacked his lips, but growled something.

'What's that? Oh, your teeth! I'll get them. You drink your tea and you shall have hot buttered toast with your second cup, I shan't be a minute.' She flew upstairs.

While the bread was toasting, Wendy washed her hands in the little scullery off the kitchen. The scullery was scarcely more than a cupboard with a sink fitted across and a window high up, heavily barred, although it was too narrow to admit even a hipless small boy. The kitchen was not much bigger. Standing in the middle of it you could reach stove, store cupboard, bread-bin, saucepans, and the hinged shelf that did duty for a table without moving your feet. There was no back door; the window looked on to the railwaymen's allotment strip and the roofs of electric trains shuttling through the cutting below the cindery slope.

Wendy washed her hands meticulously; she could not bear to leave a speck of the factory dirt, although they would be just as dirty again within five minutes of her arrival tomorrow. The oily dirt always lodged in that old screwdriver cut. She scrubbed away at it like Lady Macbeth, continuously stepping into the kitchen to watch the toast, which was no use to her father if it was a shade darker than the exact golden-brown.

When it was buttered, she covered it with another plate and opened the oven door to get her own food, which her mother always kept hot for her, as Mr Holt would not wait for his tea until Wendy got home. The gas was out and the shepherd's pie congealing on the plate.

'You never kept my food hot, Mother,' she said, more as conversation than reproach as she sat down to it at the sitting-room table. It wasn't very nice but she was hungry.

'But Wendy, I did, dear. I put it in the oven.'

'I turned out the gas,' said Mr Holt complacently, his teeth shifting up and down on the toast. 'I never saw such wicked waste. If she is late for meals, she must expect to find her food cold, I say.'

'But, Dad, you know I can't get back earlier.'

'Perhaps,' ventured Mrs Holt, whom forty years of marriage seemed sometimes to have taught no prudence, 'it would be better if we waited until Wendy got back –' Dark-blue veins knotted and swelled in her husband's head and his Adam's apple bolted up and down his throat. Quickly, before he could swallow his mouthful and speak, Wendy changed the subject with: 'How's the toast, Dad?'

He was understood to mutter that it was all right, and passed his cup for more tea. He ate in silence, his eyebrows working with his jaws, while Wendy and Mrs Holt whispered together at the other end of the table.

'All right, ask him then, Wendy, but I really think it would be better to stay in tonight. We can go next week.'

'But the picture won't be on next week. Dad!' she cleared her throat and spoke louder. 'Dad, you wouldn't mind if Mother and I just popped round to the Odeon for an hour, would you?' He snorted a little cascade of toast crumbs on to the tablecloth. 'And what am I supposed to do meanwhile, eh?'

'Well, you know you're supposed to go to bed early. I'll make you ever so comfortable with a hot bottle and your big cushion and the paper. You wouldn't even need us if we did stay in, and you've got Lassie to keep you company.' Lassie was a grotesque, naked mongrel, with starting eyes and a rat tail, who long ago had decided it was politic to suck up to Mr

Holt. She sat by his chair now, sickeningly attentive, while he dropped titbits carefully into her mouth from time to time. She was the least attractive, but the favourite of his three slaves. What affection there was in his nature exhausted itself on her.

'Well, can we?' pursued Wendy eagerly. He had not said no.

'Since you evidently don't mind leaving me at the mercy of housebreakers and murderers . . .' There was a lot more in that strain, but he had not said no. Wendy cleared the table quickly. They could wash up when they got back. She urged her father to bed, helping him up the stairs, for his joints were silted up with rheumatism. He was maddeningly slow getting to bed, and they would miss the beginning of the picture, but at last they were in the hall, and Mrs Holt had lowered on to her hair the hat that would have to be unseated again in the cinema if there was a troublesome film-goer behind. Wendy wore a blue pixie hood. They were both excited at the expedition.

She turned out the hall light and opened the front door. 'Got your torch, Wendy?' said her mother, holding on to her arm. 'It's pitchy dark.' As they stepped outside, a shout made them both jump and turn round to look up the black staircase. Wendy shone her torch, and there in the wavering spotlight stood the furious, pyjamaed figure, menacingly fore-shortened, his hair on end, Lassie staring from the crook of one arm, the other pointing at them like the finger of judgement.

'Where are you going?'

Wendy stepped back inside the hall. 'You said you wouldn't mind if we went to the cinema.'

'I never said anything of the kind! How dare you go off and leave me – a poor defenceless cripple? As God is in His Heaven I tell you, you'll be punished for this! You never think of anything but your own wicked, selfish amusement – the pair of you are no better than –'

'Oh dear.' Wendy shut the front door and switched on the hall light. He was in for one of his attacks. She squeezed her mother's arm. 'Never mind, Mother, we'll go next week.' She went wearily upstairs towards the shouting, stamping figure, and Mrs Holt took the pins out of her hat and lifted it carefully off her hair.

CHAPTER 4

THE first time Edward heard one of the girls say: 'What's the good of asking him? He won't know what the limit is on that bearing,' he pretended not to mind. Why should he know what the limit was? He couldn't learn everything at once. A few days later, when he heard one of them say: 'He's about as much use as a charge hand as my Aunt Fanny. I wish we had Tommy Presser back,' he told himself that it was ridiculous to care what a shrew like Ivy Carter said.

He would not have cared if she had not voiced his own opinion of himself. Every day in the Inspection Shop was strengthening his conviction that he was not and never would be any use as a charge hand; they should never have given him the job. The responsibility of it weighed on him like a thunderstorm. It was all very well for the girls; when they came up against something dubious, they simply slung it at him with: 'Take a look at this, Ed,' and shifted the responsibility for a subsequent mistake on to him.

And there were mistakes. The A.I.D., the body of technical purists installed by the Air Ministry in all aircraft factories to supervise the work and drive the foremen demented by their preoccupation with quality rather than quantity at the expense of the Output Bonus, had jumped on Edward several times. He got a persecution mania about Mr Rutherford, who brushed his hair up at the sides like a devil, and seemed always to be hovering over the engines that Edward's bench had inspected, beckoning him over with malevolent glee if he found anything wrong.

There was so much to learn. Edward knew some of the units thoroughly, but others only sketchily. He spent hours poring over blue-prints and modification sheets and littered the table at night with text-books when Connie wanted to cut out a blouse, but there were certain things which he could never know until he came up against them in practice. Bob Condor was no help to him. Stimulated from above, he was having one of his periodic production drives, which involved rushing agitatedly about the shop all day, with a don't-bother-me-I'm-busy attitude to every question.

Edward could go for advice to Jack Daniels, the charge hand on the other bench, but after he heard Ivy say: 'Look at little Eddie, running to Mother. We might as well save time and ask Jack ourselves,' he became self-conscious about going over. He would stroll across, pretending to be going for a light, with a gear concealed in his hand, but he felt their laughter on his back. It was not only Ivy who despised him. With the possible exception of the rabbit-girl, who never took her eyes off her work, he felt that they were all watching him to see how he would shape, resenting him as an interloping fitter.

He saw with envy the way Jack Daniels's girls treated him, hanging round him with endearments and accepting his word as law, instead of going and asking somebody else afterwards, like Edward's girls. Dinah was nice to him, but then she was nice to everyone. The others were seldom more than polite, if that. His nervousness of them made him call them Miss So-and-so, which they thought silly, and his carefully thought out jocularities turned to ashes in his mouth.

He should never have been given the job. He would probably lose it soon, with the unfavourable reports of him that must be going through. Worry made him moody and the factory remained with him when he left it at night. He no longer enjoyed his walks to and from work; the very air seemed to have lost its freshness and his legs were tired from scuttling about the shop.

'You look tired, dear,' Ruth Lipmann said to him when he went in for some pickles. 'Doesn't he, Ma?' she yelled across the shop full of people. Everyone turned to look at him and Mrs Greening made sympathetic gurglings in her throat. Mrs Lipmann approached to inspect him with her hands on her hips, swinging her head from side to side disapprovingly. 'Working too hard,' she said. 'You were my boy, I should make you take a rest.'

'How could he, Ma,' shouted Ruth, 'working in a factory? He's on essential work. Going to have the gherkins, dear, or the mixed?'

'Ach, this war,' said a very old refugee, with a moustache but no teeth, from the bench under the sausages, 'the old ones can do nothing and the young ones must do too much. It is very sad.' Everyone said how sad it was and Edward left the shop feeling momentarily a hero and ten years younger than thirty-five, instead of ten years older, as he had for weeks. Care soon returned, however, as he remembered that tomorrow was Friday, and time for his weekly talk with the Department Manager. Next time he walked down Church Avenue, he might be a charge hand no longer. Well, he wouldn't be sorry, but how could Connie take the smaller pay packet again?

Even his pleasure in his rabbits was tainted by the thought of having to go to work next day. He could not whole-heartedly enjoy Queenie's litter, who were promising superbly, and even *Backyard Breeding* had lost some of its potency. He no longer snatched it out of his pocket at every odd moment on Thursday. There had been no odd moments today, anyway, with his bench two engines behind and a girl short, with Paddy King away ill, and Mr Gurley, the Department Manager, incessantly shooting up the little window between his office and the Inspection Shop to shout about Production. Even at tea-time, when everyone else was sitting down, Edward had to run about the Fitting Shop with a half-eaten bun in his hand trying to locate, before the A.I.D. did, an engine that he had passed through without a new modification on the wheelcase.

No chance to read that evening either, as it was Thursday. The card players had taken to having their meal earlier with him, as Dorothy got so hungry these days. 'Just like me when I was carrying her,' droned Mrs Munroe. 'Eat, eat, eat, you couldn't satisfy me, especially being wartime. But with Connie now, that was different – remember, John? I could hardly keep a thing down.' . . . She sighed. 'It was a very trying time.'

'I'm sure I'm very sorry, Mother,' said Connie, 'if I caused you any inconvenience.' Don Derris guffawed and then broke off, seeing Connie's face. Had she meant it to be funny?

The chief topic of conversation as usual was Edward's new job. His reluctance to talk about it had stimulated their interest, which would otherwise have been negligible. Dorothy wanted to know what the girls looked like and whether they had to tie up their hair; Don just wanted to know about the girls; Mr Munroe wanted to know about the work, simply as an opening for his own engineering reminiscences of the time when he had been apprenticed to the Turnery; Mrs Munroe wanted to know what the snags of the job were. Edward didn't want to talk

63

about the factory. He wanted to try and forget about it until tomorrow morning. It was going to be hard enough next week to make his demotion sound anything but ignominious. He got more and more glum and monosyllabic and Connie chose to play the loyal wife apologizing for him: 'I'm sure I don't know what's the matter with him. He's tired, I dare say. And then, of course, having this new position – he's in and out of the Manager's office all day, you know – well, perhaps he's forgotten how to talk to just ordinary people.'

'Oh, for Heaven's sake, Connie,' Edward stood up suddenly, 'it isn't that at all. You do say the silliest –' The expression on Mrs Munroe's face was like a hand on the volume control of the wireless and his voice trailed away to a mutter as he picked up the tray and went out to the kitchen. What was wrong with him? he wondered, still muttering as he tipped the dishes into the sink. It wasn't like him to flare up like that, nor to have this insane desire to dash to the ground the vegetable dish with the two compartments that held too much for one person and not enough for two.

When he went back into the living-room the air was heavy with what they had said about him. After tea, they played cards, so he was unable to settle down to *Backyard Breeding* until the following evening. Mr Gurley had been at the Air Ministry all day so his weekly talk was postponed until tomorrow. Reading the advertisements for rabbits, Edward realized with a shock that he had never done anything about that doe in kindle, although his increased pay quite justified it. 'There's something wrong with you, my lad,' he thought. 'This job's getting on your nerves.'

It was. He woke in the middle of the night to the sweating remembrance of having told Reenie provisionally that that ten thou. endfloat on the control shaft was passable, and of having forgotten to look it up before her report went through. Well, that was nothing to wake up about; he would put it right tomorrow. It showed what a state he was in, when the job began to prey on his subconscious. Silly of him to forget that though, his head was like a sieve these days. Lying awake, Reenie's endfloat kept coming round as the events of the day circulated in his brain. If the A.I.D. caught him out again, they would be sure to report him to Mr Gurley – if they hadn't already. Perhaps he had better make a note to remind him in the morning, then he might be able to stop thinking about it and get some sleep. He listened for a moment to Connie's breathing. Yes, she was asleep all right. Before the excuse of the Doctor's veto, she used sometimes to pretend to be asleep, when she sensed him turning towards her in the big bed, but he had always known when she was pretending, because she clicked in her nose when she was asleep.

The blackout was not up, so he couldn't switch on the light, but it was a clear night and four squares of moonlight lay on the carpet and across the peak of Connie's long foot under the counterpane. Cautiously, he swung his legs to the floor and crept barefoot to the chest of drawers where his watch and his money lay with the oddments from his trouser pockets. He took pencil and paper to the window, made his note and stood for a long time looking out at the unfamiliar beauty of Church Avenue. The little bitty houses opposite were dignified chunks of blackness topped by shining roofs and chequered chimneys. Their solid shadows filled the front gardens and ended in a sharp outline on the road which looked like white, untrodden sand.

Edward had the idea of going out for a moonlight walk. It might clear the muddled worry of his head, but he would never get dressed without waking Connie. Looking back at her lying uncomfortably, well on her side of the bed, sleeping competently to the measured click of her breathing, her hair pinned up under a thick hair-net, Edward felt a sudden surge of loneliness and misery rush to his eyes in a pricking of tears. He had an impulse to make a noise so that she would wake and he could cry out: 'Oh, Connie, I'm so unhappy!' and in a luxury of tears, fling himself upon her to be cuddled and comforted. He longed with a physical ache for bare arms closing round his back, a soft, breathing breast and long, heavy hair that would fall suffocatingly round his face.

But of course, it wouldn't be like that at all. The moment had passed and the tears receded without ever reaching the surface of his eyes. Thank goodness he hadn't acted on that impulse and done anything silly. That's what came of prowling about in the moonlight; it made you hysterical. He tiptoed round to his side of the bed, holding his breath as a board creaked, and slid carefully under the clothes. As he lifted the sheet to cover his shoulder, Connie muttered impatiently and turned, dragging the sheet away with her. Edward didn't pull it back. She was the last person he wanted to wake and talk to him. He lay very still, with his eyes open. He wasn't going to go on like this. He was going to turn in the job. He hated it.

The next day, he looked up the control shaft endfloat, retrieved Reenie's report from the typing office, and put her in a whirl by making her alter it with much sucking of pencil and smudging of a dirty rubber. She didn't know what endfloat was and it was no use trying to explain to her, because instead of listening, she would merely stare and repeat: 'I'm sure I don't know why they want to make it all so complicated.'

'Ledward!' shouted somebody, and Edward looked round to see Mr Rutherford beckoning from another bench. 'Here, you explain to her, Dinah,' he said. 'What you want to do?' said Dinah, 'give the poor girl a brainstorm? You leave her alone. She's done very nicely up to now without knowing what end-float was, haven't you, dear?'

'I should say,' said Reenie stubbornly.

He had covered that mistake, anyway, but Mr Rutherford had discovered another, so Edward might have saved himself his midnight worry.

'How long have you been on this job?' asked the older man, taking off his horn-rimmed spectacles in a way he had, like a prosecuting Counsel.

'Only two weeks.'

'Must be damned hard to pick up at first, if you haven't had the experience,' said Mr Rutherford, putting the spectacles on again, so that his eyes dwindled behind the thick lenses.

Damned hard for a fool like me, he means, thought Edward moodily, watching him make for the Old Man's office.

At lunch-time, he ate overdone mutton, two hard potatoes, a mound of cabbage, followed by steamed date pudding and custard sauce, not because he was hungry, but because there was nothing else to do until one o'clock. He didn't want to go down to the Sports Club Canteen and drink beer and be pally round the dart board. He couldn't remember having been so depressed as this for years. He was tired too, from lying long awake. He took the folded magazine out of his pocket and re-read Allan Colley on winter feeding.

How simple to be Allan Colley and to know where you were – at the top. It must be very contenting to be sure that you knew enough to be able to lay down the law to other people. Edward at the moment had gloomy doubts even about the Ledward Strain, which had seemed such a winner. He was probably quite mistaken about the likelihood of size in Queenie's family. Who was he to judge?

At tea-time that afternoon he sat on a vacant stool next to Paddy King. She was less off-hand than usual, and when he made a joke, she laughed as if she were really amused, and repeated it across the bench to Dinah, who laughed too.

Well, he could make them all laugh if they would give him a chance. He saw himself for a mad moment as the wit of the bench with people repeating his latest *bon mots*. Perhaps he'd give the job another chance before he told old Gurley he wanted to chuck it. Perhaps they were going to accept him after all.

It was not Ivy this time, but Paddy whom he overheard saying: 'Honestly, as a charge hand, he's a dead loss. Whoever put him on this job must be a fifth columnist.'

Without thinking twice about it, Edward walked straight through the double doors on to the track and in again at the next door which led to the passage between the glass offices. Mr Gurley was sitting on the edge of his desk telephoning somebody called 'Cartwright Old Man.' Edward waited, feeling sick.

'Yes, Ledward, want me?' Mr Gurley was wiry and brisk, with a bony jutting forehead and a face full of energy. He walked about the office, opening and shutting filing cabinets, picking up a damaged gear that was lying on his desk and playing with it while Edward talked.

'So you see, Mr Gurley,' he concluded, 'I'd like to resign from the job before you ask me to. I know as well as you I'm not making a go of it.'

'My dear Ledward,' said Mr Gurley, tossing the gear up and down with little flicks of his wrist, 'I never heard one man talk more rot in one minute than you. What's the idea? Don't you like the job? Girls too fresh?' He winked and began to roll the gear along the desk, snatching it up and rolling it again.

'Oh no, but –' said Edward, 'but after what the A.I.D. have reported about me – and they're quite right, I have made a lot of mistakes – Well, I knew you'd be chucking me, so I thought I'd save you the trouble.'

'A.I.D.?' said the Manager irritably. 'What the devil are you talking about? As far as I know, they don't know you exist. If they did, you don't suppose I care a damn for their opinion? And if you think we've got nothing better to do all day than take down our back hair over people like you – well, God help Russia, that's all. Get out on the bench. You're doing a good job of work. Mistakes? Of course you make mistakes when you're new to the job. If Bob Condor wasn't such a drip, he'd have helped you a bit more.' The telephone rang and he stretched across the desk to pick up the receiver. 'And listen,' he said, as Edward was going out of the door. 'Get some work out of those girls. Get them cracking; that's what I put you there for.' He tossed the telephone receiver and caught it up by his ear. 'Gurley here. . . . Now look here, old man . . .'

Edward went groggily back to the bench. He felt stunned. Had no one really noticed, then, what a mess he had made of the job? Did they understand how difficult it was at the beginning and expect him to make mistakes? Perhaps other people had done the same. Perhaps even the girls' beloved Tom Presser had muddled his way to omniscience. He had imagined so much that now seemed unfounded, perhaps he had also exaggerated the girls' hostility. Not Ivy's – she would be hostile to anyone – but perhaps the others had been just taking the mike out of him to see how he would stand it.

Well, he'd show them. He straightened his shoulders and made for the bench, fully prepared to bellow: 'Come on, you lazy women! This job should have been done an hour ago!' It was just as well that Dinah interrupted him as soon as he opened his mouth, because his voice had emerged several keys higher than he intended.

'Shut up, Ed,' she said, 'and come round here.' She planked a bearing into his hand and goggled up at him while he looked at it. Miraculously, he knew what to say 'Scrap it,' he said, without hesitation.

'Thanks, darling,' she said, '*I* couldn't make up my mind about it. I say, can I have an early pass to go at five?'

'No,' Edward heard himself say. 'You've got another engine to do tonight.'

'Oh, but Edward, my old man's coming home and I must get to the shops. I'll catch up in the morning.'

'No,' he said firmly.

'Ed, you are a swine. What's wrong with you? Are you coming out of your shell or something? You used to be easy meat for an early pass. I suppose it was too good to last.'

Care was rolling off Edward like a tangible weight. His face lifted in an uncontrollable grin.

'Ed!' called Sheila across the bench. 'Ed! Let him go, Dinah, I want him.' He strolled round to her. She was really rather a sweet-looking little thing. Why had he thought her so supercilious?

'Look,' she pouted. 'I can't get this nut undone. If you can't, we'll have to get a fitter over.'

'Give us a rag.' He grasped the nut and it turned sweetly, magically in his hand.

'Strong man, huh?' said Sheila.

CHAPTER 5

'WHERE on earth is Edward?' said Paddy peevishly. 'He drives you mad hanging around you fiddling with studs, and then when you do want him, he's disappeared.'

'Ed-*ward*!' Dinah sent a hoot into space. They whistled for him sometimes, as if he were a dog, and once Dinah had put two fingers in her mouth and let out a piercing blast, which brought Bob Condor bustling up with his pigeon-toed gait, one eye apprehensively on Mr Gurley's open window, to ask her if she knew where she was.

'Eddie!' she shouted on a rising note, which cracked into her morning smoker's cough.

'Never mind, Di,' said Paddy. 'He's deaf as a post anyway.' She was cold. The chill of her walk to work through a raw, drizzling morning was still on her, and the Shop was always colder on a Monday morning, after a Sunday free from breathing bodies.

They had not started the heating yet, although the weather had decided that the end of October was the beginning of winter. People would keep leaving the double doors open. Twice Paddy had got up to shut them and each time a triumphant labourer had opened them again immediately to wheel in a trolley, righteous in the execution of his duty. Charlie was one of the astutest shirkers and managed to spend hours in undiscovered sleep behind the spring-testing machine, so that when he did happen to be working he made a lot of show.

'Mind your backs!' he shouted hoarsely – the early morning was death to his catarrh – deliberately steering his trolley down the gang-way where the girls were sitting.

'Mind your backs!' chorused his two henchwomen, one young and grubby in dungarees and the other older and grubbier in a long black overall and derelict shoes. They both strained behind the high trolley, providing the motive power, while Charlie, as the master mind, pushed with one hand, directing its course.

'Mind your backs, darling!' shouted the younger propeller, visible only as a straining blue behind and rounded back, her head buried in a tray of sparking plugs.

'Oh, curse you,' said Paddy, getting up and shoving her stool under the bench, 'why don't you go down the other gangway? And you might shut the door, Charlie. There's a frightful draught.'

'If you worked a bit harder, you wouldn't feel no draught,' said Charlie. 'Mind your backs there!' sharply, to Grace concentrating so earnestly on an overheated valve that she was about to be run over.

'All very well for you,' said Paddy, sitting down again as the trolley passed her. 'You're moving about. We have to sit still and shiver.'

'Now look here, girl,' said Charlie, abandoning the trolley and coming back to frown at her censoriously from under the cap that never left his head all day and possibly all night. 'Mr Condor he says to me, he says: "I want ten engines over from the dismantling before dinner-time." I'm rushed off me feet as it is, without playing nursemaid to you girls.' Deep down in his throat began the preliminary gurglings and hawkings that brought a chorus from the bench: 'No, Charles! Not in here! Charlie – no!' Unperturbed, he spat deliberately, plumb in the middle of the gangway. Someone threw a rag down on top of it and he ambled away after the disappearing trolley.

Would this war never end? thought Paddy. 'Oh, where *is* Edward?' she wailed. 'I don't know what to do about this race.'

'Let's have a look,' said Dinah.

'No, thanks. The last time you had a look, I got a black mark from the A.I.D.'

'Considering I taught you the wheelcase –'

'Yes, just how badly I've since discovered. Another black mark, that was, for a missing roller on the cam bevel, when you told me the gears always made "that funny noise" when they were dry.'

'Well, damn me –'

'Oh, shut it, you two,' said Freda, her legs astride, swinging the heavy supercharger over as if it were made of cardboard. 'Anyway, I think the whole system of black marks is grossly unfair. I'm going to bring it up at the next T.U. meeting. We're all supposed to be working together for the war, so why should some people have the right to get us into trouble? We ought to be allowed to black mark them at any rate. And if they fine us, as they talk of doing ... It ought to be exposed, you know. There's something radically wrong with the whole system.' Freda was a Communist. That is to say, she had been to two meetings in Trafalgar Square and had a small hammer and sickle pasted on the lid of her tool box.

'Lend us your C-spanner, Comrade Freda,' said Dinah. 'I can't get this ring nut off.'

'Coming over,' said Freda. 'Here, you'll never do it like that. Let me do it for you.' She struggled with the nut, her square hands knotted, her face going through red to purple.

'Now look,' said Jack Daniels, coming up with his pipe hanging out of the corner of his face. 'You don't want to do that; you'll hurt yourself. You know you're supposed to get a man to help you with anything tough.'

'I can do it,' muttered Freda, a gland swelling in her neck and her feet nearly leaving the ground with the intensity of her effort. Dinah leaned easily against the bench and watched her with enjoyment. Jack, who was a good-natured man with a huge nose that turned sideways at right angles to his pipe, was instinctively chivalrous towards anything in skirts. Freda wore pin-stripe trousers that did up in the front, but he couldn't bear to see her struggling.

'Don't be an idiot,' he said, taking the spanner away from her when she slackened for a moment to draw breath. 'Dammit, you've been making it tighter.' He grunted, flicked his wrist and the nut came off. Freda, panting on her stool, glowered at him as he walked away. 'Damn you, Dinah,' she said, 'you knew all the time it was a left-hand thread. Why didn't you tell me?'

'Did I, darling?' said Dinah. 'But you're not very tellable, you know, when you're in an athletic mood.'

'You know what you'll do,' said Reenie, 'you'll bring down a rupture. My aunt did, pulling up a window. They had to take it out for her at St Mary's.'

'Don't be silly,' said Sheila, listening across the bench. 'You don't take out a rupture, you undo it or something.'

'Oh, don't you then?' said Reenie. 'Then what's she got in a bottle on her bedroom mantelpiece, I'd like to know?'

'Oh, where *is* Edward,' said Paddy, turning up the collar of her overall, as Charlie slid the doors even wider apart to admit a minute trolley with a load of rags.

'Can I help you?' asked Madeleine, leaning over her and breathing down her neck. She hated to see Paddy in a temper. She knew what it was to be so worried that sometimes you hardly knew what you were saying. She herself had been quite rude to Kitty yesterday, pretending not to hear her friendly chattering because it made her head ache. She had been prostrate with remorse five minutes later and had had to pretend she didn't want a cake at tea so that the child could have two, only to find that Kitty didn't even want one as she had brought something from home. Which showed how much easier it was to commit a wrong than right it.

'I want Edward too,' she said sympathetically. 'I'm worried about this Mod. 229. I never seem to know if it should be in or not. It's terribly confusing.'

'It isn't a bit,' said Paddy, who had taught her the fuel pump. 'Honestly, Mad, I've explained it a million times.'

'I know, you've been very patient, but I've got such a silly memory these days. I had a wonderful head when I was your

72

age though. In the factory I was in the last War, I had it all at my finger-tips, you wouldn't believe.'

It had all been so different in the Ordnance Factory. Was it only because she was younger that the work had seemed easier and she had loved every day of it and had such fun? Nowadays, everything was so much more complicated and scientific, with people trying to teach you to read micrometers, and even the girls seemed to be different from what she and her contemporaries had been. They had never had these off-days and moods and complicated temperaments that had to be humoured. They had grumbled, of course, but only in fun. They had been such a jolly lot. She remembered how they used to sing choruses while they worked.

She had suggested this one day and the girls had looked at her blankly.

'Sing what?' Dinah had asked, breaking off the snatch of crooning that had reminded Madeleine of the old days in the cheerful Filling Shop.

'Well, you know – choruses, dear. We always used to in the last war, and a fine row we made too. The foreman used to come and tell us to be quiet, he couldn't hear the machines. But we didn't take much notice, I'm afraid. We were regular terrors for mischief.'

But girls these days were funny. If one did start to sing, as like as not another would start a different song in another key. The rage was all for being different. They even chopped and gathered and pleated their grey overalls to make them look un-alike. At the Ordnance Factory, she remembered how proud they had been of looking like an army in their brown overalls and scarves. She could see herself now, short and neat – not so fat in those days. Funny, she hadn't even met John then, and as for Martin, he wasn't even thought of. A thought struck her. Life did go in cycles. She was back again now where she had been more than twenty years ago, in a factory, with neither John nor Martin – well, as good as no Martin. All that had happened in between had not led anywhere except round in a circle. Perhaps she would go through another cycle of years as eventful – two years of John and twenty years of Martin – and still come round to a factory again at – let's see – sixty-five she'd be.

73

'Did you see that piece in the paper,' she said chattily to the bench at large, 'about the Granny who works in a factory up North? Worker of the Week, she was. She made a record – turned out more screws on her machine than anyone ever had before. It said how she got a medal and the Queen stopped and spoke to her when she was going round the factory.'

'Fat lot of good that did her,' said Freda.

'I bet she was on piece work,' said Dinah.

'You girls always scoff at everything so,' said Madeleine, 'I know you don't mean it, but –'

'That's to disguise the fullness of our hearts,' said Paddy. 'Oh, Edward, where *are* you?'

'Tea up!' shouted someone and everyone dropped what they were doing, grabbed their mugs and made a dash for the tea trolley being trundled down the gangway by Hilda from the canteen, in an overcoat and a crooked Nippy's cap. Charlie was there first, with a mug the size of a small bucket. Wendy Holt was last in the queue and there were no rolls left. She had had no breakfast, as there was only just enough bread for her father, so she took an enormous stale bun and retired to her stool, holding both hands round her mug to revive her dead fingers.

'That settles it,' said Dinah. 'Ed must be locked in the Gents'. I've never known him miss his tea.'

Edward, however, was not locked in the Gents'. He was locked in solemn conference with Dick Bennett in the Final Assembly Shop.

Edward leaned on the cylinder cover of the engine that Dick was assembling, while Dick fitted priming pipes on the opposite side. Each engine was assembled by two men, working as a team. Dick's mate, a leathery gnome called Joseph, did the fiddling jobs while Dick did the reaching and heavy stuff. Joseph was squatting out of sight at the moment, doing things to the bottom of the supercharger.

'Advertise,' Edward was saying. 'That's what we've got to do. There must be lots of breeders in Collis Park. It's only a question of bringing them together. I wonder nobody thought of starting a Club here before.'

'You want to be careful who you get mixed up with,' said Dick. 'We don't want any of these crook dealers.' He was a huge, slow man, who breathed heavily through his nose and put down his words with the same weighty deliberation as his feet. He was as keen as Edward about this Rabbit Club, but he had to raise objections from time to time to stop Edward going too fast.

'The Pros won't join,' said Edward. 'Why should they? They get their commercial bran ration, and they've already got their markets. It's the little fanciers we're after. Once we've got enough members to get registered with the B.R.C., we'll get the bran and an assured price for the stock we sell for flesh.' He spoke eagerly, jabbing at the cylinder cover with his forefinger.

Dick Bennett tightened a nut, wiped it with a rag, re-tightened it, wiped the spanner and applied it again with the whole force of his great shoulders until the crankcase rocked in its cradle and the nut creaked round another ten-thousandth of an inch. Aircraftmen all over the world were in danger of rupture from undoing engines which Dick Bennett had assembled. He hammered the lockwasher tight, wiped the nut again and spoke.

'But look here, old man,' he said. 'I don't breed for flesh. I breed for showing and to sell to breeders. There's twice the money in that as breeding for flesh. Besides, people don't like rabbit. My missus can't even cook it without she heaves.'

Edward leaned forward. 'You know what you're doing? You're drowning Merchant Seamen. And there's lots of people like you,' he went on quickly, before Dick's chesty protest could reach his lips. 'That's why every district ought to have a Domestic Club. It benefits the fancier and saves shipping by increasing the meat supply.'

'Here,' said Dick, with sudden perspicacity, 'what've you been reading?'

Edward pulled his folded copy of *Backyard Breeding* out of his overall pocket, opened it on the cylinder cover and, folding it again in a well-worn crease, began to read while Dick pitted his strength against another tiny nut.

'Your Wallop at Hitler.' He looked up to see whether Dick were listening and met his face across the top of the engine, purple, with staring eyeballs. Dick grunted, relaxed, wiped his hand and stopped work to listen. 'Britain,' continued Edward, 'has not enough feeding-stuffs to breed more cattle and sheep. She must therefore find a substitute, and what will fill the bill better than the humble rabbit? This country is still not rabbit conscious. It is the business of every fancier to forswear selfish breeding and to play his part in this vital section of the Home Front. Keep a nucleus of your best stock for show-breeding so that when the piping times of peace come once more you can keep your place in the show ring, but meanwhile, join Domestic Rabbit Clubs and obtain foodstuffs which will provide you with bran on your pledge to sell half your stock for flesh. It is your duty for the honour of the Fancy.'

'Who wrote that?' asked Dick.

'Allan Colley.'

'Ah,' said Dick, impressed. Like all Flemish breeders, Allan Colley was his god. 'Then there's a poem,' went on Edward, '"Sent to me," he says, "by a reader from Woolbreeding." Shall I read it?' Dick nodded. He was fond of poetry.

> 'I'll starve them all out,' said Hitler the Hun,
> With my U-boats and E-boats and eighty-eight gun.
> So long live our Clubs and pay up our subs.
> He's forgotten Brer Rabbit and Bernard the Bun.'

Joseph's head appeared under Dick's left arm. 'Can we have the job over?' he said. 'I want to get at the top of the blower.' Other people turned the engine upside-down to get at the bottom of it; Joseph had to have it upside-down to get at the top.

'Stand away then, Ted,' said Dick and swung the engine over in its cradle as easily as if it were a toy. Joseph squatted down like a happy native. He preferred squatting to standing, which didn't make him much taller anyway. After years of working at knee-level, he could recognize people by their trousers and could say: 'Morning, Mr Gurley,' or 'How's the garden, Alf?' without looking up.

Dick Bennett, now presented with the underneath of the crankcase, contemplated it for a few moments as if he had never seen it before, and finally took the oil pressure pump from the trolley behind him and lowered it carefully on to its studs.

'You do see how important this Club is, don't you?' persisted Edward, putting *Backyard Breeding* back into his pocket. Dick was looking for nuts on the trolley. He was maddeningly difficult to rouse. If Edward had not known that he was really as enthusiastic as himself, he would have ceased trying long ago and gone ahead with plans for the Club on his own. But he needed Dick's technical knowledge, and there had to be two people to start it – one to be Treasurer and one Secretary. Dick was going to be Treasurer because he had a head for figures; he kept his wife's accounts for her down to the last halfpenny of bus fare in a series of red threepenny cash books. There were two boxfuls of them dating back over the last ten years, and mountains of old bills threaded on wire in the cupboard under the stairs, all of which Dick refused to send for salvage, because you never knew.

Edward was to be Secretary of the Club, because he could write a bit. Unknown to Connie, he had written a few short stories from time to time. He received them back from the magazines to which he sent them with no surprise and put them carefully in a drawer until it was their turn to venture out again. His favourite story, 'The End of a Perfect Day', had been travelling through the post at intervals for years. He renovated it every so often when it was getting old-fashioned before sending it to the next paper on his list. It was going now to wildly unsuitable trade papers in the North of Ireland and Parish Magazines in Lincolnshire. It would soon be time to start again with the big Dailies.

Edward was to be Secretary of the Club, and when they had got some members, one of them would be made Secretary and Edward would become President. If they ever got big enough to have a line or two in the 'Domestic Club Doings' of *Backyard Breeding*, that would be made a Presidential not a Secretarial duty. His dreams were a long way ahead of Dick Bennett's, which were still churning over the amount of the subscription.

Edward was already planning a Club Show and had marked down the hall in which it would be held. They would have a guest judge, someone like – well, not Allan Colley, of course, he wouldn't look at a potty little show like theirs, but someone with a name in the Fancy, who would make a speech which might be reported in *Backyard Breeding* even if the results of the classes were not.

Dick had found his nuts and was screwing them on to the studs by hand, preparatory to the straining process with the spanner.

'I must get back to my section,' said Edward, 'or those girls

77

will be getting into trouble. Is that understood then? I'll write the advertisement and get it in *Backyard Breeding* and the local paper, and you'll definitely back me up if we get any response at all. You won't let me down?' he persisted, as there was no reply from Dick. 'You do want to be in on this, don't you?'

Dick rested both hands on the belly of the crankcase, breathed heavily and said: 'I don't mind.' He had not been so enthusiastic about anything for years.

'Good,' said Edward. 'I'll send off the advertisement tonight, then.'

Dick called him back as he was walking away. 'We'll pay for it,' he said importantly, 'out of funds, when we get the first subscriptions in. Let me know how much it is meanwhile, so I can enter it on the books.'

As he came off the track into the Inspection Shop, Edward's eyes went at once to his bench of girls. He was beginning to feel quite possessive about them. They were in his charge, and if the A.I.D. threatened to make trouble for one of their mistakes, Edward would cover up for them and make excuses and even put the blame on himself, if necessary. After all, you had to make allowances for girls. It was not like working with men. Girls had nerves, which were always playing them up. He knew that from Connie.

'Edward!' called Paddy, sighting him. 'Where on earth have you been? I've been wanting you for hours. You are a – pest,' she added when he was close enough for her to lower her voice. He didn't mind them abusing him. It was all in fun, really, and meant that they felt they knew him so well that they didn't mind what they said to him. It was funny, but they talked to him more familiarly than Connie – his own wife. Not that he wanted her to swear; it would sound wrong on her lips, but these girls somehow made it sound friendly. His eye took in the whole benchful of them as he approached, smiling. It always intrigued him to think of the ten of them, day by day, clocking in and clocking out, their factory life running like a machine irrespective of the course of their private life. Anything might have happened to them the night before, yet there they were, perching on their stools at seven-thirty, caught up in unsought intimacy, until the bell scattered them to their separate fates at six o'clock. Sometimes Edward used to make up little stories about them, imagining what their real lives were like. He was as intimate with them as sixty hours a week could make him, and yet the part of their life he knew was only an interlude. One day he was going to write a story about them. They intrigued him.

He didn't go straight home that night. He had an idea.

Don Derris's barrage balloon was tethered on Collis Common. Don and the boys lived in a semi-circular tin hut, ridged like a sandwich loaf, surrounded by a narrow area of cultivation. It was this allotment that had given Edward his idea. If the balloon's crew had time to dig and hoe, they also had time to keep rabbits, and furthermore the cabbages and potatoes with which to feed them. Allan Colley had said that it was the duty of the initiated to inspire the uninitiated, so Edward was going on a trolley bus to inspire Don and the boys. It would mean an interesting little letter for 'The Fancy's Forum':

Dear Sir,
    I wonder how many Domestic Clubs can claim as members the crew of a barrage balloon? In the Collis Park Club, whose membership incidentally has just reached the so-and-so mark. Etc., etc.

Collis Common was a stretch of dingy grassland between three arterial roads. Besides the balloon site, it held two football fields, one of which was now cut up into allotments, several wooden benches, a couple of shelters facing the wind and a shallow pond, gradually silting up with leaves and sodden refuse. Getting off the trolley bus at the corner, Edward struck across the grass in the waning light, turning up the collar of his macintosh, for it was windy on the open ground. The balloon was not up, and he could just see it, straining and wallowing like a sick elephant trying to rise in its stall. Two squares of light fell on the ground from the windows of the tin hut, but as Edward approached, skirting the white rail of the pond, first one and then the other was blotted out. The little settlement wore an air of desolation; the tethered monster struggled and moaned in an agony of abandonment.

As Edward approached the barbed wire, a grey figure detached itself from the greyness on the other side and began to loaf towards the hut. Edward kept pace outside the wire, peering to see who it was. It was too fat for Don, and had not his swaggering walk. Edward cleared his throat.

'Excuse me,' he said diffidently – he never knew whether these visits were officially allowed – 'excuse me, but could I possibly speak to Corporal Derris, if he's there?'

'Sure,' said the stout figure, 'he's inside. Hang on and I'll give him a shout.' Edward had not yet thought what he was going to say to Don. He would be sure to laugh at first, because he laughed at Edward's own rabbits, but he might eventually take to the idea out of boredom, especially if the business side of it were made clear. The door of the hut opened and Don came out, dropping casually down the steps and sauntering over to the barbed wire, kicking at the grass.

'Hi, Ed,' he said, facing him across the wire with his hands in his pockets. 'You've heard the news then?'

'News? What news?'

'Oh, I thought you'd come to offer your condolences. You haven't heard then that little Don's all set for the great open spaces? No more will Collis Common resound to the clink of beer bottles and the gurgle of ale in the airman's throat. No, everywhere there will be the rustle of skirts, the tantalizing glimpse of a dainty ankle and the exotic scent of perfoom.'

'What on earth are you talking about?'

'You mean you haven't heard that the knell has been struck, the Last Post sounded, the hammer of doom, the finger of fate –'

'Look here, Don.' Edward was cold, and it was difficult enough to talk in the deepening twilight across the barbed wire which made you feel you were visiting someone in prison, without Don putting on one of his nonsense acts. Sometimes he'd go on like this for hours – stuff he'd read in magazines – maddening if you were trying to discuss anything sensibly with him.

'My dear old soul,' said Don, irritably. 'I'm telling you that the powers that be have ordained that women – W.A.A.F.S. – tarts – whatever you like to call 'em, are to release men as balloon crews. Corporal Donald Derris, No. 23894, R.A.F., starts his embarkation leave a fortnight Saturday. I'm on duty at the moment or I'd come out and have a beer with you on the strength of it.'

There was not much to say. Edward commiserated and they both agreed gloomily that it was tough luck on Dorothy, and

Edward said well anyway, now he had a better chance of having a crack at Jerry, which seemed to leave Don cold.

'Well, no sense hanging about, I suppose,' said Edward. 'I'll be shoving off home to break the news to Connie. Cheer up, Don. Not dead yet, you know.'

Don mumbled something to the effect that he soon would be, said 'Ta-ta' and turned to go back to the hut. Edward watched his uniform merge into the dusk, saw the door open and heard a voice from inside before it banged shut and the settlement was once more abandoned to noises of the wind torturing the balloon, more eerie than silence. Edward felt sorry for the W.A.A.F.S. He doubted whether they would feel like keeping rabbits.

He walked up Church Avenue in the dark and had to fumble outside his front door before he could get the key in. He would have taken his torch if he had known he was going to be late. Connie would tick him off, but at any rate he had a bit of news that would pin her ears back.

'Connie!' he called, switching on the hall light as he shut the front door. From the sitting-room came the sound of noisy crying, and as he stepped quickly forward to investigate, his mother-in-law came out of the room with a face like the sole of a boot. As far as she was concerned, Don was already dead.

'It's Dorothy,' she said in answer to Edward's inquiring glance. 'I'm afraid she's had very upsetting news. We came straight round to tell Connie. We've just heard that –'

'I know,' said Edward. 'I've just been up to the Common to see Don and he told me he's being sent abroad, if that's what you mean.'

'Oh, so you know then.' Mrs Munroe's face fell another foot. She had been waiting about to be able to break the bad news to Edward. He smiled encouragingly.

'I don't see what there is to smile about,' she said, 'with that poor child in there nearly out of her mind with worry.'

'Oh, come on, Mother, it's not a tragedy.' Edward wondered whether he could bring himself to pat her drooping shoulders. 'Lots of people go abroad. It's the least you can expect. Don's been very lucky up till now to be so near home, though for his sake I should think he'd be glad to get a bit nearer the fighting.'

'Well, you're a nice one to talk, I must say,' said Mrs Munroe, who although she knew that Edward had sought and been refused his release from the factory, always held it against him that he was not in uniform. 'That poor Don, so nervous and sensitive as he's always been. You mark my words, he'll come back a changed man – if he comes back at all.' Connie came out of the sitting-room looking cross.

'Do go to her, Mother,' she said. 'I can't do anything with her and she's getting hysterical. It's ridiculous to carry on like this just because he's going abroad. Anyone would think – Oh, there you are, Ted. Where on earth have you been? I never knew anyone so inconsiderate. I might have been worrying about you for all you knew.'

'I went up to see Don. It's bad luck, but I agree with you, there's no sense in Dorothy carrying on fit to make herself ill.'

'What do you mean? I never said that.' She took a step nearer to her mother, and they both regarded him balefully. 'You can't expect a man to understand, I suppose,' said Connie. 'Come in and have your tea, Mother.' The two women went into the sitting-room together, leaving Edward alone in the hall. He took his torch off the shelf under the hanging mirror and went out to see the rabbits,

It was all very well waking up with a hangover; it was at least a memory of last night's gin. But Mrs Urry felt cheap these mornings even when she hadn't been near the Prince Albert. That nagging pain, which she used to accept as part of the price you paid for gin, came now after nothing more than a cup of tea. In fact gin seemed to be the only thing that would lay it.

Laying the pain took nearly all Mrs Urry's earnings from the Acropolis Dining Rooms. Matches were not doing so well these days, unless Urry was up to some trickery with the takings. The demand was there all right, but not the stock to meet it. He could have sold his supply twenty times over, but the little Jew wholesaler was cutting down his allowance every week. Time and again, Mrs Urry had urged him to strike out in flints or bootlaces or even cachous, but Mr Urry was adamant, doubtless because the sooner he sold out, the sooner he could leave his pitch for some warmer retreat, returning to Holborn Circus before his wife came to collect him.

'One day,' she said, 'I'm going to stick to beer for a week. Beer! I could put another name to that coloured water if I wasn't such a lady – and have a real good meal. I owe it to my system, Urry, though I must say I've no appetite for it.'

'You don't need it at your age,' grunted Mr Urry. He was sitting on the lower bunk, lacing his boots. He kept them on at night, but would not dream of going to bed without unlacing them.

'All very well for you,' said his wife. 'I know you gets your bit of fish dinner from that soft Mrs Ewins. I don't know what her old man would say if he knew. You can't run a fish and chip shop on charity and so I'll tell her if ever I meet her, which God forbid I do, because her face makes me stomach turn over and look the other way. 'Urry up, Urry, it must be getting on. 'Ere's young innocent coming down already with everything on 'er face but the kitchen stove. 'Ullo, dear,' she grinned at Sheila with her gums. 'Just in time. The chauffeur is bringing the car round now.' She cocked her head to the approaching rumble of a train. Sheila made herself smile and say something friendly. Mrs Urry's appearance was getting more fearsome every day. Her face, which was like the uneatable kernel of an old walnut, seemed to be shrinking, the yellow hands rolling up the blankets were like roots and her body looked as though it would crumble into dust at a touch.

'Well,' she hitched up the bundle and prepared to follow her husband towards the Exit. 'I must go on my way rejoicing. Ta-ta, love.'

'Good-bye.' Sheila stepped into her usual carriage, third from the end. She was glad the train windows were covered with anti-shatter net. The boy with the limp might think her queer if he saw her talking to the Urrys.

The Urrys made for the Cosy Café – 'COME AND GET IT. Prop: Samuel Snagge', who allowed them to leave their bedding there during the day.

The Cosy was a small wooden shack in a street off Theobald's Road. It stood in what had once been the entrance to the yard of a warehouse, long since dwindled out of existence with the death of its proprietor. Nobody had wanted the yard enough to face clearing it of its unsavoury junk, so the Cosy Café stood propped between two tall shops, its chicken-house roof askew, a curtain over the doorway and above the curtain a board saying: 'Teas, Light Luncheons and Minerals' which Sam had picked up cheap at the sale of effects from a teashop foundered through over-gentility. If the Cosy ever foundered, it would not be for that reason.

Inside were four linoleum-covered tables with benches, and the counter behind them, cutting Sam off at the waist and bearing crockery, two urns and a case of stale cakes and pies. The floor was the original cobbles of the yard. Sam swept it occasionally, dislodging interesting relics of food between the cracks.

When the Urrys pushed past the curtain, there were already a few regulars brooding over their tea. Two men who worked on the roads, a man employed by the Borough Council to clean out telephone boxes, but had never yet been seen doing it, the night watchman from the excavations, a rosy old man with split shoes and a bright line in pornographic magazines – the usual crowd.

'Morning all,' said Mrs Urry perkily. She carried her bundle behind the counter and through a low door into the shed that leant on the leaning café and held two gas-rings, a cold tap and a tin bath for washing up.

She rejoined Mr Urry at the table. Sam reached down two cups from the shelf behind him. He was a long, stooping man with a face that always looked as if he were about to cry. When he laughed, his face puckered up, his eyes watered and his mouth turned down instead of up. His appearance bore no trace of the inward joy that had been his ever since the death of his wife enabled him to sell the goodwill of his vegetable barrow and erect the Cosy. His face would torture itself into a laugh even now when he thought of that murderous trek to Covent Garden before dawn and the windiest corner in Holborn which had been his wife's idea of a good beat.

'The usual?' he asked, dipping milk into the two cups from the bowl of tinned milk on the bread board.

'That's right, dear. Two nice cups of, and four slices.' They drank their tea and ate the bread and butter in silence. The warm, stale air made Mrs Urry feel sleepy. 'Tell you what,' she called to Sam, 'I'll have to speak to them about running that first train a bit later. Me nights is too short.' Sam stared for a moment like a child after a fall, weighing the advantages of tears or bravery, then his face puckered up and he doubled over the counter, enjoying the joke. 'Oh, that's good – that's good!' he gasped, wiping his eyes and holding his middle. He never make a joke himself and was in agonies of delight at anyone else's humour. Mrs Urry sat back, basking in his amusement, and when he looked like recovering, set him off again with an allusion to her footman. She loved to be thought a wit.

A van driver shouldered his way past the curtain and sat down heavily at her table. 'Morning, Wally!' she said. He grunted at her, passing his hand over his face. 'Cup of, Sam, two rashers on and two slices,' he said over his shoulder.

'Coming up!' Sam doubled up to get through the low door to his gas rings.

Seeing Wally eat his bacon and potato reminded Mrs Urry of her intention to have a good meal. She would try and get out one dinner-time and see what Urry was up to at Mrs Ewin's fish shop. But there was not much chance of the Greek letting her out dinner-time. He was short of plates and they had to be washed as soon as they came off one table and rushed back on to the next one.

The Acropolis didn't do breakfast, but Mrs Urry had to be there at half-past seven to do the cleaning, wash up whatever had accumulated after her departure the night before, peel the vegetables that the Greek was going to cook for lunch and as often as not do a bit of mincing, if it was rissole day.

Having parked Mr Urry firmly in his angle between two walls, with his tray round his neck, Mrs Urry went off up Holborn with many backward glances, as if she were training a dog. She had never yet caught him wandering away, but she had her suspicions. Someone would nab his pitch one of these days.

Entering the frosted glass doors of the Acropolis Dining Rooms, she went straight through to the kitchen without a glance at the Greek, reading the paper over coffee and rolls at a corner table. He had already been to the market. There was a pile of vegetables and some large lumps of meat on the worn table that filled the centre of the low, smoky kitchen. Mrs Urry investigated. Pork again! Black Market, of course. And all those raisins – it was evidently going to be steamed fruit pudding again. Well, she'd better get the fire going as the pans went on early, steaming days. She took off her cape, but kept on the beret and wound herself into an apron that had only gone once round the last washer-up, but went twice round Mrs Urry and bunched out at the back like a bustle.

She went into the scullery. The sight of the piled dirty plates was too familiar to be disheartening. The water was still quite warm from last night, so after she had lit the kitchen range, mumbling and muttering at it and finally pouring on some paraffin that nearly blew off her few remaining eyebrows, she began on the washing-up.

The Greek's daughter, a dressy, pig-faced girl with a figure that burst out above and below the waist, came into the kitchen and began to pick over the raisins. Mrs Urry leered at her over her shoulder through the adjoining doorway.

''Ullo, Ellen, I saw you last night going in the pictures, when Urry and I was going to our 'otel. 'E's all right, whoever he is. Where d'you pick that one up?'

'Oh, he's a fellow I know,' said Ellen, popping a handful of raisins into her mouth. 'He comes in here sometimes as a matter of fact. I wonder you haven't seen him.'

'Fat chance I get to see any of the customers with your Pa around,' said Mrs Urry, scraping at a bit of mustard, abandoning it, and slinging the plate into the rack that was too high for her. When she was washing a pile of plates, she developed quite a rhythm as she swilled a plate, then up on her toes to reach the rack, then down to swill another, then up again to the rack; swill and reach, swill and reach, up and down jauntily went the bustle of her apron.

'When you were away that time,' she went on, raising her voice against the running tap, 'he and Victor were run off their feet, but would they let me have so much as a look inside the dining-room? No, they would not, and once, when there'd been a soup ordered, and I'd served it out and no one to fetch it, in I popped – as a favour, mind you; don't think I fancy being a Nippy. Well, in I popped, as I say –' she got worked up even now when she thought of it – 'and there was your Pa coming at me as if I was murder and disease and sudden death all in one. Out he comes here after me and we had a real set to. I told him straight. It don't need me to take away their appetites. You'd think this was the Ritz 'Otel, wouldn't you?' She turned off the tap. 'Wouldn't you?' she repeated.

'I daresay,' said Ellen, who hadn't heard a word. 'He's quite a nice fellow,' she went on, following her thoughts. 'He works on a newspaper.' Mrs Urry turned on the tap again and began to wash forks, several together in bunches. Newspapers to her were things that you wrapped round other things.

The Greek came out and began to mix suet pastry in an enormous bowl. When Mrs Urry made for the potatoes to take them to the scullery to peel, he threw back an imaginary lock of hair, stabbing at the dough with his fingers like an impassioned impresario. 'Please, Mrs Hurry,' he called, in his high voice, 'the dining-room is not yet done, I believe?'

'You mean you want it done,' said Mrs Urry, facing him with a butting stance, beret well forward. She didn't believe in sideways talk. She collected her bucket and mop and the precious bits of rags she secreted at the back of the cupboard and went out to slosh over the marble-topped tables and fix the dirt to the floor by wetting it. Laying the dust, that was called.

Victor was sitting behind the counter, where stand-up snacks were served, writing out menu cards in a looping violet hand. He was a Frenchman, a vague relation of the Greek's, who had escaped from Occupied France in a dinghy. He had wandered into the Acropolis one evening and had stayed there happily ever since, as if he had escaped from a labour camp and endured the hunted, starving journey across France for nothing else.

He spoke English badly, with a Cockney accent. Strangers to the Acropolis thought when Victor took their order that it must be quite a continental place – until their order arrived.

'Bonjewer,' said Mrs Urry proudly, swatting at a table with a damp cloth.

'*Bon jour, vieille putain,*' said Victor, and Mrs Urry bridled as at the wildest compliment.

On Fridays and Tuesdays, Sheila knew that the curly-haired boy with the limp would be in the third carriage from the end. It was not as if she got into the same carriage deliberately, because, after all, she went in it all the rest of the week; it just happened to stop opposite to where the stairs brought her on to the platform. She got up a bit earlier on Fridays and Tuesdays, so as to have time to put on eye-black.

She got into the train this morning just like any other Friday, ostentatiously averting her head, after making sure that he was there and staring. He never pretended to be reading the paper, and peeped round it as some men did, and if she looked at him, he didn't look away, but went on staring, so that she had to turn her head and hope that the hot feeling in her face wasn't a blush coming.

He sat at the end of the carriage and she sat half-way down on the opposite side. She wondered a lot about him. What did he do, and why did he only do it twice a week, and what could he possibly do at Earls Court? That was where he always got off. Whatever it was, he looked as if he were overworking. Perhaps his limp meant that he was discharged wounded – a pilot, perhaps – and his face was tired because the wound hurt him. His clothes looked as if they had started life right. He was well-built, with a small head, a short nose and lively eyes, a curly mouth and that crisp, light brown hair that grew so absolutely the right way. All this she had gleaned from furtive glances twice a week and a more sustained scrutiny of his back view when he was getting out.

Sometimes she squirmed to peer through the diamond opening in the window netting to watch him walk up the platform, but once he had turned as he came level and looked her full in the eyes. She was not sure whether he had seen her or not.

This Friday morning was just like any other. She read her paper self-consciously, taking care not to frown, scarcely seeing a word she read. After nine months of this tedious journey, she knew all the stations by heart, so when the train stopped at Earls Court, she allowed a decent interval for him to get up and walk to the door and then raised her eyes to watch him get out. When she looked up this morning, he was gone. It was unusual for him to get out so quickly. He always waited until the train had completely stopped, because of his limp. She squinted through the window, and when she turned back, saw him still sitting in his seat at the end of the carriage. For the first time, he dropped his eyes, almost guiltily. What was so guilty about not getting out at Earls Court? Perhaps he had suddenly decided not to go to work; perhaps his leg was hurting him and he just couldn't get up. She toyed with another idea. Perhaps he was going to travel on to see where she got out.

The train was running above ground now and the carriage was filling up. She recognized one or two people from Canning Kyles. By the time they neared Collis Park, he was hidden from her by a mass of swaying bodies. He might have already got out for all she knew.

But when she stepped on to the platform, there he was in the crowd just ahead, looking back. In a sudden panic, Sheila spotted Grace and seized on her, chatting with self-conscious vivacity all the way up the steps that led from the railway cutting to the road. She was sure he was following her. As they walked towards the Estate, she took Grace's arm, hanging on it so that she could not walk too fast, because of his limp. Grace had begun on the saga of her bathroom curtains. Sheila listened charmingly and once turned her head full towards Grace to say: 'No, really?' so that she could look sideways behind her. He was following them. It was terribly exciting. She wanted to boast to Grace, but at the same time she knew she would have only one opinion of men who followed girls.

What did he mean to do? Was he just going to follow her to see where she worked, or was he going to come up and speak to her? Surely not with Grace there. She must lose Grace. She thought of pretending to have dropped a glove, but Grace would be sure to come back and help her look for it, because she was so kind. In any case, what should she say to him? She must obviously be fairly cold and dignified, but she couldn't be too putting-off in case he was sensitive. It was rather a cheek, really, to follow her like this.

They turned through the gates on to the Estate road, and Sheila, gushing towards Grace again, saw him turn in behind her. The crowd was thickening. Even if he did accost her now, she couldn't stop and parry words with him. Someone she knew would see her. She wouldn't be able to do herself justice. He'd have to be quick though, they were only a hundred yards from the clockhouse – fifty yards and still he had not done whatever he meant to do. Perhaps he only wanted to see where she worked. You couldn't say he was not persistent. He would be terribly late for his own work.

As they reached the clockhouse, and the stream of people compressed itself to crush through the narrow entrance, she dropped behind Grace and deliberately looked back. She was going to give him one dazzling smile. It was the least he deserved.

She just caught a glimpse of his sports jacket going through the gate that led to the big office building. Craning her neck, standing firm against the jostling crowd, she saw him speak to the doorman, and saw the doorman nod and step aside to let the sports coat through, before she was swept by the current into the clockhouse, and was clocking in, looking at the figures 7.28 without taking them in and was out on the track with her brain reeling.

It was still reeling two hours later, and refusing to concentrate on work 'A penny for 'em,' said Edward, finding her staring into space, one hand idly turning the big gearwheel round on its stand.

Bob Condor was fussing about, finding jobs for anyone who was idle for a moment. One of the managers was on his way round.

'Finished this engine, Sheila?' he asked.

'What? Oh – oh no, Mr Condor, not quite.' She began hurriedly to fill in the report card, holding her arm over it to conceal how little she had done. Burrs and slight damage on teeth. What was he doing in the offices? Trim up splines . . . Who was he? Oil seal unserviceable, cracked . . . Had he or had he not been following her? Clean out thrust bearing . . . Where had he got to now?

She heard voices behind her, and when she looked round, there he was.

Sheila got such a shock that she swung straight round again on her stool and began to examine a bearing feverishly, like a monkey looking for ticks. She could feel the blush creeping up into her head; the back of her neck and ears must be scarlet. He was being shown round by the Works Manager. Who *was* he? He must be a pilot, or somebody important.

'This is the reduction gear,' the Manager was saying, studiedly casual, as if it were just a little thing he'd run up in his spare time. 'It reduces the revs of the crank, you see, to a suitable speed for the airscrew.'

He couldn't be a pilot then, or he would know that. Why didn't he say something and let her hear what his voice was like?

'See this big wheel?' went on the Manager as Bob Condor's scandalized voice hissed in Sheila's ear: 'Get up, Sheila. Don't you see Mr Wrigley's here?' She had to get up then and turn round, keeping her eyes low, unwilling to look up and see him laughing at her.

If only she could have met him as an equal at a party, perhaps, or at somebody's house at Swinley, or even in the train. Here he had her at a disadvantage. He was in the world of men in black hats and thick spectacles who came round poking at things with umbrellas and told the workers afterwards in the canteen that they were putting up a jolly fine show but were going to have the honour of being asked to do better still, while she was in the world of dirty hands whose only retaliation was a rude gesture after the departing figure.

Mr Wrigley was standing on his heels, jingling the keys in his pocket, while he indicated salient points to his guest. They had to be very salient for him to know them. Bob Condor hovered assiduously, ready to turn a nut or hand a bearing.

'What's this do then?' asked the boy with the limp, picking up the dual drive casing. His voice was like his hair – absolutely right.

'Well go on.' The Manager stepped back. 'Ask the girls anything you want to know. Talk to them. That's what you're here for, isn't it – not to talk to me?' He had had his hour of holding forth.

So Sheila had to come forward and tell him, conscious of his eyes on her dirty, broken nails, and that she was making a fool of herself. Her explanation got more and more involved until it trailed off limply with: 'Well, it's called the dual drive because it sort of drives two things, you see.' She had never imagined talking to him for the first time like this, with Mr Wrigley benevolently critical, Bob Condor hovering like an anxious exhibitor, the girls on the bench staring and giggling and herself red to the hair and with a vocabulary of about three words. He was very polite, but his questions were awkward enough to be deliberate.

'What two things does it drive?' he asked earnestly, as if the key to life were in her answer.

'Well, the constant speed and the V.P.' She knew that.

'V.P.?'

'The – er, the – er –' The word would not come.

'Oh, Sheila, Sheila, what's the matter with you?' broke in Bob Condor. 'She really knows the unit very well. She –' He turned to Mr Wrigley, explaining her away.

'Oh, yes, of course,' she said, 'the variable pitch –'

'Oh, ...' went Bob Condor, and even Mr Wrigley began: 'But surely –'

'I mean the – yes, the variable pitch – no I mean the vacuum pump, I mean –' They had got her so muddled she didn't know what she meant.

At last the ordeal was over and she could sit down on her stool with her palms against her burning cheeks. It was over, yes, but so were her illusions. If he had ever had any interest in her it must be stone dead by now.

He was at the far end of the bench now, talking to Dinah, who was making him laugh. They didn't seem to be talking about the engine at all. Dinah cared nothing for Mr Wrigley, nor for Mr Canning or Mr Kyles themselves, presuming they existed. She was perfectly at home and so was the boy with the limp. He never once looked back to Sheila's end of the bench.

Edward, who always lurked unobtrusively when authority was about, now came up rubbing his hands and said pleasantly: 'Well, you had quite a little session, didn't you? I hope you aired your knowledge. Who was it?'

'I don't know.' Sheila shrugged her shoulders indifferently.

Edward laughed. 'Look at old Dinah making her number!' He had an embarrassing habit of using service expressions and had been known to speak of an incorrect entry in a log book as 'Duff Gen'.

Sheila went on filling in her report card. Well, that little episode was over. She would take care not to go in the third carriage from the end again on a Friday or a Tuesday.

Mr Wrigley was getting restless. He usually reckoned to make the tour of the factory in half an hour, without lingering. In the preliminary talk in his office, he always said: 'Happy at their work? My dear sir, come and see for yourself. Talk to the girls; ask 'em questions. I'm not afraid of what they'll tell you,' confident that most people would be too unnerved by the din and the brawny feminine forearms and trousered bottoms in the

Machine Shop and the bevy of grey overalls and sophisticated coiffures in the Inspection Shop, to take him at his word. Unabashed people like this young man upset the timetable. You couldn't hustle them too much in case they thought you were trying to hurry them past something you didn't want them to see.

'We'll go into the Fitting Shop now,' he said.

Mr Gurley snapped up the little window of his office. 'Oh, God, the Old Man,' he said to someone inside. 'I suppose he thinks he's keeping up morale,' and snapped the window down again.

'We'll go into the Fitting Shop now,' repeated Mr Wrigley, taking the young man by the arm and easing him down the gangway, jingling his keys on their chain like a jailer doing the rounds.

'Excuse me a sec.,' said his guest, 'there's just one question I'd like to –' He broke away and limped round the end of the bench, surprisingly quickly. Sheila wondered if he could see the breast pocket of her overall jumping to the thudding of her heart.

'I say,' he said, loudly enough for everyone to hear, 'you'll think me an awful idiot, but would you mind showing me that dual what's-it again? I haven't got it quite straight.'

'Of course not,' she mumbled, pulling the dual drive tray towards her. He picked up the casing and bent down to scrutinize it. 'Look,' he said in a low voice, 'you'll probably think this awful cheek, but I feel I know you quite well, because I've seen you in the train. I've always wanted to speak to you and never dared. I didn't like to say anything before with those parties hanging about, but I've been looking at you twice a week for months, though I don't suppose you've ever noticed.' He was fingering the dual drive all the time, pretending to be discussing it.

'Well, I don't know.' Sheila picked up a gear, keeping up the pretence. She suddenly felt very cool and mistress of the situation. 'Well, I don't know,' she said casually. 'I thought you looked rather familiar. I suppose I must have seen you without noticing it.'

Mr Wrigley was waiting in the aisle, swinging his keys in a circle and tapping the toe of one shiny fat shoe. 'Look, I must

93

go,' said the boy with a limp, 'but next Tuesday, do notice me. Come and sit by me; I get so sick of that dreary journey. And I say – wear that red jacket.'

You were not supposed to go and wash your hands until five minutes before lunch-time. The 'toilet' was three hundred yards away from the Inspection Shop and contained six basins for about sixty girls. There were three alternatives: 'You could wipe your hands on a piece of rag and try to pretend that your lunch didn't taste of oil; you could run the three hundred yards among the sheds, fight your way in among the backs lined up at the basins like a litter of feeding pigs, and have a quick scrub with a hairless nailbrush and a swill in someone else's dirty water before it was time to run back again; or you could sneak out before the lawful time and risk finding Bob Condor stationed outside the door, behaving as if the war was lost or won according to whether you entered the toilet.

You could always tell when it was approaching twelve o'clock without looking at the time. The Inspection Shop was still apparently working, but restlessness stirred in the air. Girls had risen from their stools, powder-puffs appeared, surreptitiously or defiantly, the crankcase section were throwing spanners into the tool chest. George, who tested cylinder blocks for leaks, shut off his high-pressure steam and the sudden silence made you realize for the first time that the noise had been in your ears all morning. People who had washed touched things daintily so as not to get dirty again, overalls were untied, shoes changed, bags and gloves came out of drawers. Charlie and his women, who had been advancing relentlessly down the centre aisle behind a trolley had suddenly disappeared, leaving the trolley stranded, a curly oil pipe sticking up from a tray on top like a surprised eyebrow. The whole shop was fidgeting, every ear tensed for the first impact of the clapper on the bell.

Bob Condor occasionally had a pogrom and pounced on one or two people for stopping work before the bell, but it was like trying to step on locusts in a swarm. He could not hope to have any effect on the universal restlessness. Nothing short of a machine-gun could stop the swaying towards the corner where the coats hung, the furtive steps that burst into a mad rush as the bell jangled and everybody flew, struggling into coats and tearing the lining, jamming on hats and haring off down the track with swinging belts and flapping shoe-laces.

There was no time to stop and wonder why you were running. Once outside in the road, you might slow down and saunter, or even stop and chat, but you always came out of the place as if you were running for your life instead of your dinner.

Sheila, Paddy and Dinah galloped out of the clockhouse with wild hair, then pulled up and stood for a moment irresolute.

'Canteen?' Paddy made a face. 'Not after that fish yesterday.'

'King's Head?'

'No,' said Dinah, 'I couldn't hold any more malt after last night. How about Mike's?'

'I'm sick of sausages,' said Sheila. 'Milkers then,' said Dinah starting off. 'I've got to go to the shops anyway.'

They walked along the main road to the Milk Bar, which stood in a line of shops under a block of modern flats. The shops had a here-today-and-gone-tomorrow look about them. They were always changing hands. A Delicatessen Store would go bankrupt and become almost overnight a teashop, which having quietly run through a lady's life's savings would emerge as a tailor and dressmaker with half the window blacked and Ladies' Own Materials Made Up.

Only the Chain Store Grocery was constant, and the Milk Bar, which was well patronized by the neighbouring factories. Canning Kyles came out earlier than most, so the three girls were able to get stools at the counter.

'What's on, Lou?' Dinah asked the sharp little ginger-haired girl who darted up and down behind the counter like a shuttle. She paused to snatch an aluminium cylinder out of the mixing machine. 'Cornish Pasties – hot,' she said, putting a head on the Horlicks as she poured it into the glass, 'or you can have processed egg and mashed.'

'No chips?'

'No chips.' She darted away. When she had paused in her flight long enough to give them coffee and sandwiches, they sat with feet tucked under them, elbows on the counter, savouring the moment of relaxation that made it more difficult to go back and click into the rhythm of work. Three youths in overalls came in from the electric bulb factory and went straight to the automatic gramophone. Guffawing and shoving each other, they put a penny into the middle of a rising sun, the glass box lit up revealing a pastoral backcloth, and the turntable revolved among a bed of little green marbles.

'My Mommo done told me,' said the box.

'When I was in knee pants,' sobbed one of the youths, making a few tentative jitterbug passes.

'Oh, that tune again!' Dinah looked over her shoulder and caused a certain amount of scuffling and tittering.

'The Bloo-ooes – in the night,' throbbed the box.

Sheila stared happily at her reflection in the mirror beyond Lou's flying head. It was Tuesday. She had been bursting to talk about it all morning. 'I say,' she said suddenly, putting down her cup and turning sideways to face the other two, 'remember that chap who came round with old Wrigley – last week, or the week before or sometime.' She toned down her voice to casualness.

'Which one?' said Dinah. 'The old Daddy who called Freda Girlie?' She laughed at the memory of it.

'No, that young one – you know. He talked quite a lot to you – with a limp.'

'Oh, that one. Yes, I remember. Amusing bloke.'

'Yes, well, wasn't it funny, I met him in the train this morning. We had quite a long talk.'

'What a time of day to pick anyone up,' said Paddy. 'How could you be bothered?'

'Oh, no, it wasn't that. He –' She decided to suppress the first part of their acquaintance. 'He recognized me from coming round the factory. And what d'you think? He works on a newspaper. He came down to get a story on "The Girls Behind the Planes". It's going to be in on Friday. I'm longing to see it.'

'Well, if he puts in what I told him, it ought to make hot reading,' said Dinah. 'Thank God for that,' she added, as the automatic gramophone whirred and stopped. The three youths scuffled before it, reading the labels of its repertoire.

'Are you boys having anything?' asked Lou severely, appearing opposite them. 'You can't come in here and play that thing without ordering something.'

'Three teas, then, Miss,' said the tallest one. Ring-leader in dare-devilry, he produced another penny and inserting it into the rising sun, twiddled a knob expertly.

The Jitterbug one took up the tune with joy as it speeded into intelligibility.

'. . . When I was in knee pants.' Sheila smiled at herself in the mirror, remembering certain remarks. Dinah groaned. 'I'd like to smash that machine. Well, go on about your boy-friend. What was he doing this morning? Coming down here again?'

'No, going home apparently. He has to stay on at night twice a week to do an article that gets cabled over from America from some frightfully famous general. His name's David Fielding. You've probably read articles by him.' She named the daily paper for which he wrote.

'That rag?' said Dinah. 'I wouldn't use it to wrap me fish.'

'I think it's a jolly good paper,' said Sheila, who had hardly ever read it. 'Anyway, it's frightfully interesting, his job, he was telling me about it. He meets lots of famous people.'

'A woman's a thing that leaves you to sing

The Bloo-ooes in the night . . .' The machine throbbed behind their talk.

'He asked me to meet him tonight for a drink,' announced Sheila defiantly. 'I said I would.'

CHAPTER 6

IF Kitty had realized how thick the fog was, she would have left her bicycle in the car park and walked home. It had not seemed so bad when she left the factory; it was darker than usual and the air was full of raw, swirling vapours, but she had been able to see her way among the crowd coughing up the Estate road and telling each other what a rotten night.

But half-way between Canning Kyles and her home in Barnardo Road, the semi-circle that left Collis High Street at Boot's corner and came back to it at the Public Library, Kitty coasted down a hill into a patch of fog so dense that she began to ring her bell wildly in alarm, jammed on her brakes as an enormous figure loomed right ahead, and fell into the road with the bicycle on top of her. The enormous figure turned out to be a foreigner in a tent-like overcoat, who helped her to her feet and asked her the way to Blen-hime Crescent, of which she had never heard, even on a clear night. She found the edge of the pavement and began to wheel her bicycle cautiously along, making wide detours at lamp-posts, the foreigner keeping step in the road on the other side of the bicycle.

'Which way are you going?' he asked. 'If I may walk with you? I have no light.' She could not see his face; there was only the vast blurred bulk of him, the plop of his feet and his voice, which she was sure was German.

'I don't think I'm going your way,' she said. Her mother was convinced that rape stalked the mild streets of Collis Park. 'I'm going to the High Street.'

'Blen-hime Crescent?' he insisted. 'Number thirty-four. Mr and Mrs Maxwell-Steed. You know them?' He couldn't believe she did not. Mrs Maxwell-Steed was a so cultured lady with two sons, one in India and one in Ireland in the Unti-Tanks, and a daughter who was married to an M.P., whom, of course, Kitty must know. All this he imparted in his suspicious accent, while they were fumbling their way through the deepening fog. It was like walking into a wall that retreated always a foot from your nose, and instead of penetrating it, Kitty's bicycle lamp was thrown back on itself. Her hands and feet were frozen, and her nose was beginning to run, but it was better to sniff than take off a glove to get out your handkerchief. Mrs Maxwell-Steed's friend was making unpleasant snorting noises to keep the fog out of his passages.

Disembodied footsteps passed, figures manifested themselves at startlingly close range, a stick went tapping by like a blind man's and screams of feminine laughter announced that some-one thought it the funniest thing that had ever happened. Distance was non-existent, but they should long ago have come to the cross-roads with the lighted island. From time to time, a train thudded by on the left, so they must be on the right road. Unless they had already passed the island, it had taken half an hour to cover a distance which normally took ten minutes. Thinking of her mother's anxiety, she quickened her steps and a pillar-box ran into her left cheek. The slap in the face brought tears smarting to her eyes, but she fought them down. Her companion might want to come round to her side of the bicycle if he thought she was hurt.

He was still occupied in reaching down branches of the

98

Maxwell-Steed family tree for her benefit. He seemed quite happy, although he was probably going in the wrong direction.

She knew where she was now, after the pillar-box. 'We have to cross the road here,' she said. 'At least I do. I only hope we find the other side. Look out.' She turned her bicycle wheel and struck off at right angles, feeling very insecure without the kerb, as if at any minute she might walk straight into a yawning abyss.

'You cannot,' said the foreigner chattily, 'see your face in front of your hand,' and was suddenly lost. From one instant to the next, the fog had taken him unto its own and Kitty was alone in the middle of the road. It must be the middle, because she could hear water gurgling under a grating. She said: 'I say!' tentatively, and 'Where are you?' but he was gone as completely as if the yawning abyss had been more than Kitty's imagination. Feeling very much alone and quite missing him, she shuffled on into the eerie yellow blanket until she stubbed her toe on the edge of the pavement. She walked along it, sniffing, with her bicycle in the gutter. She must be nearly at the High Street by now, but in that case, what was that train doing far away on her right, when it ought to be close to on her left? She stood still, gripping her handlebars and looking all round her into nothing, realizing in complete panic that she had not the slightest idea where she was. She tried crossing the road, but when at last she did strike the other side, she met trees. She could think of no road with trees. She waited for another train, and when it came, turned so that it was on her left and began to walk forward.

As a blind man is aware of furniture in his path, she heard rather than saw the air-raid shelter, just in time to avoid another smack in the face. All the streets in which she might conceivably be had their shelters down the middle of the road. She took off her glove to get her handkerchief out of the bag in her bicycle basket, and her hand was numb before she put it on again. She went forward blindly because it was better than standing still, snivelling to herself like a lost child. She saw herself wandering about until morning, or fainting, perhaps, and lying senseless in the road until someone stumbled over her. Would they send out an ambulance on a night like this? They'd have to. How the ambulance men would curse – or perhaps they would think it an adventure. She might have broken her leg; that would make it more worth while them coming. By the time she was lying in a high hospital bed with the sheet drawn very smooth, unable to move her head, but following with her eyes the affecting entrance of her mother into the ward, she was crying in earnest. She ached for her mother. Sometimes she thought of Len and hoped he was safe indoors and wondered whether he were at home and mad with anxiety, but it was her mother for whom she ached. If I ever get home, she thought, I'll never be rude to her again. If I ever get home, God, I swear I'll pray – yes, every night, and do it kneeling before I get into bed and not lying down so that I go to sleep in the middle.

She wandered dolefully on into the freezing unknown that was like a nightmare from which you awoke sweating and lay almost panting with happiness that it was not true. But this was true and she knew now that she would never get home. She began to review her life, like a drowning man, but before she had got beyond that deliriously exciting last term at school when she had been a prefect and vice-captain of netball into the bargain, a sound of which she had despaired of ever hearing again brought her back to life.

The sound was: 'Cooee! Cooee!' Like a child playing hide-and-seek. Kitty stood stock-still and listened, her tired eyes straining. The fog played tricks with sound. It wrapped it up and moved it, so that the second faint 'Cooee!' seemed to come from behind her. She swung round. Only one person said Cooee, when she meant Hullo or, Where are you? Kitty listened again so intently that she seemed to hear the fog itself pressing and humming about her ears. There was nothing else. She must have imagined the voice. It was just a memory of the days when they used to take their tea on to the Common after school. She could not possibly have heard it where she was now – wherever she was.

She was lost. Lost, and crying with the same abandonment of despair as that time on the beach at Lyme Regis, when she had suddenly looked up from shrimping to find that everyone had disappeared and a great cloud was over the sun ... 'Cooee!' said the voice almost on top of her. 'Cooee – Childie!'

'Mummy!' A blur of yellow light melted the fog, and in an instant, the familiar smell of her mother's old macintosh was all round her and Kitty was clutching on and laughing and gasping and gabbling everything that had happened to her, her legs melting with relief.

Mrs Ferguson had been out for more than an hour, cooeeing and casting in what would seem to anyone else a hopeless way on such a night.

She brought Kitty home with the triumph of a hunter and paraded her in the sitting-room before her father and fiancé.

Leonard had groped his way round to Barnardo Road immediately he left work, and finding Kitty not back had been setting out to meet her, when Mrs Ferguson forestalled him, sweeping by him in the hall in her macintosh and shapeless wet-weather hat and telling him to go and warm up by the fire that instant, did he think she wanted her daughter to marry a consumptive?

When the excitement of Kitty's homecoming had died down, Mr Ferguson, who had never stopped treading and shedding sawdust in a gentle heap on the carpet, inquired mildly what time they were going to have supper.

Kitty went and kissed him. 'Poor dad. You shouldn't have waited for me.'

'Oh, I don't mind, Katie, but I didn't have any lunch.'

'You didn't have any –!' His wife was round on him in a flash, her loose bun coming to bits as she pulled off the wet-weather hat. 'I never heard of such a thing. What on earth were you doing?'

He blew the sawdust off the piece of wood on his fretsaw. 'Oh, I didn't want any, and I had to get a haircut, and go down to Dobbie's for some oil and things.'

'But if you'd only told me, I could have given you something the minute you got home. You could have had dripping toast or some cake – no, we finished that yesterday – but I would have opened you a tin of pilchards – anything! I'll go and get supper ready this minute.' She hurried out as if she expected him to drop dead of starvation before she got back.

'Kitty!' she called from the kitchen. 'Go and take off your things. Stockings too. I should put on your bedroom slippers if I were you. And when you wash your face, give your nose and ears a good clean to get the fog out of them.'

'Come up with me then, Len,' said Kitty, 'and talk to me while I wash.' He followed her out and when they were in the hall, she turned to him and he kissed her. He never kissed her in front of her parents.

He was not much taller than she, and slighter, a pale, serious boy, who had been an old-looking child. Kitty with her health and bounce and tight, glowing skin made him appear even quieter and less robust by her side, though all the time he was drawing warmth from her. He was quite content to sit and watch her for long stretches at a time, basking in her vitality like a lizard in the sun.

He sat on the edge of the bath and watched her now while she tucked her hair behind her ears and plunged her face in the basin, then soaped it vigorously.

'What a night!' she said, looking at him in the glass, while she massaged soap into her cheeks. 'I'm sure there's never been one like it in history. I was frightened, were you?'

'I wanted to come out and look for you, but your mother wouldn't let me. I nearly came out anyway after she'd gone, only I hadn't got a torch.'

'Good thing you didn't. She found me all right – trust her, and I don't suppose you ever would, considering you even get lost yourself between here and Manor Park in broad daylight.'

'Darling, that was years ago,' he said seriously, 'and I've told you dozens of times, it wasn't my fault. If that man at the bus terminus hadn't told me –'

'All right, all right,' Kitty laughed. 'I was only teasing.' She dried her face and turning round, bent down and kissed him. She smelt almost unbearably young and clean. Her skin was like china. He would have liked to be tremendously tall and well-built, like a Guardsman, so that he could pick her up without dropping her as he had the only time he had tried. Or even tremendously rich, perhaps, so that he could marry her straight away and give her things to make her happy instead of hanging around always having colds when she wanted to go out, with the wedding date hovering in the nebulous future of 'when Len gets his rise'.

What he had done this afternoon had seemed so right. Now he was beginning to be not so sure. Perhaps he was only taking the easy way out. Well, he would tell her and see how she took it.

He was hardly ever completely natural and at his ease with her. Although they had known each other for five years, had been going out together since they were grown up and had been engaged now for a year, there were sometimes long silences between them, when they would find themselves making conversation as if they were strangers. They were shy of each other.

He waited until she had turned round again to wash her hands and then said diffidently: 'By the way, I applied for a Medical Board this afternoon – the Air Force, you know. I may have a chance of getting in as ground crew, even if I'm not fit enough to fly.'

'Len!' She turned round with black horror in her face. She had never considered this, with Len in his reserved job as a skilled engineer. 'But Len, you don't have to go; you're reserved. They'd have called you up if they wanted you.'

'Oh, well,' he looked at his feet and rucked up the bath mat with his toe. 'I wanted to join up. Somehow – I don't know – it seemed all wrong to be earning three times as much as blokes in the Services who are working a damned sight harder. We had a pilot come round the works the other day. He'd had half his face burnt off. It made you think, you know.' He stopped embarrassed, as he had been when he had seen the pilot's face, and had realized he was staring.

'Well, we have pilots come round too, but I don't go and join the W.A.A.F.,' said Kitty pouting.

'Of course,' he went on gloomily, 'it'll mean I get a lot less money. I don't know about our getting married ... I hate having to ask you to wait.'

'Well, why should we?' said Kitty suddenly, sparkling. 'Suppose they do take you, we could get married quickly before you go, so's we could have all your leaves together.'

'Kitty!' But he looked down again, determined to see all sides of the idea. 'But you'd be awfully lonely, and we wouldn't be able to afford much of a place. It wouldn't be much fun for you while I was away.'

'But we wouldn't have a place of our own, silly. There wouldn't be any point. I'd live on here with Mum and Dad, and go on working at Kyles. We could have the spare room as ours for when you came home. In a way it would be a nicer way of starting marriage – not such a break. Then, after the war, of course, which won't be long, *every*body says so, we can have our own place, just like we planned.' She was warming up to

103

the idea. She pulled him up off the bath. 'Come on, let's go down and ask Mum what she thinks of it. I'm starving, anyway. Of course,' she went on, as they went down the stairs, 'I might not be able to have a white wedding, but I wouldn't mind, honestly. I could have blue, to go with your uniform. Oh, I *like* the idea. Do let's get married!' She jumped down the last three stairs and ran into the sitting-room in front of him. Her mother was putting things on the table, fussing round with dishes and tablespoons, getting a bottle of sauce out of the dresser, standing back to see what she had forgotten and dashing at the table again with the cruet.

'Come along, come along everybody,' she said, cutting bread and butter horizontally, with the loaf on end as if it were a school treat. 'Come along, Charlie, put that away. It's not often we get a joint, so you might as well have it while it's hot.' Mr Ferguson could carve bookends and pipe-racks and even delicate work like penholders, but he had never carved meat since his marriage. Mrs Ferguson was an expert carver. The little joint went round although she gave everybody more than they wanted.

'I should think we're all ready for our supper,' she said, heaping potatoes on to Kitty's plate.

'Mum, I don't want so many potatoes. Do take some back.'

'I don't know why you're suddenly so down on potatoes, especially with the papers telling you you should eat them, though I could have told them that years ago. There's nothing to touch a potato for nourishment, I always say.'

'I can't digest so many, and for another thing, they're fattening.'

Mrs Ferguson gave an exclamation and threw down her knife and fork. 'I thought so! It drives me to despair when I hear that sort of talk. Apart from your health, which you might ruin for good and all, men don't like these scraggy girls, now do they, Leonard?'

'I don't think so,' he said.

'Of course not. And there's Kitty,' looking at her plump and dimpled daughter across the table, 'nothing but skin and bone already and talking about dieting! Well, I despair.' She sought solace in roast mutton, sitting slightly back from the table to allow clearance. Her size was more than middle-aged spread, but it was not glandular or unhealthy, it was not symptomatic of anything but food. Kitty mouthed silently at Len: 'Tell her, now,' and her father, seeing it, raised his eyebrows inquiringly. Kitty nodded and smiled at him reassuringly. Len was just opening his mouth to speak, when Mrs Ferguson said:

'I tell you one thing, my darling. You're not going to work tomorrow unless the fog's cleared, is she, Len?' As Len never contradicted her, it was quite safe to make these kindly appeals to his opinion. She was very fond of Len.

'But I must, Mother. You get a pink slip in with your clock card now when you stay out, to say you're helping Hitler. It makes you feel awful.'

'I don't see that it'll help Hitler very much for you to save your life instead of risking your neck in this death trap as you did tonight. Who's for a little more meat? Pass your plate, Charlie; I gave you a very small helping.'

'Not for me, Alice,' he said. 'I'll have a bit of cheese presently, perhaps, if we've got any.'

'Of course we've got cheese but just have a slice more meat first. You really should, you know, as you went without your lunch.'

'No, really, dear. I've had quite enough.'

'What's the matter? Don't you like it? Is it too underdone for you? Look, let me cut you a slice and just pop it under the grill. It won't take a second.'

He kept his temper, because he had no temper to lose. He refused her offer politely, still smiling.

'Well, a spoonful more vegetables then,' she said, reaching over to heap them on to his plate. He began obediently to eat, without taste or distaste. She had made him gastric anyway in the first ten years of their marriage.

Kitty's stomach, being young, had merely been stretched by the constant overloading. She passed her plate for more without being asked. She gave Len a dig while her mother was carving and mouthed again.

Leonard swallowed what he was eating, pushed back his hair, cleared his throat and said: 'Did Kitty tell you I put in for a medical for the Air Force this afternoon?'

'Of course I didn't, silly,' said Kitty, cutting in on her mother's ejaculation, 'I haven't had a chance. But it's true,

Mother, he really wants to go, and we thought perhaps it would be better not to wait but to get married quick before he goes.' She got it all out in a rush. 'What do you think, Dad?' she asked, seeing that his face was more favourable than her mother's.

'You know what I think, Katie,' he said in his kind deep voice that lifted his moustache up and down like C. Aubrey Smith. 'Ask anyone who was through the last war. Take your happiness while you can, they'll tell you. And as for Len's going in the Air Force –'

'As to that,' broke in Mrs Ferguson with the carving knife poised, 'I thought he was in a reserved job.'

'Yes, but, Mother, he wants to go,' said Kitty sharply, wishing that her own first instinctive remark hadn't been that about being reserved. In the moment's shock of his announcement in the bathroom, she had seen all sorts of pictures: Len killed, Len wounded, crippled for life, perhaps, Len being torpedoed in a troopship. The remark which she now was ashamed of her mother for making had been jerked out of Kitty like a growl from a tigress defending its young. Since then, the visions in the bathroom were being replaced by other pictures. Len in uniform, herself going proudly to the post office to draw her allowance, stamped as a service wife by the brooch he had given her. Len a hero – there was even a quick shot of Buckingham Palace and herself being photographed holding a baby with a medal on its matinée coat.

She was well ahead of everybody else and could take up the cudgels with conviction: 'You ought to be proud that he wants to fight,' she said. 'I am. You didn't make any objection to Gerry going, though he was your son and Len's only your son-in-law, and not that yet.'

'Childie, childie, don't take me up so,' chided her mother. 'I never said I had any objection. Though if I had, Gerry has nothing to do with it, because he was in the Army already in peace-time. It's his career. What about Len's career? That's the only thing I'm worried about. It's natural for a mother, I suppose, to want to see her daughter safely provided for.'

'Well now, as to that, Alice,' said her husband, 'you know we can always help them if the worst comes to the worst. I haven't touched my money yet, and I shan't till I'm satisfied my children won't want it.' He got up. 'I'll just take my plate out to the kitchen, dear, and get the cheese.'

'What do you think young legs are for? Kitty, dear, run and get the cheese for your father.' But he was out of the door before she could get up; it was a ruse to get rid of his plate before his wife could see how much he had left on it.

'And so you see,' Kitty was saying when he came back. 'I shall go on living here, and when Len comes on leave, we can have the spare room – if that's all right with you.'

'Fancy asking such a thing of your own mother!' beamed Mrs Ferguson. 'Oh, not that bit of cheese, Charlie. That's last week's I'm keeping for cooking. Kitty, run and get this week's cheese; it's hanging under the shelf in a damp cloth. And get my chocolate ration out of the dresser drawer while you're there. No, not you, Len. Kitty likes to go. Funny scrap,' she said, looking after her. 'Fancy asking me if I minded your having the spare room! As if I wouldn't give her the roof off my head, if she asked for it. I might have the spare room done up. It needs new curtains anyway, and I've still got all my coupons, though Kitty'll have to have some for her trousseau. I'll make that room really nice, and I want you to feel that this is your home whenever you can come.' She laid a podgy, hard-working hand on his arm. 'Perhaps I can give you the home your mother never gave you.'

He bit his lip and looked down at his plate, trying to edge his arm away imperceptibly.

'Well, what d'you think of the idea?' asked Kitty, coming back and banging the door behind her.

'I don't see why you shouldn't do it,' said her mother, un-wrapping her chocolate, 'provided they do take Len in the Air Force. Dad and I will talk it over, of course, but you know we only want what's best for your happiness.' She broke off two squares of chocolate and gave one each to Kitty and Len, in supreme token of her benevolence.

The more she thought about it, the better she liked the idea of this marriage. Her minds eye visualized the spare room, seeing it with a new eiderdown and curtains hanging from a gathered pelmet. She would get her mother's wardrobe out of store, where she had been keeping it until Kitty had her own home. The room was quite big enough to take it. Yes, and it would be big enough to have a baby in, too; they could always have a gas-ring fitted in there for boiling kettles.

Len was silent. Things were going well, but in the wrong direction. He had anticipated opposition, but this was almost worse. The main thing was for Kitty to be happy, and she certainly looked it now, arguing with her mother about the length of her wedding dress. But the high spirits which had made him indulge his amateurish whistle as he walked to the recruiting office at lunch-time had long since evaporated. The existing prospect of freedom from the factory which for so many years had confined him in its noise and smells and arguments was giving place to a regret for its familiarity. He had never realized before how many friends he had there. Regarded honestly, would the Air Force mean more than the same work that he had been doing for years, but with less responsibility, more discipline and discomfort and less pay? His leaves he could see only too clearly, unless he could manage to save up enough sometimes to take Kitty to a hotel.

Two days before Kitty's wedding, the other girls on her bench came back early from lunch, spilled all the pipes out of her tray and festooned them with streamers and ribbons. They hung a naked celluloid doll on one induction pipe and an old shoe on the other, and on her light, shaking with mirth at their own humour, they hung a placard saying: 'All right tomorrow night.'

When Kitty came back from lunch, everyone was looking at her as she approached the display, giggling and crimson, and finally let out a hoot as she saw the placard and hid her face in her hands, shaking her hair from side to side.

People were staring and calling out from all over the Shop. A man on the cylinder section was standing up to see better at one end of a rig that cradled a cylinder block.

'What's up?' asked his mate, who had come in late, tugging at his overall.

'They're razzing one of the girls on the bench. Got her pipes all tied up with ribbons and things.'

'Let's look.' He climbed up on to the other end of the rig. 'What's the idea?'

'She's going to be married.'

'Oh, is that all?' The man who had come in late climbed down again, swinging the rig so that his mate fell off and impaled his shin on a stud.

Edward had difficulty in getting the girls to settle down to work. They were fooling about excitedly and had begun flicking rubber piston rings about, which was good fun, but liable to put somebody's eye out. Kitty was still in helpless paroxysms and unlikely to be good for any work for some time. That could be overlooked, since she was getting married on Friday, but Edward trotted round the bench trying to round up the others into some semblance of order before Mr Gurley should shoot up his little window.

'A joke's a joke,' he pleaded, 'but you must shut up now and get down to work. . . .'

'My little Eddie!' crooned Dinah, hanging round his neck and leaving lipstick on his cheek. She had been drinking beer instead of eating at lunch-time. She could drink it like a man, opening her lovely throat and tipping in the beer like pouring swill down a sink. She dived under the bench, crawled to the other side, bit Reenie in the leg and came up filthy.

'Dinah, your *hair*!' said Grace in horror. She herself had one special day a fortnight for washing her hair; it came between the day for polishing the furniture and her husband's black day, which was stove-cleaning day, when not even a cup of tea could be brewed. Thinking how she herself would feel if she got her hair unexpectedly dirty and had to upset her whole routine by washing it, she was horrified for Dinah.

Edward wiped the lipstick off his cheek and left a smear of oil instead. He liked a joke as much as anybody, but Bob Condor was bearing down on his toes from the far end of the shop.

'Shut up!' said Edward, knocking on the bench with a mallet, 'and get cracking!' He loved the girls to be in high spirits, but he also loved to think that they paid some attention to what he said. Whenever they came to him for advice, trustingly submitting a part for his ultimatum and either scrapping or retaining it on his word without a murmur, his heart glowed. He loved it when they couldn't turn a nut or get a gear off a shaft, and he could do it for them. If he failed, he could always take the part into the Fitting Shop, get one of the fitters to do it and come back as if he had done it himself. It made him smile when he thought of his first fear of them. Of course, he still made mistakes, but then to err was human, as he frequently told Wendy Holt when she made one of her muddles with the rockers. It was natural that she should make mistakes. She could never be mechanically minded like Freda, for example. Bearing in mind that this was the most difficult work for a girl so feminine and fragile as Wendy, Edward spoon-fed her and protected her from the ravenings of the A.I.D., who, if they pounced on Dinah, would get answered back, but if they pounced on Wendy, usually reduced her to tears.

'Why haven't your girls started work?' asked Bob Condor, his eyebrows where his hair would have been if his hair had not started so far back.

'Just a bit of fun,' said Edward. 'After all, it's not every day –'

'What d'you think this is – a nursery school? Nice thing if someone were to come round the factory and see this going on. No wonder your bench gets so many black marks, Ledward, if you let them fool about like this.' He picked up a pipe with a blue bow on one end, tore off the ribbon and ground it underfoot.

'That's unfair,' said Edward, incensed. 'We've had fewer black marks than the other bench this month.' He was sure of this because it was written on his heart every time the name and crime of one of his girls was entered in the A.I.D.'s black book. Kitty was feverishly tearing the trimmings off her pipes, and hiding the oddments in her tool box. The placard was lying on the bench and Edward quickly turned it upside-down.

Mr Gurley's little window went up with a crash as if he were trying to shatter his glass office. 'Condor!' he bellowed. He had had beer for lunch, too, but it was all very well for him. He could sit back with his feet on the desk if he liked and still leave his mark on Production by raising his voice.

Dinah didn't feel like getting down to work. She was suddenly so bored with her slipper gears that she wanted to scream and hurl them from her, following them up with the gearcase. Bill was working on nights all this month, their flat had a leak in the side wall which the landlord refused to mend, and Dinah's mother's only theme, in letters and conversation, was that her pension was inadequate to the increased cost of living.

'Look here, Dinah,' said Edward. 'Even if you feel as lousy as you look, there is a war on.'

'Oh shut up, Ed. This is a bum engine anyway. Is it a write-off?'

'Yes. Right off the map,' said Edward, but she didn't laugh. 'Get cracking, for Heaven's sake,' he said. Perhaps he would not have used his Air Force expressions if he had realized that he had picked them up from Don Derris. It was mean of him, he knew, but Thursdays had been a lot less irritating since Don went abroad.

'Only our fun,' said Dinah, yawning. 'We had to give poor little Kitty some sort of show. By the way, thanks for turning the card over. Bob would have died of shock.'

'Come to that,' said Edward, sitting down on Reenie's vacant stool and squinting along her control shaft, 'I was a bit shocked myself. I mean, a joke's a joke, and I'm no prude as you know, but this seemed a bit nearer the knuckle for someone like Kitty. Why, she's hardly grown up.'

'The Indians do it at twelve,' said Dinah, 'but honestly, I never thought about it. We always stick up something like that. I suppose it is a bit crude. Still, I bet he's been let in for something a lot cruder at his aerodrome or wherever he is.'

'No,' said Edward. 'I don't think men do get teased like that – not about the girls they marry, I mean.'

'Oh, women are awful, Ted. When you come back from your honeymoon, they stare at you, to see if you look any different. You'll see, they'll do it with Kitty.'

'Nothing sacred, eh?'

'Not a thing. The questions you're asked – it's indecent. But most women don't seem to mind. In fact, they'll tell you without waiting to be asked. I think they get more kick out of talking about it than out of the actual thing.'

Edward was amazed. 'You mean they discuss their husbands?'

'Of course. Try and stop 'em,' said Dinah. 'And their boy-friends too. My poor Ted, haven't you learned by now that women have no shame? Why, I bet your own wife – No,' she said on second thoughts, having met Connie once when she was visiting her aunt in the ground-floor flat, 'perhaps not her. But one girl on this bench, for instance. I won't tell you who it is, but between you and me, she's having her first fling and my

God, have I had all the details! I might be having an affair with the man myself, the amount I know about him, and it just couldn't be more boring.'

'Who is it? Do tell me.'

Dinah laughed. 'Oh, no, you don't get that out of me, manure-hound. Anyway, I thought men were so lovely and pure and didn't care to discuss that sort of thing. Get up, anyway, here comes Reenie. She's been down the First Aid to get her leg disinfected, because I told her she'd get hydrophobia.'

That evening, Edward and Dick Bennett had a date at the Marquis of Granby with a Mr E. Dexter Bell, 'Uanmee', The Rise, Collis Park. At present, he was no more to them than that, but from the sound of the letters with which he had answered their advertisement and subsequent correspondence, he looked like the future nucleus, if not the entire enzyme of the Collis Park Domestic Rabbit Club.

The other replies held mostly more obstacles than enthusiasm. Some people only wrote to say that they could not join, and at great length why. One woman even wasted a stamp to state that she lived at High Barnet, so how could she join a club at Collis Park, although no one had asked her to. Edward's little notice in the glass case outside the Lipmann's shop had so far produced two answers; one from a schoolboy, and one from a woman who said that as a life member of the Anti-Vivisection Society, the R.S.P.C.A., and the National Society of Vegetarians, she must protest against the wanton slaughter of God's innocent beasts of the field and had they tried vegetable hotpot as advertised by the Ministry of Food, and also Carrot Flan, which did, indeed, taste just like bananas?

But Mr E. Dexter Bell was far higher game. He had answered the advertisement with a long typewritten letter, efficiently set out and scattered with symbols like (I) (a), cf., sup., viz: – On the last page, he gave a list of his stock, in columns with full pedigrees. On the first page, he gave a list, also in columns, of notable members of the Fancy with whom he was acquainted. 'Only the other day,' he said, in conclusion, 'I was talking to Mr "Bucky" Buckingham, the well-known Havana man and popular judge (cf. above) and bemoaning the fact that no Collis Parkian had yet had the enterprise to start a club in this district.

I myself, would, of course, have done so long ere now if business affairs had not made so great a claim upon my time. However, now that you, Mr Bennett, and you, Mr Ledward, have undertaken the initial groundwork, I shall be only too happy to place my knowledge, experience and *enthusiasm* at your disposal. I am, sirs, with heartiest good wishes,

Your fellow fancier,

E. Dexter Bell.'

Edward would soon be able to be President of the Club because here was its obvious secretary. He sounded like a gift from Heaven. From his stock list, he was evidently in as large a way as an amateur may be without being a professional.

They were to meet tonight and discuss what Mr Bell called 'The Campaign', as if it were Congregational electioneering.

He didn't sound a bit like the sort of man who would live in a house called 'Uanmee', and at first sight of him in the private bar of the 'Marquis', he didn't look it either. If it was his wife's idea, that made her the Mee and him the U, and he looked more like the Mee.

He was sitting at a round-corner table with a glass of whisky, conveying the impression that since he was reading the *Evening Standard*, the *Star* and the *News* might have saved themselves the trouble of going to press.

Even if he had not been wearing a small yellow carnation and a tie of 'equi-distant blue diagonal lines on a black ground' as promised in his last letter, numbered: 'C.P.R. Club, No. 5. re. appt.', it could have been no one else. 'There he is,' said Edward at once, as he and Dick Bennett pushed aside the curtain and came blinking into the light, but Dick would not commit himself until he had considered and rejected two trousered women in turbans drinking port, a strawberry-nosed old man in a bowler hat and a Canadian soldier trying to put some life into a plain girl in a macintosh, who were the only other occupants of the private bar.

Mr E. Dexter Bell uncrossed his legs as Edward and Dick approached, half rose, with a hand on each knee and sat down again, folding up his paper.

'Messrs Bennett and Ledward?' he said. 'My name is Bell.' They all shook hands and Mr Bell invited them hospitably to sit down. He was a well-fed, well-dressed man, with thick tortoiseshell spectacles with side-pieces like shoe horns, and a wide mouth that opened and shut flatly, like a toad catching flies. A loop of key chain hung out of his trouser pocket, and another little chain, such as Americans wear, lay across his tie.

'What are you gentlemen going to drink?' he asked.

'No, allow me.' Edward got up again. 'What was yours – whisky?'

'That's all right,' said Mr Bell. 'Sit down, there's a good chap. Harry!' he raised his voice, and Harry came round the partition from the Saloon Bar with more alacrity than he had ever given Edward when he stood at the bar with only the width of it between them.

'Double whisky, Harry,' said Mr Bell, and glanced inquiringly at the other two.

'The same for me,' said Edward, and Dick said, after a pause: 'I'll take whisky,' as if it were something new he had thought up. 'Only safe drink these days,' said E. Dexter Bell. 'I know for a fact that all the gin is doctored, and as for the beer – ye gods! Interesting thing, I met a chap the other day, who's by way of being an analytical chemist. He's been working on some Government tests at the various breweries and he assured me that the average maximum percentage of alcohol content was lower by – let's see, was it five point five, or five point ought five? – forget my own name next – than two years ago.' He stared at Dick Bennett through his great spectacles and Dick nodded his head slowly, impressed.

When Harry appeared behind the bar with the drinks, Edward was getting up to fetch them, but Mr Bell restrained him and Harry lifted a flap and came through with the tray. 'There you are, Mr Bell,' he said, wiping the table, 'three doubles and a large soda. How's business?'

'Don't speak of it, Harry, I'm a ruined man.'

'Aren't we all?' said Harry, going gloomily away with the tray on which was the money with which Mr Bell, shocked at the idea, had forestalled Edward's hand as it went to his pocket. Dick Bennett had previously allocated a certain amount out of petty cash to pay for these drinks, so this upset his calculations. They would have to have a second round to put them straight.

After talking about anything and everything except rabbits

for ten minutes. E. Dexter Bell said: 'But we didn't come here for idle gossip, however pleasant it may be. To work, gentlemen! I want to hear all your progress and plans for this Club. Spare me nothing, however circumstantial, I'm a business man myself and I apppreciate business details. I may say I'm interested, extremely interested in your little project, so go ahead, Edwards, and spare me nothing. Tell me exactly how you're going about it,' he said and then proceeded to tell Edward and Dick, almost without pause, how he would go about it if he were they.

In all the conversation, Edward was hampered by a ridiculous impulse to call him sir, particularly when he was talking about his rabbits, which made Edward's own collection seem about as impressive as a schoolboy's hutchful. Mr Bell had spoken often in his letters of his champion stud Flemish, one Dexter Royalist. Edward had marked him down as a likely husband for the best of Queenie's grand children, who already at seven months was showing promise of the size after which Edward was striving. But even if his master agreed, Champion Royalist would never look at so humble a bride. Why should he, when groomed and pampered lovelies from harems all over England came in patent travelling boxes to his bridal couch?

'You know,' Edward said to Dick, when Mr Bell had left them to see a man about the proverbial dog, ha-ha, 'I almost wish we hadn't got mixed up with this man. He's right out of our class. If we let him have his way, he'll try and make the thing too big; he'll take it out of the reach of the little breeder and the novice, who are the people we really want to get at.'

Dick was drawing patterns with a ring of spilt liquid on the table. 'On principle, old man,' he said, 'I've no doubt you're right, but the way I looked at it, he's just the man we want to get us going. You can't run a Club without capital. You heard him offer to put up the money for our first show, if we needed it? He's a real sportsman.'

'All the same,' said Edward, 'I can't quite say why, but I don't like him, you know.'

'*Don't* you?' said Dick, whose accent always broadened into a trace of Yorkshire when he was surprised. Mr Bell came back. He had flat, important feet and fat thighs that stretched the trousers of his chalk-stripe blue suit. He walked with his hands in his pockets, his legs rather wide apart and had a trick of loosening his shoulders inside his coat as if he were feeling the power of them. Dick Bennett got up to fetch the drinks that they had ordered in his absence, and came back to the table, the glasses looking small and breakable in his huge fists.

'Oh, not for me,' said Mr Bell smiling. 'I've had my ration. Never take two before dinner. Doesn't do the old system any good, you know.'

Dick Bennett looked up worried from the account book in which he was entering the price of the drinks.

'Oh, come on,' said Edward, 'since it's here.'

'Positively not, Edwards, thanks very much all the same. I must be getting along in any case. I can't tell you how much I've enjoyed meeting you and hearing your plans. We'd better make a date for next week, so that you can keep me *au fait* with progress.' He had told them that he used to go to Paris on business; staring into space and shaking his head sadly, he had added: 'Ma pauvre Paree. What have they done to you?'

Edward finished his drink, offered the third unwanted one to Dick and when he shook his head, drank it himself and stood up. He had told Connie that he would be late, but there was no sense in being too late. He was taking Dick back to supper with him.

'Which way do you go?' asked Mr Bell, shrugging himself into a greenish-brown teddy-bear coat with a belt.

'Church Avenue,' said Edward, taking his macintosh off the peg. 'Along Arthur Road and down the hill.'

'I'll walk along with you. It's on my way,' said E. Dexter Bell, settling his hat at a good angle. Outside the door, he switched on a torch like a lighthouse.

'I say,' said Edward, 'that's a bit bright, isn't it? You'll have the Wardens after you if you go about with a light like that.'

'Not me,' said Mr Bell, making the light suddenly dim. 'You see, I keep my hand over it when there's anybody about, and get the full benefit of it in the quiet streets, where you need it. I don't want to break my neck.'

'Yes, but a light like that could be seen from the sky,' said Edward, as they turned into a side street and Mr Bell uncovered the beam. 'You're spoiling the whole blackout.' Three double whiskies had made him feel truculent.

'Oh, they're a lot less particular about the blackout than they were,' said Mr Bell lightly. 'Anyway, there's not a Hun within miles tonight.'

Dick Bennett was in a quandary. As a part-time Air Raid Warden, even off duty, it was up to him to do something about the searchlight which preceded them down Arthur Road; as treasurer of the Collis Park Domestic Rabbit Club, it was up to him to keep in with Mr Bell. He struggled with himself. Edward, who was annoyed, had begun to hum. To cover his embarrassment, Dick said heavily: 'That's a very fine torch.'

'I believe you,' said Mr Bell. 'You wouldn't find one like it in the shops, I can tell you. You have to know where to go for these things. But I'm not telling. No names, no pack drill, as they say. By the way, Edwards, you won't forget to let me have a look at that form the B.R.C. sent you, before you send it in? You want to be careful how you fill up a thing like that, you know. I might be able to put you right on one or two things. When it's a question of allocation of rations, you want to know how to deal with these people. Tell you what, I'll just pop along to your house with you, if you're only in Church Avenue, and pick it up. Perhaps I could have a look at your stock.'

Edward let them into the hall of his house, and switched on the spectral blue light. Mr Bell pretended to fall over the umbrella stand and switched on his torch, spot-lighting Connie, who had come out of the kitchen beyond the stairs, to tell Edward and Dick that they were very late and must not be surprised if the fish was spoiled.

'This is Mr Bell, dear,' said Edward. 'Mr Dexter Bell.'

'How d'you do, Mrs Edwards?' said Mr Bell. 'Forgive the intrusion, but I'm a fellow-fancier of your husband's. We've been making great plans, Mrs Edwards, great plans.'

'How do you do?' said Connie. 'The name is Ledward. Won't you take off your coat?' Another of these dreadful rabbit men. Edward might tell her when he was bringing in strangers. Here she was, caught out in her stringy old green jumper. She never bothered to change for Dick Bennett.

'Mr Bell's only just looked in to fetch a paper and have a squint at the rabbits,' said Edward quickly, before she could think that he had brought him to supper. 'Let's go out to them,

117

shall we? You'd better bring that torch. I hope you don't mind going through the kitchen.' Dick and Mr Bell in his teddy-bear coat took up a lot of room in the narrow hall, and Connie had to step inside the living-room doorway to let them go by.

'Hullo, Dick?' she said without enthusiasm. She distinctly smelt whisky in the air.

Mr Bell distinctly smelt fish in the kitchen. He stopped short, while Edward was unbolting the back door, and sniffed. 'My,' he said, 'something smells good. What is it?' I *will not* ask you to supper, said Edward to himself, pretending not to hear and going out into the back garden. 'Come along,' he said. 'we're showing a light if I don't shut the door.' They stood in the cold, quiet darkness for a moment until Mr Bell's torch violated the blackout once more. He flashed it on the first hutch and its occupant, the nervous little grey doe who was like Wendy Holt, shrank against the back wall, blinking.

'All right, little thing,' said Mr Bell shading the torch, as he crouched down to look at her. 'They don't like a bright light, you know,' he said to Edward, who had just been going to tell him that. They both squatted in front of the doe, with Mr Bell going: 'Hm . . . hm . . .' as he considered her points. 'I thought you said you were going all out for size,' he said.

'Yes, I am, really,' said Edward. 'I like her, though. I don't want to get rid of her.' He knew he should have done so long ago, when he began to concentrate on the Ledward strain. She had never been anything but a loss, because even when her litters were not sickly, she was so nervous that she frequently killed them within the first day or two. She was almost impossible to get into kindle too, as the train journey upset her so much that she would resist the buck like an outraged spinster. But although she was not really worth food or hutch space, he refused to part with her. He had recently changed her name to Wendy. Since he had become so fond of the girls on his bench at Canning Kyles, he had named rabbits after all of them. Three of Queenie's latest litter were called Paddy, Madeleine and Sheila, and the great bouncing young doe, who challenged cats through the wire netting and came back from her honeymoons with a rollicking eye and a tremendous appetite had long ago been changed from Princess to Dinah.

Mr Bell got up and moved on to the next cage. 'You're absolutely wrong,' he said. 'With a small collection like yours, you must, you simply must cut out the dead heads. If you're going for size, chuck out anything that doesn't promise to be big. If it's coat you're after – same thing applies. Chuck out anything shabby. It's the only way to get results. That's just the difference between the amateur and the professional, you see. The amateur so seldom has the courage of his convictions.'

'Oh, but I do,' said Edward, 'it's only just that particular doe –' He followed Mr Bell down the line of hutches, trying to justify himself, while Dick Bennett followed behind them, breathing heavily in the darkness.

'Now this is a good buck!' exclaimed Mr Bell in surprise, as if Edward didn't know. He shone the torch full on to the great blinking Masterman, the pride of Edward's stock. He was only young yet, but he was going to keep him as a stud buck. He had all the qualities necessary for a founder of the Ledward strain.

'Yes, sir,' said Mr Bell, and lowered himself on to his fat haunches to have a closer look. Edward couldn't help being gratified by his admiration, because after all, he did know something about rabbits. Dick Bennett was impressed too. He squatted behind them like a great bear, whistling softly through his teeth. 'You haven't told me about this one, Ted,' he said enviously. 'You sly old devil, I'd no idea you'd been keeping something like this up your sleeve.'

'It's Masterman, Dick,' said Edward, 'you've seen him ever so often.'

'Have I? Surely not. He's never been as big as this. He must have grown at a tremendous rate then.'

'He has,' said Edward happily. 'I've been trying him on a new diet and it seems to be working. As a matter of fact, I've written a letter about it for *Backyard Breeding*. I'm hoping they'll put it in this week.'

'*Backyard Breeding?*' said Mr Bell, getting up and yawning to disguise the noise of his bones cracking, 'sound paper that. A propos of what I was saying about chucking out, Edwards, you ought to read my friend Allan Colley; he's very hot on selective breeding.'

'I know,' said Edward. My *friend* Allan Colley. 'Do you know him, then?'

'Know him? Why, bless your heart, we're like *that*,' said Mr Bell crossing two fingers in the beam of his torch. 'Known him for ages, met him at shows all over the country. Oh, he's a great lad is the old collie dog. He's forgotten more about Flemishes than you or I will ever know. Grand chap.'

'He must be,' said Edward. 'I've always wanted to meet him.'

'Well, no reason why you shouldn't. He might be interested in our little venture. He likes to encourage new enterprise. I might bring him along some day. He lives quite near here as a matter of fact – Raynes' Park. He's got a fine place; house in its own grounds, and his wife –' he blew a kiss into the air, 'what a peach! They entertain a lot.'

'I'd love to meet him,' said Edward, thrilled to the core and suddenly back in the second eleven, watching the Captain of the school bearing down on him across the field at half-time to congratulate him on a lucky goal. He viewed Mr Bell in a completely new light.

'Well, let's just have a quick dekko at the others while I'm here,' said E. Dexter, 'and then I must be off, or my sister will be thinking I've gone under a bus.' His sister? Was she the U of 'Uanmee'? Come to think of it, he had never spoken of a wife in all his conversation about himself.

'There aren't any more,' said Edward. 'That's the lot.'

'Oh,' he said and turned to go indoors, falling over a dustbin on the way and conveying by his oaths that at 'Uanmee' you didn't have to go past dustbins to get to the rabbits.

In the kitchen, he began to sniff again, and even opened the oven door to look inside. 'I thought so,' he said, smacking his lips. 'I know a herring when I smell one. My favourite fruit. Why d'you have 'em baked though? I always say they're a frying fish.' So did Edward but he only said: 'My wife can't touch fried food, never has been able to.'

When he had sent them up to the bathroom to wash, Edward went into the living-room to brave Connie, sitting upright at the laid table, knitting very fast. 'I'm terribly sorry, dear, but what could I do? He simply asked himself. And he could see there was enough for four.'

'What do you mean, he could see?' she asked, knitting faster. 'The dish is in the oven.'

'Yes, but he opened it to have a look.'

120

'Well, what a cheek! Did you ever hear of such a thing? Who is this Mr Bell, anyway? Someone from the factory?'

'No, he's in business as a matter of fact. I'm not quite sure what. Quite well-to-do though, by the sound of it. I'm awfully sorry, Con. If I wasn't such a fool, I'd have found some way to get rid of him. I'll go and get the extra plate and things, while you dish up. They're just coming down. I'm sorry, Con,' he said again, and smiled at her.

'That's all right.' She rolled her knitting round the pins and stabbed them through the ball of wool. 'I suppose I can't object to you having guests in your own house, though I must say, it is a bit difficult when you never know whether you're to provide for three or thirteen. I'll get the plate,' she said going to the door. 'If I've got to go to the kitchen, anyway, there's no point you running about like a flea in a fit.' She went out. 'And by the way,' she said sternly, putting her head into the room again, 'don't offer butter with the cheese, or even marge, because we've none to spare. Cheese they can have, though if they eat too much, you'll have to have your macaroni plain tomorrow.'

CHAPTER 7

THERE were no placards but only, as Dinah had foretold, a lot of looks and remarks about circles under the eyes, when Kitty came back from her honeymoon, looking faintly surprised but otherwise no different.

Why should she? thought Dinah. It would take more than three days with Leonard Bright to make anyone look different. One week a year was the maximum leave allowed to Service wives, and Kitty and Len had decided to save four days of it in case he suddenly got Embarkation Leave later on.

Edward felt sorry for her. There she had been on Wednesday, with her pipes *en fête*, blushing and giggling among the ribbons, radiantly excited; and on Monday, almost before they had had time to notice she was gone, there she was back again, perching childishly on her stool and being called *Mrs Bright*, with emphatic wit. And that was marriage. To Edward, she symbolized the pathos of every wartime bride. Feeling sentimental about her, he tried to think of ways in which he could lessen what must be the burden of that first day. He inspected some drain-taps for her while she was doing the pipes, and she was grateful, unaware that the A.I.D. would be back with them tomorrow with sarcastic inquiries about Mod. 202. All day he kept coming up and asking her if she wanted any help, and once, after she had booked three oil pipes missing on her report, he came trotting back from the dismantling shop where he had taken them to clean, and she had to rub everything out.

She had expected it to feel queer to come back and work there after three days of being married, but by the end of the day she found it almost impossible to believe that she had ever been away. The day had been so exactly like other days, no more nor less tedious. She had gone through all the usual phases: cold and depressed at first and inclined to wish that whoever it was had never invented the internal combustion engine, softening towards him after tea and a margarine roll at half-past nine had brought her fingers alive at last, bearing up until at about eleven-thirty it became evident that lunch-time would never come, quite lively after the hour's break, but falling away after an early tea into the state that made her shake her watch unbelievingly at half-past four and at intervals afterwards, until at half-past five she struck an interesting patch of work and looked up suddenly to see that it was five to six and she would have to fly for the toilet if she wanted to be out when the bell rang.

She felt no different. She had to keep telling herself that she was married and looking down at her ring, because she didn't feel married at all. Going listlessly through an unexcitingly perfect set of pipes, she thought again of the week-end behind her that had made her into a married woman, with an Air Force allowance book and a new identity card, and tried to make it seem real. Long before she met Len, she had always visualized her honeymoon as the peak of her life – Paradise at the time and living in beautiful memory for years afterwards, with some fading photographs and a pressed flower, perhaps, and a menu card. Well, she had got the hotel bill, which her mother had described as highway robbery, but as for living through the years, the memory of her week-end honeymoon was already growing faint after one day. The factory and the girls, and even

122

Edward in that familiar maroon tie, seemed much more real. The other was just an interlude: impossible to believe that it could have any effect on the course of her life.

It had been over almost before she knew it had begun. On the Thursday she had been to the hairdressers and then come home to soak her nails and write a few laboured letters to aunts and to Mr Sommers at her father's firm, thanking them for presents that would remain packed away until she and Len got their own home after the war. Then she had stood fidgeting for hours with her mother kneeling at her feet, talking through a mouthful of pins while she adjusted the hem of her wedding dress. In the evening, Len had turned up for supper, but Mrs Ferguson had sent him laughingly away, saying that it was bad luck. He had told Kitty afterwards that he had rounded up some pals for a drink, but she didn't think he had had any supper.

After their own meal, which she had chosen – sausages and chips and jam fritters – Kitty had gone out to the telephone box on the corner and rung up Len's aunt, with whom he was staying. It seemed very important to speak to him, as if in that last minute she could find out what he was really like, but he was not in. She had gone home and had a bath, and her mother had made her drink hot milk in bed, although she was still full of jam fritters. Her father had come up to kiss her good night, which was unusual for him, as his sciatica didn't take him up and down stairs very easily. She had fallen asleep to the burr of his treadle fretsaw coming up through the floor under her bed.

All the part in the church and afterwards at the buffet lunch at home, where everyone had declared they didn't know how Mrs Ferguson did it and they had never seen such a spread in wartime, had seemed unreal even at the time. When she and Len were in the taxi on the way to the station, they had suddenly looked at each other, awe-stricken, and then begun to giggle. They seemed to have giggled a lot in the next few days: in the train, when the woman in the W.V.S. uniform and the man with the drop on the end of his nose had a row about opening the window; at the hotel at Banbury, when the sweet was called *Crême Montecarlo* and turned out to be cold rice shape with raisins in it; and again in the train coming home, when they had to stand in the corridor and the man next to Len had kept falling forward and bumping his nose on the window. What had they done all the time in between?

They had got up late – that had made the morning go quickly. Then there was lunch in the big crumby dining-room, which took a long time as there was only one waitress. Afterwards they had sat in the lounge looking at the papers and each begged the other to say what they wanted to do, fortunately discovering at last that they both wanted to take the bus into Oxford and go to the cinema. On Sunday they had gone for a walk in the rain, and Kitty had discovered that her new shoes let in water. Lunch had been roast beef that day, followed by hot jam roll, which Len enjoyed. It was nice to find something he did enjoy, because he was fussy about his food as a rule, but the waitress would not allow him a second helping. Now that she thought about it, Kitty had really been hungry all the time they were there, in spite of the buns which they had bought in Oxford and eaten afterwards in the bedroom. When they were packing on Sunday, they had found a bun left over and after some discussion, had thrown it out of the window in case the maid, finding it in the wastepaper basket, should think it odd.

When they got back to London, Len had wanted to take her out to dinner, so they had gone straight to the West End from the station. They had tried several places, but everywhere was full. Len was for going back and queuing at the Regent Palace, but Kitty had suddenly stopped dead in Leicester Square, put her bag down on the pavement and said: 'I'm awfully sorry, Len, but I'm tired. Let's go home. Mother will give us something to eat, and after all, she'll want to see something of you before you go back to Wales tomorrow.' They had had quite an argument, stepping on and off the pavement to avoid being knocked into by people and cars alternately.

When they did get home, Kitty's mother had worn that look that she had seen on the faces of some of the girls this morning – but only for an instant. The next, she had taken her into her arms with a scything movement and was hugging her and rocking from side to side while Len put down the bags and hung up his gas-mask and greatcoat.

It was a good thing they had come home, because it turned out that her mother had been expecting them all the time. There was a fluffy fish pie in the oven, and some trifle left over from the wedding. Mr and Mrs Ferguson had already had high tea, as it was his evening on at the Warden's Post, but Kitty's mother sat at the table while they ate, watching every mouthful on and off their plates and picking absent-mindedly at the loaf while she plied them with questions. It was a bit awkward after supper. When Mrs Ferguson was in the kitchen, Len had said to Kitty: 'Let's go upstairs, darling,' but they had not liked to go up to bed together. In the end, Kitty had gone up first, while he said he would just have a smoke and look at the paper. Her mother went up and talked to her while she undressed. Much later, when they were in bed, Kitty had heard her father come home, but instead of coming in to kiss her good night, like other Sundays, she heard his shoes creak to a stop outside the door, and after a pause he had tapped softly and said: 'Good night, Katie. Glad to have you back.'

Kitty put the last pipe back into the box, wiped her hands, and thought of this morning and how odd it had been to wake in the spare-room, that was now called Len and Kitty's room, and had new rust-coloured curtains and a new rug over the worn patch of carpet by the bed. The note of the alarm had been the same and she had smothered it at once as usual and dozed guiltily for a minute or two. When she did open her eyes, she couldn't understand at first why she was looking at the brass handle of a dark-brown wardrobe door instead of at the picture of St Christopher carrying Christ over the stream, which she had had for her Confirmation.

She dressed very quietly, but when she came up to the bed to wake Len to say good-bye, she saw that he had been awake all the time and watching her. He would be gone when she got back tonight. There were so many things she wanted to say, but no time to say them. As it was, he made her very late, and she flew downstairs, cramming a folded piece of bread and butter into her mouth on her way through the kitchen to get her bicycle. It would never do to clock in late this morning; she could imagine the remarks.

Her mother, with her pigtail hanging down the back of her black quilted dressing-gown, brought her sandwiches out to the gate as usual, bewailing 'all that good bacon in the oven'. It was so like ordinary days that it was almost impossible to believe that behind that bow window up there her husband lay in bed, with his uniform folded neatly over the back of a chair and his brushes on the chest of drawers. He was very tidy with his things. His toothpaste and sponge-bag were never in a mess like hers, and after he had shaved, he put everything away in an oilskin bag instead of leaving them soapy and scattered as her father did.

Tonight, when she got back, he would be gone. As she pedalled away into the cold wind, with her lamp going out at each bump and coming on again at the next, he was gone already and she was Miss Ferguson again, too fat in navy-blue trousers and a red jersey, with her lunch in greaseproof paper in the basket of her bicycle.

Bob Condor had recently taken to coming up at a quarter to six and asking Edward: 'Where are all your girls?'

Edward couldn't very well say 'Washing', because that was not allowed until five to six. He looked innocently around as if the bench were not empty except for Grace, still checking valves like an automaton, Madeleine re-reading her report to make sure it was right, and Wendy Holt scribbling notes on what she had inspected, because she knew she would never remember until tomorrow. 'By the way, Condor,' said Edward craftily, 'I'd like to ask your opinion on this rotor. D'you think they can salvage those vanes, or are they too far gone?' Bob could never resist an appeal for his opinion, but even the business of fitting his jeweller's spy-glass into his eye and calling for emery paper and digging at the rotor with a little steel pick and saying 'I'd make them redundant for poshible shalvage,' failed to divert him. Putting down the rotor, he looked at Edward with the spy-glass still in his eye, as if he were trying to see into his brain, and said again, 'Where are all your girls?'

'Oh – somewhere about,' said Edward vaguely. 'Here's Madeleine and Grace and Wendy ... and here come Sheila and Dinah,' he added, wishing that they were not so blatantly carrying soap and nail brushes.

'Shee here, Ledward,' said Bob, unscrewing the spy-glass, 'if you've no control over the girls, as apparently you haven't, you might at least persuade them to go over to wash in ones and twos, and not the whole ruddy bench at a time; then if the old man or anybody came round, it wouldn't notice.' Edward agreed and wandered away. With the whole Shop packing up and easing itself towards the moment when the six o'clock bell should send them flying, why did Bob Condor always pick on him? Why not the chalk-test girls, who were already winding scarves around their heads and turning out the lights? He suspected that Bob had a down on him because he was well in with Mr Gurley.

As it was Thursday, Edward was in no particular hurry to get away. He sauntered over to the coat pegs behind the scuttling crowd and stood unhurriedly winding his scarf round his neck and calling out 'Good night' to his girls as they rushed by him. Dinah was the first away, half in and half out of her coat, a loaded string bag bumping around her knees. Bill was home early tonight, and she wanted to get the beds and a semblance of housework done before he came in and tried to do it. Freda was close on her heels. She never wasted time over anything, much less putting on clothes. The collar of her tweed overcoat was turned in and the laces of her brogues untied. She had not combed her hair since this morning, and possibly not since she went to bed last night.

''Night, Eddie!' Sheila ran off, looking clean and pretty in a halo hat. She had taken a long time washing tonight and had come out of the toilet looking quite different from when she went in. She was meeting David in a bar and they were going to be what he called 'civilized people' and have dinner somewhere smart to celebrate his having sold a story. Ivy passed Edward without a word on very high heels, her hair tied into a turban and the collar of her hard fur coat turned up round her thin neck. Edward often wondered what she got up to out of working hours and was sure it was no good, whether she was with that drunken swine of a husband or somebody else. She always left the factory and returned to it with a secret, hostile look, as if defying anyone to inquire into her private life.

Kitty had told Edward that her husband would be gone when she got home, but she would have been surprised to know how sad he felt for her as she trotted off in her red scarf and thick gloves, looking like a child sent out to play in the snow.

'Good night, Madeleine!'

'Good night, Edward. Don't be late in the morning!' That was one of her little jokes. Since Christmas, Madeleine had

127

taken to wearing trousers. With them, she wore a mauve crochet jumper with a butterfly brooch, court shoes with buckles and Louis heels, a dark-green waisted coat with a fur collar and her best black winter hat with the little veil. Paddy, following her out, wondered how she could ever have thought it funny, when now it just made her despair. She was going to go to bed early tonight and make up last night's sleep. The American Army was all very well, but it had brought with it to London its New York habit of 'going on some place else' and never seemed to have heard of going to bed. She would put off her letter to Dicky just one more day, until she could concoct something a bit more inspiring than her last two, which, she recollected contritely, had been too full of complaints to bring cheer to a man in the desert who had only a gallon of water a day to wash, shave, drink and fill his radiator.

Grace and Reenie went off arm-in-arm, looking waistless. 'Good night, Edward,' they said and Reenie giggled, because, she didn't know why, but the name Edward always sounded funny. Grace was pulling her along, her mind on the Hoover with which her husband had won her undying love shortly after marriage.

Edward was into his Burberry and had lit a pipe to keep him warm on the way home. A skinny labourer in dungarees was running his hand down the light switches and the shop was almost dark before he saw that Wendy Holt had not yet gone home. She was bending over something in a corner under the hanging overalls.

'Not gone yet, Wendy? You'll miss your bus.'

She looked up, her face pale for an instant and then obscured as the labourer reached the last switch and hopped down from his step-ladder. 'Oh, I don't go by bus – there's not one goes near. I walk. It isn't very far.' She bent again to the bundle on the floor, half-kneeling over it, tugging at a cord impatiently.

'What on earth are you playing at?' He felt taller than usual as he stood over her. 'Can I help you?'

'Oh, no – it's all right, really. It's only these blankets. I bought them at lunch-time today and the girl in the shop tied them up so I could carry them, but now the string seems to have slipped.' She tugged again. 'I'll never get them home unless I've got something to hold them by.'

128

'Here, let me do it.' Edward squatted down beside her. She had tied the string tightly around the middle of the blankets, but they were coming unfolded and falling out all over the place. Wendy held his torch while he struggled to undo her knot.

'Oh, thanks *aw*fully,' she said, when he stood up with a moderately wieldy bundle under his arm, and held out her own arms for it.

'I'll carry it down to the clockhouse for you,' he said. 'You shine the torch.' They picked their way round a bench and past a trolley abandoned in the gangway by Charlie and his women when the bell struck. The darkness was full of brooding, metallic shapes. Here and there a gear grinned or a polished shaft gleamed in the light as Wendy's torch passed over them. Drawn up by the door were the humped, headless torsos of assembled engines, shrouded in canvas like bodies in a morgue. Hitching up the blankets, Edward held open the little door inside the big door for Wendy and then stepped through himself, backwards, bringing the bundle through after him. The Shop stretched away into vaults of gloom: it might have been a hundred yards long, or limitless. Quiet as a cathedral, but packed from end to end with the potentialities of a noise so great that two men sitting cheek by jowl behind it would have to speak to each other through microphones.

Edward shut the door and joined Wendy out on the track. 'It's lighter out than in,' they both said at once, and then laughed. The gate-keeper in the clockhouse looked at them cynically as they each made their separate 'ping' in the silence that ten minutes before had been an orchestra of pings.

'Looks bad,' said the gatekeeper, 'comin' out a quarter of an hour later with blankets over your arm.' Pleased with his joke, he repeated it. 'I say, it looks bad coming out a quarter of an hour –'

'Been working overtime,' said Edward, crisply. 'Good night!'

'Overtime I don't think,' said the gatekeeper to the boy who was collecting the cards, as the door swung to behind them. 'I say, overtime I don't think, or you wouldn't catch 'em clocking out a minute before the quarter but a minute after, so's to get the credit for the next quarter. Ah, yes – there's some funny things goes on in this factory. I've seen more than I care to tell about.' What he did tell about was so much that if he had really seen it the factory would have been closed down long ago. His family were all adenoidal from listening open-mouthed to the stories he brought home.

Edward was carrying Wendy's bundle up the Estate road. 'This is much too heavy for you,' he said. 'I can't think how you managed to get back with it lunch-time.'

'It was a bit of a struggle. I had to keep stopping to hitch it up. I expect you noticed I came in late. I'm awfully sorry.'

'Good Lord, I don't mind,' he said. 'If all the girls were as good timekeepers as you, there wouldn't be as much difficulty. You haven't had any time out since I've been in your Shop, have you?'

'No, I don't think so.' Wendy never even took the hour off that they were allowed once a week for shopping. It meant missing the overtime bonus, and she couldn't afford that. When they got to the main road, she said: 'I'll take the blankets now. It was awfully kind of you to carry them.'

'Which way d'you go? Perhaps we go in the same direction?'

'No, we don't.' She shook her smooth tail of hair. 'I turn up to the right and you go straight on, don't you? I've seen you.'

'Well, I'll walk along with you a bit. I'm not in a hurry. You can't possibly manage these in the dark; they're much too heavy.'

'Oh, yes, I can,' she protested, pulling at the bundle. 'Do give me them. I don't want to make you late: you go on home.'

'Wouldn't dream of it,' he said, holding the blankets more tightly. The feebleness of her tugging made him feel masterful. 'Where do you live?' he asked sternly.

'Queensdale Road, but –'

'Queensdale Road! That's nothing, hardly out of my way at all. Let go the blankets or I'll drop them. Come on. I'll take you home.'

He strode ahead, while she trotted beside him, still protesting. Presently he slowed down his athletic stride, but he noticed that she still took two steps to his one. She had tiny, useless ankle-bones that skittered under the weight even of so slight a body. They talked about the factory for a while, and then walked in silence. He knew very little about her outside the factory. Once or twice he had brought his stool up beside her at tea-time, but they had only talked about the news or how it would soon be Christmas, or, more recently, what a long time it seemed since Christmas and hadn't it gone in a flash.

She was wearing a grey coat with a nipped-in waist and a full skirt. Her small feet looked chunky in ankle socks and flat shoes as they moved unobtrusively beside his. He had a sudden impulse to tell her that he had a rabbit at home called Wendy, but instead he said:

'D'you live with your people?'

'Yes,' she said.

'What, mother and father, eh?'

'Yes.'

'Just you alone, or have you got brothers and sisters?'

'No,' she said. 'We've got to cross here and go down that road on the right. That brings us into Queensdale Road. I'm afraid you're going to be awfully late. Do give me the blankets now. I can easily manage them just that little way.'

'If it's such a little way, it won't make much difference to my being late,' said Edward. On the corner of Queensdale Road, she stopped and said again, 'Let me take them now. You could turn off here and get down into the High Street.' Edward walked on, pretending not to hear, because he wanted to see where she lived.

Queensdale Road was a cul-de-sac, ending in a corrugated iron fence topped with spikes. Wendy lived at the end near the fence, in a little house with a grey slate roof, flush on to the road like a miner's cottage. Edward could not see much else about the house, except that the front window showed chinks of light at the sides of the curtain.

'You ought to have a better blackout than that, living so near the railway,' he said, resting the blankets on his hip while Wendy fumbled in her bag.

'I know,' she said, 'isn't it awful? I had such trouble fixing it up, but every time anyone draws it, it seems to get torn. Anyone being her father, who cared nothing for air-raid Wardens, though a great deal for German bombers, and always turned out the light at the main when an air-raid warning was on.

Wendy opened the door and stood aside for Edward to put the bundle down in the hall. He stepped back on to the doorstep, and she made no move either to invite him in or show him out.

'Well, good-bye,' he said. Although they called each other Ted and Wendy at the factory, somehow they had not been able to since they had left it. They were more like people just introduced than people who had spent nine and a half hours together six days a week for six months.

A door opened and Wendy's mother came into the hall, flustered at the sight of Edward, whom she took for the Wardens again.

'Oh, dear,' she began.

'This is Mr Ledward, Mother,' said Wendy. 'From the factory. I bought those blankets I told you about at Ringers today and he's carried them home for me.'

'Well, that *is* nice,' said Wendy's mother, coming forward with her old-fashioned walk that looked as if she had no feet. 'How do you do, Mr Ledward? I'm sure it's very nice of you to help Wendy.' He noticed that she kept looking behind her at the closed door, as if she were afraid of something. She spoke in a low voice and Wendy answered her in the same way, so that Edward found himself almost whispering, too. They were like three people talking outside a sick room, and Edward wondered if it were Wendy's father who was ill.

Suddenly Wendy said: 'Why don't you come inside and shut the door? It's quite cold, Mother, I think the least we can do is give him a cup of tea before he goes home, don't you?' They both glanced swiftly at the closed door.

'I don't see why not,' said her mother, hesitantly.

'Oh, no, really,' murmured Edward. 'Please don't bother. I wouldn't dream –'

'Yes, you would,' said Wendy. 'I'm sure you'd love one. Anyway, it's the least we can do after you carrying those blankets all the way home, isn't it, Mother?'

'I – yes, of course, dear,' said Mrs Holt, with her eyes and her mind on the door. Whatever had come over Wendy to risk such a suggestion? Surely she was not going to take him into the living-room? There had been circus enough last time when Dad had come down from his bedroom to find the War Savings lady in there. She blushed now to think of the way he had carried on, as if the poor lady were trying to rob them.

132

That had been bad enough, but he would be even worse with a man, because he thought all men were after Wendy, and to take him into the sitting-room where Dad was settled with the evening paper. It was sheer madness. Whatever would this Mr Ledward think?

But Wendy was saying, 'Come on, then. D'you mind coming into the kitchen. It's warmer there.'

'Yes, he could come into the kitchen,' breathed Mrs Holt more hopefully. It was so long since they had had anyone to the house, it would be quite a treat to have a little company. 'We could all have some tea in the kitchen.' They could have another cup later on with Dad, and he need never know.

'It's very kind of you, Mrs Holt, but I really ought to be getting along.' Edward was terrified of disturbing whoever was so ill behind that door. They stood in the dark hall like three conspirators plotting anarchy, and when Wendy finally overcame his hesitation, they tip-toed past the door as if they were on the way to the Vaults of the House of Commons.

Once safely in the kitchen with the door shut, everyone breathed more freely, although there was hardly room for the three of them to move in the tiny room. Mrs Holt spoke in a normal voice, and Wendy began to hum softly as she turned up the flame under the kettle and reached in the cupboard for cups, which she could do without moving. There was nowhere to sit, so Edward leant against the flap-table, with his legs crossed and his arms folded, trying to appear at ease. Every now and then, Mrs Holt would glance towards the door, as if she expected to see the Frankenstein monster walk through it.

'I got the fish, Mother,' said Wendy, calculating how strong she could make the tea and still leave enough until Saturday. 'It's in my string bag over there.'

'I'll just wash it then, shall I?' said her mother, peering about for it without putting on her glasses, 'and put it on the stove, otherwise we shall be late with your Dad's supper and that would never do.' She tried to imply a beloved figure stamping home from work and bellowing jovially for the attentions lavished on him so willingly by his women. 'That would be too bad,' she said brightly, her face betraying just how bad it would be. She took her gold-rimmed oval spectacles out of the bag that dangled at her waist, and in three paces was at the scullery sink.

Wendy made the tea and poured out with a great show of domesticity. 'Sugar? We've got lots,' she lied, prepared to drink hers unsweetened for the sake of hospitality. Mrs Holt brought in the fish, dripping through the colander on to the floor and Wendy put it on to boil. Both she and her mother gave their souls for fried fish, but Mr Holt had once read an article saying that frying destroyed nourishment and they had had it steamed or boiled ever since. Of all the truth and nonsense that he read in the paper and frequently decried, certain things like this stuck in his brain and became a ruling passion. Sometimes it worked the other way: he was so incensed by what he read that he went all out for the contrary. No carrot was allowed near the house since the Ministry of Food had started their campaign.

It was quite a party in the kitchen. They all stood close together, and sipped their tea, and nodded and chatted. Edward leaned against the flap table, Wendy against the stove, with the steam from the fish saucepan dampening her hair, and her mother, who was built all in one piece and the wrong shape for leaning, stood by the window with her little finger well crooked, feeling very social. Edward was telling them about his rabbits. Most interesting it was, and drew from Mrs Holt tut-tuttings and exclamations of 'Well, I say!'

Wendy wondered what the other girls would say if they could see her entertaining Edward. She knew they liked him, although they laughed at him and called him indelicate things behind his back, but they had no idea what he was really like. No one had ever heard him talking seriously and interestingly like this; at the factory he was always making jokes. She herself scarcely ever spoke to him about anything but work, but perhaps now he knew her better they would have some interesting conversations. It would be nice if he sometimes brought his stool to her end of the bench at tea-time, because she had nobody to talk to at her end except Ivy, who despised her, and Sheila, who was always shouting up at Dinah at the other end. True, she had Grace opposite her, who talked untiringly on the fascinating subject of housekeeping. Wendy liked to hear people talk about

134

their homes and compare them with what she would have, but Grace overdid it. She had a way of opening her eyes very wide at you, as if she would hypnotize you into listening. Wendy had once spent nearly an hour in a kind of coma induced by the saga of Grace's linen cupboard, and had come to to find that the other girls had finished the engine and left for the next bench, while her hands had been lying idle among the rockers. Edward, now, was what you would call clever, and Wendy admired clever people because she knew she was not clever herself.

The atmosphere in the little kitchen was conducive to another cup of tea all round. Wendy wished she could offer something to eat, but they had no biscuits or cake, and although there was plenty of bread, you couldn't swindle butter as you could tea. Edward, who had been about to say that he really ought to go, was started off again about the rabbits by his second cup. No one had ever shown such a gratifying interest in them before; even people like Dick Bennett, who were in the Fancy themselves, only listened in order to be able to talk about their own stock.

'Oh, I *do* wish I could see them!' Wendy said. 'They sound so sweet!'

'Pretty dears –' chorused her mother.

'I tell you what,' said Edward, looking from one to the other enthusiastically. 'you ought to come along and see them one day. Wendy and I could pick you up after work, Mrs Holt, and take you along. Oh, no – it would be too dark. You'd have to come on a Sunday, any Sunday – I'm always there. Why don't you? This next Sunday, if you like.'

'Oh, I'd love to!' said Wendy spontaneously, and Mrs Holt looked as wistful as if it were a treat of the first order. 'D'you think we could –?' she began.

'Of course!' said Edward heartily, thinking she was doubting him, not herself. 'Do come this Sunday. You ought to come soon, because I've got a litter just at the perfect age – like toys, you'll think they are. And wait till you see my Masterman! I'll guarantee you've never seen a rabbit like that in your lives. And he's tame, too, Wendy. You can have him in your arms and do anything you like with him.' In his enthusiasm, he was raising his voice.

'It would be lovely!' Wendy and her mother looked at each other with shining eyes.

'Say you'll come on Sunday, then?'

'Yes, we will.' Wendy nodded eagerly. It really seemed for a moment as if they could, but in the next moment, while they all stood there smiling, delighted with each other, the door from the hall was wrenched open and in the doorway stood a little man with baggy knees and a shock of white hair standing off his head like a cockatoo's crest. His face was working, and so was his voice.

Wendy took a step nearer to her mother, and Edward looked for a place to put down his cup, and, finding none, went on holding it awkwardly. The three in the kitchen stood transfixed as if they had been found in each other's bedrooms. For the life of him, Edward could not think what he had done wrong, yet he could feel the sense of guilt creeping over him.

Mr Holt was shouting as if he were in the Albert Hall instead of two feet away from his panic-stricken audience. 'What in the name of all the saints in Heaven? . . . mean nothing to you that I should perish of starvation before you'll lift a finger . . . as God sees me, this is my house, and I will not – I will not, I say, have it used as a hotel . . . I will not –!' There were a lot of things he would not, but one thing he would, and that was to know who, in the name of all that was just and Holy, was Edward.

Edward had never been so embarrassed in his life. His one thought was to get away, but the gabbling, gesticulating figure stood between him and freedom. There was not even room to retreat from it, so he had to stand in the line of fire smiling foolishly, with the cup and saucer held before him like an offering.

'Father –' Wendy stepped forward when he paused for a long whistling intake of breath. 'Father, this is Mr Ledward from the factory – he carried some things home for me.'

'We were just having a cup of tea, as it's so cold,' put in Mrs Holt, with her instinct for fanning the flame. She burst into tears as it leapt forth at her. Mr Holt began to jig up and down in his rage. With only a vague idea of what he was angry about, he had already worked himself up to the pitch of only knowing that he was angry. It didn't matter what he said, but he said everything, and went all out for hysteria. Edward began to wonder if he were quite normal. So this was why they had whispered in the hall.

Suddenly Mr Holt leaped aside and stood with quivering knees and arm outflung towards the front door. It was obvious whom he meant, and Edward was only too thankful, with an apologetic glance at the other two and a few uncertain passes with his cup, which eventually landed it on top of the stove, to make for safety. Wendy was close behind him, hurrying him on. She was almost in tears.

'I'm so sorry,' she kept saying, 'I don't know what you'll think. I'm so sorry!' Passing him, and turning to look up at him with her hand on the doorknob, she said: 'You'd better go' – as if anything could have stopped him. The noise continued from the kitchen, where Mrs Holt was still cornered. Edward racked his brain for something to say to show Wendy how sorry he was for her and that he did not think it funny, but nothing came. And he did think it funny: dashed funny!

'You'd better go,' she repeated, opening the door. 'The doctor has said he mustn't get excited, but the least little thing upsets him. He's been ill, you know. His nerves have been in a terrible state ever since the blitz; he had a Nervous Breakdown.'

'Yes, of course – a Nervous Breakdown,' said Edward, grasping at the magic words which dignify hysteria into a disease. 'Well – good night,' he said. She would want to shut the door before the neighbours heard the noise. There was no need for either of them to mention next Sunday.

'Good night,' she said, sadly. The ranting voice filled the shadows behind her. It was like leaving a sacrifice in the lion's den. 'Are you sure you'll be all right?' said Edward on the doorstep. 'Wouldn't you like me to get a doctor or – or something?'

'Oh, no!' She gave a little laugh. 'There's nothing to worry about. He'll be perfectly all right after a good night's sleep.' She laughed again, nervously, as if she could laugh off the blare from the kitchen which proclaimed how all wrong she was.

Edward could hear it even after the door was shut and he was on his way up Queensdale Road. The tin fence seemed to amplify it and throw it about his ears. But long after he was out of

137

its range, he kept hearing it and mopped imaginary sweat from his forehead and said aloud 'Phew!' and wondered how Wendy was getting on.

He seemed to be dogged by noise tonight. When he let himself in at his own front door, an hour later than his usual time, voices came out to meet him from the half-open living-room door. They were arguing about something, and they were eating too; he heard the noise of knives and plates and hoped there was something left for him. He thought he would go and wash first, but as his foot was on the bottom stair, Connie called out: 'Is that you, Ted? Where on earth have you been?'

'Come in here, my boy!' boomed his father-in-law, 'and explain yourself. Counsel for the Prosecution will now cross-examine you?' When he laughed, he said 'Ha, ha, ha,' just as it is printed.

Edward went in and stood before them like the little boy in 'When Did You Last See Your Father?' which hung over the mantelpiece. They had all suspended eating for a moment to look at him and hear what he had got to say.

'Sorry I'm late, Con,' he said easily. 'Fact was, I had to see a man about the Rabbit Club. I didn't tell you because I didn't think I'd be long, but he kept me talking hours!' The camera turned once more and the scene came to life. Dorothy's mouth began to chew again, and Mrs Munroe's fork continued its journey to her mouth and descended, while she digested his information along with the baked cod.

'Oh, that awful Rabbit Club,' said Connie, dismissing it. 'He's mad about it, you know,' she said to her family, like a parent excusing a child.

Mrs Munroe swallowed, and her face was once more flat between the heavy coils of hair. 'You'll run into trouble with that Club if you don't look out. You never did have a head for business. Every day you read about somebody starting one of these crackbrained schemes and going bust.'

'The trouble is, ' said Mr Munroe, 'you've got no capital. Can't start a club without capital. Why, I remember when I founded our Whist Club –'

'But we *have* got capital,' said Edward. 'I told you about Mr Dexter Bell. He's willing to advance us anything we need until the subscriptions start coming in.'

'Oh, a Jew, eh?' said Mrs Munroe, to whom anyone connected with finance was a Jew.

'No, he's not, as a matter of fact,' said Edward, and discovered that Connie was saying it, too. 'He's quite well-to-do, though, I should say,' she continued. 'I can't think why he bothers with this daft little idea of Ted's and that awful Dick Bennett.'

'Something fishy somewhere,' said her mother, removing a bone.

'Oh, I wouldn't go so far as to say that,' went on Connie. 'He doesn't seem that sort of person. He's got his own business – estate agents, didn't you say, Ted – somewhere in the Bloomsbury district, I believe. Do get on with your fish, Pa. You're terribly slow, and you'll only want some more after we've all finished.'

'Estate agents, eh?' he said, ignoring her request and beginning to cut his bread into maddening squares. 'Must be making a mint of money. I met a chap the other day who told me that every flat that's let in London now could have been let twice over and then again, The City's choc full. You've only got to go into the restaurants and see the queues.'

'Well, we know that, Pop,' said Dorothy. 'We've all been to the Tuck-Inn and we've all stood in a queue and we all know that when we did get a table there wasn't anything hot left, because you've been talking about it ever since.'

'Well, there wasn't anything hot, was there?' He turned his slow aggrieved eyes on her. 'I had to have Spam and had a thirst all night in consequence that got me out of bed three times to drink out of the jug on the washstand. I can't see the harm in stating a fact that happens to be true, and there was nothing hot, and I don't care who asks me, if it was the Prime Minister himself, I should tell him: we stood in a queue for half an hour at Tuck-Inn and there was nothing hot left.' He popped a small square of bread into his mouth and chewed as if it were a mouthful.

'Oh, all right, all right, all *right*!' said Dorothy. 'Nobody minds your saying that – it's just that you keep on and on and on about a thing, till a person could scream.' She opened her eyes very wide and half opened her mouth, but as no scream was forthcoming, she shut it again and went on eating. Dorothy was normally the most placid girl – almost cowlike she had been two years ago, when she planted her unbudging devotion and admiration at the feet of Don Derris, who could not be bothered to avoid marrying her. As a maiden, she had been peaceable in the home and never noticed her father was there. Now that she had come back to it after a year of emancipation with Don and in a condition which her mother described as 'So', her irritability increased with her size.

'Dorothy, dear,' said Mrs Munroe, and wagged her forefinger.

'Leave him alone, Dorothy,' said Connie, 'or he'll never finish. Ted, your fish is in the oven if you want it, though I don't know what it's like by now.'

'Well, my boy,' said Mr Munroe, as Edward was going out of the door, 'how's the factory?' Edward had once tried to tell them about his new job and the responsibility of it and how he was getting hold of it and working up quite a position for himself in the Inspection Shop, but the wireless had been on at the time and they hadn't really listened. They'd be surprised, he thought, if they could see him at work, passing judgement on complicated bits of mechanism, like a Solomon. He had never been particularly enthusiastic about his job in the Fitting Shop, and if they thought he still felt like that, never mind. They probably could not understand that you could enjoy your job. Although he knew that if he passed anything faulty, it would go through a lot of hands before it got into the air, there was always the chance that all those hands might miss it, even the A.I.D., whom he was discovering now to be not so omnipotent as he had thought when he was new and callow. But he was not going to embark on an explanation to his family-in-law of the exhilaration involved in telling yourself that on your word alone, perhaps, depended whether an engine might pack up at five thousand feet over the North Sea or bring its fighter pilot safely home time after time.

So when Mr Munroe said 'How's the factory?' Edward just said 'Oh, mustn't grumble,' and went on into the kitchen to get his food.

They were back at their old argument when he came back to the table. The call-up of childless married women had recently been announced and the argument was whether or not it affected Connie. Mrs Munroe thought it did, and prophesied immolation in the scullery of an A.T.S. kitchen: Connie thought she was just over age.

'But it doesn't depend on that,' said Dorothy, 'It's whether you've got any children. They're going to take all the ones without children first. You are silly, Connie, never to have had any. They can't take me.'

'Of course,' said Connie, with dignity, 'if they call me up, I shall go and gladly.' Edward raised his eyebrows. 'But I still maintain that they'll not call me up.'

It was a silly argument, anyway, which could only be settled by an official pronouncement. He let it play around him while he ate steadily through his plateful of fish and potatoes. He was hungry. It seemed ages since he had been in that scene at Wendy's house. Was it really only a little more than an hour ago? Might be a bit awkward seeing her tomorrow morning. He wouldn't say anything about it, of course, unless she did, but it would be rather embarrassing seeing her for the first time after having seen her in tears. He would think of a joke to pass it off.

'Very nice fish, Con,' he said, pushing his plate away and easing his waistcoat. 'I wish we could sometimes have it fried, though. I must say, I love a bit of fried fish.'

'You know I can't touch fried food,' said Connie, as if it was his fault. She was not particularly nice to him during the rest of the evening, so that it was with something more than surprise that he found her well in the middle of the bed when he got into it and announcing shyly that she had been to the doctor again and it was all right.

He had always believed that the doctor was only an excuse for her aversion to him as a husband. He had not thought for a long time whether he loved her, but now, what with shock and pride and contrition at having so misjudged her, he thought that he loved her very much, and completely forgot that for the last hour he had been yawning his head off and living only for the moment when he should put his head on the pillow and fall like a stone into sleep.

CHAPTER 8

LIVING in sin might be preferable to marriage, as David, who had tried both, always said, but it was much more complicated. Not that Sheila felt in the least sinful or guilty, but although she was learning many things from David, she had not yet quite achieved his indifference to the rest of the world. After that first Saturday night, when he had come to the flat for dinner and still been there at breakfast-time, nothing could have been more natural that than he should move his typewriter and much-labelled bags from his uncomfortable lodgings in Earls Court to Sheila's sixth-floor flat near the British Museum. They had hardly even discussed it. Sheila was in a state of delirious acquiescence in anything, and if he said it was all right, it was all right.

She had gone down to Earls Court one evening to fetch his things, as he was busy. His idea of packing had been to throw in a few books and shoes and then lose interest and go off to the office. Sheila didn't mind; she asked nothing better than to exercise her right to fiddle around among his things. Even his shirt collars gave her a thrill, and intimate things like his tooth-brush and the razor blade he had used that morning affected her strongly. His landlady had manifested herself in the door-way, registering neither approval nor censure as her eyes followed Sheila about the room. The unfortunate nape of Sheila's neck had begun to give her away as a novice by reddening, but she had brazened it out, she flattered herself, like an old hand.

'I said I was your sister,' she told David afterwards.

He laughed. 'You needn't have bothered, darling. She wouldn't care. You've no idea of the unbridled licence of Earls Court. Anyway, it's no business of hers.'

'Oh, but she believed I was your sister. She even called me Miss Fielding.'

'That pleased you, I bet. Swinley rearing its ugly head again.'

He always said that when she made little gestures of respectability. The night porter was her friend and seemed to approve but the day porter, who had a glass eye, had taken to giving her searching looks with the other one whenever she went in or out. She was careful always to wear gloves, but Swinley had reared its ugly head and prompted her to suggest that she might have a ring from Woolworth's. Nothing had come of that, but he had said, laughing at her, that she could call herself Mrs Fielding if she liked.

But then it was so complicated with ration books and identity cards. The owners of the flats held a check-up every few months and it was silly to call herself Mrs Fielding when her identity card said Sheila Blake, single. They might get suspicious and think she was an alien. The rations were an awful nuisance. David was registered at Earls Court, and she had to leave the train there on Saturdays and get his rations before going home to get her own. His landlady had registered him with all her friends, who kept rickety little shops in Warwick Road and never had anything but tinned plum jam and cheese in silver paper. She was going to be very efficient and re-register him when the next period started, if she could find out how it was done. She had enough trouble with the milkman, who was as obstructionist as a whole Government Department, and they had had to share her ration of milk for weeks while his landlady was getting all his.

These details, however, were of no importance beside the fact that she was ecstatically happy and that life was more exciting than she had ever imagined in her wildest girlhood dreams. Living with David might be tiring, but it was never dull. He hated making plans, and would suddenly ring her up in the evening as she was cooking their supper and ask her to meet him in some bar in ten minutes' time as they were going to the theatre and dinner afterwards. With a rueful glance at the wasted kidneys, for which she had spent all her lunch-hour searching, she would tear off the becoming overall in which she had arranged herself against his homecoming, fly to do things to her face and hair, wail hopelessly in the streets for a taxi and plunge underground, scattering old ladies on the escalator, and arrive breathless at the rendezvous to wait for him for half an hour.

Or again, when they had planned to go out to dinner, he would come home tired and in a domestic mood and expect to find a full course dinner waiting in the oven. Whenever Sheila went home to Swinley, she surreptitiously rifled the larder for tins of food against these contingencies. But best of all she liked Tuesdays and Thursdays, when he had been working all the night before and slept during the day. She liked to come in and find him safely asleep. She would let herself into the flat quietly and, creeping into the bedroom, sit down on the edge of the bed for the joy of having his arms go around her neck simultaneously with his waking. There was a lot to be said for living with a man, in or out of sin.

Her mother had never taught her anything about housekeeping, and it was a great worry to Sheila at first. She wished she could confide in Grace, who was always talking about 'Managing', and ask her how one Managed. David would eat all his week's butter in two days and then be surprised that there was no more, and he was frightfully extravagant with toilet paper and soap. Still, he worked so hard that you couldn't expect him to bother with silly little details; that was the woman's job, and Sheila was proud to do it. There was a certain fascination about being ridden by domesticity, and she was beginning to understand why some women never talked of anything else. She cultivated Grace's company and always travelled home with her.

She would have given anything not to have had to go to work. Apart from the difficulty of sleeping with the alarm under her pillow so as not to wake him and either dressing in total darkness or in the bathroom, his work as Feature Editor of a daily newspaper entailed peculiar hours which left him free sometimes in the middle of the day and hankering for her. He was very naughty about her job, and if he woke in the morning when she was dressing would do everything possible to make her late. She was getting a lot of pink cards that said: '*YOU* are helping Hitler! Why are you late clocking in?' Once, he had actually rung her up at the factory and she had had to take the call in Mr Gurley's office, with Mr Gurley listening. David was telling her to come over faint and come home at once, because he was going to Oxford on a story and she was going with him. He had booked their room and it was going to be fun. It had been terrible having to damp his enthusiasm and confidence that she would come. It was impossible to try and explain and at the same time give Mr Gurley the impression that she was dealing with a family crisis, because you were not supposed to be rung up. David never understood that her work at the factory was at all important, nor that in wartime you couldn't come and go as you pleased. 'Let someone else count the . . . nuts and bolts for a bit,' he said, and she had to jam the receiver hard against her ear so that Mr Gurley couldn't hear.

She felt she had let him down and was miserable for the three days while he was away. The flat seemed so wrong without him. How had she ever lived there alone before? She had not the heart to cook herself anything to eat, but lived on coffee and toast. She thought he might be angry when he came back, but that was what was so lovely about David: he never brooded. He could be furious with her one minute and shout so that Colonel Satterthwaite would knock on the wall, and the next he would seize her round the waist from behind as she sulked over the stove in the kitchen and demonstrate his affection for her so exuberantly that Colonel Satterthwaite would knock on the wall again.

He came home on Friday evening in tremendous spirits, and Sheila forgot her three days' unhappiness in an instant. He had a bottle of gin under one arm and a whole tinned ham under the other. Sheila's eyes nearly came out of her head.

'*Ham*, darling! Where on earth –? You didn't steal it?'

'One of the Subs sold it to me. He's got a girl who smuggles him out trifles like this from her father's eating-house. He's an Armenian or a Greek or something, and knows all the dodges to get stuff.'

'But that's Black Market! D'you think we ought –'

'You're crazy! If somebody's going to have it, why not us?' He threw the tin into the air and dropped it, making a dent in the bedroom door.

'Oh, David, look what you've done.' Sheila rubbed at it ineffectually.

'One more thing to explain to Kathleen when she comes home.'

'Oh, I know. I can't think what she's going to say when she sees the coffee stains on the carpet and that awful burn on the mantelpiece.'

'She won't mind. Tell her I did it. I say' – he limped into the kitchen to get the corkscrew – 'it's going to be hell if she ever does stop being evacuated. We'd have to find somewhere else.'

'It would be awfully difficult,' she called from the bedroom, where she was replacing her lipstick. 'They say you can't get flats for love or money.'

She had a sudden vision of herself staying out from the factory to tramp from agent to agent, viewing one impossible flat after another. She could almost feel her feet aching. Supposing she didn't find anywhere? They couldn't afford to go to a hotel for long, and at the thought that he might drift away from her if they were separated, the round eyes looking at her from the mirror grew rounder with fear.

'Oh, you'd find something!' he called. 'I can't get the ice out of the fridge.'

Yes, she would find something, because he expected her to. That was at once the tiring and exciting part of being in love, living up to what was expected of you.

'I can't get the ice out! What on earth have you done to this thing? It's like an iceberg. Come and get it out, because we're going to celebrate!'

'I'm coming.' The face in the mirror relaxed. She smiled at herself. Really, she was not looking at all bad these days. Love seemed to make your hair do what you wanted and your make-up stay on properly.

Later that evening, she said dreamily: 'I'd give anything not to be going home tomorrow night.'

He was furious. He protested that she had never told him.

'I did, darling. You've forgotten.'

'I never forget. I don't see why you have to go just when I get back. What am I supposed to do all the time you're away?'

'It's only one night. You'll be all right. I've left you lots of food. You'll only have to get your breakfast on Sunday, which you do anyway on other mornings. Think, you'll be able to have all the Sunday papers. I thought you'd probably go out for lunch, and I shall be back in the evening.'

'Don't go.'

'Darling, don't be unfair. You don't think I want to? I haven't been home for ages. I simply must go, or they'll begin suspect something. Mummy's already beginning to say "What are you up to?" in her letters.'

146

'Tell her what you're up to, then. Do her good!'

'But, David, you don't understand: I couldn't. They'd simply die of shame. They – oh, I couldn't!'

It was a fantastic suggestion.

It seemed even more fantastic next evening in the blue-lit train approaching Swinley. She laughed to herself at the mere idea. To start with, they would never believe it. David teased her enough about 'The Stately Home of Swinley', but he didn't really understand just how remote its life was from life in Museum Court, WC2. It was not that it was rich or stately; it was just a house that knew what was going to happen in it at every minute of the day. Her parents were not even the Blimps he imagined; they were just two people who had never gone abroad because of leaving the dogs. They might know less about life than their youngest daughter did at the age of twenty-two, but they knew what one did and did not do. She could never tell them.

The train made four stops at little stations on the way to Swinley, and as each one was called out there accumulated around Sheila more and more associations to draw her back to the life from which she had escaped.

'Cot'nam!' That was where they always clanged milk cans about on the daytime trains. 'Ardrey Bridge!' They had once got out there and driven four miles in a governess cart to have tea with some people called – Rogerson, was it? – whose son was six years old and couldn't feed himself. He had been a family joke for years afterwards,

'Park Halt!' Funny to hear a woman calling that. That was Mrs Munday, who lived in the cottage by the level crossing and had dozens of tattered children swinging on the gates. The children were grown up now and gone away. Some were in the Forces, perhaps. Sheila remembered one little boy who always called 'Yah!' and made a rude face at the train. She had seen him once when he was older, holding open a gate when she was out hunting and looking as if he would still like to say 'Yah!'

By the time she had passed 'Six Elms!' with its memories of trips there to buy a special sort of red sweet, and was reaching for her case as the train slowed down for Swinley, she was so steeped in the old atmosphere that she might have been ten years old, or any age. She half expected to see her legs stepping on to the platform in black woollen stockings, so exactly did she feel as if she were coming home from school for the holidays. The thought of David and the flat brought up her head and made her walk with conscious poise to the gate. She was different now, a visitor from Town. She was someone from Town looking at the country, instead of someone from the country looking at Town as a place where you went to buy clothes and see matinées and have tea at the underground Fullers below Jaegars.

She was someone to whom things had happened, who knew what she was alive for. Why, then, as she stood in the station yard, trying to see which of the lights were the lamps of the dogcart, did she feel as if she belonged here, where nothing ever happened? If I don't look out, she thought, I'll start feeling guilty, and I've managed to avoid that up till now.

The dogcart had been brought out of retirement when it became apparent that if Mr Blake were going to drive to his office in Worcester in the car there would be no petrol to spare for anything else. There was no question about his taking the car, for apart from the round-about train journey there was a quaint Victorian custom in the Blake family that Father had first go at everything, including the red gravy under the joint.

He was the senior partner in a firm of solicitors which had the confidence of every local family whose secrets were worth knowing, but was disappointingly stuffy about betraying that confidence in the home. With a brother-in-law and cousin as mature junior partners, he could have retired by now, but he had nothing better to do.

So the dogcart had been brought out of the barn, where it had rested so long on its haunches with its shafts slung up to a beam, dreaming of the days when it used to develop a rare turn of speed down Swinley Hill, especially when Nigger shied at the goats half-way down. But Nigger was gone long ago, to shy at goats from between the shafts of a job-master's buggy, and gone, too, was Noakes, the town-bred groom, to whom all horses were potential criminals, controlled only by a lot of jabbing and whacking and come-hupping, you Devil.

Although they were both country people and dressed and spoke the part, Mr and Mrs Blake did everything wrong in the country. They engaged the wrong sort of groom, because he had the right sort of references and transfixed them with a glib line of talk. They bought the wrong sort of horses – showy chestnuts with pale slender legs which buckled at the mere sight of a road, pretty, tricky ponies with little mean eyes on whom the children sat for delightful photographs, but by whom they all, except Roger, the eldest, who had no imagination, were put off riding for life.

The Blakes always had the wrong sort of dogs, too, untrained gun dogs that had got sloppy through living indoors, spaniels, with limpid eyes, and ears infested with canker. There was usually a shrill terrier about, so bad-tempered that he was a burden to everyone including himself, and in a permanent state of moulting white hairs all over the furniture. The furniture at Swinley Lodge was not quite right, either: it was neither comfortably homely nor elegantly formal, but just inelegantly uncomfortable. Chairs and sofas repelled you forwards instead of inviting you backwards, tables were ill-proportioned things with legs opposite all the chairs, the fireplaces let in draughts and let out heat, and all the flower vases were too tall and narrow.

The house itself, over whose threshold Mr Blake, who always did the right thing, had staggered with his substantial bride in 1901, would have been more at home in Dulwich than in the black-and-white Worcestershire village. It seemed to have got there by mistake, like a day tripper who has missed his train home and is stranded in the country in all the wrong clothes. Its red brick had darkened but never mellowed, and threw off creepers before they had reached the first floor window-sills. The garden was on a slope, with lawns that devoured a gardener's energy like vampires and a summer-house that lost the sun at midday. There was a vegetable garden and a fruit cage, but the rose garden had chronic greenfly and the flowers in the herbaceous borders all bloomed at different times.

The Blakes had had four children at regular intervals: a boy and a girl, a boy and a girl, all free from squints or harelips or embarrassing complexes. They had all gone to the wrong sort of schools at the right sort of fees and been taught the right recreations by wrong people like Noakes, the groom, who would 'shake 'em down in the saddle' by beating tin cans behind the pony's rump and sending it scuttling and bucking away with a child in floods of tears clinging on by reins, mane or arms round its neck. Everything possible had been done for their happiness. A pool had been dug and cemented in the upper lawn, too deep for a paddling child and too shallow to swim in. Beyond the thicket of evergreens that darkened all the windows along one side of the house there was a tennis-court, end-on to the evening sun, made of a special substance which melted in the heat and went into tarry whorls if you turned your foot quickly.

By living in such a house in such a village as Swinley, which was three miles from the station at the end of a single track line, the Blakes managed to combine the disadvantages of the country with none of its advantages. One by one the children had gone away, but Mr and Mrs Blake continued to live, in the country yet not of it, in expensive inconvenience which grew more expensive and more inconvenient with the coming of another war, It never occurred to them to make any radical change like moving to a cottage which could be run with one servant, or having fewer courses for dinner. Things were not given to occurring to Mrs Blake. Had it ever occurred to her to wonder for what purpose she rose each morning and dressed carefully in cashmere cardigan sets and heather mixture stockings, she might never have risen at all.

Unlike most country houses, the front door at Swinley was locked, and Sheila had to ring and be admitted by the female half of the 'Good Little Couple' whose male half had driven her the chilly three miles behind the common, slovenly cob. The Good Little Couple were both tall and gaunt and evil-visaged and reminded Sheila of the gardener in Nathaniel Gubbins's column who spent all day with his feet on the kitchen stove reading Karl Marx and prophesying Armageddon for his employers. But her mother, who had acquired them through an advertisement one dreadful week when it had seemed she would have to do all the housework and her husband's shoes, was convinced, in spite of evidence to the contrary, that they were the real old retainer type and that the Good Little Couple, whose name was Geek, would stay for ever and defend Swinley Lodge with their lives in the event of invasion.

Mrs Geek took Sheila's case without a word and disappeared down the hall with a martyred back, although Sheila had intended to carry the case herself. Geek shut himself out into the frosty night and Sheila heard him swearing at the cob. The grandfather clock whirred and said 'Nine o'clock', and across the hall, where a bar of light shone from under the drawing-room door, the wireless was switched on to the announcement of the News.

It was ages since Sheila had listened to the News. There was no need to with David; he always knew it already, with some sort of confidential embroidery tacked on. She was impressed by his grasp of the war and would listen devotedly while he expounded on something complicated like the Caucasus or Inflation, agreeing with him heartily but stumped if he asked her a question that he had not already answered himself. Then he would laugh at her and they would talk about silly things instead of the war.

She longed for him now and wondered whether he felt as low as she did. He was probably in a restaurant, one of their own haunts, even, for he was not sentimental about things like that. Perhaps it was just as well for them to be apart now and again. Sheila had read in a magazine that you should never let your man get used to you. Make your life together as exciting as those halcyon days of courtship.

Their courtship, which had only lasted a week, had not been particularly halcyon from Sheila's point of view. Its working hours had been spent in making mistakes because her mind was elsewhere – wondering why he had not written or telephoned, or worrying over the implications of his most casual remark, and in her off duty she had not moved from the telephone except to meet David at whatever peculiar hour or place he might suggest. However, she followed the magazine's advice faithfully, changing her hair style and the colour of her lipstick, and greeting him one evening in a gingham apron with a ribbon in her hair and the next in a sophisticated black dress with her hair swept up and earrings.

Her hair was tousled now by the scarf she had worn on the drive, and she tidied it before she went into the drawing-room in case her mother should think it was meant to be like that and beseech her to go to a reliable hairdresser. Mrs Blake herself came up to London twice a year for a perm, and at other times was shampooed and set by a man called I. B. Littlejohn in

Worcester, whose sets, no matter what style he attempted, always came out looking the same. The ladies who patronized him in preference to Dorée Smart, whose assistants wore apple-green overalls and said 'Righto, dear', had heads which resembled both each other and the wigs in I. B. Littlejohn's window. Mrs Blake's head was too large for the amount of hair she possessed, but I. B. managed to eke it out into his basic set: a side parting, showing a wide lane of pink scalp in her case, one deep scallop over the right temple, descending in gentle waves to a curl well forward over the ear, backed by a double row of curls in various stages of tightness or ravel, according to the age of the client's perm.

Mrs Blake had been, it was said, a handsome girl, and was now a fine woman, but, then, horses are fine and handsome, too. She had a square chin and a large nose with curving nostrils, red inside like a rocking-horse; she carried her head high and her bosom well forward. She was always dusting things off her lapels, or shaking them up or hoisting and lowering her double pulley of pearls, unconsciously titivating this proud portion of her anatomy. When Sheila came into the drawing-room, she looked up and said 'Ah!' and her husband, who had Sheila's runaway chin and a pair of pince-nez on a chain, looked up and said 'Ah!' too, and they both waited in their chairs to be kissed, as if they were not consumed with a degree of pride and affection which she had never suspected.

She had been full of things that she was going to tell them, oddments of news about the factory and the flat, but there was no need, because her mother started right in on local news. Her father went on listening to the wireless, sitting facing it, with crossed legs and a patent-leather pump dangling from one toe, nodding approval if it said anything sensible. Sheila, with her coat still on, sat thawing on her own tapestry stool in front of the fire, and as the atmosphere of her home closed around her as familiarly as hot bath water, she was no longer the girl from London, David's girl, whose life was hectic and blissful. She was once more the yawning girl in a plain expensive jumper and tweed skirt, sleepy from a too-heavy lunch, looking at magazines or playing with the dogs' ears, passing the time until a stubborn parlourmaid should bring in the tray with the silver pot and the spirit lamp, hot anchovy toast and two home-made cakes.

It was no stubborn parlourmaid, however, but the herring-gutted Mrs Geek who answered the bell when she rang for her dinner. David said that in the next world, by which he meant the world after the war, the people who pressed bells so confidently were going to find that nobody answered them. Sheila and he both agreed that this would be a good thing, but it did not prevent them from going to expensive hotels and restaurants whenever they could afford it and pressing bells without a qualm.

Mrs Geek stood in the doorway in a long, unbleached apron, like Death come for them all.

'My whisky, please,' said Mr Blake.

'And Miss Sheila's dinner,' added his wife. 'She can have it in here on a tray.'

'I 'ad laid it in the dining-room,' said Mrs Geek, implying the Herculean labour of transferring two knives, two forks and a spoon from the dining-room table to a tray.

'Yes – well,' said Mrs Blake, 'she's going to have it in here.'

'And a fresh syphon,' said Mr Blake. 'There was barely enough at dinner time. I do wish you'd keep a full one always on the sideboard. I've asked you so often.' How dared they speak to her like that? Sheila wondered, as the door closed. Didn't they know that if the Geeks chose to leave they would never get another maid? But her mother didn't seem aware of these things. She was constantly being surprised in shops by being unable to buy hot-water bottles or lemon squash.

Sheila got up. 'I'll go and get my dinner,' she said. 'I don't see why she should bother.'

Her father looked at her, surprised. 'We haven't quite come to that yet, my dear,' he said.

'She really hasn't got much to do,' said her mother. 'We hardly ever have anyone to dinner, and most of the bedrooms are shut up.' She lowered her voice automatically, for the Billeting Officer was her bogey.

'Why don't you take off your coat, darling? D'you know, it smells terribly of oil or something? You'd better leave it down here and let me get it cleaned for you.'

'Sorry,' said Sheila, 'I came straight from the factory. The

153

fire draws it out, I expect.' She went to the back of the room, where it was cold, and hung her coat over the back of the only comfortable chair in the room, which was never sat in because it was so far away from the fire. Nobody had ever thought of bringing it closer.

'How is the factory?' asked her father.

'Oh, it's all right. We're working quite hard. We're doing a new type of engine now; it's a lot more complicated.' She could never make it sound interesting or amusing, as she could when she talked about it to David. She could usually make him laugh, but when she tried to be entertaining at home, she could hear herself being a bore.

While she ate her dinner, her mother watched her, sitting with her thick legs well apart and her skirt high, showing grey silk directoire knickers. 'You're too thin, Shee,' she said. 'It doesn't suit you.'

'I like to be thin,' said Sheila. 'Clothes look better.'

'You'll lose your looks. I used to love you in that blue velvet. I've been keeping it in the landing cupboard in a moth-proof bag, but you could never wear it now; you'd look scraggy.'

'I wouldn't want to wear it now,' said Sheila, 'or ever again. It was a hideous dress.'

'Oh, no,' said her mother, with a smiling, grown-up shake of the head. 'I remember you in it at that last Christmas party before the war. You looked a dream.'

'A jolly solid one,' said Sheila, with her mouth full, remembering and blushing for her bouncing, bulky girlhood. The blue velvet dress might have been all right once, but she had come a long way since then. Her mother and father didn't seem to have progressed at all. They were still living, with minor unavoidable alterations, exactly the same life, when here before them at last was this wonderful chance to live differently. They didn't seem to want to live differently. They thought that the next world – after the war – was going to be exactly the same as the dull, expensive, privileged one they had always known. Sheila knew it was not. David had said so. She wouldn't tell them yet about communal feeding centres and no first class on trains and public schools open to East Enders, because it was no good upsetting them sooner than necessary. She wasn't quite sure what would happen to solicitors. She would have to ask David.

'Enjoying your dinner, Girlie?'

'Yes, thank you, Daddy – I was starving.'

'What had you for lunch?'

'Oh, I don't know, Mummy – sandwiches or something.'

'Now, Sheila, you don't mean to tell me that you only –'

'Oh, no – I remember, I went to the canteen,' she lied. She had actually had a stale cheese roll and coffee made with essence at a workman's café on the main road with Dinah. She was enjoying her dinner. It was roast mutton and cauliflower and rhubarb tart with the top of the milk, which was like cream down here. There was something to be said for having food brought to you under silver covers when you were hungry and tired, instead of having to clear up the breakfast mess and start opening tins and discover that you were out of milk.

Mrs Geek brought in her coffee and picked up her tray as glumly as if it were a bedpan.

'I'll wash up if you like to leave it,' suggested Sheila. 'I expect you want to get to bed.' She wanted to have a quiet session in the larder to see what tins she could take home. Mrs Geek's lips tightened as if she knew this. She hated anyone in her kitchen, and if you went through with an order she would stand and talk to you in the doorway so that you couldn't get in.

'Thank you,' she said, 'but Geek and I don't go to bed just yet. We haven't finished.' She went out, her long feet crushing the carpet like the treads of a tank.

The telephone rang surprisingly, with its continuous rural trill.

'Sandow about golf,' said Mr Blake, without looking up from his book. He thought of a message to give. He had established the tradition that he never telephoned, which saved him a lot of bother.

'For Miss Sheila,' said Mrs Geek, reappearing. 'Mr Fielding.' Sheila blushed scarlet, scrambled up and flew into the hall, banging the drawing-room door behind her. She was still flushed when she came back five minutes later, but shivering half with pleasure and half from the draught. The telephone was on a wall bracket in the kitchen passage, where people knocked into you with trays as you leaned either against the banisters or among the coats and ulsters on the other side. She had had to speak quietly because the kitchen door was open and she knew the Geeks were listening.

'Who was that, dear?' said her mother, pleasantly. She was writing a letter at her desk.

'Oh, just someone I know – someone in London.' Sheila sat down on her stool again and stared at the fire, smiling.

'Long call to make from London,' said her father. 'He must be either very devoted or very rich.' He laughed his silent laugh, which went on inside his face without emerging from it. Sheila's smile grew slightly rueful as she thought of her telephone bill. With David in residence, it was staggering. He was so used to being able to pick up a telephone in the office and get through to Glasgow or even New York at will that he thought nothing of trunk calls in the home. He always said 'Let me know what it is, darling, and I'll pay you back,' but, of course, she wouldn't dream of asking him for the money.

'What did he want, dear?' asked her mother, whose life was so dull that even somebody else's phone calls were interesting.

'Oh, nothing much. He wanted to fix up a date for dinner.' It would be lovely to be able to talk about David, just drivel on to somebody sympathetic. She indulged this craving sometimes to Dinah, but lately she had had the suspicion that Dinah, who was certainly no prude, oddly did not approve. In any case, no one who didn't know David could understand his perfection. They would never believe that any man could be quite all the things he was.

'You never tell me about any of your London beaux,' complained her mother, licking an envelope saver with a wry face. 'I'm sure there must be somebody, because Timothy's mother says you never write to him; he's told her so in his letters.' She sighed. 'You know I always thought you two would make a go of it. Perhaps you will yet, when this maddening war's over. I must say I shall be glad when we can use proper envelopes again. I'm sure these sticky things are poisonous.' Sheila smiled indulgently, thinking of Timothy with his voice that urchins mimicked in the street and the thinness of his legs in riding breeches. How she ever could have even toyed with the idea! But she hadn't known David then.

'By the way, he said – this man who rang up – to be sure and listen to the Midnight News. He couldn't say anything over

156

the phone, but apparently something pretty exci
pened.'

'Oh? And how does he know?' Her father took off h
nez, raised his eyebrows and replaced the pince-nez. 'The
nothing on the Nine o'clock News.'

'Well, he's on a newspaper, you see. They hear things at
office before they're announced officially.'

'Journalist, eh? What's his paper?' Sheila named it, antici-
pating the answer, which came: 'That rag! Well, I hope he's
not as common as his paper, that's all.'

'Don't be silly, Daddy. Just because you don't like the paper,
it doesn't mean to say that everyone on it is common. It's
owned by a Lord, as a matter of fact.' She nodded at him confidently, but he said 'Newspaper Peers!' and disposed of them
with a snap of his fingers.

'Anyway,' said Sheila, who, true to her upbringing, had
always scorned the paper until she met David, since when it had
been her Bible, 'I don't think it's a rag at all. I think it's a very
clever paper.'

'Oh, now, darling,' said her mother, whose greatest sorrow
had been the passing of the *Morning Post*, 'you can't really
think that. Your father says it looks bad even having it for the
kitchen, but the Geeks seem to like it. I think it's a disgusting
paper. It simply encourages people not to be educated.' Sheila
might have asked her how she knew what it was like, and discovered that she always read it if she found it in the pantry
when she was doing the flowers, but she was too indignant to
think of that. Her parents had both stopped what they were
doing, and she sat between them with burning cheeks while
they seemed to be goading her deliberately, almost as if they
suspected something.

'I'd like to meet this man,' her father was saying. 'After all,
it's bad enough for us to have you living all alone in London
at your age, without thinking that you're getting mixed up with
goodness knows whom.' Mr Blake would as soon have spoken
a grammatical error as written one.

'Oh, Daddy, don't be a *fool*!' said Sheila, with rising warmth,
ignoring her mother's 'Ssh, you mustn't call your father a fool.'
'Why, I – I hardly know him. You talk as if I were having an
affair with him or something.' She laughed unnaturally. 'And,

157

case, he is *not* common. He happens, as a matter of fact,
  very nice,' she finished airily.
  What is he — a man of about forty?'

'No, he's quite young, about Geoffrey's age – thirtyish.'

'Ah!' Her father took off his pince-nez and leaned forward
to make his point. 'Then why isn't he fighting for his country?
I suppose writing filth for the illiterate masses is a reserved
occupation? Wouldn't surprise me!'

Sheila struggled to control herself, but tears were pricking at
her eyes. How dared he talk about David like that? In what she
hoped was a coldly biting voice, she said: 'He happens to be
medically unfit, and I don't mind telling you that no one minds
being out of uniform more than he does.'

'What's wrong with him?' asked her mother, who, being a
stranger to ill-health, always suspected it in others.

'He had a football accident when he was a boy and got T.B.
in the bone of his leg. It's never cleared up. He limps,' she said
sadly, more to herself than them, looking into the fire. They
seemed to be satisfied. Her father went back to his book and
her mother to her letters. Sheila had just decided that she had
imagined their suspicions, when her mother, who was a great
one for plugging a subject, said: 'This man – Fielding or whatever his name is – is he in love with you?'

'Good lord, no!' Sheila, taken by surprise, brought out the
unnatural laugh again, much too loud. 'I've told you, I hardly
know him. I can't think why you make such a song about him.
He's the most ordinary person – rather dull, really.'

'My dear Sheila,' said her father, in measured tones, 'nobody's making a song about anyone. We were merely taking
a polite – and, I think, quite natural – parental interest in any
friend of our daughter's, but you got so excited about it –'

'I didn't get excited,' began Sheila, crossly.

'Leave her alone, John,' said her mother, 'she's tired.'

'If you ask me, she's overdoing it at that factory. She's as pale
as a ghost. I've half a mind to ask Dr Lewis to have a look at
her tomorrow; he wouldn't mind coming round on a Sunday.
He might give her a certificate to say she's got to have three
weeks' rest in the country. That's what she really needs.'

'I know. I really get very worried about her. If she goes on
like this, there's no knowing what she may let herself in for.

She's got a nasty cough now as it is, and we've always got your poor grandfather to think of.' They went on talking about her over her head as if she were not there until Sheila, unable to stand it any longer, burst out: 'What d'you suppose would happen if all the girls who were tired decided to take three weeks' rest? Who'd make the planes? You don't seem to realize there's a war on. What would you think of a soldier who felt tired and took three weeks off to recuperate? And I'm not tired. I never felt better in my life.'

'My darling child,' said her mother, with an indulgent little laugh, 'we all know you're very patriotic and I think it's *quite* the right spirit, but you mustn't lose your sense of proportion. I dare say you're doing quite an important job, and doing it very well, too, I've no doubt, though you've never explained to me exactly what you do, but I can't believe that your being away for three weeks could seriously alter the course of the war one way or the other. You've got to consider your health, you know – it's only fair to others, apart from yourself.'

'Well, what about the other girls?' repeated Sheila, heatedly. 'Don't you think they're tired? Much tireder than me? You've no idea how some of them live – the married ones. They've got to get their children dressed and get their husband's breakfast before they go to work, then they trail around to a day nursery with the kids, rush to the factory, work like stink all day, and miss their lunch probably because they've got to do all their shopping. Then in the evening they've got to go home and put the children to bed and do the housework and get their husband's supper, and he probably comes home drunk and beats them,' she added, with a flash of imagination to give colour.

Her mother laughed uncomfortably, and her father said: 'Quite the little Communist, aren't we? You see, dearest child,' he went on, patiently, 'it isn't as if we didn't know how marvellous some of these people are. We do. We all know that there's a great deal of suffering and hardship, even today. You, of course, being young, think that you're the only person to have discovered that there's anything wrong about it. It is a phase all young people go through. I did myself.' He laughed in silent reminiscence, studying his nails. 'You'll grow out of it.'

'Well, if everyone knows it's wrong, why don't they do something about it, then?' said Sheila sullenly.

'My dear –' again the whispered laugh, 'Rome wasn't built in a day. If you read the papers – I mean the *News*papers, not that tabloid to which you seem so attached – you'd see that some of the greatest brains in England are already applying themselves to the adjustment of post-war social conditions. Good luck to them but they've got an uphill struggle. You see, Sheila, what you don't realize is, apart from the question of whether they *ought* to have better conditions, half these people don't want them.' He reached to the table at his side and took the stopper out of the whisky decanter.

'Daddy, how can you say such a thing? You've got no idea – you don't know how these people live – you've never –' Oh, how she wished she had David here! He would know how to confound her father. She knew what she wanted to say, but could not find the words to say it.

'Far from having no idea, my dear Sheila,' continued her father, unruffled, pouring himself a generous tot of whisky, 'I have a very good idea. I'm not speaking idly when I say that some of these people don't want better conditions. Take the case of our own city of Birmingham. You know the wonderful great blocks of flats they put up – at enormous cost – in place of some of the worst slums? Well, I'd like you to see those flats now. A pigsty, I might say, but that would give you no idea. I tell you –' He splashed soda into his glass, held it to the light, then splashed in half an inch more, 'I tell you, they've made a shambles of the place. They've done their very best to turn those clean, healthy flats into the replica of the slum dwellings from which they have been unwillingly uprooted.' He cleared his throat and took a sip of whisky, like a public speaker refreshing himself with water at the conclusion of a telling passage.

'Yes,' put in his wife, who had not liked to interrupt him before on his oratory, 'Give them a bath, they put coals in it. They do, you know.'

Sheila felt suddenly very tired, as tired as her mother imagined she was. She felt, too, that she had let down the people for whom she wanted to speak, by not being able to confound her parents' ridiculous arguments. But you couldn't argue with them, because they simply had no idea. 'Come the Revolution,' David always said, 'no one will be more surprised than the people who find themselves being massacred.'

Mr Blake seemed to have stopped for the moment, so his wife went on: 'You see, darling, what you don't realize is that it's not quite the same for you as for these other girls working at the factory. It's bound to come harder on you.'

'Why?' said Sheila, quite rudely.

'Well, don't you see, because they're used to it. They expect to have to work these dreadful hours. They'd have to do it whether it were peace or war, but it's different for you. That's why I worry about your health. You're not brought up for this kind of life.'

'No?' Sheila turned round on her angrily. 'And whose fault is that?'

Her father began to tap his foot. 'Sheila, Sheila –' he said, threateningly, 'a good, sound argument is all very well, and no one knows better than I do that everyone is entitled to his own opinion, but rudeness to your parents, and especially to your mother, is a thing I cannot and will not tolerate. However, we know you're tired, so we'll excuse you tonight, but please don't spoil our enjoyment of your visits home again – Heaven knows they're rare enough. You'd better go to bed. Good night, child.' He inclined his face upwards for her kiss. 'I'll come and tuck you up,' said her mother.

As she pulled herself upstairs by the banisters, feeling exactly like the child who had pulled herself up the same stairs to the night nursery in disgrace, Sheila was crying those same, frustrated tears that had run down that child's grimacing face. The same feeling of being in the wrong, no matter how right you were – they had not lost the power to inspire it nor she to feel it. Only now there was no Nanny hovering in the shadows behind the gate on to the nursery landing, with: 'Never mind, my pet, Nanny knows. You didn't mean it. You come into Nanny's room and see what she's got in her tin, and then perhaps she'll read to you in bed – only don't you tell a soul, mind.' This conspiracy had been Nanny's triumph.

Oh, David, David, David – I need you so! How did I ever exist without you?

The next day went smoothly enough until after lunch. Sheila slept heavily, woke to find a cold cup of tea at her side, and was startled out of bed by the breakfast gong. At Swinley Lodge everyone was expected to breakfast downstairs, fully dressed, even on a Sunday. Dressing hurriedly in her cold room with its bulky, old-fashioned furniture, Sheila thought regretfully of Sunday mornings at the flat. It was one of the best times of the week. They would sleep late; if she woke first, she would lie happily still, watching David until he woke. By stretching out a hand, she could turn on the electric fire, and when she did get up there was no huddling about in a dressing-gown as she was doing this morning. She would throw the papers in at David while she was getting the breakfast, so that by the time she came back to bed with the tray, he would have finished with the serious news.

When they eventually got up, they would spend ages over baths and dressing, wandering about the flat, and often only emerging just in time for late lunch in Soho. That was the way a Sunday morning should be spent, thought Sheila, going downstairs in the country clothes which her mother would insist on steeping in moth-balls while she was away. When she lived at home, it used to be her father's reproving joke to say: 'Good evening,' when she was late for breakfast, but now, as a concession to her hard-working week, he indulgently let it pass without comment. She kissed the smooth cold side of his face which he offered and her mother's well-powdered cheek, and helped herself at the sideboard.

'Kippers, Mummy! Where on earth d'you get them? I haven't seen one for months in Town.'

'We've had quite a lot lately. Mr Carnegie always keeps me some when he can. And so he should, seeing what wonderful customers we've always been.'

'We've always paid our bills promptly; that's what counts,' said Mr Blake, extracting a long kipper bone from between his teeth, examining it and placing it in the parallel row of others round his plate.

There were only two Sunday papers at Swinley Lodge. Mr Blake had one and Mrs Blake the other. Sheila ate her breakfast, wishing that it were coffee instead of tea, and glanced at the news on the backs of the papers her parents were reading.

'Isn't it marvellous what the Russians are doing?' she said. 'D'you want the last bit of toast, Daddy, or can I have it?'

'No, I've finished, thank you, dear. Yes, I must admit I take my hat off to the Bolshies, but don't forget they could never do a thing if we weren't diverting the Huns in Africa. People are only too ready to exaggerate Russia's effort and minimize our own. And don't make the common mistake of forgetting that they signed a non-aggression pact with Germany. I shall never forgive them that, no matter how many adulatory programmes about that villain Lenin the B.B.C. asks me to listen to.'

'All the same,' said Sheila rashly, 'they stopped us losing the war last year. They despise us – at least, they did before we started to attack.'

Her father lowered his paper and removed his pince-nez. 'My darling child, you talk more nonsense than anyone I've ever heard. Who on earth told you that?' David had told her; she was quoting him verbatim, but she said: 'No one told me; that's what I think.'

Her father looked at her, laughed silently, then replaced his pince-nez and shook his paper into position again.

After breakfast, Mr Blake took the *Sunday Times* away to his study where he kept his tobacco in the jar he had had at college; Mrs Blake dusted the drawing-room, which with two W.V.S. sewing parties a week and suffering blackout and rationing uncomplainingly comprised her war effort; Sheila helped Mrs Geek make beds, which the latter did as if she were laying out a corpse. Sheila had the feeling that she would rather have made them alone, but Mrs Geek had said neither 'Yes' nor 'No' to her offer, but simply thrown the corner of an underblanket across to her and gone on tucking in her own side as if Sheila was not there.

'How d'you like the country, Mrs Geek?' ventured Sheila, when they were making her father's bed, a job which almost called for precision instruments. The Geeks were evacuees from Rotherhithe.

'It's all right, I dare say, Miss,' said Mrs Geek, puffing up a pillow which Sheila had already done. 'It'll serve for the time being.'

'You wouldn't stay here, then, after the war?'

Mrs Geek smiled grimly at the mere idea. 'I'll thank you for that other pillow, Miss.'

'Where will you go, then?' pursued Sheila, as they moved over to her mother's bed. 'Back to London?'

163

'That's right, Miss. When my boy comes home from the sea.'
She made it sound as if he would rise from the deeps, with sea-weed hanging around his drowned, bloated face.

'Your boy! I never knew you had a son at sea. What is he –
in the Navy.'

'Merchant Service, Miss.' Sheila wished she wouldn't keep
calling her 'Miss' and stressing it ironically.

'But how exciting!' she said, folding her mother's pre-war
satin nightgown. 'What's his ship?'

'Ask me no questions, Miss,' said Mrs Geek cagily. 'I tell
no lies.'

'You must be very proud of him,' continued Sheila, deter-mined to be friendly.

'Yes, Miss,' said Mrs Geek, implying 'if you say so.'

They were putting on her mother's counterpane now, over
the eiderdown instead of under it as Sheila liked. 'What's he
like, your son? I'd love to see a photograph.' It didn't seem pos-sible that the barren-looking Geeks could have borne fruit.

Mrs Geek mitred the counterpane corner. 'Oh,' she said,
'he's not much. He's never been a good boy. He and Geek
didn't speak for six months after he got us into our trouble.'
She walked out of the door, leaving Sheila seething with con-jectures about the Geeks' past. It just showed what people
missed by never talking to their servants.

Sheila and her parents walked to church in bulky clothes and
sensible shoes, and afterwards Major Saunders came to lunch
and was jocose at Sheila as if he were in the conspiracy to forget
that she had ever gone away from home and grown up.

It was after lunch that the day ceased to go smoothly. Sheila
was in the drawing-room, wondering what to do until tea-time
and wishing that there was a train to London before six o'clock.
Her mother came in, in the purple jumper which was such
good quality that it had lasted ever since King George V died.

'D'you know, Shee,' she said, 'I think I'll come up with you
tonight. I was going to Town tomorrow in any case to look at
sheets, so we might as well go together. I want to see the flat, too.
I never have, you know. You could put me up, couldn't you?'

'Oh, but there's only one bed,' said Sheila, in a panic.

'But you've told me you had that girl from the factory to
stay. Isn't it a double bed? I wouldn't mind sharing it.'

'Oh, you wouldn't like it, Mummy, it's – I don't think you'd better stay. I mean, it's an awfully small bed – it really isn't a double bed at all.'

'Well, I could manage on the sofa, I dare say, or you could.'

'There – there isn't a sofa.' Sheila's mind was in a whirl. Even if David were not waiting for her in the flat tonight – which he would be – it would take her hours to clear away the traces of him before she could possibly have her mother there.

'Well, it seems a pity, Sheila. I would have enjoyed spending the night there with you. And as Barbara's coming to tea and going to drop you at the station afterwards, I thought I might as well come, too. We could have taken up some tinned stuff and had a cosy little supper there together. I tell you what – I'll ring up the Wigmore Hotel; they'll let me have a room. Then I could still come up with you and see the flat and just go there to sleep after supper.'

'Oh, you'll never get a room,' said Sheila quickly. 'London's terribly full; you've no idea.'

'I'll get in there all right. The manager promised last time I was there. He'd always fit *me* in, he said.'

'Oh, but Mummy –' Sheila didn't know what to say. Wild ideas to prevent the catastrophe were rushing through her brain.

'I hear your mother's going up with you tonight.' Mr Blake came into the room, still carrying the *Sunday Times*. It took him all day to read it. No one else ever got a chance until after dinner.

'Oh, no, I don't think she –' began Sheila, but her mother was already saying: 'I'm just going to ring up the Wigmore and see if they can let me have a room, as it seems that Sheila can't put me up, after all.'

'I'll do it for you, Mummy – let me,' said Sheila, getting up and hurrying to the door, meaning to pretend to ring up and find there was no room.

'That's my nice girl. I'd love you to get through for me. The Exchange is awfully tiresome on a Sunday, but I'll speak to the hotel. They know me.'

'They know me, too,' said Sheila, in the doorway. 'I'll speak to them.'

'No, I think I'd better. Call me when you've got through.'

Leaning up against the wall in the draught, while she waited to get through to London, Sheila made frantic plans. Her mother meant to come straight to the flat from the station, so there was no hope of going on ahead and clearing it up. She would have to ring up David and explain – he'd be furious – and tell him to put all his things into cases and take them away and not come back until late that night. Could she telephone from here without being heard? The Geeks would listen, even if her parents remained safely shut in the drawing-room. It was risky. She would have to talk quietly and be very cryptic, and the line was sure to be bad. David might not even be in, and if he were, would he realize the urgency of it? He was always saying: 'Let me meet your parents, darling. I don't see why you're so furtive.' He never understood that it would absolutely be the end of the world if they found out.

But after her mother had finished with the Wigmore Hotel, who said: 'But, of course .... any time Madam wishes ... only too glad ...' and Sheila had firmly shut both the drawing-room and the kitchen doors, there was the sound of a car on the gravel outside and the cheery voices of her sister Barbara and her doctor husband who had come over to tea.

'Number, please?' said the girl at the local exchange for the second time, but Sheila hung up the receiver. She would have to telephone from the station; that was the only chance. At least, there would be privacy in the phone box, but she would have to pretend that the clocks were slow so as to get them started for the station in time. What would happen if David were not in, she didn't dare to think.

He was in, bless him – but the line, curse it, was terrible. She could hear him all right, but he kept saying: 'I can't hear a word you're saying. Tell me when you get back,' and threatening to ring off. At last she managed to make him understand. He said, as she had feared he would: 'Well, what about it, darling? Good opportunity to break the glad news to her. I'll get the place tidied and make something nice for supper, hm?'

'Oh, David, *No!*' Any minute now the train would be coming. Her sister's round, florid face was already mouthing at her through the glass of the box. At last she managed to convey something of her urgency to him. He grumbled, he protested, he offered other ideas. He was making it more difficult than it already was. Did he think she liked having to make him turn out like this? Did he think she wanted to miss their lovely Sunday evening?

'There's the train!' she shouted, while Barbara thumped on the box with a fur-gloved hand. 'You *promise*?' He promised. She felt physically exhausted as she picked up her gloves and bag and ran down the platform to where her mother was getting into a carriage.

'Come along – come along!' They all beckoned to her with wide sweeps of their arms as she approached. 'Why on earth you want to telephone now –' said her mother. 'Why didn't you do it at home?' And her sister, who was still to all appearances Captain of Hockey at St Brenda's, Bexhill, said: 'You are *mad*, Shee. You nearly missed the train.' Too breathless to answer them, Sheila sank into her seat, while her mother blocked the window exchanging last-minute urgencies.

Sheila sat in suspense all the way to London. She could not relax until she had opened the front door of the flat and satisfied herself that all traces of David were gone. Would he remember his shaving things? And his typewriter? Even his books might give him away, but it was too much to hope he had taken them. She would have to say they were Kathleen's. What about his gas-mask? He had a Service one in the hall cupboard. There was no telling where her mother might be moved to look. Pipes? Even the smell of tobacco – he would never think to open the windows. She sat fidgeting, distraught, unable to read, and scarcely answering her mother coherently. If she had never felt guilty before, she felt now like a criminal. Living in Sin: she and David had laughed at that often enough, but for the first time she felt that it was true.

They managed to get a taxi at the station. She was not sure whether she would rather put off the evil moment or get it over as soon as possible. Sitting well forward on the seat, tensed, while her mother sat solidly back and talked comfortably about White Sales, Sheila formed a plan between King's Cross and Bloomsbury. It all hung on one thing: whether the night or the day porter were on duty at the flats. It was eight o'clock – just about the time they changed over.

It was the night porter. She could have hugged him. Lolling out of his hutch to see who it was, he winked at her as if he admired her brazenness in bringing her mother to her Love

167

Nest. Looking him full in the eye and daring him to contradict her, she said to her mother: 'I'm afraid you'll have to walk upstairs. They don't run the lift on a Sunday,' the porter raised his eyebrows and dropped his jaw, and seemed about to speak. Sheila winked at him with all the muscles of one side of her face, took her mother by the arm and propelled her towards the stairs. He played up. She had judged rightly that he would enjoy being in on a conspiracy. Looking back at him, she saw him laughing darkly. He had not shaved that morning or that night, or whenever a night porter did shave.

'That's right,' he called after them. 'Got to save fuel, you know.'

'I wonder you don't turn out the light in the lift, then,' remarked Mrs Blake, nodding towards the lift, sitting blandly inviting them with its doors wide open and its lights blazing, but beginning nevertheless to plod unsuspiciously up the stairs.

'It's five storeys, Mummy,' said Sheila. 'I hope it won't kill you. You take it easy, and I'll run on ahead and light the fire and do the blackout.' She darted up the stairs as if on wings. Amazing what one's body could do in an emergency. She was hardly out of breath when she was at last outside her own front door and fumbling desperately for the key. If only nobody rang for the lift now. The porter might stop them getting in downstairs, but he could not prevent them summoning the lift from another floor.

She burst open the door, shut it behind her and said 'David!' in an urgent whisper. Everything was dark. There was no one there, and she could admit to herself now that she had been afraid he would not even have gone away. How could she have thought that of him? Darling David, he hadn't let her down. She rushed to do the blackout, and switching on all the lights, went frantically about the flat. He had done his best, poor darling, but you couldn't expect a man to notice little things. His comb, one sock on the floor, a bottle of hair cream, some typewritten notes, all these and other oddments she hurled into a drawer, locked it and shoved the key under the chest of drawers. Thank goodness she had come up first! It would be all right now. The bed was unmade, but she could say she had left it like that on Saturday morning, and the same with the breakfast things in the kitchen. She gave one more quick, comprehensive glance through the rooms, tore his gas-mask from its hook in the hall cupboard and buried it under some blankets in the linen cupboard, and was able to open the door, smiling, as her mother toiled up the last flight of stairs, with her hand on her bosom and her breath wheezing.

'Oh, dear, oh, dear –' She stood still for a moment to catch her breath and rearrange her lapels. 'I can't be as young as I was. I tell you what, Shee, my wind's shocking. I believe your father's right; I do smoke too much.'

'Come on in, then, Mummy, and sit down.' Sheila hustled her in, for on the floor above she heard a front door bang and a voice say: 'Damn – I've forgotten my torch. Shan't be a sec, George.' She had her mother safely inside her own front door before they could ring for the lift, and start that tell-tale whine and hum.

Everything went off all right. Her mother, as she knew she would, poked all round the flat and discovered nothing more suspicious than a bottle of laxative, which let Sheila in for a lecture on not having needed anything like that in the country and not getting enough exercise. There was one tricky moment, when Sheila saw the Sunday papers lying in disorder on the bed, but her mother's mind, not being sharpened by anxiety, never thought to inquire why they were not lying neatly folded just inside the front door.

They opened the tins which Mrs Blake had brought, and had an amicable supper over the sitting-room fire. Relief had made Sheila happy and affectionate, and her mother found her so unusually willing to chat about all the things which usually seemed to bore her that she was loth to go back to the well-bred discomfort of the Wigmore Hotel. Seeing the bed, she had said: 'But, darling, that *is* a double bed. I don't know why you thought we couldn't share that.'

'It's not really meant for two people, though. The springs are terribly weak – and in any case I kick like anything. Dinah says so. You wouldn't sleep a wink.'

'The springs feel all right.' Mrs Blake had bounced on them, and Sheila had said: 'They won't be if you go on doing that,' and made a joke of it to distract her.

At ten o'clock, she said: 'Mummy, I think you ought to go or you'll miss the last bus.'

'I'll get a taxi.' Mrs Blake leaned farther back in the comfortable armchair with her heather-mixture legs stuck out to the electric fire.

Sheila laughed. 'Shows what a country cousin you are. Taxis simply don't exist at night. You'll never get one. Come on – I'll walk with you to the bus. You can get a 7 or a 73 right down Oxford Street and then you're nearly there.' She had told David not to come back before eleven, but you never knew.

Her mother was maddeningly difficult to get organized. Even after Sheila had got her out of the front door, she had to go back twice for her gloves and scarf. Once more offering up a silent prayer about the lift, she hurried her downstairs and did not breathe freely until they were past the porter and safely into the street.

'That man didn't turn out the lift lights,' said Mrs Blake. 'Deliberately, I expect, because I suggested it. I've never known anything like the independence of these people nowadays. Why, even that good little Mrs Geek . . .' The story of Mrs Geek and the milk book lasted until the bus stop in New Oxford Street. It was bitterly cold and they had to wait ten minutes. Mrs Blake insisted on wailing 'Taxi' at every passing light, even if it were only a bicycle.

'Are you sure you can't get off and have lunch with me tomorrow?' she asked Sheila for the tenth time as the bus loomed up.

'Positive, Mummy. I'm sorry. I really can't.'

'Well, it's a pity. I might have got you a hat at Marshall's, but it's no good getting one without you there. Now, promise me, you won't overdo it. Your father and I –'

'No, no – of course not! Hop on, Mummy. Good-bye, and get home safe!'

'Come home again soon, darling.' Her mother turned with one foot on the bus and one in the gutter. 'We do love having you.' The conductress cut across the hint of wistfulness in her voice with: 'Come along there, *please*!' and a hoist under Mrs Blake's right elbow that landed her on the platform as the bus started away.

Sheila had hoped that David might be in when she got back, so she did not stop when the porter tried to detain her but sped

170

upwards in the lift. He was not yet in, but it was only ten to eleven. He was doing everything she had said.

She had a bath, she brushed out her hair, she washed her face and powdered it again. She put on her prettiest nightdress, she put coffee on to the stove and arranged herself in an armchair with the wireless playing soft music.

She woke with a start to the smell of burning and a voice announcing the Midnight News. She switched off the stove, threw the burnt-out saucepan into the dustbin, turned off the wireless and crawled into bed. He wouldn't come back now. He was probably staying with Toddy, but she left off her hair-net just in case, although her hair wanted setting.

She went to sleep with the alarm clock under her pillow as usual, and when it woke her next morning, silenced it hurriedly, as usual, and turned over to make sure it had not woken him.

She thought he had come home in the night, but it had been a dream. He wasn't there.

CHAPTER 9

IT was to be quite a little show. That was how Edward and Dick Bennett wanted it: just a few select classes for members of the Collis Park Rabbit Club only. If outsiders wanted to enter, then they must join the Club; that was a ruse to get the new members they so badly needed. Three months after its foundation, the Club had a nice little kernel of members, but although some of these were experienced fanciers with interesting stock, others were no more than one-rabbit men or schoolboys with a pair of Utilities in a converted soapbox.

However, they all paid their subscription, drew their rations of bran and dutifully sold half their young stock for flesh. The Club was also a market for their breeding stock, which they bartered through the medium of Edward or E. Dexter Bell, who although he insisted that he was too busy to be Secretary, was not above dabbling in the more attractive functions of the office. Edward had to deal with all the correspondence, long-hand, because the clacking of his old-fashioned typewriter set Connie's nerves on edge, but Mr Bell liked to feel that he was

171

the master-mind behind it. Edward could hardly object to his supervision, as he paid, among other things, for the notepaper and stamps.

Dick Bennet sometimes annoyed Edward by remarking that if it had not been for Mr Bell's solid backing he didn't know where they would have been.

'I reckon it was a rare stroke of luck getting in with him,' he would say, breathing heavily with a hero-worship which Edward could not share. Dick was all for making Mr Bell President, but so far Edward had managed to avoid this. The three of them called themselves Joint Unofficial Presidents, or in Mr Bell's moments of sticky *bonhomie* in the Marquis of Granby, The Three Musketeers.

It had become an established thing for them to meet roughly once a week, either at Edward's house, or at Dick Bennett's (not often because the children were so noisy), or in Mr Bell's sanctum on the first floor of 'Uanmee'. They would hold a kind of informal board meeting, going over the correspondence and the pamphlets from Ministries, drafting advertisements, making plans or simply talking shop. Often they would talk far into the night, until the room was stale with tobacco smoke and Connie or fat, sloppy Mrs Bennett or stylish Miss Bell had long since gone to bed.

'Quite a little show,' Edward was repeating thoughtfully one evening. 'Not a big do: more like a get-acquainted affair for our members. Being the first, we've got to set the pace for the Club's future, don't forget. We're not catering for the big breeders and the high fliers. Quite a little show, that's how I picture it. Friendly. We could get St Mark's Hall; they throw in flags there for nothing.'

'Hm,' said Dick Bennett and Mr Bell said: 'St Mark's Hall! My dear good chap, we want to aim a bit higher than that. Friendly by all means, no one's keener on that than Yours Truly, but as you say yourself, we've got to set the pace for the future. My point is this: properly handled, this little Club of ours could go a long way. Now I'll tell you what I had in mind for the Show.' He tilted back his head and his Adam's apple pumped the beer out of his glass.

They had had supper at the Four in Hand and were now digesting it in the upstairs sitting-room of 'Uanmee'. Miss Bell, who was the Assistant Manageress of a Secretarial College and moved upright along tracks of sexless competence, had told her brother that an occasional supper party was all very well, but once a week was another matter. Sandwiches she could undertake, but no more. Mr Bell respected his sister's decrees because she made him comfortable.

The room in which they sat was all that a bachelor could desire. He had chosen the suite himself: two arm-chairs and a settee in a thin, synthetic leather that evoked the casualness of the traditional study or library without the traditional shabbiness. These three pieces toed the edge of a black poodle rug in front of a gas-fire contrived to look like glowing coals. It was a pleasantry of Mr Bell's to make as if to knock his pipe out into this fire and then recollect himself with : 'Damn thing's so life-like it nearly takes me in! Honestly now, you'd never think that wasn't the real thing, would you? It's the only sort of fire to have, I'm convinced of that. All the advantages of a coal fire, with none of the inconveniences.'

You didn't contradict him, any more than you contradicted his assurance that the pale polished table behind the settee was as good a piece of oak as you were likely to see in a day's journey. There was something special about the seam apparently, but you agreed without understanding, hypnotized by Mr Bell's possessive confidence.

Bookshelves ranged the lower part of the walls, some holding books lying horizontally to fill up the space. Above them, the wall paper was regularly spaced with pictures. There were one or two hunting scenes with rather blobby horses and irresolute background, wild duck in flight, after, but not catching up with Peter Scott, and some of the better-known sporting prints, like 'The Moonlight Steeplechase' which had been with Mr Bell from boyhood and were referred to as 'my friends'. The mantelpiece held pipe-racks and tobacco-jars and photographs of women, some theatrical and inscribed. The mirror above was stuck round with snapshots, invitation cards, visiting cards, prize cards from rabbit shows, newspaper cuttings and similar interesting personalia. In one corner stood a fine radiogram, fluted and polished and inlaid, and beside it a little cupboard on legs, which Mr Bell had bought because it was labelled 'Cocktail Cabinet', held albums of catalogued records.

173

A typical man's room as Mr Bell always proudly apologized to new-comers.

Although it was early April and the evening quite warm, the window was shut and the gas-fire round which the three Unofficial Presidents were sitting was being a coal fire at full blast. A saucer of water, which Mr Bell thought was his original idea, stood in the fender to keep the air from getting dry. Beer bottles and ashtrays stood on the poodle rug. Edward was on the settee with a pile of papers in his lap, Dick Bennett was in one arm-chair, apparently for life, and E. Dexter Bell was in and out of the other according as he was moved to put on a record, tune the radio with howls and squeals through a rapid succession of stations, or lean heavily on Edward's shoulder, stabbing at one of his papers with a square, manicured finger.

They were still discussing the Show, when the clock struck ten and Miss Bell came in with a plate of sandwiches in each hand and her library book under her arm, for she was on her way up to bed. Edward got up and Dick Bennett, who was wedged between the arms of the incapacious arm-chair, struggled and heaved. He had got himself half upright with bent knees, when she fortunately said: 'Please sit down', and he was able to subside again before he was completely unstuck.

Mr Bell said: 'Sandwiches – ah, bless you, Muriel!' and rubbed his hands. 'I always say,' he went on, 'there's an art in making sandwiches as in everything else. Muriel's got it all right. What are you feeding the Brute with tonight, Mu?'

'Liver sausage, and cheese,' said Miss Bell, putting them on the table as she spoke, rubbing at an imaginary spot with her finger, inspecting her finger and wiping it on the handkerchief tucked through her belt.

'It's very kind of you,' said Edward, who was still standing, with some of his papers clutched to him and others falling on the floor, 'you really shouldn't trouble.'

'No trouble at all,' said Miss Bell. Her voice was pitched on a permanent note of surprise and her face never altered in expression. She had small features, neat, and somehow unphysical. You could never imagine her nose running or her eyes watering, or saliva forming in her mouth at the smell of bacon cooking. Her little flat ears would always be clean even if she never washed them and the short hair waved behind them would never straggle in the rain. She may have worn a little powder and colourless lipsalve, but no one of either sex had ever witnessed the secrets of her toilet. She had no close friends and seemed to need none; she had never betrayed nor given a confidence. She was as self-contained as a modern flat and about as inhuman.

She stood there, waiting to see if anyone had anything further to say to her, listened politely and without comment to Edward's résumé of the day's weather and Dick Bennett's groping beginning of a sentence that collapsed without ever coming to anything.

Mr Bell had already leaned over the back of the settee and helped himself to a couple of sandwiches together before passing them round. With his mouth full, he blew a kiss into the air indicative of appreciation.

'Well, I'll say good night,' said his sister. 'Don't forget to turn out all the lights and put the chain on the door, Edgar, before you come to bed.'

When she had gone, Edward, who didn't want to return to the subject of the Show, turned up the pile of letters which were the week's queries from members. Some of these Edward could answer himself, others were forwarded to the proper sources of information, in spite of E. Dexter Bell, who saw himself as the Dorothy Dix of the rabbit world and never lacked an answer. When the query was 'What would you recommend as a suitable mate for such-and-such a doe?' or 'What buck would give me such-and-such a characteristic?' the answer was always simple: 'One of the Bell bucks.' How could any fancier be in doubt?

The subject of the Show did not come up again until their next meeting, which was at Dick's flat. Mr Bell's snuggery was being spring-cleaned and Edward did not like to impose too often on Connie, although she had been surprisingly complaisant of late.

The Bennetts' flat was the converted upper part of an old damp house, in which none of the doors and windows fitted. The floors didn't seem to fit either. Domestic noises and rumbling voices rose from the ground-floor flat to mingle with the noise of Dick's family about its daily life. As the three of them sat round the table, where Mrs Bennett had given them a hearty and delicious meal, roars came from the baby in the front bedroom, hammering from the schoolboy's room, shrieks and giggles from the room where sixteen-year-old Peggy was dressmaking with a girl friend, and an alarming noise from the kitchen where Mrs Bennett was washing-up.

'Touching this question of the Show,' began Mr Bell, raising his voice and his eyebrows as an unexploded landmine appeared to fall in the schoolboy's room, 'I've had a great idea.'

'I've been in touch with the lessors of St Mark's Hall,' began Edward doggedly, but Mr Bell waved this aside and continued: 'My point is this: "Let's have a show," you say. "Let's have a so-and-so class, and a so-and-so. Let's have a this and a that." Certainly; nothing finer. "Let's advertise," you say. "Let's get a lot of exhibitors to come and –"'

'No,' said Edward, 'that's just it. We don't want a lot of outside exhibitors this first time. I want the members to get the prizes.'

'My dear Edward, I thought the idea was to rope in a lot of new members?'

'Oh, yes, of course. Everyone's welcome, *provided* they join, but look here, Bell –' He had been repeatedly urged to call the man Edgar, but had never been able to bring himself to it.

'Well then. Where was I? Oh, yes, well now, having done all that and laid all your plans, even booked your hall, apparently, though it'll never do – having done all that, – he leaned his arm on the table and waggled his finger at Edward – 'there's just one, just one little infinitesimal detail that you've overlooked. Infinitesimal, I say, but I might describe it as the most important item in the whole schedule.' He leaned towards Edward, thick lips slightly open, spectacles gleaming with triumph.

'Why, I don't know – I don't think I –'

'The judges, man! The judges!' roared Mr Bell, and the baby echoed him, crescendo.

'Oh,' said Edward. 'Yes, of course, the judges. Well, I hadn't really thought –'

'Ah!' Mr Bell leaned back, nodding contentedly, and taking off his spectacles. 'I thought so. Now here's where Yours Truly is going to make his humble suggestion. I think it's a winner,' he added diffidently, and taking out a silk handkerchief, began to polish his spectacles slowly to create suspense.

'Fire ahead,' breathed Dick, his great face agog.

'Well I was turning over this little question in the watches of the night when I says to meself, says I –' He paused again and eyed his audience. 'Why not ask my old friend, says I, my very good friend –'

Edward leant forward. 'Allan Colley?' he said excitedly.

'Edward, old lad, you're a mind-reader. None other than my old friend, Allan Colley.'

'But he never would, surely,' said Edward. 'A little unknown affair like ours. I mean, he judges at the big County Shows and all that. Oh, I don't think he would. But how marvellous if he did.'

'He might,' said Mr Bell casually, 'if I asked him as a favour. Do anything for me, the old collie dog would.'

'I say, it would be marvellous,' said Edward in the tones of the schoolboy whose hammering had just been stopped by a yell from the kitchen of 'Ar*thur*! I'll pat you if you don't stop that and get to bed. Go on and say good night to your Dad!'

'Wouldn't it be grand, Dick?' said Edward. Dick's face was flushed with pleasure, as he nodded, but before he could speak, a dirty object in shorts and a green jersey had hurled itself into the room, butted into its father's stomach with close-cropped head so as not to have to look at the visitors and hurled itself out again with a great clatter of boots.

'My eldest son,' said Dick, gazing after him with his face collapsed in sentiment, the Show and Allan Colley forgotten.

Edward heard no more about it until they met at his house one evening when Connie had been given a chicken by her uncle from Barnet. Edward had thought that she would want to have it on Thursday when her family came, but when he mentioned that Dick and Mr Bell might be looking in one day after supper, she had surprisingly said : 'Well, what's the matter with my cooking? Isn't roast chicken good enough for your precious Mr Bell?'

It was quite a party. Mr Bell arrived with half a bottle of sherry in the deep pocket of his overcoat 'to drink the health of my friend, Allan Colley, who's promised to come and judge our show.'

'*No!*' said Edward.

'Aha, yes!' said Mr Bell, knocking his arms against the walls as he struggled out of his coat in the hall.

'You mean he's really promised to come and judge for us?'

'Well, I told you he would, didn't I?'

'Yes, but I never thought – I mean, such a small affair – it couldn't possibly interest him.'

'Who said it was going to be a small affair?' Mr Bell sagged at the knees to look in the mirror and quiff up his side hair with the flats of his hand. 'With a draw like Colley, we'll get the big breeders in the neighbourhood, and some from outside too, unless I'm mistaken. I say, can I go and wash, boy? I stink of the city's dirt.' He ran upstairs. He was quite at home in the house by now, and Edward followed him up and hovered on the landing while Mr Bell sluiced water lavishly over himself and the floor. He was a large man, and though not outsize, he had the knack of making things look small. Edward's house seemed to shrink as soon as he got inside it, and now, using the bathroom basin, he gave the impression that he was washing his hands in a pie-dish.

'Yes, sir,' he was saying. 'We'll certainly have to put up a good show for the old collie dog. I know for some reason or other you were set on a little show, Ted, but this puts a different face on things, doesn't it?'

Edward was silent. He had never dreamed that Allan Colley would accept, and he was still adjusting himself to the impossible fact that he had. He had to adjust himself too to the defeat of his plans for a cosy, encouraging little show. Mr Bell had undoubtedly scored a point.

'Now my idea is this,' he began, saturating as if it were a pocket handkerchief the towel which Edward handed him. 'To start with, I thought the Victory Hall –' He elaborated his plans and Edward had no choice but to agree. After all, Allan Colley was coming, that was the main thing, and it was up to them to give him something worth coming for. They went down to the living-room, where Dick was reading the paper, Connie took off her apron and came in from the kitchen and they all had sherry out of the set of glasses that had hardly been used since their wedding day. They drank: 'To the Show!' and then filled up and drank: 'To the Collis Park Rabbit Club!' which even Connie drank quite willingly. She liked sherry. Then Dick

cleared his throat and said: 'Here's to you. All you've done –
Edgar,' which made Edward look at him sharply, it sounded
so odd.

As the evening wore on, he found he was minding less and
less that he had lost his battle about the show. After all – Allan
Colley. And if the humbler members of the Club were eclipsed,
well – do 'em good, perhaps – give 'em a bit more ambition.

The evening was a success. The roast chicken was perfect, Mr
Bell said that the potatoes excelled even his sister's, and the gravy
was rich and brown. Mr Bell kept mopping his up with bread,
'*à la* Continental', he said and smacked his lips. Connie told
him about Wenduyne and Edward was surprised that she remembered so well. They had not talked about it for a long
time. He kept looking at her and thinking how young she
looked and how pretty in that pink blouse thing. Dick, of
course, had to go and make her frown by asking: 'Heard any
more about the Call-up, Mrs L?' It had been mentioned when
he was last there.

'Oh,' said Mr Bell, passing his plate for more treacle tart.
'They won't take you. Don't worry about that.'

'I'm sure I don't mind if they do,' she said. 'I should be only
too pleased, if I thought that they would really make good use
of me.'

'Aha,' he said, 'there, with a woman's perfect intuition,
you've hit the nail on the head. If they'd make good use of you
– but the point is, would they? The wastage of labour that's
going on is a scandal. I tell you what you ought to do, if you
really want a job, though it seems to me you've got a full-time
job being a housewife – and a darned good one too.' He held
up the last piece of tart on his fork, nodded at it and engulfed
it. Connie bridled.

'What ought she to do?' asked Edward.

'That *was* a treacle tart,' said Mr Bell, putting down his fork
and pushing back his chair to stretch out his legs. 'What ought
she to do? Why, pick her own job, something that won't waste
her capabilities. If you really think they're going to call you
up, though I can assure you they won't yet –' he had his finger
on the pulse of every Ministry – 'you want to cheat them by
getting yourself fixed up first. I tell you what, you know, you
ought to come and work for me. I'd give you a job in the office

179

any day. We're rushed off our feet with work – could do with any amount of help.' Connie got up to go and make the tea, giving no indication of whether she liked the idea or not.

'But surely that wouldn't exempt her?' said Edward. 'An Estate Office – that's not reserved?'

'Not reserved? My dear old boy,' Mr Bell laughed tolerantly. 'Of course it's reserved. One of the most important things in the war, housing people.' He really made you believe it, too, sitting back with his spectacles in his hand, his tongue excavating the remains of Connie's excellent meal from inside his flat, wide mouth.

While he was undressing that night in their room, Edward said: 'Would you like to have a job, Connie? Would you like to work in Bell's office? I think he meant it, you know.'

She was doing her hair at the dressing-table, fixing each little sausage in a loop of wire. She laughed with a curler in her mouth. 'Oh, it was only a joke. I wouldn't care to particularly, anyway. I'm all right.'

'I've sometimes wondered, you know, dear,' Edward stood looking at her with his braces hanging down while he took out his cuff-links, 'whether you wouldn't be happier with a job. I mean, it's lonely for you, alone all day –'

'I'm all right,' she repeated. 'I'm sure I've plenty to do.'

'Yes, I know, but – tell you what, Con,' he said quickly, 'I wish we'd had a child. You'd like it, wouldn't you?'

'We couldn't afford it,' she said without looking at him.

'Oh, I know we said that at first, and then that business of your illness came, and what the doctor said. But we could afford it now, you know.' He was scrutinizing himself in his little mirror on the chest of drawers, with the same studied attachment as she was in hers. 'I mean, do you think you ought to go and see the doctor again?'

She dealt very carefully with a curl at the back of her head, turning it up so that the bristles showed where the underneath hair had been cut.

'I'm sure there's nothing wrong with *me*,' she said. 'I don't know what you mean.' He sighed. He couldn't get her to say one way or the other whether she wanted a child.

She put on her hair net, stood up and took off her dressing-gown, was revealed for a moment in the V-necked Celanese nightgown that gave her a bit of a tummy, and then kicking off her slippers was into bed.

'Hurry up, Ted,' she said, hunching the clothes over to her side, 'I never knew a man take so long to get to bed.'

'And how many have you known, pray?' he asked, but she was not in a mood for joking. The cheerfulness in which she had spent the evening seemed to be passing off.

'Don't be silly,' she said. 'And do hurry up. I want to get some sleep.'

'Just got my teeth to do.' While he was in the bathroom, sedulously doing his forty strokes on each side, up and down, not across, he turned things over in his mind. He had put out of his head so many years ago the dream of having a child that he hardly dared to bring it back. He had always known that she never wanted one, although she had made the excuse, first of money, then of the doctor. But just recently, since she had been being 'Nice to him,' as he put it to himself, he often wondered: did she consider the possibility and not mind it, or had the doctor perhaps told her she was safe?

When he came back the room was in darkness. He went to the window, drew the blackout, opened the window at the bottom and stood for a minute or two doing his exercises and breathing deeply through his nose. The exercises ought really to be done in the morning, but there was never time. This was better than nothing. When he had done his twenty arms bend, arms stretch and had touched his toes with difficulty five times, he shut the bottom window, opened it a foot and a half at the top, felt his way round the end of the bed and slid under what was left of the clothes. He didn't think she was asleep, she was not clicking.

'Connie,' he said into the darkness, 'suppose we did have a baby, would you mind? I know you were never keen on it, but now that you – now that we – *you* know – I wondered perhaps if it meant that you wanted one after all.'

'What do you mean?' she asked in a strangely defensive tone. 'What are you driving at?'

'Nothing,' he said surprised. 'I only wondered. Nothing to get huffy about.'

'I'm not huffy,' she said crossly, 'but it's enough to drive a person mad the way you keep on, question, question and cross-examine.'

181

'I'm sorry,' he said, and put out a hand. 'Con –'

'Oh, don't keep *on*,' she said, kicking him with her feet as she turned farther away from him.

When she had no shopping to do, Wendy Holt usually lunched in the canteen. Although the shilling dinner cost more than her usual cheese roll and tea at the milk bar or one of the local cafés, it was more economical in the end. Having had a good hot lunch, she and her mother could manage on bread and cheese and cocoa in the evening. Her father could always have soup, or a little bit of fish or an egg perhaps. Wendy and Mrs Holt usually gave up their egg ration to him; they didn't much care for eggs anyway.

In the torrent of people that was released from the Shops by the twelve o'clock whistle, those who were going to the canteen ran as fast as anybody. There were usually two meat courses: joint and some made-up dish, so unless you had a passion for rissoles or savoury pie, it was as well to get there early. The canteen was at the far end of the track, but the men from the Machine Shop, who had the shortest distance to run, managed to be queuing up at the counter almost before the whistle had died away.

There was hardly ever any joint left when Wendy arrived. The canteen was already full when she came in, breathless, to join the queue for tickets at the cash desk. Conversation that had been pent-up all morning, rabid knives and forks and a roystering lunch-hour programme from the loudspeaker vied with each other in the thick savoury air. The counter was arranged like a Totalizator. Files of people approached it empty-handed and countermarched back on the other side of the little railings with a heaped plate in one hand and a knife and fork in the other.

'Any fish?' asked Wendy hopefully. There was fish and chips sometimes.

'Only rissoles now, dear,' said the steamy woman who was pushing plates steadily through the hatch as if she were feeding a machine. Wendy took her plate and a knife and fork from the box and walked down between the tables looking for a place. It was a mystery to her how people managed to get there so early. Some were half-way through their plateful and some even, with eyes bolting out of their heads as the last mouthful bolted in, were half on their feet to make a dash for the pudding hatches. Wendy found a place at one of the farther tables, opposite a man who was eating absent-mindedly with a fork, absorbed in a folded paper propped against the vinegar bottle in front of him. She had sat down before she saw that it was Edward. He looked up and smiled, offered her the cruet and went on reading.

Wendy hoped he didn't think she had followed him here on purpose. She had been painfully shy of him since that awful night when her father had turned him out of the house. They had neither of them alluded to it, but although he had been as polite and considerate to her as usual, and even brought his stool alongside hers sometimes at tea-time, their conversation had never recaptured that spontaneous intimacy of the tea party in the little kitchen.

After what had happened, it was nice of him to talk to her at all. He couldn't possibly like her, especially if he thought she was trailing him in his lunch-hour. She would have liked to move to another table, but that might look funny, so she stayed and ate in unobtrusive silence, hoping she was not disturbing his reading.

It was Thursday and Edward was combing the show announcements of *Backyard Breeding* to see whether the proposed date for their show clashed with another in a neighbouring district. 'Egliston Open Sweepstake Show. May 9th' . . . 'Briar Park and Hadleigh Open Table Show. At the Crown Hotel, May 14th. Calling all the Rabbit Fancy. Show Secs. DO NOT CLASH!' . . . 'Wilford and Dis. Rabbit Club will hold a Members' Show for the Red Cross on April 30th.' . . . 'Morley Ann. Show aff. B.R.C. Spec.: Chinchilla Classes. Chin. fanciers keep yr. chins up!' No, it seemed to be all right. Good. He smiled, refolded the paper and put his knife and fork together on his empty plate. He was properly aware now of Wendy opposite him, picking her way among the surplus potatoes. Nice of her to come and sit at his table, and nice of her to sit there quietly while he was reading. Most girls would have started to chatter, stung to conversation by the sight of someone absorbed.

'Hope you didn't think me rude,' he said. 'I was just finishing something.'

'Don't let me disturb you.'

'Oh, no, I've finished.' He put the paper in his overall pocket. 'I'll fetch you your sweet, shall I? What are you going to have? There's –' he looked over his shoulder at the menu on the blackboard. 'There's hot jam roll or prunes and rice.'

'I'd like jam roll, but please don't bother. I'll get it.' She wiped her mouth with her handkerchief and started to get up.

'No, sit down, I'll get it. Give me your ticket.'

He came back presently with two plates of prunes and rice. 'Sorry, jam roll's off as per usual.'

'It doesn't matter. I like prunes.'

'Do you? So do I as a matter of fact. Not many people do though, do they?' Having agreed that this was so, they passed on to a discussion of other food and found they had quite a lot of tastes in common.

'Cigarette?' said Edward. 'Oh, no, you don't smoke, do you?'

'Not often, but occasionally I do. I would rather like one now if I may.' She smoked it cautiously, in short puffs, and he thought a cigarette made her look more old-fashioned than ever, instead of more modern.

'How are your rabbits?' she asked, tapping non-existent ash into the ashtray. 'Have you still got – Masterman, was it?'

Edward was delighted. 'Fancy you remembering!' He told her about Masterman's latest litter and went on to tell her about the show. The canteen was beginning to empty now; there was no one else at their table. She was far easier to talk to here than at the bench, where she seemed so reserved and the other girls were always listening or chipping in.

'You and your mother were going to come and see the rabbits, weren't you?' he said, forgetting for a moment what had shattered that project. 'I do wish you would. Perhaps you'd like to come to the Show? It might be rather interesting. We've got a very famous rabbit man coming to judge for us.'

'I'd love to,' said Wendy, 'but I'm afraid I might not be able to get away. My father's not well, you know –'

'Yes, of course,' he said quickly. He didn't want to talk about that horrible old man with the prawn's eyebrows and the working face. He didn't want Wendy even to have to admit that he was her father. 'Still, if you could ever get away, do come and see them. I'm sure you'd like them.' He saw the clock. 'Gosh, I'd no idea it was so late. Come on, we'll have to run for it if we want to clock in on time.' He hung back for her as they ran along the track, but in the crowd round the clocks, he lost her, and after looking for a moment, clocked himself in just on time.

By the time Wendy struggled to her clock against the stream of people coming in from outside, it was a minute past one and she had lost a quarter of an hour.

Before going back to the bench, Edward slipped up to the Final Assembly Shop to show Dick his draft for an advertisement. He read it over to him while Dick, who always started work dead on time, was assembling a control shaft.

The little collars and split pins which fixed the control levers to the rods were impossible for Dick's hands, so Joseph, who was fiddling happily with the sump, had to keep popping up to do them. Every time Dick grunted: 'Pin, Joe', Joseph's little head of a pickled mummy would appear inquiringly round the supercharger, he would straighten his knees, jump on a wooden box and fix the pin with a twist of his delicate wrist.

'"Grand Inauguration Show", d'you think, or "Gala Inauguration Show"?' asked Edward frowning.

'What does *he* say?' asked Dick. He was really getting very tiresome.

'I haven't asked *him*,' said Edward with wasted sarcasm. '*I'm* doing the ads.'

'Oh,' said Dick and thought. He took a mixture control rod from the trolley behind him, looked at it without enthusiasm, put it back in the tray and took out another one. 'Just read it through again, old chap,' he said.

'I've read it once,' said Edward. 'I can't stop up here much longer or the girls'll be getting themselves into all sorts of messes.' He hadn't really come up here for ideas from Dick, but only for corroboration of his own opinion that the advertisement was rather telling. '"A Unique Opportunity",' he began. 'Or, I say, Dick, ought it to be "An Unique"?'

'Pin, Joe!'

Dick rumbled the words over, while Joseph manipulated the split pin. 'A unique . . . an unique . . . a unique . . .' He shook his head. 'That's a nice point, Ted. I'd better look that up for you. I'll call in at the Library on my way home.' He hitched up his overall, produced one of his red notebooks and wrote: 'Memo: Query An, A unique. Publ. Lib. 6.15. April 18th.'

'Right you are, Chum.' Joe hopped back to his native level and Dick tried the tightness of the collar by laying on it a strain far greater than it would ever know.

Edward finished reading the advertisement and put it back in his pocket. 'You think it's all right, then? I've got to get back now. I'll pop up again if I think of anything else. Why don't you come down to me sometimes? You never do.'

'Down to the Inspection Shop?' said Dick and shook his head. 'Too many girls. Pin, Joe!'

There was something going on when Edward got back to his bench. Instead of being spread out at their places, the girls were all clustered up at the wheelcase end, chattering. Some problem for him to straighten out. He felt bad about holding them up by not being there. He really ought not to do it, but there was so much to arrange and so little time to do it out of working hours. Dinah's head looked up out of the crowd of bending grey backs as he approached.

'Eddie!' she called, beckoning. 'Where on earth have you been? Do come here.'

'What's up?' He strolled up to the group, feeling indispensable. Paddy King was sitting in the middle of them blushing. He had never seen her blush before; it clashed with her hair.

'Well look,' said Dinah, 'it's the most exciting thing –'

'What is?' asked Edward. 'Found another German bullet or something?'

'Don't be a twerp, Ed,' said Dinah, 'It's nothing to do with work. It's Paddy, she –'

'Yes, Paddy's had a letter, isn't it marvellous?' cut in Kitty, gabbling, her hair all over her face and her nose shiny. She was beginning to look a very funny shape already, though Edward supposed he ought not to notice it. It made her look younger than ever, and she carried her figure as if she didn't know what to do with it.

'What, what, what?' They were all talking at him at once and he couldn't understand, and then suddenly they stopped and Paddy said quietly: 'Oh, it's nothing. It's a silly fuss. It's only that I've heard my husband's coming home.'

'Only!' shrieked someone. 'After two years! Coming back as a Captain to some frightfully important job –'

'Shut up, you mustn't say that.'

'Well, he did, in the letter.'

'He didn't. He only hinted it. But honestly, Ed, isn't it marvellous for her? I'd be half mad if it was me, but no such luck, with my old man sticking around at home being a key worker – oh, we didn't tell you – he's going to get a medal, isn't he, Paddy?'

'She'll go to the Palace.'

'Look at her, she doesn't care.'

'Not much she doesn't.' They hung around, teasing her, while Paddy sat with her usual stoop, fiddling with a gear shaft and not saying much. Edward had never seen her shy before. It must be a bit embarrassing to have this horde on top of you when all you wanted was to be alone and think and glow inside yourself. He was filled with affection for her. She had never seemed a happy person, and no wonder: two years away! Some people had all the tough luck. It would be grand now to see her happy. She'd get leave of course. His mind raced ahead and saw her dressing up, meeting a train. He could see it all; the young man in uniform stepping down – he ought to have his arm in a sling by rights.

Gradually, he managed to chivvy the girls back to their jobs. It was nearly knocking-off time on Saturday afternoon, when nobody felt like work, anyway, but Bob Condor, though locked in solemn conclave with some of the A.I.D., kept looking sharply over towards them and obviously wishing that ethics did not forbid him to walk out on the conclave.

Edward came back to Paddy when the girls had dispersed. 'I'm awfully pleased,' he said. 'It's wizard for you.'

'Thanks,' said Paddy, without looking up.

'Yes,' went on Edward, 'it really is the most wonderful news –'

'Oh, for the Lord's sake,' said Paddy, suddenly, shrugging him off with her back. 'Give the thing a rest. Anyone would think nobody's husband had ever come home before.' Edward went understandingly away, refusing to be offended. It was her nerves, of course, after two years of worry, and then the shock and excitement ...

Madeleine laid her hand gently on Paddy's arm. 'I didn't say much when the girls were around,' she said. 'But I just wanted to tell you, Paddy, dear, how very, very happy I am for you.'

My God, thought Paddy, what is this? A conspiracy to make me feel bad? Don't they know that Dicky and I have never got on so well as since we've been a thousand miles apart? Isn't it enough that I'm dreading going back to that endless bickering, that I don't even really know whether I want him back or not, without having it rubbed in? I'll count ten and then if she doesn't take her hand off me, I'll scream.

'So very, very glad,' urged Madeleine softly.

Paddy's left arm was tense. Now she's giving me the Look. I can't look at her. Oh, Lord, she's going to cry, and I'm going to cry, too, and she'll think it's for the same reason and want to wallow. She bit her lip and then suddenly the angry muddled tears rushed away from her eyes and she heard with cold horror what Madeleine was saying:

'I wasn't going to tell you, but I must tell someone. It only came this morning. Just "Missing", that's all it said, so it could be worse – it – I'm glad it was me and not you. It's worse for a wife than a mother, I always say, but Martin wasn't – isn't – married. I'm so sorry, dear, I didn't mean to tell you. I didn't want to spoil your happiness.'

As E. Dexter Bell was paying for the advertisement, Edward had to show him the draft copy before he sent it to the local paper and *Backyard Breeding*.

Mr Bell barely glanced at it. 'My dear old boy,' he said, 'you needn't worry your head about that. I've already had one set out by my Mr Upshott at the office, who does all our ads. I've got it on me somewhere.' He slapped his pockets. 'I brought it home for you so that you could send it off and get the posters printed.'

'Posters?' said Edward.

'Yes, of course, must have posters. Let's see, about five hundred you'll want. Get 'em up all round the district – shops, hoardings, walls, pubs – *you* know.'

'But how am I going to put them up? I'm at the factory all day and it's dark soon after I come out.'

'Good heavens, don't ask me; that's your job. I've done all

the donkey work for you as it is. Get hold of some kids. They'll do it for a tanner.' Edward could not see the youth of Collis Park taking kindly to this suggestion. They all seemed to be scufflers in the gutter, jeerers and ringers of bells, and the refugee children from the railway district were no more than bandits. He read glumly through the advertisement, which was geometrically set out with a mapping pen in red and black ink. He thought it compared unfavourably with his own. It was professional all right, and clever: 'The Collis Park Rabbit Club will hold their Annual Show,' as if they had been going for years, but it had no magnetism. You believed no more that the show was an 'Outstanding Event' than you believed that a gaunt, inconvenient house was the 'Commodious Gentleman's Residence' of Mr Upshott's usual advertisements.

Edward liked his own much better. It was modelled on some of the more attractive ones from *Backyard Breeding*.

'Are You Getting Your Exhibits Ready,' it said, 'For Our Unique Show at the Victory Hall?', etc., etc. 'Our Unique' was the solution to the 'a unique' or 'an unique' difficulty. Dick Bennett had looked it up in his own Public Library, but then, travelling to the next borough for corroboration, had found that the dictionaries differed.

Edward returned the bit of paper to his pocket. If Mr Bell's ideas were so different, it was just as well he had not looked at it. He would probably think it amateur.

'Right you are. Do that then,' said Mr Bell with the confidence of a man used to having orders carried out. Edward noticed that Mr Upshott, no doubt under instruction, had put 'Presidents: E. Dexter Bell, Esq., R. R. Bennett, Esq.; Hon. Sec.: E. L. P. Ledward, Esq.'; but he folded the paper and put it in his pocket without comment. Whenever he felt like kicking against the totalitarian Bell influence which seemed to be creeping into the Collis Park Rabbit Club, so democratically planned, he reminded himself that it was through Mr Bell that he was at last going to meet Allan Colley. There couldn't be much wrong with a man who was on such intimate terms with Colley.

As a fancier, too, Edward had to admire him. Whenever he returned from Mr Bell's rabbitry, scientifically housed in the outbuildings and garden behind 'Uanmee', he viewed with dissatisfaction the hybrid hutches in his own crowded strip of garden.

Not all Mr Bell's rabbits were quality, and some were undoubtedly inferior to Edward's best stock, but they differed subtly as Hollywood film stars differ from English stars. They had glamour. Even the utility does who were used as foster-mothers had it. They knew they were Bell stock, therefore their coats were silkier, their eyes more bold and bright; they basked in the nimbus of their owner's pride. It may have been only that Edward usually saw them by electric light. All the out-buildings were wired, and when they were looking at the outdoor hutches, there was the searchlight torch to spotlight each occupant with a theatrical effect that Edward could never achieve in his garden with a bicycle lamp.

When he got home tonight from meeting Mr Bell, he went straight through to the garden. Connie was neither in the living-room nor the kitchen, but he didn't stop to call upstairs to her. He wanted to reassure himself by a sight of the latest litter sired by Masterman, his best yet. The doe was an enormous animal of the same strain, and these youngsters seemed to Edward to be outstandingly big for their age. He measured them every week with a tape measure, and had sent up statistics to Allan Colley's 'Inquire Within' column, and had received the answer that – yes, they were certainly very sizey, but Edward must not be over-confident as these early growers sometimes stopped before they reached maturity. With the Show in view, Edward had them on a forcing diet. The Lipmann's spring vegetables were coming along nicely and Ruth often had something under the counter for him. He always went in there ostensibly to buy something and pretended to be surprised when Ruth beckoned him behind the other customers' backs.

'I don't see why you keep bringing home all this potted meat,' Connie would grumble. 'You hardly ever eat it, and what you do open goes mouldy before you finish it. Wicked waste I call it.'

He shone the bicycle lamp on the wire run against the far wall. There were three bucks and two does and he was going to exhibit them all except one at the show. Following his fancy of calling the rabbits after the girls at the factory, he had called the biggest Freda, because her whiskers were so fine. He was pinning all his hopes on her winning one of the Flemish classes. She would have romped home at a little show, but with all these big breeders exhibiting, you never knew what she might be up against. Would Colley like her? 'If Colley doesn't like you, Freda,' he said, thrusting a cabbage leaf at her nose which she was trying to screw through the wire, 'I'll put you in a pie and go in for cavies.' He might, too, though he would never put Freda in a pie. But he had often toyed with the idea of extending his fancy to guinea-pigs, if only he had the space. There was money in them and they were useful to the government in wartime.

He went back into the house and called up the stairs for Connie. Both the bathroom and the bedroom doors were open, but she might be pretending not to hear because he was so late home. Perhaps she was doing something in the spare room. She sometimes raised dust madly there and shifted the furniture about and shook out rugs before leaving it to settle down again under its dust-sheets until the fever was on her once more. He went up and opened the door, but there was only the shrouded furniture and the stale smell and the neat pile of newspapers on the floor waiting to go in for salvage.

'Connie!' He wanted his tea. He looked once more in the living-room, but the blackout was not even drawn in there. The table was not laid and her sewing was strewn on the arm-chair as if she had abandoned it in a hurry. Dorothy had probably come round and taken her off to a cinema. In that case, she might have left something hotting in the oven for Edward, or she might not.

She had not. Pity he had got home too late to go to the Lipmanns' and get something tasty, because he was hungry. Mr Bell had been talking about the leg of pork his sister was going to give him for dinner, and Edward had been looking forward to haddock, because it was Friday and they nearly always had haddock on Friday. Mr Arles at the fish shop usually kept one for Connie.

There was the haddock, too, still wrapped in its newspaper on the dresser. Perhaps Connie meant to cook it when she got back from the cinema; she might bring Dorothy in. She would be annoyed if he had already had something else for his tea and didn't want to eat fish with them. That would be wasting food. But he couldn't possibly wait until half-past nine or later; he was starving. Perhaps he'd better just lay his appetite with a slice of bread and butter while he looked forward to the haddock a little longer. But supposing she had had tea before she left, or was going to have something out and leave the haddock for tomorrow? He would have waited and starved for nothing. If he was going to sit down to bread and cheese when she did get home, he might as well sit down to it now. He opened the cupboard door and lifted the cover of the cheese dish. Underneath, in contrast to the dish, which was shaped like a generous wedge of Cheshire, sat a small cracking lump with green dust on the edges. Of course, the new ration came tomorrow. The jam was also at the end of its tether. The pot would have to be scraped to make it do for breakfast. Edward sighed and considered the Lipmann's potted meat jars. Two were Austerity and were labelled reticently 'Fish', and 'Meat'. The third was called Lobster and Tomato, but it had already been opened and was now covered with a bloom of fungus. He threw it into the dustbin, remembering afterwards that you were supposed to save glass jars.

He couldn't keep his eyes off the parcel of haddock, which was just asking to be cooked. How pleased they would be when they came back from the cinema to find a tempting dish waiting for them in the oven. Yes, but would it be tempting? All he knew about cooking was from watching Connie, who hated to be watched and would put her back between him and whatever she was doing and would answer questions like 'How d'you make pastry?' with 'Oh, it's a knack. You'd never do it.'

Still, haddock ought not to be difficult. He had seen her put it in the oven with water and milk and simply leave it. He could tell when it was done by tasting it, and if it was ready before they got home, he could have his without spoiling the dish. And if Connie had not meant to have it tonight, well, it would hot up all right tomorrow, wouldn't it? In any case, it was his haddock. He had paid for it, hadn't he? He unwrapped the haddock defiantly and stood looking at it for a moment, wondering about the skin and those fins and that backbone and those gristly shoulder bits. They never appeared on the finished article, but at what stage were they removed? They would probably be easier to take off when it was cooked, but supposing it was right to do it first, and Connie came in before the fish was done?

He turned the fish over and began to saw at the skin with a fruit knife. That was one thing he did know: you must never touch fish with anything but silver. Nothing happened. The knife did not even penetrate the skin. Eventually he managed to jab the point in, but the thing was impossible. You needed three hands, one to hold the tail of the fish, one to work the knife and one to peel the skin back as you cut it. If men had to do the cooking they would see that all this trimming was done at the fishmonger's, but women liked to make things as difficult as possible and then be martyred. Abandoning the skin, he tore off the fins with his naked hands. The haddock was now beginning to look a bit battered, so he put it in the dish that Connie used and covered it with water and milk. He put the dish in the oven, lit the gas and washed his hands. Cooking was rather fun. It was nice to be able to mess about in a kitchen undisturbed. For one mad moment, he contemplated making a cake. The papers said you should use the oven for more than one thing. He even got as far as getting out the flour bin and mixing bowl and a cookery book, but fortunately all the recipes called for eggs, so he put everything away again.

'Season to taste.' A phrase in the book caught his eye. He knew there was something he had forgotten. He took the fish out again, gave it salt and pepper, tasted the lukewarm liquid with his finger, and added more pepper. Of course, it would taste different when it was cooked. He hoped it would not take too long. It would be grand to have it ready when Connie came home and see that incredulous look that came to her face when he achieved anything like mending a fuse or unstopping the sink.

He went into the sitting-room and drew the curtains, then got the cloth out of the sideboard drawer and laid the table. He laid it for three, in case Dorothy was coming; it looked more hospitable. It was soon done. Why did people make such a thing of it, flapping the cloth and rattling knives and crockery when you were trying to listen to the wireless? Might as well see if there was anything on now. He looked at the clock. Of course, Tommy Handley. It was Friday and getting on for half-past eight. He might get the chance to listen to it before they got back. Connie didn't think Tommy Handley was funny. She didn't like Max Miller, or George Formby, or Arthur Askey either, and as for Bob Hope, well, if that was what America was like, she was sorry, but give her the Germans. She liked Dennis Noble and Peter Dawson and the man who sang about being a roving vagabond, and she liked anyone and everyone who played the cinema organ.

Passing before the mantelpiece to turn on the wireless, Edward's eye was caught by a sheet of paper leaning against Dorothy's wedding group. The old girl had left him a note. Now he'd know what time she'd be in and whether he'd done right about the haddock.

The note said: 'V. bad news. Come round to the Buildings straight away. I have gone there.'

Schoolbred Buildings was an immense hollow block of Trust Flats, red brick and flat-topped, with rows and rows of windows. It was not very homely. The only way you could tell where one flat ended and another began was by the different curtains, or a row of plants perhaps, or an old lady parked in the window all day like an exhibit. You entered under an archway past the caretaker's door into a courtyard made hideous all day by children and at night a dark well of noise from the surrounding wireless sets. Two entrances led out of it on each side, with stone stairs beyond.

Edward sped across the courtyard and into the corner doorway on the left, clattering up the stairs with his heart thumping. He had run all the way from the trolley bus. He turned off at the third floor, along the corridor, knocking into a couple who said: 'Well, I must say –' and turned the screw bell of No. 84, which went 'prring!' and then sprang back and caught your fingers.

His mother-in-law opened the door with a face like a slice of doom. Edward didn't know what he had expected. He had been prepared to hear them crying half-way up the stairs, but instead he found them all sitting round the table in silence, drinking tea.

'Well, here you are at last, then,' said Connie. 'I did think you'd come straightaway.'

'But I did,' said Edward. 'At least, as soon as I saw your

194

note. I didn't see it at first, I – but never mind that. What's happened?' He looked from one to the other. They were all there, anyway.

'You tell, Mum,' said Dorothy, her face heavy and her eyes unfocused. Mrs Munroe sat down in her place and began to stir her tea. 'It seems funny everybody doesn't know. We've known now for hours. But you not coming round. . . . It's Don,' she said. 'He's gone.'

'Gone? said Edward, dully. 'But how d'you mean – what happened? Is it definite?'

'Well, of course it's definite,' said Connie sharply, almost as if it were Edward's fault.

Edward didn't know what to say. He tried to convey his sympathy, but they didn't seem to accept it. The four of them were withdrawn into a world which he could not enter, a world which had known for hours that Don Derris was dead. They had been through the shock and the tears and the futile conjecturing, the hope and the protestations of despair, until now there were no more left. Tired, they watched him to see what he would do.

'But what happened?' asked Edward again, and watched the spoon going round and round inside Mrs Munroe's cup while she told him. 'He was like a son to me,' she said, and Edward, looking at her, saw that she really believed it. Why not? He had been fond of Don, too, how fond he had never realized until now it was too late to show it. Poor old Don! He could hear him saying: 'Think of me where the sands of the desert grow cold,' and now he was drowned without even having got there.

'I knew he'd never get there,' said Mrs Munroe. 'I always said so, didn't I, Connie? Didn't I, Dorothy?'

'Oh, shut up, Mum,' said Connie. 'It doesn't matter what you said. That won't bring him alive.' She put her arm round Dorothy's shoulders, where it lay awkwardly, Dorothy neither welcoming nor rejecting it. They had never been affectionate sisters. They had bickered when they were at home together and criticized with an even clearer perception since they had been apart.

Mr Munroe opened his mouth to speak and was instantly shut up. He was seldom allowed to speak when all was well, so he could hardly hope for a hearing under the circumstances.

However, he went on talking although nobody listened to him until it became clear that he was making the quite sensible suggestion that Dorothy should go to bed.

'Oh, I couldn't,' she said. 'I shouldn't sleep a wink.'

'But you must try, dear,' said her mother getting up. 'Come along, I'll settle you down with an aspirin.'

'Oh, no, I don't want to.' Dorothy clung to her chair as her mother took hold of her arm.

'I'm only thinking of your good, Dorothy. It's your duty to try and sleep. You must think of baby. After all,' she said, 'he's all you've got now.' Dorothy began to cry, her face still swollen and stained from her last tears. 'I don't want to – I couldn't. Not here, where I've been with him. No, Mum –'

'Now, now, now,' said her father. 'Do as your mother tells you.'

'I tell you what,' said Connie, 'why don't we take her back with us? Edward can go in the spare room and she can sleep in with me. Would you like that, Dorothy?'

'I don't mind,' she said. 'I don't care where I go. I wish I was dead.'

'Yes, of course you do, dear,' said her mother. 'And I'm not surprised either after what the child's been through. Enough to drive anyone out of their mind, I'm sure.' Dorothy cried harder and Connie stood up.

'Come on,' she said, 'you're coming back with us. You get your coat on and I'll get your things together. Edward, you'd better go down to the phone box and ring for a taxi.'

'You'll never get one,' said Mrs Munroe, but Edward was quite glad to go. When he got back, Dorothy was in her coat, looking enormous and pathetically plain in a beret that Connie had put on for her too far forward.

'Well, I don't know, I'm sure,' Mrs Munroe was saying. 'I don't like you going where I can't have my eye on you. You never know what may happen after a shock.'

'You come round tomorrow, Mum,' said Connie. 'And don't you worry. You'll be all right here with him, won't you?' She jerked her head at her father, who was hovering in the background, making passes towards Dorothy and her case as if he wanted to help.

'I suppose so,' said Mrs Munroe. 'Though I can't say I like

it. Still it doesn't matter about me so long as Dorothy's all right. I don't want you to worry about me, Dorothy. I dare say I shall be all right.'

'Yes,' said Dorothy, who had no intention of worrying.

It was apparently Edward's fault that there was no taxi at half-past nine at night in an outer suburb of London. They were half-way home on the trolley-bus before he remembered the haddock. As they walked down Church Avenue, he said to Connie: 'You take Dorothy straight upstairs; she's yawning already. I'll come up in a sec. and move my things.'

'What's that smell?' said Connie, as he opened the door for them.

'What smell? I don't –' but it was too strong to ignore. 'Oh, that, I burned some rubbish in the boiler, that's all.'

'Well, you shouldn't,' said Connie, 'it clogs it up,' but she was really only thinking of getting Dorothy upstairs. As soon as they had rounded the turn by the bathroom, Edward shot into the kitchen and shut the door. He turned out the oven and when he opened it a blast of scorched air hit him in the face. The haddock was in a terrible way, blackened and charred and as inseparable from the sides of the dish as the clothing of a burnt man from his skin. The liquid had long since boiled away, but it had first boiled over and encrusted itself on the floor of the oven. The dish scorched his hand through the thick oven cloth. He hurried outside with it and tipped as much of the haddock as would come away into the dustbin. What to do with the dish? Back in the kitchen, he heard footsteps on the stairs, so he quickly shut the dish outside the back door and was in the hall with the kitchen door shut behind him before Connie had reached the last step.

'What are you doing?' she said. 'Never mind the boiler now, I want you to come up and get your things. Dorothy's in bed already. I believe she'll sleep. She's absolutely worn out.'

'Just coming up now.' He took her arm and bore her up with him. He collected his pyjamas and brushes and the things he would want in the morning and kissed Dorothy, giving her shoulder a squeeze and covering her up and tucking her in as if she were a child.

'You going to bed now?,' he whispered to Connie. 'Have you had anything to eat?'

'I couldn't touch anything. I'll get to bed now. I may have a bad night with her.'

He kissed her. 'You've been a brick,' he said and went out shutting the door. It seemed callous to think of food when everyone else was too upset to eat anything, but he was absolutely starving. When Connie was safely in bed, he would go down and remove all traces of the haddock and find himself something to eat. It was very cold in the spare room and there was no bulb in the light. He took one from the landing, but Connie had taken down the curtains and there was no blackout. He switched off the light, pulled the dust-sheet from the bed and took his things down to the bathroom. He came up again in his pyjamas and dressing-gown and listened outside the bedroom door. There was no sound, but he opened the spare-room door and shut it, in case Connie was awake.

He crept downstairs, feeling like a burglar in his own house, and went quietly about his cleaning, holding his breath when the dish knocked against the side of the sink and running the taps on to the dishcloth to deaden the sound of the water. Once having lied about the fish, it would look so silly if she came down and caught him. The whole business, anyway, seemed so inappropriate to the tragedy of the evening. It looked now like a stupid little schoolboy prank to make trouble where there was trouble enough.

By dint of scraping and scrubbing, he at last got the oven clean. He left its door open to clear the smell and he would open the window before he went up. His stomach was knocking with hunger now. He got out bread and margarine and scraped the green part off the cheese. Then he sat down at the table and ate steadily and ravenously, but without pleasure. It was just a duty to his body. While he ate, he stared at nothing and thought about Don.

He was feeling so bad about Don that he thought that if he went on feeling like this, he would never have any peace of mind again. It was not only his remorse but the selfishness of it that kept nagging at him. He could not forget that when Mrs Munroe had said: 'Don's gone,' his instant reaction had been not sorrow for Don, nor for Dorothy, but for himself who had never bothered to like Don and now had no chance to make up for it. He had felt cheated. If only someone had told him what

198

was going to happen he could have been friends with Don. He had never even written to him, and now it was too late.

And much, much too late to make up for all those things when he had priggishly shouldered off Don's gestures of goodwill. Those 'Parties with the Boys', which he had always congratulated himself on avoiding, those 'Quickies' and 'sprints round to the local before supper' which he had always declined because Don bored him. Much too late too to unsay all the things he had ever said to Connie.

'Every time I look at that chap, the back of my hair goes up.' He could hear himself saying that after one Thursday evening. He had not really meant it at the time, so why did he have to go on remembering it now? Why couldn't he stop tormenting himself with regrets?

Sorrow was one thing; there was something noble about sorrow. When his mother died, a year after his father, when Edward was not yet eighteen, there had been something ennobling about the completeness of his grief. He had worn his loss like the black band on his sleeve, buoyed up by the picture of himself as a tragic figure, a man of grief.

But there was nothing noble or sustaining about remorse. Remorse was bitterness and shabby, secret self-pity.

He was not a religious man. He had hardly been to church since his wedding. Brought up to believe there was a God, he had accepted that fact unthinkingly without doing anything about it. He had sometimes prayed, but only as a schoolchild recites poetry, or superstitiously, to ward off evil, but he prayed now properly for the first time, chewing on a bit of bread without knowing that he was eating.

It was a bit out of the Bible: 'Let this cup pass from me. Don't let me go on feeling like this. I'll be good – I'll do everything for Dorothy, but don't let me go on feeling bad about Don. It won't help him now. Let this cup pass from me.' He sat for a long time, with thoughts going round in his brain until suddenly he found that he was thinking about nothing. His brain was blessedly at peace. Was this the answer to prayer? Was prayer and the answer to it nothing more than a state of mind?

He went upstairs and the shrouded furniture looked at him dispassionately as he got into the bed and was instantly asleep.

CHAPTER 10

AFTER a time, Edward became quite attached to the spare room. When the curtains were up and the furniture unshrouded and the drawers filled with his clothes, it gradually relaxed from the resentment of a room too long unlived in and began to take character from himself. It even began to smell of him. It was nice to be able to do his scalp massage at his dressing-table instead of in the bathroom. Connie had never liked the smell of his hair tonic in her bedroom. She had not liked him to put his trousers under the mattress either, nor to read in bed, nor to open the window at the bottom, however warm the night.

All these things he could now do. There was a lot to be said for marriage, but there was also a lot to be said for having your own room. The bed was narrow and harder than the big double-bed, but it was a change to be able to sprawl and not to be woken out of your best sleep by a prod to stop you snoring.

He sometimes wondered, without undue fervour, whether Connie was ever going to start being Nice to him again. Dorothy would be going home presently when the baby was due.

But Dorothy stayed on, and gradually it became established that she was going to have the baby right there in the front room. Connie seemed to like having her. It was company for her, and it put her one up on her mother. She balanced the extra work it made by skimping on the work she used to do. She never made cakes or scones now for Edward to take to work and it was as much as he could do to get a sock mended. When he was almost down to his last pair, the others being piled in Connie's workbasket or the dirty clothes basket, he once asked mildly after supper if she would do some darning.

He was sitting reading at the table. Dorothy was in his easy chair, which was the only one in which she could get comfortable and Connie was in hers at the other side of the painted screen in the fireplace. The two women were knitting, the moaning undertow that had come into their voices since Dorothy wore mourning dragging at their conversation.

'Your socks, Edward?' said Connie. 'Surely you've got

plenty to wear. I can't do them tonight, anyway. I want to get this finished so that we can match it for ribbon tomorrow. You don't realize what a lot there is to be done if this baby's not to look neglected, poor little soul.' Dorothy turned on him her look of a reproachful cow.

It had been the same the next time he asked, and finally he had been driven to wearing a holey pair round to Dick's and pretending the holes had only come that day at work. Mrs Bennett, flushed and maternal, had darned them for him while he sat in Dick's slippers allotting numbers to the Show entries. The plans had reached this advanced stage by now and the Show was less than two weeks off. Entries were coming in excitingly; Edward never got used to finding a lot of letters in the letter cage when he got home from work. Some quite big people seemed to be taking them seriously and there were several exhibits coming by rail. A lesser judge, a lady called Miss Violet Seeds, had been engaged to assist Allan Colley. The Victory Hall had been booked and the sticky eartags ordered. Edward had spent seven coupons on a white overall.

There was still plenty to do, and on top of that Canning Kyles was having one of its pep periods. Mr Gurley's little window went up and down so often that it seemed to have discovered the secret of perpetual motion. The goaded labourers pushed trolleys at twice the speed and slung bits of engines about with reckless clangs. Old Charlie's younger female mate grew straddle-legged from staggering under too heavy loads, and the elder one cut the split sleeves out of her overall and wore it like a jerkin over one of her late husband's flannel shirts.

Charlie had not had a wink of sleep for days; his nook behind the spring-testing machine was filled now with crankcases which had been inspected so fast that the Fitting Shop was not ready for them. No sooner had the girls signed their names to one report than they were up and away to another bench, tool box under one arm and stool under the other. Things went so fast for Reenie that she found herself writing the report of one engine on the card of the next. Freda's arms were bare to the elbow and she tackled even delicate jobs like a blacksmith and told people that at last they were working one-tenth as hard as the Russian women. Edward scurried about among them like a sheepdog, clearing up muddles, helping Wendy when she got behind, chasing a gearwheel that had been sent for polishing six engines ago and never reappeared.

He was busy all day long as well as most of the evening. He liked his life to be full, because his body took on fresh vitality to meet it. He ate enormously, slept like a log in the narrow spare-room bed and wished the walk to and from work were twice as long. New things kept cropping up. There were letters from manufacturers of patent foods and hutches, friendly letters from secretaries of other Clubs, inquiries from breeders with names well known in the Fancy. He had even been on the telephone to the editor of the local paper about sending along a reporter.

But when he looked at Dorothy, he felt bad about feeling so well. Each evening as he put his key into the lock, he toned himself down to a more suitable pitch for the atmosphere of his house. The baby was due any day now and Mrs Munroe was practically in residence. She often came round to breakfast – mercifully after he had gone – and was nearly always there when he got home. Sometimes she had parked Mr Munroe elsewhere, sometimes he was with her and cumbering some corner while the women droned and planned as if he were not there.

Edward would come in bursting with something to tell and be fidgety all evening for the lack of anyone to tell it to. They were not interested in the Show and he understood that they thought it callous of him to be so wrapped up in it. Dorothy might have been interested. She had asked him once or twice about the Show when they were alone and even went out occasionally to see the rabbits until her mother fetched her in with a warning about the deformities of babies whose mothers got their feet wet. She and Connie watched Dorothy like a hawk. Whenever the sun shone or she enjoyed a meal or the natural self-absorption of her condition made her forget about Don for a while, her mother or sister was on hand to remind her.

One of Mrs Munroe's most common remarks was: 'Where's Dorothy? I'm sure she's crying.' If Dorothy was out of her sight, she would roam the house listening for the sound of tears and once when Dorothy had gone out for a walk on a delicious May morning, her mother had trailed her to make sure she was not heading for the river.

'Why should she?' Edward had asked Connie, with a wave of his hand to the flooded gravel pits beyond the garden. 'With the Ponds so close?' He saw at once that his flippancy was a mistake. He gradually adapted himself to the conditions of his home by keeping his full, absorbing day outside it and just being as little trouble as possible inside it. He often stayed out to supper. His rations were probably of more use to Dorothy than his presence. His heart yearned with pity towards her but there seemed to be nothing he could do to help. He was allowed to do nothing for her. He had offered once to take her to the cinema and fancied he saw a gleam of interest in the jelly of her eye but Mrs Munroe had been so shocked as if he had suggested hot music at a funeral service. What would people think?

The doctor said they might expect Dorothy's baby on May the 22nd, but Mrs Munroe knew better. The twenty-second was a Monday, and didn't the old saying say: 'Thursday's child is full of woe?' He would come on the twenty-fifth.

The main line station for Collis Park was Cleave Hill, some two miles away near the gas works, and thither Dick Bennett drove in a small Ford lorry, on a wet Sunday morning in May. His job, whose responsibility was making him grip the steering wheel tightly, was to collect the rabbits which had been sent by rail and take them to the Victory Hall in time to be penned and labelled before the show opened at eleven o'clock. Mrs Bennett's brother, who was a builder, had hired the van to Dick and Edward at cut prices, any scruples about using the petrol being drowned with several Olds. After the third pint, Dick's was already a mission of national importance; he should almost have a label on the windscreen saying 'Urgent'.

'My point is this,' said Edward, who had unconsciously picked up some of E. Dexter Bell's phrases, 'rabbit breeding is important in wartime. Am I right?' Dick Bennett nodded, staring into his beer 'The Government encourage it, don't they?' said Edward truculently, as if someone had contradicted him. 'What about all those pamphlets they keep sending out? Well, how are you going to keep up the breeding standards without shows? Answer me that. And if shows are important, it's presumably important to get the exhibits *to* those shows. Important? It's a national duty.'

'Oh, quite, quite,' said Dick's brother-in-law. It didn't matter to him what the van was used for if he happened to have petrol to spare. 'What I always say is,' he signalled the barmaid by waggling his little finger, 'I always say the harm's been done by the time the petrol reaches the consumer. The chaps at sea have already risked their lives, so it don't make a ha'p'orth of difference to them whether the stuff's used for aeroplanes, rabbit shows or the wife and me to visit her sister over at Croydon.' An argument that was subsequently to get him fined ten pounds after being stopped by a policeman on the Eastbourne Road.

But this had not happened yet and no policeman stopped Dick Bennett as he coasted down Station Hill and into the yard with elaborate hand signals. There were about twenty little boxes and baskets waiting for him, labelled 'LIVESTOCK WITH CARE' and Dick gave them so much care that the woman porter who was helping him made two journeys to his one from the platform to the lorry. He had frequently to adjure her to mind what she was about.

'There's some very valuable stock here, Miss. I'm taking them to the Show.'

She swung a luxury basket from a well-known breeder in Finchley over the tailboard as carelessly as if it had contained a dead cat.

'The Collis Park Rabbit Club, you know,' said Dick. 'Fur and Fancy Show.'

'Oh, yes,' she said. Rabbits did not interest her, except that she had never been able to eat them from a child; that was interesting and she told Dick about it as they returned to the platform for the last lot. Before he could get started on his painstaking explanation of the difference between flesh and show stock she had slammed up the tailboard of the lorry and walked off whistling with her cap on the back of her head. Dick pulled himself up into the driver's seat and let in the clutch with great delicacy.

He drove to the Victory Hall, leaning slightly forward, with his cap worn quite straight on his head and his lips pursed, blowing his horn at stray, early church-goers and stopping dead at every deserted cross road to look right and left before he crawled across. Whatever Edward thought, Dick was certain that Mr Bell was right in insisting on a fair-sized pen show instead of a potty little table show. The fact that these big breeders had bothered to send entries by rail justified the daring of the enterprise, which had almost numbed him with worry at first.

The inside of the Victory Hall, still in chaos, brought on some of the numbness again. The hired pens, which came in lengths of six partitions, were stacked anyhow in the middle of the floor. A line of them was only just beginning to take shape along one wall under the hands of two of the Club members, a schoolboy and a little bow-legged man called Simkiss, who bred Chinchillas on his allotment. Edward, in his shirt-sleeves with his soft light hair on end, was helping to erect the judging table under the platform at the end of the hall.

'How goes it?' asked Dick.

'Capital, capital,' said Edward abstractedly. 'It wants to come up a bit at your end, Mr Marchmont. We'll have to put a couple of blocks underneath.'

'At the show they had at Iver,' said Mr Marchmont, who wore hairy terra-cotta plus-fours and a cap to match, 'they didn't have trestles like this. They had some sort of solid erection. I must say it seemed very satisfactory.'

'Well, I've brought the rail stock,' said Dick proudly.

'You've brought the – good heavens man, you haven't left them outside, have you? Here, let's get them in straightaway. You never know what might happen.'

Edward hurried out, with Dick following in alarm, visualizing the entire lorry gone, although he had its ignition key and rotor arm in his pocket.

Gradually the hall took shape. As more Club members arrived Edward set them to work. Some of them only got underfoot and asked questions and fussed round their own entries. Mr Marchmont kept asking why hadn't all this been done the night before and Edward had to keep telling him that the night before the Victory Hall had been full of a Flannel Dance. Dick Bennett, who was the most underfoot of all, was eventually stowed away behind the table where Miss Hemming was checking the entries and issuing the numbered eartags to Mrs Ledbetter. Miss Hemming was secretarial, with neat clothes and an expensive fountain-pen, and Mrs Ledbetter had large masculine features and wore a navy blue tricorne and a dirty white apron tied round the skirt of her best afternoon marocain. She handled the rabbits like an expert, balancing them in one hand while she stuck the little round labels inside each transparent right ear. She was one of the Club's most solid members, who bred pofitably, in a back garden where her husband would have liked to grow vegetables. As it was, he had to content himself with tomatoes and dwarf beans in window boxes. She had brought him along this morning to help, and he had been given to Mrs Bennett, who was running a small refreshment bar up on the platform. He was cutting open rolls, while she spread them and put cheese and beetroot inside, her eyebrows and the front of her hair singed from a slight contretemps with the Primus stove.

At ten o'clock, Miss Hemming put on a small round hat and slipped away to church, leaving Dick happily making lists and collecting entrance fees in a tobacco-tin. Edward had changed into his new white overall and had time to look at some of the entries. He inspected the Flemish Giants with concern, going back to Freda's pen to reassure himself that she was bigger and better. He kept popping outside to scan the road for Allan Colley, who was not due for another hour, and returning to stand in the doorway and look round the hall to see how it would strike him. Would the whole thing seem amateurish after the big shows at which he had judged?

Edward himself was impressed with the scene; the Show was taking shape. The pens were built in a double tier along two walls, the travelling boxes were stacked tidily in a corner, Mr Simkiss was laying out a table of leaflets and handbooks, and the judging table was covered with sacking and was level at last, although Mr Marchmont still didn't like the look of it. Just when there seemed to be some hope of the Show being able to open by eleven o'clock, in walked E. Dexter Bell in a blue flannel chalk-stripe suit with a flower in the buttonhole and announced that the pens must be in the middle of the hall so that people could circulate.

Mr Marchmont was delighted, because that was how they had them at Iver, and he had said so all along. He told Mr Bell this, but Mr Bell was not listening, because having got everybody working like beavers to rearrange the hall, he was unwrapping on Dick's table the small silver cup which he was presenting for the Best Rabbit in the Show. A girl in a flowered dress, who had brought two Havana Rexes in the basket of her bicycle, hovered by with little cries of admiration.

'Look at the *cup*, Mrs Ledbetter,' she cried. 'Isn't it smashing?' Mrs Ledbetter picked up the cup, disclosing that it was lighter than it looked, replaced it on its stand without a word and hurried back to work, her hips working under the tight white apron.

Edward had taken off his white overall and was in his shirt-sleeves again, and Mr Bell came and gave him a blow between the shoulders as he staggered across the hall with one end of a row of pens complete with rabbits.

'Splendid work, old boy,' he said. 'You've done a great job here. Sorry I couldn't get in before to give you a hand, but I've been tied up with work all morning. Can't even reckon on my Sundays these days, like you can.'

'Easy!' said Edward to the schoolboy at the other end of the pens. 'O.K., put her down. Perhaps you'd give me a hand with some of these then,' he said, straightening up. 'This lad's got plenty to do.'

'My dear old boy, I can't. I've got to rush off. I only just looked in to see what I could do to help. Good thing I did, too. Those pens would never have done as you had them. I'll be back in good time, though. Don't worry. Colley'll probably come round to my place and I'll bring him along with me.'

But at a quarter to eleven, Edward, who was going through lists with Dick, looked up impatiently as Mr Marchmont's tan golf stockings with the yellow tassels came straddling into his vision.

'Colley's here I see,' said Mr Marchmont. 'Spotted him at once. He was at the Iver Show.'

'Is he?' Edward jumped up. 'Where? I ought to have been there to –' he looked round, not liking to admit that he didn't know what Allan Colley looked like.

'Over there by the Chins.' There were three men looking at the Chinchillas; one was a Club member, another was a tubby man with wiry grey hair and a square moustache who looked as if he had just wandered in by chance, and the third was obviously Allan Colley, tall and sporting with a high complexion and heavy brogues. Edward hurried up to him.

'How d'you do, Mr Colley?' he said, holding out his hand. 'I'm so sorry I wasn't at the door to meet you. I understood you were coming with Mr Bell.'

The tall man stared. 'Watson's the name, sir,' he said. 'Watson and Dolmeny's Rabbitries of Slough.' He pulled a card out of his waistcoat pocket, which Edward took without looking at it, turning in embarrassment to the short man.

'Then – oh, excuse me – are you – I mean, I'm expecting Mr Allan Colley.'

The grey-haired man's eyes went small and twinkled when he was amused. He held out his hand. 'I'm Colley,' he said. 'My fault for not introducing myself. I was just having a look round. You're the Secretary, eh? Bell didn't tell me your name.'

'Oh, that's all right. I mean my name's Ledward. I'm terribly sorry – you must think me very rude, but Mr Bell told me you were going round to his place and coming on with him.'

'Good Lord, no. I don't even know where he lives. I've only met him once or twice as a matter of fact, but I'm grateful to him for having asked me to come and judge here. I understand this Club's quite a new venture, and I'm keen on that.' They moved away from the tall man, who had been listening with his eyebrows raised. Allan Colley strolled with his hands in his pockets, chatting to Edward as if he were an equal and rapidly dispelling his confusion. Edward kept sneaking back with pleasure to the thought that Allan Colley, E. Dexter Bell's 'old pal the collie dog', hardly knew Mr Bell.

The other judge, Miss Violet Seeds, arrived with more pomp. She stood in the doorway in a white macintosh and a porkpie hat, looking about her and tapping a brogue until people came hurrying up. It was obvious who she was. Under her macintosh she was all ready for business in a green overall with the badge of a famous club on the pocket. Allan Colley had changed into a worn white coat. They knew each other. The two of them chatted technically for a few moments, while Edward sent for the rabbits in the first class, and then the judging began. They each took a class at one end of the long table and Edward stood between them with the record book in which he entered the numbers and results in duplicate. As each class was finished, he tore off the outside column and an eager schoolboy dashed off with it as if it were the midnight Russian Communiqué to the table where sat Dick Bennett and Miss Hemming, now looking holy.

Spectators were not allowed on the judges' side of the table. When E. Dexter Bell arrived, he had gone straight round to the sacred side where Allan Colley was holding a rabbit upside-down to look at its belly fur. 'The other side, please, if you don't –' he had begun politely, without looking up at him, but Mr Bell cut in with: 'My dear Colley, how are you? Do forgive me for not being here to greet you. One of the world's workers, you know.'

'Oh, hullo, Bell,' said Allan Colley, turning the rabbit right side up and ruffling its back. 'How are you?'

'Fine, fine,' said Mr Bell, as if he had really wanted to know. He was smoking a small cigar and wearing a short white overall that stuck out round his fat hips. He moved along to greet Miss Violet Seeds with gallantry, and then remained on the judges' side of the table, clearing his throat loudly to keep his presence obvious, and making sounds of approval as the rabbits were gradually weeded out and the final six graded as Commended, Highly Commended, Very Highly Commended, Third, Second, and First.

The rabbits were held on the other side of the table by Club members, wearing red rosettes which said 'STEWARD'. As one class was finished, Edward called out the numbers of the entries for the next, and the Stewards went off to the pens to collect them. Mrs Ledbetter was invaluable. She returned in an instant, always with the right rabbit, which was more than could be said for Mr Simkiss. She held three rabbits at once, cradled on the table between her arms, stroking them expertly, so that they lay still, with their ears sleeked back and their eyes calm, only their noses moving. The girl in the flowered dress was at Miss Seeds' end of the table. She only held one rabbit at a time, and by dint of letting it go and catching it as it moved forward, as a cat plays with a mouse, contrived to make the rabbit she held appear an intractable demon, controlled only by her skill.

'You naughty thing!' she kept saying to a blowsy Angora, which was squatting like a log. 'Keep still, you bad one.' It was too overfed and well-trained to want to do anything else, but by prodding and tweaking, she managed to make it move a step forward, when she clutched it back to her, stroking it feverishly and looking round in triumph.

'You can soon tell a rabbit that hasn't been handled,' she said. 'Be still, you wicked bunny!' The Angora went into a kind of coma, unmoved even when Miss Seeds pulled it forward by the ears and turned it upside-down. It lay on its back, praying at her with front paws neatly together, and then squatted while she took liberties with its hips, blinking as if it were an old story. It knew it had won prizes at many shows: and it knew it would win this one, which it did, returning to the toothy girl to be told as she carried it back to its pen that it was a wicked bun and didn't deserve it – 'Ah, scratch me, would you?'

When the first Havana Rex class came up, the toothy girl tried to hold one of her own rabbits, looking innocent until Edward discovered it. She handed it over to Mr Marchmont and held another, trying to spoil its chances by making it leap in the air.

As each class was judged, Miss Hemming filled in award cards and the eager schoolboy dashed to fix them on the pens. Mr Bell's rabbits were getting a lot of cards. He occasionally moved away from the table to stand in front of them so that he could tell admirers who was the breeder, in case they could not read Miss Hemming's writing.

At last it was the Flemish Adults. Freda lay, smug and enormous, between Mr Marchmont's terra-cotta sleeves, ears well back and great dewlap folded on the table. Edward had trained her *ad nauseam* to lie properly, and she was not letting him down. His heart swelled with pride as he looked at her covertly, terrified of giving away that she was his, for a small girl who had shrilled: 'That's my bunny!' had been severely reprimanded by Miss Seeds and almost got her rabbit disqualified.

'That's a sizey rabbit,' said Allan Colley and hopped her over two others to the head of the line as if he were playing Halma. Edward's eyes nearly came out of his head as rabbit after rabbit was sent back to its pen until only three remained. For the sake of the spectators, who were crowding round, some with cups of tea in their hands and their mouths full of Mrs Bennett's beetroot rolls, Allan Colley now delivered one of his little lectures. Size was paramount in a Flemish, he said. Edward's heart leaped. But size was not everything. Edward's heart sank a little but rose again as he said: 'But this is a quite exceptionally large doe. She starts with a great advantage. If she has the quality' – he turned her up and round about, he prodded and fingered her like a butcher, he pulled her ears apart and stared her in the face – 'and she has –' Edward wondered whether people could see it written all over him that he had bred her. 'On points,' Allan Colley pulled a panting brindle rabbit out of Mrs Ledbetter's arms, 'on points, this one's her equal, but –' he balanced them, one in each hand, Freda's great front paw, which was as big as a dog's, hanging limply down, 'but there's no question about which gets First.' He put Freda down, where she lay in perfect position. 'That one First,' he said, and Edward could have died for him. He wrote '1st' very deeply against Freda's number in the book, and almost forgot to record the decision between second and third, it was so unimportant.

When they broke off for a quick snack at Mrs Bennett's counter, Edward wanted to talk to Allan Colley about Freda, but she was eligible now for Best Rabbit in Show, so he could not claim her yet.

It was the last class of the Show. All the First Prize winners of every breed were lined on the table and Allan Colley and Miss Seeds judged them together. Mr Bell had two up there, a Chinchilla and a jazzy Dutch, and most of the others came from the big breeders who had sent by rail. Edward realized that the actual members of the Collis Park Club had not done very well. He heard Mr Marchmont say: 'Personally, I don't think it's right. They shouldn't have let the outside competition in. The Iver Show was only for members.'

From Edward's point of view, the quality of the competition only made Freda's prize more glorious.

He had left his place on the judging side of the table and now stood with the crowd at one end, his lips dry, his fancy already racing ahead to himself taking home the cup and showing it to the family. He might even take it to the factory to show Wendy. Later, he would have it engraved; he could see the spot on the mantelpiece where it would stand. Allan Colley liked Freda. He kept putting her up to the head of the line, and Miss Violet Seeds kept changing her for Mr Bell's Chinchilla, a gross-looking animal that could hardly breathe for its coat. Miss Seeds was a well-known Chinchilla breeder. It was soon obvious that it was between these two. One by one, the others were sent back to their pens until at last there were only Freda and the Chinchilla and an aristocratic Havana left on the table. The judges didn't pay much more attention to the Havana.

Edward was aware of heavy breathing over his shoulder. 'Looks like it's you or me, old boy,' said Mr Bell, his eyes like marbles behind the thick lenses.

'But you can't win your own cup!' It had only just occurred to Edward.

'Can't I? You watch me.'

That was the maddening part. He knew he was going to win. Even when Allan Colley and Miss Seeds were conferring together *sotto voce* and apparently arguing, and Edward could hardly breathe for suspense, Mr Bell affected to turn away and light another small cigar. Miss Seeds was being didactic with a square-nailed forefinger. At last, Allan Colley shrugged his shoulders and stepped back, turning away as if he had no more interest. 'Best Rabbit in the Show,' said Miss Seeds in a voice which Edward thought grating, 'No. 66, the Chinchilla.'

'That lets him out if he hasn't paid for it,' said Mrs Ledbetter to Miss Hemming, as Mr Bell wrapped up his own cup again and bore it away, making the V sign. She untied her white apron, and called Mr Ledbetter from the washing-up to help her box her own rabbits.

Mr Bell had his car outside and was going to give Allan Colley a lift, but Edward managed to catch the judge in a corner where he was taking off his overall.

'Oh, there you are, Ledward,' said Allan Colley. 'I wanted to thank you for putting up such a good show. Thoroughly enjoyed myself. Not every club does so well the first time.'

'Thanks awfully,' said Edward. 'I'm glad it went off all right. It was terribly good of you to come along. I say, excuse my bothering you, but that Flemish, the one that was runner-up for best rabbit –'

'Should have been first, if I'd had my way.'

'I bred her,' said Edward, blushing with pleasure.

'You did? Congratulations. Got any more like her, or is she just a fluke?'

212

'No, I've got some youngsters coming along that promise even better. I'm going all out for size, you know.'

'Good, good.' He seemed really interested. 'You may be starting something really big, you never know. Concentrate on your stock's best point; that's what I'm always saying, but people simply will try and get everything at once and then wonder why they end up with nothing.'

'Oh, no,' said Edward smugly. 'I'm concentrating on size.'

'Good man,' said Allan Colley. He had his jacket on now and they were walking towards the door, where Mr Bell was holding forth to a few admirers.

'Who's going to do the write-up?' asked Allan Colley casually.

'The write-up?'

'Yes, for the papers. Ought to put a bit in *Backyard Breeding*, you know. Give the Club a bit of a fillip.'

'Would they put it in?'

'Of course they would. I'll see to that. You going to write it? Good. Send it along to the editor with a little note mentioning my name. They have an awful lot of stuff they can't print, of course, but I'll see that this gets in. Keep it short.'

'About how long, and when should I –' But they were at the door now and Mr Bell had claimed Allan Colley with a hand on his arm and: 'Come along, my dear chap, mustn't let the horses get cold – fourteen of them – ha, ha, ha.'

Allan Colley allowed himself to be led away, looking back to smile good-bye at Edward.

Edward saw them off from the door and then, turning back into the hall, took off his overcoat and rolled up his sleeves, and got down to the job of removing all traces of rabbit from the Victory Hall before the Boy Scouts moved in with their concert.

The conductress on the trolley-bus stared at Edward's two big baskets. He held the one containing Freda on his knee and put the other on the seat beside him. The conductress was feeling chatty. The bus was almost empty and she was nearing the end of her run, so she lingered after punching Edward's ticket.

'What you got in there, dead babies?'

'Rabbits,' said Edward, giving Freda's basket a little pat. 'Two in each.'

213

'Rabbit pie for supper, eh?' said the conductress, who had ginger curls and an impudent mouth.

Edward laughed. 'No fear,' he said. 'These are breeding stock. As a matter of fact, I've just come from a show with them.'

She asked it. 'Win any prizes?'

'Didn't do so bad on the whole. Got a First and she was runner-up for Best Rabbit in Show. Should have won it too.'

'Well, I say,' said the conductress, 'I'm ever so glad. Did you breed them yourself?'

'Oh, yes, that's the whole point.'

'I had a cousin once,' she said, leaning on the back of the seat in front of him, 'who used to breed mice for shows. Chocolate or something, he called them.'

'Oh, yes, Self Chocolate,' said Edward, who had read of them in *Backyard Breeding*. 'A very interesting Fancy, I believe.'

'Come again?' said the conductress.

'I said it was very interesting – the Mouse Fancy,' repeated Edward.

'Fancy that!' She laughed, and swinging herself on her hands, one on each side of the aisle, she launched herself down the bus to greet a pair of old women with nodding hats and loaded leather shopping-bags.

The trees in Church Avenue were full of birds. Number Seven's almond blossom was coming out. Even the pavements smelled different at this time of year as if the spring rains had cleansed them of contact with the soles of people's shoes. Carrying his baskets home, Edward was still going over the high spots of his day. 'You may be starting something big,' Allan Colley had said. He had liked them, definitely he had liked them. A man like Colley would not say that unless he meant it. He was the type to speak his mind. Bit of a rough diamond really. Fine chap, though. His thinking Freda the best in the Show made her the best, whether she had won the prize or not. Miss Violet Seeds indeed! He must get started at his report of the Show tonight if Colley was really going to get it into the paper for him. He saw himself writing it at the table after supper and being asked what he was doing. He might get some of those short stories of his sorted out and brought up to date. It was time some of them went out on the rounds again. It was only a question of luck, everyone knew that. Once you got a start, it was easy to sell stories. His luck had put him in the way of Allan Colley, and why should it stop there?

Humming under his breath, he put down the baskets on his doorstep, opened the door and lifted the baskets into the hall. Opening the lid of Freda's, he took her out and held her fragile skull against his cheek, looking at their reflection in the mirror. E. L. P. Ledward and his champion Flemish Giant, Ledward Freda. No reason why she shouldn't be a champion, one day. He was going to carry her into the sitting-room and hold her out to Dorothy saying: 'Take a look at a first prize winner!'

There was no one in the sitting-room except Mr Munroe, who was doing the children's crossword in the evening paper, so Edward held out Freda and said his piece to him.

'Well done, boy, well done,' he said. 'That's a fine rabbit if ever I saw one. I used to know a deal about rabbits, you know, when I was a lad.' Edward knew this, because his father-in-law told him so every time the subject cropped up, but he said: 'Did you?' politely and began to tell him about the Show. People did not often tell Mr Munroe things, because of his habit of digressive interruption, so he was pleased to have this attention from Edward and only remembered after five minutes why he was sitting alone here downstairs.

He jerked his head towards the ceiling. 'Dorothy's started,' he said. 'Taken bad about three o'clock. I didn't think she looked well lunch-time. I said to your mother-in-law –'

'But I thought it wasn't till next week?'

'Ah, you don't want to pay much attention to what the doctors say, especially these young chaps. I remember when I had my kidney trouble –'

'I'd better go up and see if there's anything I can do.' Connie was coming down the stairs as he went into the hall with Freda in his arms. She looked shiny and some of her sausage curls were coming unwound.

'Oh, there you are at last, Ted. What on earth are you carrying that rabbit around for?' Her voice sounded tired. 'I want you to go round to Dr Simmons. He promised to come three hours ago, but there's no sign of him. I expect that girl of his hasn't given him the message.'

'Is she bad?' asked Edward anxiously.

'Of course she's bad,' Connie looked at him as if he had no right even to inquire in matters that concerned him so little.

When he came in from putting the rabbits away, Connie was in the kitchen, putting on the kettle. 'Ted, I thought you'd gone. I asked you to go round to Dr Simmons' straight away. Whatever have you been doing?'

'I had to put the rabbits away, Con.'

'You and your rabbits. Still, I suppose they are more important to you than Dorothy's baby.' He didn't stop to defend himself, but ran all the way to Doctor Simmons. The doctor was out and the maid looked at Edward as if he were the father of the baby and it was an old story and promised to tell the doctor as soon as he came in, meaning as soon as he'd had his supper. Edward ran most of the way back to Church Avenue to find the doctor's car already outside his own front door.

There was nothing he could do. He had heard plenty of jokes about anxious husbands: 'We've never lost a father yet,' but he knew now just how they must feel. The doctor went away and came back again later. When Edward opened the door to him, he just nodded and ran upstairs. Connie and Mrs Munroe remained closeted with the mystery in the front room, dashing every now and then for kettles. Every time he heard one of them on the stairs, Edward would jump to his feet and start out into the hall with an inquiring face, but the harassed figure would pass him by with a shake of the head and sometimes without even that. Edward would go listlessly back to the living-room and go on playing backgammon with Mr Munroe. How bored he got of both Mr Munroe and backgammon that night!

Round about eleven o'clock, Connie opened the door and focused her tired eyes on them with difficulty. 'You'd better get yourselves something to eat,' she said.

'What about you, Con?' said Edward, getting up. 'I'll get you something.'

'We've had something,' she said and went out.

Edward and his father-in-law had tea and bread and cheese, which Mr Munroe ate as fumblingly and crumbly as usual, taking full advantage, as he had all evening, of this unrivalled opportunity for discourse. Towards midnight, Edward fell asleep in his arm-chair and woke with a start when Mrs Munroe came in and said accusingly to her husband: 'Well,

you're a grandfather now. I hope you're pleased, I'm sure.' It
was a boy, cannon-fodder for the next war in Mrs Munroe's
mind.

Connie came down presently and looked surprised to find
them still there. Mrs Munroe was having the spare-room bed,
but before he and his father-in-law set out on their forty
minutes' walk to the Buildings, Edward, to everyone's surprise,
produced a bottle of Empire port which he had been saving for
this very occasion. They all drank the health of little Donny –
the poor little mite, doomed by only two minutes to be a
Saturday's child that 'works hard for his living'.

'Born in sorrow,' Mrs Munroe kept saying, sitting slackly at
the table with the placket of her skirt undone and one of her
earphones of black hair coming uncoiled. 'Born in sorrow.'

CHAPTER 11

Now that his home had been turned into a temple of worship,
whose god was Dorothy's Poor Little Mite, now christened
Donald Hector John, Edward spent more and more time in
the garden in the lengthening summer evenings. When he got
home from work, he always went first to visit the baby in his
swinging cot with the regal canopy of muslin and bows with
which, in spite of the washing, Dorothy would not dispense.

Donny was hairless, with a great pear-shaped head like his
grandfather's, tight polished skin and Dorothy's circular, wide-
open eyes. Edward's heart warmed to him. He never could think
of anything to say, but he would make friendly stabs, thrilling
with pride if the fat hand clutched his finger or the china eyes
seemed to recognize him. If Donny laughed, it would make
Edward laugh, too, and he would look over his shoulder
quickly in case anyone were coming in. If one of the women
were with the baby when he paid his visit, Edward would affect
indifference and say something like: 'Gosh, isn't he an ugly
little brute?' which never failed to get a rise.

After tea, when every chair in the living-room had knitting
on it and the kitchen was full of the smell of boiling nappies,
Edward would go straight out to the garden and potter about

while the clear evening air thickened imperceptibly into twilight until suddenly it was too dark to see and the dusk was full of imaginary wires stretched at the height of your knees. Going from hutch to hutch, with his basin of warm potatoes and bran and the sack of grass cuttings from the Lipmann's lawn, Edward was like a benevolent matron doing her round of the beds, with a kindly word for each and a longer sojourn with the favourites. Old Masterman, gross now and coarsening, was the patriarch. Many of his sons were stud bucks now in their own right, but he was still in his prime and his incestous unions with various great-granddaughters and great-nieces were always a success. When he died, Edward was going to have him stuffed, mounted in a naturalistic case perhaps, and honoured as the founder of the Ledward Strain, now well beyond the stage of dreams and experiments. Litter after litter contained rabbits of a size that bore out the careful mating. It was no longer a question of chance. Edward knew that, as Allan Colley had said, he had 'got something'.

'You'll all be famous one day,' he told a young mother, stirring the basin while she clamoured at the wire netting, fondly imagining that if she kept to one corner of the hutch he wouldn't notice the stirring nest in the other corner. 'You're making history,' he told her. 'There you are, Kitty. Dinner's served.' He spooned in some of the mixture through the little slot at the bottom of the wire – a patent device of his own – and moved to the next hutch without getting up from his squatting position. He had not been able to resist calling that doe after Kitty, although it seemed a bit crude. They had both carried themselves in the same inexpert way, as if they were looking for somewhere to deposit their burden.

When Edward had christened the rabbit, Kitty had already been out from the factory for two months, being stuffed with food and kept almost permanently horizontal by her mother, who was a great believer in putting up the legs. But her namesake in the hutch had beaten her to it. Reenie, who lived in the same road as Kitty, still had nothing to report.

Inspired by Freda's success at the Collis Club Show, Edward took her and two of her descendants to a much larger show, an ambitious affair in aid of the Red Cross, held in marquees on Wimbledon Common.

Besides rabbits, there were dogs, cats, chickens, cavies, mice, vegetables, flowers; it only wanted horses and cattle and brightly coloured farm machines to be a real Agricultural Show. Having penned his entries, Edward wandered about among the crowd, amassing a quantity of free literature from advertisers' stalls.

The Flemish classes were not until after lunch, so he found the refreshment tent and edged his way apologetically through the crowd which hid the counter. But reaching the counter was only half-way to getting his glass of beer and a sandwich. The three hot girls on the other side were as impervious to his diffident request as programme girls at the theatre. Whenever one came his way, he suggested: 'One Light and two cheese rolls, please, Miss,' until the words became meaningless through repetition.

Everyone else seemed to be eating or drinking or being served, but presently Edward became aware of a voice, beyond the red-faced man on his left who was drinking stout with great gusty breaths, which had been chanting in unison with his own whenever the waitress came near.

'Two sausage rolls and a large ale,' the voice kept saying in patient and strangely familiar tones. Edward leaned across the red-faced man and there, in a badly-fitting grey tweed suit, tapping hopefully on the counter with a two-shilling piece, was Allan Colley.

'Not so easy to get a drink, is it, Mr Colley?' said Edward, blushing. Allan Colley's square forehead was puzzled for a moment and then cleared.

'Why, hullo!' he said. 'It's – er, Mr – er, you're the Secretary of the Collis Park affair, aren't you?'

'That's right,' nodded Edward, thrilled that he remembered.

'How are you?' said Allan Colley. 'Bit of a – two sausage rolls and a large ale! Damn, she's gone again. Here, this is hopeless. How about slipping out and finding a pub somewhere?' The red-faced man expanded himself and filled their places thankfully as they left the counter. They were parted for a while by the crowd but met again in the doorway.

'Thank Heaven for some air,' said Allan Colley, mopping his brow. 'Let's go down to the High Street. We shan't miss much if we're quick about it.' They talked in spasms, parting and coming together again as they dodged through the sauntering crowds. 'I don't know how it is,' he said, 'but waitresses always behave as if I were dumb and invisible. D'you find that?'

'Rather,' said Edward, who would never have admitted it off his own bat, appearing round a perambulator.

In the Queen Adelaide, Allan Colley said: 'You grab that corner table, and I'll cope at the bar,' but Edward almost pushed him into a chair and rushed to the bar. He wasn't going to miss the chance of buying Allan Colley a drink.

He was so friendly, so unlike a famous man, so different, yet so very much nicer than Edward had ever imagined. They talked about rabbits over their lunch like any two fanciers. Edward had to keep reminding himself that he was really sitting chatting to Allan Colley and even being called: 'My dear Ledward.'

'Got any of your famous Giants up here today?' asked Colley, jerking his head towards the Common.

'Yes. The doe you gave first prize to and a couple of youngsters of the same strain. They're only novices, of course, but I'm hoping she may do some good, though there's some pretty hot competition.'

'I remember the doe. It'll have to be pretty hot to beat her if I'm any judge.'

'Are you judging today?'

He shook his head. 'Busman's holiday. I much prefer a little show though to an affair like this. The Pros. take all the interest out of it. I tell you what, you know Ledward, I meant to tell you the other day, but I didn't get a chance, if I were you, I should have a table show for your Club next time. Have it just for the Club members; don't let outsiders in. It's a much better way of encouraging and helping the amateurs, and after all, they're the backbone of the Fancy these days.'

'But that's exactly my own idea,' said Edward, leaning forward, his eyes shining. 'That's what I wanted that show of ours to be, but – well, other people thought differently.' Allan Colley might despise him for a sneak if he mentioned names.

'By the way, Ledward,' he said, 'I read the report you turned in about it. I thought –'

'Oh, it was only a scratch thing, I know,' said Edward quickly.

'No, I thought it was jolly well done. You gave it quite a

220

human kink, refreshingly different after the same old formula most people grind out.'

'Did you really think so? I say, have a beer? We've got time.'

'No, on me.' He got up, but Edward again beat him to the bar.

'I've been thinking – here's who!' continued Allan Colley, 'you've got a style that might lend itself to an article or so. Ever tried your hand at writing?'

'Well –' Edward thought of the drawer full of much-travelled short stories. 'One or two things you know – stories and such. Only potty little things of course.' He saw no reason to mention that they had never appeared in print.

'Thought you weren't quite new to the game. Look here, they're crying out for original little articles in *Backyard Breeding* Not necessarily very technical stuff, you know – they've got the old timers like me to do that – but chatty, helpful stuff – as one amateur to another. You know the kind of thing. Why don't you have a shot at it? I'll have a word with the editor. They don't pay much I'm afraid –'

'Good Lord,' said Edward breathlessly. 'I don't care about that, but what could I write about?'

'Oh – amateur breeding – your difficulties and what you've done about them – things that'll interest the little breeder. I tell you one for a start: How to Start a Domestic Rabbit Club. Write it from your own experience; how you went about it, what cropped up, how the Club grew, what the Government do for you – you could make it a bit humorous as well as helpful. Try it anyway and send it along. About a thousand words.'

'But I don't know whether I could,' said Edward, unnerved by the speed with which the suggestion had been made and apparently settled, but his demurring mutters were lost on Mr Colley, who had pulled out a watch on the end of a chain and was standing up and reaching for his hat.

'Ought to be getting back,' he said, 'or we'll miss your class. I want to see if my friend Armitage thinks as highly of your doe as I do.'

Mr Colley's friend Armitage, who was a jolly-looking man with hair that grew forward in a fringe like a boy's, thought very highly of Freda. He placed her second only to the famous

Montserrat Playboy, who had won at so many shows that entering him now was a mere formality. Armitage told Colley afterwards, and Colley told Edward that Freda might even have been placed first if she were not slightly past her prime.

Mr Armitage, who had a reputation as a humorist, cracked jokes all the time he was judging and made the atmosphere round his end of the bench very gay and informal. Most of the spectators crowded round him, and the judge at the other end of the bench, who went about his work in tight-lipped earnest, kept looking along disapprovingly. He would have liked to give little lectures, but there was hardly anyone at his end to give them to.

What pleased Allan Colley, and therefore Edward, even more than Freda's expected success was that Mr Armitage, with many a quip about next Sunday's dinner, placed Edward's two young rabbits second and third respectively, in a class judged by meat standards.

'As a point of interest, sir,' asked a man in a bowler hat as the bench was being cleared for the next class, 'why did you give that Second and Third? They weren't any bigger than any of the others.'

'I believe you,' said Mr Armitage. 'But the point is, they were younger. By the time they're the same age, they'll be bigger. Get it?' The man in the bowler hat nodded and went away to brood over his unplaced exhibit.

'Well what about this rabbit?' A sharp-faced, thrusting woman held out a rabbit which had been one of the first turned off the bench. 'He's bigger than any of the others. Perhaps you'd tell me what's wrong with him?'

'What's wrong with him? Well, look at him, madam. Gross. Like a pig, madam. Fat and muscle aren't the same thing, as any butcher will tell you.' He handed her back the rabbit, wrinkling his nose. 'Gross,' he repeated. The woman bore her rabbit away in a huff and Mr Armitage smiled round on his appreciative audience.

'Any more questions? Blimey, this is quite a Brains Trust.'

When Edward got home, with a basket in each hand and his blue and green cards peeping out of his breast pocket, he found E. Dexter Bell at the house. Mrs Munroe was there too, and they were all having tea with hot anchovy toast.

'Look at the lovely flowers Mr Bell brought for Dorothy, Ted,' said Connie, putting into her voice a reminder that Edward had never thought of bringing flowers all the time Dorothy was in bed.

'And a rattle for Baby,' said Dorothy, holding up a garish affair of chromium bells and coloured ribbons.

'Very kind I'm sure,' said Mrs Munroe.

Mr Bell basked, leaning well back in his chair. He seemed very much at home.

'How's yourself, Edward, my boy?' he asked. 'Been to a show, I hear. Wish I could have gone with you, but we can't all take Saturday afternoons off.'

'It's my monthly half day,' said Edward, sitting down to the cooling cup of tea Connie had poured for him. 'Dammit, we work fifty-eight hours a week, I should think we're entitled to that.'

'Oh, of course, I wasn't suggesting –' said Mr Bell passing off Edward's slight huffiness with an indulgent laugh. 'Do any good at the Show?'

'I did rather, as a matter of fact,' said Edward carelessly. 'Got a second with my doe Freda in a very hot class, and two of my young ones were well placed in a flesh class.' Mrs Munroe shuddered slightly. 'Chap from a big stud came up afterwards and made me a very good offer for one of them,' went on Edward, helping himself to toast. 'He said he'd take any more of the same strain that were going; seemed quite impressed with it.'

'Splendid, splendid,' said Mr Bell. 'That's the way to go on. Well, you young rascal, what are you crowing about?' He turned aside to Donny, whose cot was drawn up between him and Dorothy.

'As a matter of fact,' said Edward, incensed by Mr Bell's failure to be impressed, 'Allan Colley said that they were the best youngsters he'd seen for a long time.'

'Oh, was Colley judging? He told me he wasn't booked for any more shows this month.'

'No, but he was there. We had lunch together. He talked quite a lot about the Club, by the way. You know what I always said about having a little show for members only –'

'Oh, you and your old Club,' said Connie. 'Can't you talk

about anything else? It's awfully boring for us, and I'm sure Mr Bell doesn't want to be bothered with business just when he gets a little free time.'

'Look, even Baby's yawning,' said Dorothy, and they all made cooing noises at the cot, but Edward was not going to be put off.

'As I was saying, Bell,' he continued, with a black look at Connie, 'Allan Colley thinks we ought to have a little members' show. I believe he'd come and judge for us if we asked him.'

'My dear chap,' Mr Bell gave his short indulgent laugh again, 'you can't ask people like Colley to put themselves out for a potty little affair. By all means have another show soon, I'd planned that we should in any case, but don't let's go back on what we've already achieved. Even if it's not bigger, we'll run it on the same lines as the other. I must say I thought it a great success.'

'You would,' said Edward sourly, 'you won it.'

Connie said: 'Really, Ted!' and Mrs Munroe clicked her teeth. E. Dexter Bell said: 'Oh, don't mind him. It's just a slight case of our old friend the little green monster, eh, Donny? Eh, you young ragamuffin?'

'It isn't at all,' said Edward. 'It's simply that the smaller members of the Club ought to have a –' But no one was listening. The women, bored with the rabbit talk, had decided that it was the baby's bedtime. They were getting up and beginning to clear the tea-things. Connie had picked up the baby and Edward noticed with a shock how it became her to stand there holding him in his shawl, patting his back and nuzzling her cheek against his head. She posed for a moment or two, the picture of maternity, while Dorothy stacked the tray.

When the women had gone upstairs, Mr Bell said that he must be going. 'Coming round the corner to have one for the road with me?' he asked. He never seemed to notice when Edward was annoyed with him.

'No,' said Edward. 'I've got work to do. I've got an article to draft out for *Backyard Breeding*.'

'Commissioned one, have they?'

Edward did not see why he should deny it. After all, Allan Colley had promised to get it in; that came to the same thing.

'Hu*llo*!' said Mr Bell. 'We are coming on! I quite envy you.

You know, I've always said I'd do a bit of writing myself if only I had the time. I've had a book in my head for years as a matter of fact. You know what they say – there's at least one book in every man's life story? I dare say I'll get down to mine one of these days. Oh, well, I must be toddling. Sure you won't come out?'

'Oh, by the way,' said Edward in the hall, 'before I forget: this scheme of Club members going round visiting each other's stock. It's quite a success. A lot of them came here last week-end, and tomorrow we're going to Mr Marchmont. I thought we might come to you next week if it's convenient.'

'Terribly sorry, old boy,' said Mr Bell, putting on his black homburg, 'but not next week.'

'Well when?'

'Oh, I don't know. Leave it a bit. I can't say definitely.'

'I would like to give them a date. They're awfully keen on coming to you; they've heard so much about your stock.'

'Good heavens, Ledward,' said Mr Bell quite crossly. 'I've told you I can't say definitely. Good Lord, you can't expect me to throw open my place at a moment's notice to a rabble of schoolboys and God-forsaken spinsters.'

'But I've told them we're going to you soon. They'll think it so funny. I mean, everyone else had been only too pleased –'

'Let 'em think what they like,' said Mr Bell airily. 'Look here, I can't discuss it now; I've got to fly. And I promised I'd go and see Donny in his bath. I don't want to miss that. I'm a fool about kids, you know.'

He escaped upstairs and Edward stood in the hall looking after him, nodding his head sagely. A small suspicion that had been creeping into his mind for some time was being confirmed.

He thought about it all night and tackled Dick at the factory on the following Monday.

Dick was having his tea, sitting on an upturned box with a half-pint mug cradled in his hands and two Swiss buns in his lap.

His reactions were unsatisfactory. 'I don't know what's the matter with you lately, Ted,' he said. 'You seem to have got a regular down on Edgar. I must say, considering all he's done for us, I think it's damn paltry of you.'

'But don't you see,' said Edward. 'I'm beginning to think that he's only helped the Club in order to help himself. Mind you, I'm not blaming him for that; after all, he's not a charitable institution, but it does seem a bit fishy to me that he's been claiming lately for more and more breeding does. He's been getting an awful lot of the bran ration.'

Dick took a long drink of tea and swilled the liquid round and round in his mug before answering. 'Look here, Ted,' he said pompously, 'I'm in charge of the rationing scheme. Are you suggesting that I've been making false returns? Because if you are –'

'Oh, don't be a *fool*, Dick,' said Edward exasperated. 'I'm not suggesting anything of the kind. I'm only asking, have you ever had any proof that his figures are correct, and what's even more important, have we any proof that he's sending half his young stock to the butcher? I mean, it's different with the other members, because they sell their flesh through us, but as you know, Bell has always done it direct to his own man, and now I'm asking myself: Why?'

'Why?' repeated Dick obtusely, biting into a bun and looking at it while he munched.

'That's what I'd like to know. I've been thinking about it for some time, and the other night, when he as good as refused to let us come and see his stock, I must say, it got me properly suspicious. Look here, how long is it since you went round his place and saw for yourself how many breeding does he's got? I know it's months since I did, and then it was only in the dark. I honestly think one of us ought to go and check up. It could all be quite friendly, just an ordinary visit. The last thing I want is any unpleasantness, but if he's doing what I suspect, well it's – it's Black Market, that's all it is, Dick. You go. I think it's your duty.'

'I don't know about you, Ted,' said Dick slowly, 'but I personally would be ashamed to go spying like that on a man who's been such a good friend to us. As I said before, I don't know what's got into you. You never used to be one to take a personal spite.'

'Oh, Dick, you're hopeless,' raged Edward. He could have knocked him off his box, mug and buns and all. 'You're so honest yourself, you're absolutely blind. This man's got you just where he wants you. He's probably laughing at you behind your back for a mug –'

Plink-a-plink-a-plonk! The charge-hand of the Assembly Shop played a carillon with a cross bolt on the studs of a crankcase to indicate that the tea break was over. Dick put the last piece of bun into his mouth and stood up, brushing crumbs off his overall.

'We've always been good friends, Ted,' he said, 'and I'm sure I hope we still may be, but I never thought I should hear you talk to me like that. Come on, Joe. Time's up.' He lumbered off, with monstrous dignity, his little leprechaun mate hopping behind like a Familiar Spirit.

Cursing Dick's stupidity, Edward went back to his own Shop and took it out of Reenie for an innocent question about a sticking lever and was told off in his turn by Dinah for having been away for so long with the magnifying glass.

Nobody's temper was very good on the bench these days. They were short-handed and in a perpetual rush to get the engines through to schedule. Paddy was gone. When her husband came home, he had got her transferred to a factory near where he was stationed. Everyone had been surprised that Paddy, who had always behaved as if she were bored to tears with Canning Kyles, had seemed quite upset at leaving. She would not even say good-bye to anyone, but on her last day had slipped away after lunch, leaving them stranded with the embroidered teacloth with which they had planned to surprise her at six o'clock.

Her place was filled by a girl called Rachel, who was taking a long time to learn the job, as she was too busy radiating ripe sex to pay much attention. Kitty's place was vacant, but she was expected back any day. She had had her baby in the front room, or rather, her mother had practically had it for her, suffering every pain and finishing twice as exhausted as her daughter, who was sitting up having tea and toast three hours after her son arrived. The doctor had said she could go back to work in a month, but Mrs Ferguson kept discovering signs of relapse, and was being very difficult about weaning the baby to mixed feeding, which had been unheard of in her day, although in her day, as the doctor pointed out, there had not been a war on.

Meanwhile, Grace and Sheila were sharing her work, Sheila regrettably slapdash and preoccupied and Grace so conscientious that she would have taken all day over a set of pipes, given the chance.

Ivy was helping Rachel with the wheelcase job, which she deeply resented, complaining constantly about being paid to do her own job and nobody else's and absenting herself as often as she dared by way of protest. Dinah and Freda had Wendy's job to do, for Wendy had been out for the last week; no one quite knew why. Edward was wondering whether she would think it funny if he went down to the cul-de-sac by the railway to see what was the matter.

Madeleine, as ever, was a rock, coming in quietly day after day, doing her job neatly and perfectly, longing to help the busier ones, but impotent because she had never got round to learning any other job but her own. She would stand by them, maddeningly, saying: 'Isn't there some little thing –? Couldn't I test your springs, or perhaps look at a bearing? I feel such a silly useless thing.' She missed the days when they had all been so jolly together on the bench. No one seemed to have time to chat and joke nowadays; it was all such a rush. With Paddy gone, she had no one to talk to about Martin, who still had not been traced. As she never mentioned the worry that was eating her up inside, people forgot about it and there was nothing about her to remind them. She looked just the same, poor old Madeleine, coming in day after day in those sleeveless cotton frocks and that beige straw hat that everyone was so sick of, never a minute late, never lingering for an extra minute over her tea, never going out to wash before time, never making a mistake.

When one day she did make a mistake, it was a sensation. It was not only a mistake, it was a glaring, hideous *faux pas*, a great gaping crack right across the scavenge pump casing, which the dumbest, blindest novice could not have passed. But Madeleine – Madeleine, who had been on the job for two years, who knew the oil pump like her own soul, who drove the fitters mad with her minute, hypercritical reports; Madeleine, who had discovered things with her naked eye that an expert with a magnifying glass could hardly see – no one could believe it.

The A.I.D. woman, who was checking the engine, hardly

liked to bring the pump back to her, although her signature was on the report. She took it to Bob Condor.

'There must be some mistake,' she said. 'One of the girls has passed an appalling crack on the scav. casing. Mrs Tennant's name is on the report, but it must be the girl on the other bench. I mean, Mrs Tennant *couldn't* –'

'Crack?' said Bob, taking the casing, which almost fell to pieces in his hands. He went 'Whe-ee-ee-ew!' and 'Tt-tt-tt-tt-tt. Whoever passed this ought to be kicked out. She's not fit to be an inspector. But you're right. It couldn't be Mrs Tennant.' He hurried up to Edward with his tiptoe run and Madeleine, looking up from the next job, saw them talking together with scandalized faces and looking towards her. They went up to the girl who did the pumps on the other bench and she shook her head and looked righteous. They looked at the pump again and then back at Madeleine doubtfully, hardly liking to tax her with it. Like a hypnotized mouse watching a stalking cat, Madeleine sat paralysed on her stool and watched their hesitant approach.

Edward cleared his throat. 'Er – Madeleine,' he said, 'there's just a little thing here to clear up. It seems this scavenge pump went through.' He held it out to her. 'It's got your name on it, but – I mean, well, I can't believe that you –'

'Ish this your report?' Bob Condor laid the card on the bench and she read it through without seeing it, not daring to look up again at the pump, after the first quick glance which had sent her heart into a panic.

'Well, ish it yours?'

She nodded, still not looking up, twisting her hands between her knees.

'But, Madeleine, how *could* you pass it?' burst out Edward. 'You of all people! But nobody could – if they were deaf, blind, paralytic, drunk, they couldn't pass a thing like that.'

Madeleine said nothing. 'It's terribly dishappointing,' said Bob despondently, 'when your record's so good. The A.I.D.'ll be furious about this. I don't know how you could let us down so, I'm sure I don't.'

Dinah, looking across the bench to see what was going on saw Madeleine making an extraordinary, crumpled face, as if she were going to cry. Ivy stared, and nudged Reenie, who stared too with her mouth open and her pencil laid on her tongue, arrested in the act of sucking the lead.

All that day, people kept coming up to Madeleine and telling her they couldn't understand it, until she thought she would go mad. She had to go to Mr Gurley's office about the black mark, and he kept saying: 'But what the blazes happened to you? Aren't you well, is that it? Would you like time off to go and see your doctor?' She saw some of the girls surreptitiously looking at the scavenge casing, drawing in their breaths and looking at her as if she were a freak. 'Bad luck, Mad,' some of them said, 'sort of thing that might happen to anyone,' meaning that *nobody* could have – much less old Mad.

Madeleine did not usually long for the six o'clock bell. She never wanted to go home, because being at work was far better than being alone, but tonight she prayed for it to ring so that people should rush off and forget about her. Tomorrow was Sunday and perhaps by Monday they would have forgotten.

She pinned on the beige hat, put on her gloves and followed the crowd slowly out into the golden evening. Someone came up behind her and took her arm, squeezing it.

'Cheer up, Maddy,' said Dinah. 'It's not the end of the world to get a black mark, you know. Blimey, if I got worked up about all the mistakes I made I'd be in my grave by now.'

'If only they hadn't kept on about it,' said Madeleine miserably. Her face looked shrunken and yellow, like a badly-stored apple.

' I know,' said Dinah, 'that's the fault of being the Prize Girl. It's a compliment really; they couldn't believe it of you, you see.'

Madeleine began to cry. She had a handbag in one hand and a shopping bag in the other, so that she couldn't wipe her eyes.

'Oy,' said Dinah, 'you can't do that. What's the matter? Here – I had a hankey somewhere.' They were nearly at the clockhouse and Madeleine was crying so that she could hardly see: painful, unpractised, middle-aged tears. At the door, she suddenly turned and bolted across the track, between two sheds and down the three stone steps to the toilet.

Dinah found her sitting on the cleaner's chair, her arms on one of the filthy basins, her feet in the litter of paper towels and cigarette-ends that the girls had left behind.

'Look here, Mad, old girl,' she said sternly. 'You must pull yourself together. If you're going to work in a factory, you must be tough. You ought to know that by now, after the last war and everything. I mean, it's hopeless. Come on, I'll take you round to the pub and give you a drink. You can't sit there all evening like some broken down old lavatory attendant.'

Madeleine fumbled in her bag and showed her the telegram that wrote off Martin with a finality that seemed to laugh at all her months of hoping and believing. It had come the night before and been in her bag all day, but she hadn't meant to tell anybody.

Edward made up his mind to go and see what was wrong with Wendy several times before he actually brought himself to go. Even when he was at last walking down Queensdale Road, smelly after the spell of rainless weather, he almost turned back half-way. Would she think it awful cheek? Would her father kick him out and would she hate Edward for exposing her to the embarrassment of what that dreadful old man might do? He had not even the excuse of coming to inquire after her health, because she had sent word to Canning Kyles that it was not illness, but 'family trouble' that kept her out.

As he knocked at the door, Edward marvelled at himself for daring to intrude. Whatever the 'family trouble' was, they could not possibly want him. Someone might be dead; he ought not to have come. Footsteps were approaching the door from the inside, shuffling footsteps that sounded like Mr Holt's. Before Edward could turn and run, the bolt shot back and the door was opened by Wendy in bedroom slippers.

She gave a little gasp, hesitated, and then, instead of asking him in or shutting the door in his face, stepped out quickly and joined him on the pavement, closing the door without latching it.

'Ted,' she said, 'you shouldn't have come all this way. Why did you?' She looked thinner than ever. Her shoulders showed sharp through the top of her blouse and her wrists and ankles looked as though you could snap them with your hand. She had no make-up on and her ash-blonde hair was dull and drawn tightly back with a crumpled bit of ribbon. Edward suddenly realized how much he had missed her.

'You shouldn't have come,' she repeated, glancing back at the door. He had planned to say that he had come down about some tools of hers which could not be found, but instead he said: 'I was worried about you. I wanted to know what was the matter.'

'That was nice of you. I wish I could ask you in, but – No, perhaps it would be all right. Come in and have some tea.'

'No, I won't really,' said Edward quickly. 'I wouldn't dream of it. I only just wanted to see how you were. Walk down the road a little with me and tell me what you've been up to, that is, unless you'd rather not.'

She glanced down at her bare legs and slippers and touched the apron she wore. 'Oh, I can't,' she said. 'Look at me.'

'Doesn't matter,' he said, 'you look fine. Come on.' He took hold of her arm, eager to get away from the house. After hesitating, she came with him, and when she was walking at his side, he suddenly realized he was holding her bare arm, and dropped it. She padded softly in her slippers up the messy pavement, and they were half-way up the road before she began to talk.

'It was awful,' she began. 'It really was awful, Ted.' She nodded her head thoughtfully. Then suddenly, it all came out in a rush, as if she had been bottling it up for a long time for want of someone to tell it to. She talked on, in her quiet, un-emphatic voice without looking at him, and when they came to the end of the road, he steered her round the corner into the long crescent and they walked under the speckled plane trees.

It had all happened the night when the solitary raider had set the sirens wailing after months of silence. Wendy and her father and mother had been in the sitting-room, Wendy and Mrs Holt were sewing, and Mr Holt was reading the evening paper with his usual ejaculations of disgust. In five more minutes he would let Lassie out and they would all go to bed.

At first, Wendy thought it was a bus climbing the hill, but as soon as she realized what it was, she looked quickly at her father, who had raised his head with its grey cockatoo's crest and was listening with wild eyes. Mrs Holt, who was rather deaf, looked at him too and realized that something was wrong before she heard the siren.

'There!' said Wendy brightly, 'quite like old times to hear old Moaning Minnie, isn't it?'

'Was it the –' Mrs Holt's lips shaped the word siren and she

232

looked at Wendy and then they both looked back at Mr Holt.

He didn't say anything. He just sat there with his Adam's apple going up and down his long throat, slowly crushing the paper on the table in front of him. Lassie leaped off his knee and ran under a chair, with her rat's tail touching her stomach.

'No planes, anyway,' said Wendy. 'I expect somebody's leaned on the button by mistake. D'you remember that first Sunday of the war, when they sounded it just after Mr Chamberlain's speech and everyone got so excited and then it was one of our own all the time? I wonder what happened to the man whose fault it was. I expect he –' She chattered on, trying to cover the noise that was still scarcely more than a throbbing in your own head, felt rather than heard. But now as the siren died, even Mrs Holt could hear it, that familiar throbbing drone that grew imperceptibly until it filled the whole sky and seemed never to have been out of your ears.

It was no good pretending it wasn't there, or that it was one of ours, for a gun barked and then another. Every time they went off, Mr Holt jumped, but he still said nothing, even when Lassie whined. Wendy and her mother looked at each other and both knew what the other was thinking. They were remembering all the nights when the terrifying noise outside had been nothing compared to the noise within the house, how he had ranted and raved and shouted to heaven and cursed, and each night they had thought he was going mad until the miracle of daylight and the All Clear had put him into a stupefied sleep. He used to sleep all day; that was what had saved him, the doctor said, but towards evening, he would stir and groan and tremble and finally wake to go about with an expectant look in his eyes, working himself up to be ready for them with his frenzy when they came.

They watched him now. Was he going to begin that again, or was he by some miracle going to be all right? Wendy didn't think she could go through it all again.

She got up briskly. 'Well,' she said, 'I'm going to make some tea. We might as well enjoy ourselves if they're going to keep us awake.' She had thought then that he was going to be all right. When she came back from the kitchen with the tray he was still sitting quietly at the table, and it was only when she went up to him with his cup that she realized that he was absolutely tense, with every nerve in his body quivering. You could see them twitching in his face. His eyes were staring and his hands, held just off the table, were shaking lightly as if they were lying on a machine.

It was no use trying to make him drink his tea; he did not seem to be aware of her at all. The plane had passed over and the guns were now only far-away woofs.

'Let's get him up to bed,' said Wendy. 'We'll all go to bed, shall we? The All Clear'll be going in a minute. Come on, Dad, I'll help you upstairs.' He allowed her to get him to his feet and went with her like a man sleep-walking, placing his feet on the stairs without looking at them. She had her arm round him and it was horrible to feel the quivering of his body, but he was quiet and came without resisting. Mrs Holt followed behind, making little pushing movements with her hands, hardly daring to speak in case she should set him off. His tenseness was something that you felt would explode at any minute. It was like waiting in the dark for an alarm clock to go off, feeling it sprung up and sprung up yourself in expectation of the shock it would give you, you didn't know when.

They had been able to get him into bed. He didn't seem to know they were undressing him. Wendy had sat him on the bed in his pyjamas and then lifted in his legs and covered him up. Ordinarily he would never go to bed without Lassie under the eiderdown, but now he didn't seem to notice that she was not there. He never asked for her. He had not spoken a word since the first notes of the siren had set him listening.

Wendy and her mother hurried out of the room as if there were a time bomb in it, and safely downstairs, relaxed a little although they kept looking at the ceiling.

They drank their tea and congratulated each other on having got him safely through it.

'Perhaps he'll sleep now,' said Wendy, 'if only the plane doesn't come back. Oh, why don't they sound the All Clear?'

'It's coming back,' said her mother, slowly putting her cup on the table and standing with her mouth quivering and her eyes turned upward.

Mr Holt's shout and the first gun went off simultaneously. Wendy ran into the hall and there he was, standing at the top of the stairs with his pyjama trousers dropping off, clenched fists raised to Heaven, a confused torrent, half-religious, half-blasphemous issuing from his distorted mouth. He looked just like some fanatical negro teacher, yelling his libation with the whole of his jerking body. His eyes rolled and there was foam on his lips. He was insane.

Wendy stood for a moment, cold with horror. She had started forward up the stairs when the bomb fell – it must have been several streets away – and he screamed, gave a kind of twisted leap in the air and fell forward. He lay head downwards, diagonally across the stairs, the catalepsy of his body more terrifying than all its paroxysms.

The roar of the falling building faded to a rumble and in the silence that followed, the drone of the plane could be heard growing fainter and fainter, satisfied.

Mrs Holt gave a little moan and sank to her knees in the sitting-room doorway. The little dog pushed out past her and as Wendy bent over her father, it came bounding up the stairs with its tail wagging and began to go over the staring twisted face with its darting tongue.

Mr Holt was paralysed now all down one side, and the doctor didn't think he would ever speak again. Wendy had to do everything for him; that was why she had not been able to come to the factory.

CHAPTER 12

SHEILA had never considered the possibility of Kathleen coming back to London, and wanting her flat. Her office was evacuated for the duration, and beyond that Sheila did not look. She never thought about what was going to happen to her and David after the war. When she tried to think about her future with David at all, it was just an empty space. She couldn't visualize it, and she didn't let herself try. The way to live was like David, wholly in the present, and never make plans for the future. David hated making plans.

Once he had said to her: 'You know, you and I really ought to get married,' and she had caught her breath, and then said, like a fool: 'Oh, I don't know, darling. We really might be married as we are.' She was afraid that he had said it because he thought she was dissatisfied with the way they were living. Afterwards, she could have kicked herself for having lost the opportunity, because he didn't speak of it again. She couldn't mention it, in case he thought she were trying to tie him down. Still, he had the idea in his mind, that was something. Perhaps he was waiting until after the war.

Because she could not look farther than the end of the war, Sheila did not mind how long it went on. Nobody near to her was in the Services, David said there were not going to be any more blitzes, and really, once you got used to the rationing and no cars and having to work at the factory, it made very little difference to life. She even caught herself being half disappointed when the Russians advanced, and almost welcoming any setback that might postpone the end of the war. The end of the war would bring Kathleen home and then life would begin to be difficult.

When she got Kathleen's letter to say that her office was returning to London and that she was coming back to the flat, Sheila said: 'Oh!' and stood stock-still in the middle of the six square feet that was called the hall.

David was in the bath. 'What's the matter, honey?' he called. Sheila read the letter through again, unbelievingly, and then opened the bathroom door with a face of tragedy. 'Kathleen's coming home,' she said slowly, dropping the words at him as he lay smiling and unconcerned in the bath.

'Well what of it?' He began to plunge his face about in the water, splashing the floor and her feet.

'She'll want the flat!' wailed Sheila. 'Her office is coming back and she's coming back for good. Oh, I could kill her.'

'What?' He came up out of the water blinking and shaking his hair.

'She'll want the flat. We'll have to turn out. Oh, David, isn't it *awful*?'

'No, we'll have to find somewhere else, that's all.'

'But it's so nice here, and it's terribly difficult to get a flat in town. We'll never find anything.'

'Oh, you'll find something all right. Go to an agent's tomorrow.'

'But they're all shut by the time I get back from work.'

'Well, take a day off for a change.'

'I suppose I'll have to, but a day isn't much. Couldn't you try, David? You'd be much better at it than me.'

'Me? Good God, no. It's woman's work. Look out, darling. I'm coming out. Chuck me my towel.'

'Find something nice, though,' he called, going into the bedroom all wet to find a cigarette. 'And make it in this neighbourhood. I don't want to be far from the office again. I can't think how I ever existed at Earls Court. Why don't you try that place – what's it called – Chessington Lodge? It's quite a good spot.'

'Oh, David, it'd be much too expensive. We couldn't possibly. Even if Kathleen didn't let me have this cheap, I should think the Chessington Court flats are about twice as much as this.'

'Well, somewhere else then. There must be masses of flats. You'll find something.'

She would have to find something, that was all. She went into the kitchen for a cloth to wipe up the mess he had made on the bathroom floor and across the hall. She would have to start making the flat presentable for Kathleen too. That was another thing. All the broken crockery that they had slung so light-heartedly into the dustbin, the picture that David had torn down because he didn't like it, breaking the frame and making a hole in the wall, the burns on the dressing-table and the mantelpiece, the crack in the sink where they had dropped the mincer, the curtain in the sitting-room that was torn because David would never bother to move the desk and draw it properly – all these things that had seemed funny at the time would have to be put right before Kathleen came back. She would never understand how Sheila had managed to do so much damage on her own.

Sheila took three days out from the factory and returned, having achieved nothing, to a rating from Mr Gurley for having stayed away without a doctor's certificate. She didn't dare take any more time off. She had been to nearly all the estate agents in Bloomsbury and was now putting advertisements in papers at great expense, spending her lunch-hour scouring the newspapers in the Public Library and the rest of the day writing letters under cover of her report card. How could anyone take an interest in reduction gears under the circumstances? Kathleen was coming home in a week and she was as far off as ever from finding somewhere to live. David was still hopeful. He could not understand why she was making such heavy weather of it. He didn't seem to realize that there was not one hole or corner in all London, much less in Bloomsbury. She had even tried hotels, but they were all much too expensive or had people sleeping in the bathrooms. Everyone in England was living in London and Sheila was getting desperate.

On the night before Kathleen's homecoming, they packed glumly at the flat. What Sheila had been terrified of all along was going to happen. They were going to be separated. David was going to put up at some bachelor apartments with a man who worked on his paper and Sheila was going to stop on with Kathleen, as Kathleen had suggested.

'I still don't see why I can't stay on here too,' said David for the hundredth time, banging drawers about and kicking at cupboard doors. 'I wouldn't mind the sofa a bit – or Kathleen could have it and we could have the bedroom. She'd be tickled to death to have a man in the house!' Sheila was tired of explaining to him that it was as impossible to tell Kathleen they were living together as to tell her parents.

'To start with, she'd tell Mummy at once,' she said. 'She's frightfully thick with them – more than me really. She used to live down at Swinley, you know, and they were always shoving her down my neck as a friend. Look, David, you must take this old pair of shoes, even if you don't want them. She mustn't ever know.'

'She'd understand. Your unfortunate upbringing, my darling, makes you think everyone has the same outlook as you had before I took you in hand. She'll probably be thrilled to think you've grown up at last. I dare say I shall tell her myself if the water at Toddy's place isn't hot. I'll be coming round for baths.'

'David, if you dare! You don't know what she's like. She just simply isn't the sort of person that could ever understand. I mean, she wears lisle stockings and glasses and awfully good-style coats and skirts. I don't think she's ever had a boy-friend, she's probably never even been kissed –'

'Well, I might put that right for her then, mightn't I?' He was impossible. He simple refused to understand. He made it doubly difficult for her by being particularly gay and sweet and loving when all she wanted was for him to remove all traces of himself as quickly as possible. She held out against going out to dinner with him. She had to stay behind and clean the flat. At last he was ready and she helped him carry his things down to the taxi.

The night porter was on duty. 'Leaving us?' he said. He never called anyone 'sir'.

'Turned out into the snow,' grinned David and added something which Sheila couldn't hear, but which made them both laugh. She had a sudden glimpse of David telling his friend Toddy about her and then laughing. Did men talk about their women as women did about their men? Surely David wouldn't – but men were impossible when they got together. She couldn't bear him to be going back to that masculine world which he had left to come to her. She kissed him on the pavement, dragging him well out of the porter's view and watched the tail light of his taxi disappear with something like panic in her heart. It was absurd to mind saying good-bye when she was going to see him for dinner tomorrow.

Tomorrow was Saturday. She had the afternoon off and she was going once more to do the weary round of the agents.

Kathleen had arrived when she got back at lunch-time and her presence was already all over the flat. It smelled of her toothpaste – she always cleaned her teeth at least three times a day – and of her clothes, which always smelled as though they had just come back from the cleaner's, which they usually had. A Revelation suitcase was open on the bed, unpacked down to the layer of shoes, each pair wrapped in tissue paper, and every crevice filled with neatly rolled gloves and stockings. There was a patent case for dresses too, with Kathleen's dull clothes folded over a rail in the lid. The things she had unpacked were hung out all over the room to rid them of non-existent creases. Kathleen's ivory brush and comb set were on the dressing-table beside Sheila's scrap lot, where David's moulting brushes had been. Kathleen's green pyjamas were even laid out on David's pillow.

'But Shee darling, you look awful!' were Kathleen's first words as she came in from the kitchen with the china hairpin tray which she had hunted out from the dresser where Sheila had put it. 'So tired, and so thin. My dear, you're a stick!'

239

Kathleen always spoke with exclamation marks. Her conversation was very tiring.

'You haven't been looking after yourself properly. I can see that,' she went on, kissing her with her cheek. 'Hardly a scrap of food in the place, no milk or butter, and no fruit, with the shops simply stacked with it! I spent a night at Swinley on the way here and saw your people. Auntie Lena told me you were working like a nigger, and had got much too thin, but I never expected to find you looking so utterly worn out. What on earth have you been doing to yourself?'

'Oh, I'm a bit tired,' said Sheila, looking for her shoes, which Kathleen had moved.

'Tired? I should think you are! Now you just sit down. I've got some coffee making. Have you had any lunch?'

'No – yes,' said Sheila. 'I won't have any coffee, thanks all the same, Kath. I've got to rush out as soon as I've changed.'

'Rush out, where to? You ought to take it easy when you do get time off. I always do. They work us terribly hard, you know, at the Min., but I find I can take it in my stride by eating the right things and relaxing with a good book whenever I can. My dear Shee, how can you exist in those ridiculous underclothes?' she cried, as Sheila stepped out of her trousers. 'I'd die of cold.'

'Not in summer, you wouldn't.'

'Yes I should.' Kathleen picked up the dungarees from the floor where Sheila had left them and began to fold them, running her thumb-nail down the crease. 'My goodness, don't they smell of oil! I'll pop round to the cleaners with them this afternoon. They'll get them done quickly for me. They know me.'

'So they do me,' said Sheila, 'but I still shouldn't have anything to wear on Monday. You leave those dungarees alone, Kathleen.'

'Well, well, well,' said Kathleen, 'aren't we getting snappy in our old age? You've been living alone too long. It's high time I did come home, I can see that.'

'Look, Kath.' She had got to know sometime, and it might as well be now. 'It's awfully sweet of you to suggest me staying on here with you, but I know you'd much rather be here alone. I mean, there's not really room here for two,' she lied, thinking of how perfectly it had suited her and David. 'If I could just stay here for a few days until I find something, then I'll push

240

off and leave you to it. It'll be much better if I have a place of my own. I'd have gone already only it's rather hard to find anywhere in a hurry these days.'

Kathleen was staring at her. 'My dear Shee, what on earth are you talking about? You must be mad! Of course we'll stay here together. It'll be grand fun, and I'm going to look after you, see that you eat properly and go to bed early. I don't know how you could think I wouldn't want you. We shall get on famously!'

'No, honestly Kath, I don't think I will, thanks awfully all the same. It would never work. I get up terribly early. I should wake you.'

The thought of sharing the bed with Kathleen, even for a few nights, was repugnant. 'Then I go out quite a lot in the evening, you know, and I'd disturb you coming in. I should be an awful nuisance to you.'

Kathleen had very large, prominent teeth which she brought close to your face when she talked to you, buttonholing you with her eyes, staring, and watching your mouth when you spoke. 'I never heard of such a silly idea!' she said. 'Whatever would Auntie Lena say? She was so pleased that we were going to be together. She didn't like your living alone at all, you know.'

'I can't help that,' said Sheila stubbornly, moving away from her to the dressing-table. 'I've made up my mind, I really shall go as soon as I can find somewhere.' Kathleen followed her, watching closely while she hid her face, still arguing, outraged. In a minute, she'll make me say it, thought Sheila. I shall say: 'I don't want to live with you,' and then there'll be trouble.

'Well, I must say, you are queer,' went on Kathleen. 'You've certainly changed, and I don't know that it's for the better. You were never independent like this a year ago, and we used to have such fine times together. I hated going away and leaving you, you know, when you first came here. You seemed to want me so much to stay, I can't think what's happened to you. Still, I expect it's just because you're tired. I shan't worry you. I shall just leave you alone and then presently you'll drop this silly attitude and we shall both live here happily ever after. What do you say?' Things that Kathleen said always demanded an answer.

'I've made up my mind,' said Sheila getting up and putting on her jacket.

241

'Oh, well, we'll wait and see.' Kathleen smiled indulgently. 'Where are you going?'

'Out,' said Sheila, and went.

Some of the agents had shut at one o'clock and at others it was the same old story. What Sheila wanted and the price she could pay made them smile pityingly. Having no experience of flats and rents she had no idea whether it was because it was wartime or because she was asking the impossible. There must be something, somewhere. She had come down to considering anything in London. If it couldn't be Bloomsbury, David would have to put up with it. He had lived at Earls Court for ages before he knew her, and if he felt as she did he wouldn't mind where it was so long as they were together.

Towards five o'clock, she was beginning to despair. She was very tired and the extra high-heeled shoes she had put on to annoy Kathleen were making her feet ache. She would try one more agent on her list and then give up, and have to admit failure when she saw David tonight.

Bell, Watson and Lampeter were on the first floor above a stationer's shop in Kingsway. She had been there twice and thought the clerk looked at her sickeningly as she toiled up the stairs and entered the outer office. It was quite a prosperous-looking place, with a green leather sofa and chairs and a table with old magazines on it.

'If you'd care to wait just a minute or two,' said the clerk, 'Mr Bell will be free.'

Sheila sat down on the sofa and waited without hope. Presently the inner door opened and a woman in furs came out, accompanied with hand-washings by E. Dexter Bell.

'Ah, Miss – er,' said Mr Bell. 'Not found anything yet then? I'm afraid I've got nothing more to offer you, but if you'd like just to step into my office, we'll have another look.' His manner with young clients was ponderously patronizing, with older ones, if they were well off, it was unctuous, and if they were not it was belittling.

Sheila followed his broad back down the passage between the glass partitions which gave forth sounds of clicking typewriters and sat down in the chair before his desk which she had occupied, the first time optimistically, the second with faint hope and now with no hope at all. At a smaller desk in the corner, a woman in a pink blouse with her hair in little sausage curls, sat going through letters with a wetted finger.

On Mr Bell's desk was a revolving stand such as you find outside newsagents. The sections were headed: 'FURN: HOUS: UNF: MAIS: etc.,' and held overlapping index cards instead of postcards.

'Let's see,' said Mr Bell, spinning it round, 'it's a flat you're after, isn't it? Unfurnished, if I'm not mistaken?'

'Furnished,' said Sheila.

'Of course.' He turned the stand again and ran his finger down the file. 'Blah, blah, blah, *this* one might do.' He flipped out a card. 'H'm, h'm, h'm, and *this*. I'm afraid we've still not very much to offer you, my dear young lady. You're asking something when you ask for a furnished flat these days. They're as rare as a shilling tip in Aberdeen.'

'I know,' said Sheila. He had said this every time. The two he showed her were hopeless, one three times too expensive and the other a basement, which David would never stand.

'Ah!' Mr Bell clapped a hand to his forehead. 'Now didn't we have a flat turned in today? I believe – I'm not promising you, mind you, but I *believe* it might be the very thing you're looking for.' Hope leaped in Sheila's eyes. She gazed at him as if he were a god, which he enjoyed.

'Oh, I'm sure it would,' she said, prepared to take it without even hearing about it, before it vanished into thin air as all the other possibles had done.

'Let's see.' He turned in his chair. 'Did you make out the card for that flat that came in a little while ago, Mrs Ledward?' The name struck Sheila as familiar, but she was too excited to wonder why.

'Yes, Mr Bell,' said Connie in her office voice. 'I have it here.' She rose and laid it on his desk and then sat down again and went on going through her letters with pursed lips. Edward at home was just hunting vainly in the kitchen for something appetizing for his tea, but she had not given him a thought all day. Her new life as a business-woman was far more engrossing than anything that could ever happen at Church Avenue. She left the housekeeping now almost entirely to Dorothy, who was no more proficient at it than her sister.

The flat sounded quite possible. It was a miracle. Sheila had already decided to take it before Mr Bell had finished reading out the card. She could see herself telling David about it at dinner. They might even move in there tonight.

'Oh, yes,' she said, interrupting him breathlessly before he had finished with kitch., and usual off., 'I'm sure it would do. I'll take it.' She leaned forward, nodding eagerly.

'Well, well, you are an impetuous young lady, to be sure,' said Mr Bell. He looked through the card again with maddening slowness. 'I'm not sure, though. . . . We've another inquiry about it already, haven't we, Mrs Ledward?'

Connie looked through a file on her desk. 'Yes, Mr Bell,' she said. 'The client was not sure whether it would suit. She said she'd let us know.'

'Did we give her any promise to keep it open?'

Connie had lost the place in the file and went through it again from A., although the client's name was Widdicombe. Sheila could have screamed. Why couldn't they put her out of her suspense?

'No, Mr Bell, we gave her no option,' said Connie at last, and Sheila let out her breath and leaned back in the chair beaming.

'Well, then I could –' she began, but Mr Bell interrupted in a businesslike voice: 'When would it be convenient for you to see the flat in question?'

'Oh, any time. Now if you like, I mean. I don't mind taking it straight away without seeing it. I'm sure it would do; it sounds just right.'

'Oh, but Miss Blake,' said Mr Bell, with raised eyebrows, 'we couldn't let it to you without a viewing. That would hardly be fair to you, or to us. Still, as you seem in such a hurry, I see no reason why you shouldn't see it this evening. We have the keys and it's only just round the corner from here. Let's see, who could we send, Mrs Ledward? Would you be good enough to go and inquire?'

Sheila didn't like the way he looked at her when Connie had gone. His manner became quite intimate, but she couldn't be too putting-off in case he might suddenly withdraw the flat, so she smiled and played up to him, answering back when he made a personal remark about her hat. He was delighted with her, and feeling that he held her in the hollow of his hand, allowed himself more familiarity of tone than was ethical, dropping it with a clearing of his throat when Connie returned.

'I'm sorry, Mr Bell,' she said, 'but there's no one. Phillips and Mr Schilling have gone, and the rest of the staff are up to their eyes in work.'

Sheila hated her. 'Well, couldn't I go on my own if you gave me the keys?' she asked. 'I wouldn't steal anything.'

Mr Bell laughed and Connie folded her lips and sat down again, uninterested in whether Sheila saw the flat or not.

'Wouldn't steal anything, eh?' said Mr Bell. 'I'm not so sure. It's just these innocent-looking ones who turn out to be the most dangerous criminals. Isn't that so, Mrs Ledward?' Connie pretended not to hear.

'Oh, but I must decide tonight,' said Sheila. She knew that the flat would escape her if she didn't grab it.

'I tell you what' – Mr Bell looked at his gold wrist-watch, which had such a stout cage over the face that it was a wonder he could see the time at all – 'I've got ten minutes to spare. I don't mind just popping round with you if you come straight-away. We shan't need very long. I dare say the viewing will be only a formality with you as you seem to have set your heart on the place.'

'Oh, would you really?' said Sheila, looking up at him under her curly lashes as he stood up. 'It's awfully good of you.'

'Not at all.' Mr Bell reached for his hat on the stand behind him. 'Just a part of our service, eh, Mrs Ledward?' Connie smiled briefly. 'What about that letter to Lauder's?' she said. 'You wanted to get that off tonight, didn't you?'

'Oh, I'll be back in plenty of time for that,' he said airily. 'If anyone wants me, tell 'em to try again in a quarter of an hour.' He held open the door for Sheila. 'Shall we go then, Miss Blake?'

The flat was at the top of a tall, dingy house in Tavistock Square. 'Not much to look at from the outside,' said Mr Bell confidently as they paused at the front steps, 'but you can't always go by outward appearances, can you? Take me. Now to look at me, you'd never think I was a man of great artistic tastes, would you? I love beautiful things, Miss Blake,' he said looking hard at her. Sheila didn't care what he loved. All she cared about was getting inside the house and seeing the flat. Its position was perfect; her hopes were soaring. For diplomacy's sake, she smiled charmingly at him and allowed him to take her arm to help her up the steps.

The street door was ajar and they walked through a dark hall, past a glass-panelled door with a Yale lock and began to climb the stairs, Mr Bell going neither in front nor behind, but keeping level with her, step by step.

'As you see,' he said, 'these flats have their own front doors. All the privacy you want, Miss Blake, and I'm sure you do want privacy, don't you?' He leered at her in the gloom and she said brightly: 'Well, who doesn't?'

'Who, indeed?' he chuckled. 'And I know what your young man would say. I know what *I* should say if I were your young man. What's he like? Tall and handsome? – Damn him.' Sheila laughed uncomfortably. Mr Bell's body was overpowering, so close to hers, and he was breathing heavily down her neck as they climbed upward. She quickened her pace and arrived before him at the top floor in front of a white door with a Yale lock, a lovely door, her and David's front door.

'Is this it?' she said.

'Must be,' said Mr Bell, arriving slightly out of breath at her side. 'Let's see, is there a number on it?' There was no light on the little landing, so he struck a match and they peered together.

'Flat 5,' they both said at once. 'Five,' said Mr Bell, fumbling in his pocket for the key. 'The magic number.'

'Oh, do hurry up and open it,' said Sheila excitedly. 'I'm longing to see it.' As soon as he had turned the key, she pushed past him and entered the flat, groping along the wall for the electric light switch.

The hall had no windows and was quite dark. She heard him come in behind her and shut the door. 'I can't find the light,' she complained. 'Where d'you think it is? Oh, here.' She clicked down the switch, but nothing happened. 'It doesn't work,' she said. 'Oh, dear –'

'The power's off, I expect,' said Mr Bell, startlingly close to her. 'So what do we do now, come back in the morning?'

'I suppose so,' said Sheila, disappointedly. Even if she took the flat without seeing it, she and David couldn't very well move in here tonight in the dark. Or could they? Would he think it fun?

'Look, Mr Bell,' she said, groping her way back to the door. It was hateful being shut in this box with this objectionable, breathing, unseen man. 'Supposing I took the flat on the chance without seeing it – I mean, you can say I've viewed it now, can't you? Could we – that is, I move in tonight? I'll have to ask my friend. He – she, that is, my girl-friend, you know, who's sharing it with me –'

'He – she?' mocked Mr Bell, still horribly close. 'I say, you are a naughty young lady. What'll you give me not to tell, Miss Blake?'

'I don't know what you're talking about,' she said in a panic, feeling all over the door for the handle.

'Don't you?' he said. 'Don't you? Don't you think I should get something for being discreet and for bringing you all the way round here – don't you? Not even one tiny little kiss –' Before Sheila could say anything, his arms went clumsily round her and his horrible loose wet mouth was on hers. She pushed at him blindly, with all her strength, and flinging up one hand to hit him in the face heard the tinkle of his glasses as they fell to the floor.

'Damn you –' he said and clutched for her again, but she had found the door handle and felt it hit him in his soft stomach as she wrenched it open and pelted down the stairs, through the hall, down the stone steps and along the pavement, running, running, knocking into people who turned and stared, running anywhere until she saw a Tube station and bolted down it like a rabbit, worming herself into the crowd as if she could rub off on them that crawling feeling in her spine that he was behind her.

Sheila no longer slept with the alarm clock under her pillow. She hoped it would waken Kathleen, who slept deeply and healthily with her hair in a net and grease on her face, but it never did. Going down the steps of the Tube, still heavy with sleep and the worry which had now grown to be an obsession that governed all her waking hours, Sheila remembered what David had said last night. They had been dining cheaply at a place in Soho, where the knives and forks were not properly washed up, and he had told her that he was no longer sharing a room with Toddy, as another room had fallen vacant in the same house.

'It's very comfortable,' he said, 'grand bed, an arm-chair and a desk, and the old girl does me very well: bacon and egg this morning and kippers yesterday, I seem to have struck oil.'

Sheila would rather have heard that he was wretchedly uncomfortable and half-starved without her. She was losing him; she could feel it. He was slipping away from her with each day that she failed to find somewhere for them to live together.

'Can I come and see it?' she asked wistfully. 'I'll bring you along my brocade cushion and that red counterpane you like.' She wanted to leave something of herself in the room to remind him of her all the time.

'Good God, no!' he had said. 'It's the most frightfully smug establishment, a sort of Y.M.C.A. – no followers allowed. We all live like eunuchs.'

''Ullo, love,' said Mrs Urry, coming up the platform with her bundle of bedding. 'You do look cheap this morning. What's the matter with you these days – crossed in love?'

'Who wouldn't look cheap at this hour of the morning?' retorted Sheila. Mrs Urry was a nice one to talk, with her bleary eyes and ropy hair escaping from under the beret.

'Something on your mind though. I said so to Urry only last night, didn't I, Urry?' she called over her shoulder to her husband, who was still sitting on the lower bunk, fiddling with his boots. 'Blast that man. 'E's slower than a funeral. What's up, duck? Tell Mum.'

'Well, I am a bit worried,' said Sheila. 'I've been trying to find a flat, you know, and it's impossible these days. I'll be sleeping down here with you if I don't find somewhere soon. I can't stand the girl I'm living with much longer.'

'You could do worse,' said Mrs Urry, hitching up her bundle while she waited for her husband. 'H. and C. laid on, feather mattresses, early morning tea, all the comforts of 'ome. Ah, there you are, Urry, and about time. What's the game? Want me to be late at the office?'

'Shut up, you ugly old bitch.' Mr Urry shuffled up with his bootlaces untied. 'I'm poorly this morning. Don't think I'll go to work.'

'You will or else –' said his wife. 'So you're looking for rooms, eh?' She turned to Sheila. 'Tell you what, I believe that

Greek's got a couple going begging over the café.' She pronounced it to rhyme with safe.

'Really?' Sheila pricked up her ears. 'Where are they?'

'Stone's throw from 'Olborn, Thatcher Street. It ain't Park Lane, but it's quiet and central. Mind you, I ain't seen 'em, but – No,' she shook her head, looking at Sheila's clean blouse and sleek hair and brightly made-up face. 'They wouldn't be good enough for you, I dare say.'

'Oh, I'm not looking for anywhere grand,' said Sheila quickly. 'I can't pay much, and I'd be thankful to get anywhere at all.' Her ideas about flats had come down considerably in the last weeks, after some of the hovels she had seen and even, in her despair, considered. 'D'you think they're still going?'

'I could ask for you, if you like.' Mrs Urry put her head on one side. 'There's your train coming.'

'I wish you would,' said Sheila. 'Tell me tomorrow and perhaps I could go round and see them in the evening. There'd be two of us, you know. My – husband and I. Is it a double flat?'

Mrs Urry said something, which was drowned in the roar of the incoming train. The doors sighed and slid open. 'Don't forget to ask, will you?' said Sheila, looking back as she stepped into the carriage.

Mr Urry was half-way up the platform by now. He stopped and looked back balefully. 'Come *on*, Aggie!' he called. 'I thought you was in such a hurry. Rushin' me out of bed ... keeping on at a man. ...'

'Oh, shut up, for Christ's sake.' She trotted after him, and they grumbled off together, bickering all the way to the 'Cosy'.

Sheila waited for David in the hall of the Café Royal in a fever of excitement. He was late. She kept getting up to look at the clock over the lift and then going back to sit down, tapping her fingers on her bag, crossing and recrossing her legs, glancing at the evening paper without reading it, and getting up to look at the clock again. The longer she waited, the more nervous she became about whether he would approve of what she had done, trying to visualize the rooms on the second floor of the Acropolis with his eyes, defending them to herself.

They were clean anyway, and they were miles better than some of the places she had seen. She had stayed up until one o'clock this morning working on them, rearranging the furniture, strewing them with her own belongings, disguising the more unattractive features with cushions and rugs, removing the old-fashioned photographs and ornaments and hiding them on top of the cupboard, even cleaning the windows. Would he mind about the flowered carpet? Would he notice that cistern? It was only because she was excited that it had kept her awake last night. Anyway, it was done now; she had taken them, and paid the first month's rent in advance. He would be pleased that it was so small.

The revolving door went round slowly all the time. Every time it quickened, she looked eagerly for the first sight of his good leg stepping out of it. Each time she was sure it was going to be David, but each time it was hateful people, walking confidently through to the restaurant with talk and laughter, or someone alone, glancing round for a moment and then greeting a friend, shyly or casually or with obvious pleasure. None of the people sitting in the hall with her were kept waiting for long; even that woman in the macintosh and strap shoes had a husband, who came anxiously through the door with parcels, abasing himself for being five minutes late.

Sheila sat on. Jews came, foreigners came, sailors and airmen and American soldiers came, but not David. She would wait ten more minutes and then go away. She waited a quarter of an hour, twenty minutes, she went and washed her hands again, but he was still not there when she returned. Even if he did come now there would be no tables and probably no food. She was watching a family party assemble in the hall with an unnecessary lot of kissing and laughter, still keeping half an eye on the revolving door, when David, who had come in by the side door, spoke in her ear and made her jump.

'Awfully sorry, darling,' he said. 'That's what you get for going with a journalist. Let's eat, shall we? I'm starving.'

She waited until they had got a table and had ordered, and when their drinks had come, and David, who was looking tired, had put down his glass and said: 'Ah, that's better. Now let me look at you,' she said: 'Darling, guess what.'

'What?' he said. 'I like that hat.'

'I've found somewhere for us to live.' She described it to him, making it sound cosy.

'Thatcher Street?' he said. 'Pretty low neighbourhood. It's probably buggy.'

'Oh, no, it's marvellously clean. It's nothing like the flat, of course, but, honestly, it isn't bad. There's a bathroom.' She did not mention that it was shared by the occupants of the first-floor rooms. 'There isn't a kitchen, I'm afraid, but we've got a gas ring and the man who owns the restaurant says I can use the kitchen whenever I like. Anyway, it's somewhere to be together. That's the main thing, isn't it?'

'Sure,' he said, but when he saw the rooms he was not so sure.

In the middle of the night, when she thought he was asleep, she heard him turn over and thump the pillow and turn over again and groan.

'Aren't you asleep?' she said softly, putting out a hand.

'This is a damned uncomfortable bed,' he grumbled, turning over again.

'I don't think it's so bad. I expect it's because you're tired.'

'I am tired, and it's still damned uncomfortable.' The cistern chose that moment to explode and David swore. When at last he did get to sleep some men came down Thatcher Street singing, and when he dozed off again, the Greek's daughter Ellen came home and stood talking on the pavement for a long time before letting herself in and banging the door. Sheila lay awake for what seemed hours, willing the cistern to be quiet, and when the alarm clock buzzed under her ear, it seemed she had only just gone to sleep.

David woke as she was dressing and stared about him, rubbing his eyes. 'Where am I?' he said. 'Oh, God, I remember,' and closed them again. All the furniture in the bedroom was dark and looming. Either the floor, or the legs of the wardrobe or both were uneven. It leaned forward so that its door would not stay shut. The head of the bed was carved in scrolls and hung menacingly over David's restless head. He opened his eyes again as she was doing her hair at the mirror that overswung itself unless you wedged paper into the frame.

'What'll I do about my breakfast?' he asked.

'Well you can make coffee on the gas-ring in the sitting-room. There's bread and butter and milk and things in the sideboard, and you can make toast at the gas-fire; I bought a toasting-fork. Or you can go down and have breakfast in the restaurant. Mr Petrocochino said he'd give it you if you wanted it.'

'What, that place we came through last night?'

'Yes. The cooking's very good, I believe,' said Sheila brightly.

The cistern exploded and David groaned and pulled the sheets over his head.

The following night, David had his American article to do in the early hours of the morning, which meant he stayed at the office all night. He was working all the next day and when Sheila rang him in the evening from Collis Park Station, hesitantly, because she knew he didn't like being called at the office, he told her he was not coming back to sleep at Thatcher Street.

'I'll sleep at Toddy's place,' he said. 'My room's still free. I'll get some food at the canteen here and then go straight to bed. I'm dead to the world.'

'But, David, I've got some fish. I was going to do you a lovely dinner. You could have it in bed and go straight to sleep. I'd be ever so quiet. Do come home, David.' She called it home, hopefully.

'Not tonight, honey. I must get some sleep.'

'It won't be so noisy tonight. I spoke to Mr Petrocochino about that cistern, and he said —'

'No, not tonight. Yes, what is it, Sammy?' His voice went away, talking to someone in the office and then came back to her. 'Look, I must go now. I'm fearfully busy. See you soon, h'm?'

Sheila went back to Thatcher Street, to the rooms which seemed blowsier than ever with the bed unmade, and brooded over tea and toast in the sitting-room with its tasselled tablecloth and tarnished gilt clock that didn't go. Mr Petrocochino had promised to keep her fish in his refrigerator, but when she wanted it on the following night, it had disappeared and with it, conveniently, his memory of putting it there.

'But I gave it to him,' stormed Sheila to Mrs Urry in the little scullery. 'How can he have the face to pretend I didn't? He's used it in the restaurant, I know.'

'Eaten it 'imself, more like,' said Mrs Urry, who was scraping carrots. 'You don't catch a nice bit of fish like that finding it's way into the dining-room. Dog-fish is all the customers ever see, and Gawd knows what when it's fish cakes.'

'Oh, he's hateful. When you accuse him of anything, he pretends not to understand. It was just the same over the bath-water. He's vile, he's mean –'

'Mean?' said Mrs Urry. ''E wouldn't give you the drippings from 'is nose.'

'Mrs Hurry!' called his voice from the kitchen, 'how long I am waiting for those carrots?'

''Ow long, oh Lord, 'ow long,' muttered Mrs Urry, plunging her hands in the earthy water in the sink.

'You are getting too old for your job, my woman,' he said, appearing in the doorway in a collarless shirt and pot-bellied apron. She swung round from the sink, the bunch of her apron at the back quivering.

'If anyone's getting too old for their job round here, it's you,' she retorted. 'Talk about the ruins of Greece! And don't you call me your woman.'

'Carrots, carrots, carrots!' he hissed, beckoning them imperiously with a hand that had been mixing sausage-meat.

'What's all the excitement?' asked David's voice from the kitchen, where he had strolled down to see why Sheila was being so long.

Sheila, trapped in the scullery by the Greek's bulk in the doorway, hated him to see her in the middle of this sordid scene. As soon as she could, she squirmed out and found him picking bits of crust off a loaf and talking to Ellen, who was dressed to go out in a black skirt and white satin blouse with nothing underneath.

'Come on upstairs, David,' she said. 'I'm afraid we'll have to go out to dinner as our fish seems to have disappeared into thin air.' She stood waiting his leisure, while he finished talking to Ellen, who leaned voluptuously against the dresser twiddling her dark curls with one fleshy white arm raised to display her figure.

'So your boy-friend's a newspaperman?' David was saying. 'Like me. You want to look out for those guys.'

'Oh, I *like* newspapermen,' said Ellen, travelling up and down him with half-closed eyes. Sheila snorted and went upstairs.

David always seemed to have some excuse for not sleeping at Thatcher Street. He was tired, he was working late, he had promised Toddy to go back and meet some chaps in his room. On the nights when he was not there, the cistern was mute and the street outside as quiet as a country lane, but when he was there, all the devils in hell seemed to be let loose in the plumbing, cats mated at the tops of their voices and local revellers behaved as if it were New Year's Eve. Sheila would lie awake, listening to him tossing and cursing, willing him to sleep, and dreading to hear him, when he got up in the morning, wide awake, as he had never been at the flat, say: 'Don't expect me tonight, darling. I've got a late job on. I'll sleep at home.' Home, he called Toddy's, when this was supposed to be his home. She was beginning to hate these rooms as much as he did. At the flat, she had managed to feel married, but here she felt like a prostitute, waiting night after night, going to bed without cream on her face in case he should change his mind and come back.

'What about dinner, then?' she would say.

'Better not fix anything. I may not be able to get off, and I don't want to keep you hanging around. You go out and enjoy yourself.' Enjoy yourself. Who with?

One night, when she was happy, when everything had gone right and he had come back to dinner and they had had fun, just as they used to, she came down to the kitchen at about eleven o'clock to make coffee. Ellen and her young man, who had been to the cinema, had come in with the same idea. She was standing over the stove, her behind prominent in a flowered silk dress, cut on the cross, and her young man, who was rude and untidy, was sitting at the kitchen table picking his teeth with one of his fingernails, which were never clean.

'Oh, hullo, Ellen,' said Sheila. 'I just came down to make some coffee, d'you mind?'

'Of course not, dear,' said Ellen, who, given the chance, would have been bosom friends with Sheila. 'You can have some of this if you like; I've made pints. How many's it for – the two of you? Got your husband up there?' She jerked her head towards the ceiling. David was always called Sheila's husband, although she thought they all knew that he wasn't.

'Yes, two of us,' she said, putting down her tray on the table. 'Good evening, Mr Birkett.'

He made a vague salute. 'Just call me Dan,' he said without

getting up. Ellen took a long time over the coffee, insisting on letting it brew before she would strain it. Sheila wished she would hurry; she wanted to get back to David. When she was with him up there she felt that she could make him forget how beastly these rooms were. She didn't like to leave him in them too long alone, knowing from experience what powers of depression they held. It didn't matter what you did – whether you moved the furniture about, or stood vases of flowers everywhere or stuck up magazine pictures or silly dolls – the rooms lowered at you. The black marble mantelpiece in the sitting-room was a scowling brow, the half-open, convex drawer of the sideboard a sullen underlip.

David did not like being up there alone any more than she liked leaving him. Presently she heard his whistling and his feet clattering down the stairs.

'Darling,' he called from the first-floor landing. 'What on earth are you doing down there? Get a move on.' Dan Birkett raised his head in surprise and as David limped down the last flight and appeared in the kitchen doorway, he said with his dirty sideways smile: 'He*llo*, fancy meeting you!' Sheila was watching David's face, which was taken aback and trying to register unconcern.

'Oh, do you boys know each other?' said Ellen comfortably, 'That's nice.'

'Sure,' said Dan. 'We work on the same paper. That is, if you can talk about a common reporter and a feature writer in the same breath.' He did not seem to like David. 'I didn't know you hung out here though, Fielding. I thought your wife lived up north.'

'Well, she does – I mean, she did, you see, we – Oh, hell, what business is it of yours, anyway?' David, who could so easily have explained the situation away had chosen instead to turn and tramp angrily away upstairs.

'My, my,' said Dan, and he and Ellen looked at each other.

'What about your coffee?' said Ellen as Sheila picked up her tray and started off after David.

'Oh, never mind,' she said. 'Leave it. I – I'll come down for it later.'

She found David in the sitting-room, leaning on the mantelpiece and kicking the fender with his good foot.

'Damn, damn, damn,' he said. 'This'll be all over the office by tomorrow.'

'But, darling, it's all right. He doesn't know we're not married. If only you hadn't dashed off like that – I mean, there's nothing funny about two people living over the Acropolis Dining Rooms.'

'The Acropolis Dining Rooms!' His laugh was a snort. 'I was a fool not to think of it. I knew his girl's father was a Greek who kept some low café – he was the one who used to get us those tongues and things, remember?'

'Yes, but I don't see that it matters. Even if he doesn't think we're married – and I'm sure he does – why should you mind? You've laughed at me often enough for being conventional; it seems to me you're a damn sight more conventional yourself.' She sat down at the round table and twisted the fringe of the green woollen tablecloth, wanting to cry. 'I don't mind what your beastly friends think, so why should you?'

'Oh, you fool, it's not that. I don't give a damn for that. It's just the – oh, I don't know – being caught in this awful sordid hole. It's all so shabby, and sort of degrading. I shall be laughed to death over this.'

They were not really having a row. Sheila often thought afterwards how much better it would have been if they had, but David never quarrelled; he couldn't be bothered. If they had been having a row, it would have been quite natural for Sheila to challenge him with: 'What did he mean, he thought your wife lived up north? Doesn't he know you're divorced?' But as David, once he had got over his first annoyance about Dan Birkett, didn't seem to notice that there was anything wrong between them, or that Sheila couldn't see what her fingers were doing to the tablecloth because of the mist of tears that hovered on the brink of her eyes, it sounded stupid and captious when she blurted it out. She could hear how self-conscious it was as she said it: 'What did he mean, he thought your wife lived up north? Doesn't he know you're divorced?'

'What?' He took his foot off the fender and looked at her in surprise. 'Well, I'm not actually. We're separated, but there's never been anything legal. You know that.'

She didn't know it. Although they had hardly ever spoken

about his wife, she had taken it for granted that he was divorced, but she would have died now sooner than let him see that.

'Oh, yes, of course,' she said. She had torn a tassel of the cloth and was pulling it to pieces, thread by thread, without noticing what she was doing.

'Well,' said David, 'if we're not going to have coffee, I think I'll clear out before Birky comes up to ask the happy married pair down for a nightcap. Where's my coat?'

The Thatcher Street rooms were a terrible place to cry in alone. Once started, you could never stop, and you realized, then, that that was the effect they had on you all along. They had made you want to cry, and now that they had achieved their object, they stood off, more comfortless than ever, and watched darkly the tears which had been accumulating for so long reducing you to a rag.

After that, David came less and less to the rooms. He had the additional excuse now of not wanting to meet Dan Birkett. At first Sheila went on buying food, in case he should want to have dinner there, but presently she gave it up. He did suggest it one night when he was tired and they had not much money between them, but as she had got nothing to cook for him they had to go to a restaurant just the same.

They still met frequently for dinner, but afterwards, whereas it had at least been a question of was he or wasn't he coming back with her, it was now hardly ever even that. It gradually became the accepted thing for them to part at the Tube, or at a street corner, and gradually, Sheila could not quite say when, it was not: 'See you tomorrow,' or 'Ring me at lunch-time' or even 'Keep Monday.' It began to be: 'See you sometime' or Sheila would say diffidently: 'When'll I see you?' and he would say: 'I don't know. I'm going to be pretty busy. Tell you what, I'll give you a ring.'

But it was usually she who rang him in the end. The terrible part of it was that he didn't seem to notice what was happening. He behaved quite naturally, while all the time Sheila could feel him slipping out of her hands like the crumbling earth of a cliff-edge.

They began to see each other less and less frequently. Once, when they met, she heard him being polite to her, as if he had forgotten for a moment that she was not just some woman for whom he was switching on his charm. Nothing was ever said between them. Perhaps she could have saved it even then if she could have brought things to a head, but how could she bring to a head something of which he did not even seem aware?

Presently he was going to Bristol, to take over the job of the branch editor who was on holiday. 'When I come back,' David said, 'we'll have a party. It's ages since we had a good party. We might round up some of the folks and have a real do.'

'Yes, that'd be fun,' she smiled, clamouring inside herself. 'I shan't come! I shan't come! If you're bored with me, why don't you say so, instead of sitting there looking just the same as you always did? How am I supposed to stop loving you when you go on looking just the same?'

He went to Bristol on the night train and he made her have dinner with him and see him off at the station. There was another woman seeing a soldier off, and after the train had gone, Sheila saw that the woman was crying as if she thought she would never see the soldier again. Sheila had an awful feeling that she would never see David again either, but she had not even the right to cry about it. There was nothing heroic about her tears as there was about this other woman's, who walked away, looking like a symbol of the tragedy of war.

Sheila was not a symbol of anything except an unattached girl who had missed the last train home and would have to walk.

Dinah knew about David. She had heard about him *ad nauseam* when Sheila was in the first flush of living in sin. In those days to say: 'How's the boy-friend?' never failed to unloose a torrent of tedious detail, so Dinah hardly ever said it unless she were feeling so sunny that she could stand anything. But nowadays, since Sheila had become more reticent, it was safe to ask after David.

'How's the boy-friend?'

'Oh, all right. thanks. He's gone away, as a matter of fact.'

'Has he? Where to?' Dinah thought it would be nice to take a polite interest, as Sheila looked subdued this morning and had not bothered to do her hair properly.

'Bristol.'

'Oh, Bristol. Gone off on a job, has he?' There had been no need to draw Sheila out like this in the old days.

'He's working at the branch office of his paper there.'

'Pity you couldn't have had your holiday now and gone with him,' said Dinah.

'Yes, wasn't it?' said Sheila. They were washing their hands before lunch and she scrubbed absorbedly at her nails as if it were the only thing in the world that counted.

'You probably could have, if you'd pestered old Gurley,' went on Dinah. Sheila didn't answer.

'Did you try?' persisted Dinah. She knew she was being nosey, but she wanted to find out if anything was wrong. There must be something wrong to have turned Sheila recently from a babbler into a clam.

'Oh, yes,' said Sheila. 'It wasn't any good though. Damn my hands: I don't believe I'll ever be clean again.'

'Bill's away tonight and tomorrow,' said Dinah as they were drying their hands under the hot-air blower. 'We might have some food and go to the flicks or something. We grass widows ought to get together. Perhaps I could sleep at your place if we're going to a cinema up West. I've never seen your new flat.'

'I'm afraid I can't tonight, Dinah,' said Sheila. 'I – I've got to go out with an aunt.'

'I'll come another time then. I'd love to see it.'

'Yes, you must come some day. We'd better be going back, hadn't we, or the bell will be ringing.' She had no intention of letting Dinah come to Thatcher Street. Apart from being ashamed of the rooms, she didn't want Dinah to see that there were no masculine traces – nothing of David there.

She could not give up the rooms, because she had nowhere else to go. Impossible to go back to Kathleen after having been so firm about living separately. Kathleen would take her in, of course, but she would gloat. She would have her bath ready and bring her things on trays and say: 'I *knew* you wouldn't like living on your own. You were a goose!' It was difficult enough to live with Kathleen when you were happy; unbearable now that you were miserable.

She had paid the second month's rent in advance to the Greek, so she could not afford to live anywhere else, even if she could find something. She was very hard up. Dining out so often with David had been expensive, because he was hard up too. When they lived at Kathleen's flat, she had always paid the rent; this was natural, because she had been paying for it long before she met him, but they had been going to share the rent of Thatcher Street. She supposed it was natural too that he had never paid his half for the first month. After all, he had hardly been there.

So there she was, stuck in those two hateful rooms, with the use of a bath, which, when the geyser was not out of order, was always occupied. She lived bleakly on snacks, to avoid going down to the kitchen more than necessary. She was sure everybody knew about David, because they were so inquisitive. Mr Petrocochino was always asking when the 'Beautiful Husban'' would return, and Ellen was always saying: 'My goodness, don't you get lonely up there? I should think he'd be afraid to go away for so long and leave you on the loose.' Even Victor, the French refugee who waited in the dining-rooms, would question her as she went through on her way to the stairs.

'All alone again, dearie?' he would say in his Gallic Cockney. ''E don't know 'is luck. Englishmen! I tell you –' He spat into the recess behind the counter, where he kept the bowl for washing up glasses. 'Why don't you come and eat down here tonight? I fix you something special – just for you.' His manner was increasingly familiar now that she was without David. Sometimes he would come round from behind the counter and make for her as she was walking between the tables, so that she had to run through the swing door into the kitchen.

Mrs Urry was almost the worst. She had become clingingly maternal. She would watch out for Sheila coming home and pop out from the scullery to catch her as she hurried through the kitchen, intent on getting upstairs away from them all.

'Just in time,' she would say. 'We'll 'ave a cup of tea quick before that Greek comes back. The kettle's on the boil.'

'No, thanks, Mrs Urry, really.'

'Come on, love. Just a nice cup of. Do you good, a nice cup of will. Look, I've made it now, you can't say no.'

'Oh, well.' It was simpler to do what people wanted, to stop them pestering you. Then Mrs Urry would get all chummy over the cup of tea and come and stand very close, the top of her head on a level with Sheila's shoulder.

'Come on now, out with it,' she would say. 'Something's up,

ain't it? Mum knows. Tell Mum.' She had usually just been out for a quick one or two before the evening washing-up session, and having temporarily dispelled her own troubles, was anxious to dispel everyone else's as well.

Sometimes, to get away from the place, Sheila went round to Kathleen for supper. She always came away wishing she had not gone, but it passed the evening.

After one particularly depressing evening when Kathleen had given her dried-up risotto and made her listen to a radio play in blank verse about Sir Philip Sidney, the night porter strolled out of the cubbyhole as Sheila was leaving the flats.

'Hullo, stranger,' he said. 'We don't see much of you these days, do we?' She stopped and talked to him. She had always liked him and thought him a sympathetic person to talk to.

'Remember the days I used to come up to your flat and jaw over coffee?' he said. 'Seems a long time ago. We were pals then, weren't we?'

'Well, we still are.' She didn't want him to think she had forgotten how nice he had been to her when she was alone at the flat. They had been quite intimate. She had confided in him when she first met David and he had been agreeably interested in the progress of her romance. He seemed to approve of David coming to live with her. With the day porter, Sheila had kept up a feeble pretence of being married, but with the night porter, it didn't matter. He understood, and she thought he felt benevolent towards them, having been in on the start of the affair.

'Yes, rare old times we used to have,' he mused, leaning against the wall in his familiar attitude, with his chin on the loosened knot of his tie. 'And then Love walked in and I walked out, eh? How is Love by the way? Still going strong? You might give him my regards and tell him he owes me eightpence on some empties that went astray.'

'Oh, I am sorry,' said Sheila, opening her bag. 'I'll give it you now.'

He waved it away. 'Wouldn't dream of it,' he said. 'So everything in the garden's still rosy, eh?'

'Yes –' she said from habit and then paused. She was tempted to tell him. He had always been so understanding, and the strain of having nobody to confide in was wearing her down.

He was the only person she could possibly tell. She didn't think he would laugh at her or despise her or tell her she had been a fool. Almost she told him. She was turning over in her mind possible ways to start, when he went on:

'Well – it's nice to see you – and looking so lush too.' She always dressed smartly when she came to see Kathleen.

She looked down at herself. 'D'you like this dress?'

'Mm-hm.' He let his eye travel over her. 'Yes, you look pret-ty expensive.' He was talking musingly, as if he were thinking of something else and then suddenly his eyes lost their indolent smile and seemed to get smaller and brighter. His face tightened up and his voice, which had been warm and lazy, was suddenly quite hard and brisk.

'Just as well,' he said, pushing on the wall with his shoulders and straightening up. 'Just as well you do look expensive, because of a little proposition I have for you.'

In the hot weather, dinner at Swinley was taken in the loggia. Not lunch, because in high summer the sun beat too fiercely into the glass-sided loggia that would have been more at home in Dulwich than in the heart of Worcestershire. It stood open to the garden in front; beyond the two plaster pillars supporting its roof were the sloping side lawn and rose garden. At the back it led into the drawing-room through french windows flanked by ferns in plaster pots. More ferns hung in baskets from the domed glass roof, the floor was of patterned paving and in one corner were stacked the deck-chairs and the bumble puppy set, Mrs Blake's gardening gloves and the tall basket on wheels which she pushed round the garden when she went snipping dead flowers.

Towards the end of August, the midges began to make dining in the loggia less pleasant, but as it was Mr Blake who decided where they should dine and the midges did not bite him through his suit, they dined there just the same. Although they were almost out of doors, there was no suggestion of picnic. The table was laid with the same detail as in the dining-room: mats, centre piece, three silver cruet sets, unnecessary knives, empty sweet dishes and unused wine-glasses. You had to change too, even if it were only from one light frock into another. Sheila, who had been in shorts since she arrived that afternoon, now wore a flowered silk dress smelling of moth balls which she had once thought pretty.

Dinner had as many courses as ever: soup, cauliflower cheese, meat, summer pudding and dessert. The interval between each course was even longer than usual, because the loggia was farther from the kitchen. Mrs Geek silently disapproved of dining in the loggia for this reason. In any case, she could not understand people wanting to be out of doors when they had plenty of rooms to sit in. She herself hardly left the house all the year round except to go to the dustbins or the vegetable garden. Sheila had given up offering to help her fetch the dinner or hand it round. Mrs Geek seemed to think it a slight on her efficiency, and when she had gone out, Mrs Blake would say: 'It's the wrong principle, dear. After all, we pay her to do it, and they have a very easy job here.'

There was liver and bacon on this Saturday night, with waxy mashed potatoes and not enough gravy. 'Liver, Mummy?' said Sheila as Mrs Geek handed her the silver entrée dish. 'Where on earth d'you get it? You never see any in London. How d'you manage it – Black Market?' She was only trying to make pleasant conversation, but her father said quite stiffly: 'It's natural that the shop people should treat one well when one has a certain standing in the town. I dare say everyone can't get liver. We can. A little more gravy, if you please, Mrs Geek. No more? Never mind, it doesn't matter.' Sheila saw him looking at her plate and felt that she had taken too much.

'Are you getting enough to eat, Shee?' asked her mother for the tenth time since she had come home. 'I do wish you weren't living alone. I can't think why you don't live with Kathleen.'

'She doesn't want me,' lied Sheila.

'Well, that's not what she says in her letters. She says how disappointed she is that you shouldn't be together, after the great friends you used to be down here. I had a letter from her only yesterday saying that you looked tired, which I must say you do. She writes to me quite a lot, you know. More than you do.'

Oh, yes, they were very thick. No chance of Kathleen not telling dear Auntie Lena anything that she heard about her daughter. As she scratched her legs and slapped midges on her arms all through the dawdling meal, so exactly like all the other

263

meals of her life at Swinley, Sheila realized more and more how impossible it would be to let the night porter present Kathleen with a bombshell to drop on this stagnant milieu. She had got to get the money that he wanted for keeping his mouth shut about David.

That was what she had come down for this week-end. She did not tackle her father until they were sitting over coffee in the waning light. Sheila got up to switch on the light but he looked at his watch. 'No, leave it,' he said. 'Only ten minutes to blackout.'

'But it's not dark yet and they never bother about you being dead on time, especially in the country.'

'Better to be ten minutes on the right side than ten minutes on the wrong side of a fine,' he said sententiously. 'As an A.R.P. officer, one must set a certain example. People are lax enough as it is. You might just get my pipe for me, dear, if you will, and the Swan Vestas from my jacket pocket in the hall.'

'And my pills, Shee, while you're about it,' said her mother as she went through the french windows. When she returned from the errand that she had discharged every night of her life at one time, Sheila went and sat on the steps leading into the garden, with her back against a pillar and her profile towards her father.

'Daddy,' she said. 'I wonder if you could possibly let me have a little money. I'm rather short this month. The bonus hasn't been good at the factory, and – I've got one or two bills I really ought to pay off.'

'How much do you want?' he asked, giving no indication of whether he would or would not.

'Well – about ten pounds would cover it.' The night porter's ideas of blackmail were not large, but they were more than she could meet at the moment.

'Oh, darling, I knew this would happen,' said Mrs Blake. 'This comes of your being so silly and taking a place of your own. You can't possibly afford it. You'd far better go back to Kathleen where you'll only have your board to pay.'

'Your mother's right,' said her father. 'Independence is one thing, but debts are another. This settles it. You'll go back and live with Kathleen.'

'But it's got nothing to do with living alone,' said Sheila.

'I've paid the rent. It's for clothes mostly. I had to have a coat this summer and I suppose I did spend too much. Will you let me have it? I could pay you back next month.'

'Don't be ridiculous,' he said. 'I wouldn't dream of taking money from my own daughter, I'll put you straight this time but –'

'Oh, thanks, Daddy,' she interrupted, getting up to go to him. 'I knew you would.' She went behind his chair and sliding her arms down the back on to his shoulders, kissed the narrow bald top of his head.

'But you ought to be able to manage on what you earn at your work. However, I know what girls are when they get among the shops,' he said indulgently, as if he had never heard of clothing coupons. 'My proposition is this: I'll give you five pounds – and you must go back to Kathleen.'

'Oh, but, Daddy, I need ten.' She took her hands from his shoulders and put them on the back of the chair.

'You'll soon save the other five when you haven't any rent to pay.'

'But they want the money now!' The night porter had only given her a week and already three days had gone by.

He shook his head knowingly. 'Shops are used to waiting, though as you know, it's against my principles not to pay all bills on the nail. Give them something in advance, go back to Kathleen and you'll soon be able to pay the rest.'

'But I can't go back to Kathleen,' said Sheila, getting angry. 'Dammit, I've told you she doesn't want me –'

'I do wish you wouldn't swear so much, Shee,' said her mother. 'You never used to before you went to the factory.'

'Do give me the ten pounds,' said Sheila, hating to have to plead with him. 'It'd be much better to owe it to you than the shop.'

'I've told you what I'm prepared to do,' he said with surprise that she should question his decision. 'The remedy is in your hands. Go back to Kathleen and you'll be able to get straight. Of course if you choose to go on living alone and get into debt again – as you probably will – I can't promise to help you. I think that's fair, Lena?' He looked to where his wife sat in the twilight at the other end of the table.

Mrs Blake, who was longing to give Sheila the ten pounds

and more, had to say: 'Oh, yes, I think so. She really must be sensible and go back to Kathleen.' Sheila left the chair and went to the edge of the loggia to stand looking out at the garden, still and silent in the gathering darkness.

'I shan't go back,' she said. 'Thanks for the five pounds,' she added ungraciously. She knew it was no good hoping for any more. She would have to fob the porter off with half what he wanted and collect the rest somehow.

'Well, that's settled then.' Her father laid his napkin on the table and got up. 'Let's go indoors, shall we? I can't see myself think.' His little joke indicated that he bore her no resentment.

'Coming, Shee?' asked Mrs Blake, getting up clumsily and groping under her chair for her bag. 'You'll be getting your holidays soon, won't you?' she said, glad to change the subject. 'I'm so looking forward to it. You shall have a really good rest, breakfast in bed every day if you like and plenty of lying in the garden in the sun like you used to do. We'll get the court rolled and round up some people for tennis. When exactly is your holiday?'

Sheila turned round. 'Two weeks' time,' she said. 'But don't count on me coming home. I promised ages ago to go and stay with some people. I don't see how I can get out of it.' She would not dream of coming home now.

'But, Shee!' said her mother; and her father said: 'Well, I must say, that's a bit of a disappointment. You never told us you wouldn't be coming here.' She could not see their faces across the loggia, but she knew that she had hurt them. Well, she couldn't help it. They should have given her the ten pounds. Damn, damn, damn. What was she going to do?

'Come along then, Lena,' said Mr Blake, holding open one of the french windows. His wife lingered. 'Coming, Shee?' she said uncertainly.

'I think I'll stay out here for a little,' said Sheila. She heard them go indoors, and the glass door shut behind them and heard the dry scraping of Mrs Geek's long feet on the stone floor as she came out to collect the last things on the table. She stood chewing on her fingers, while night crept towards her over the lawn. What was to stop the porter going on and on wanting money? David would have known what to do, but she could never tell him now, even if she did see him again. She had got to cope with it alone. How was it going to end? What was she going to do?

They were in the milk bar, she and Dinah, sitting up at the counter as they had been nearly nine months ago on the day when Sheila told Paddy and Dinah how she had met David in the train.

Their lunch was the same: sausage rolls, coffee and a jam tart, for the milk bar's repertoire was not inspired. The same girls from the rope factory in turbans and blue jeans were chattering over pies and chips at the corner table, the same sheepish young bloods were lounging round the automatic gramophone, whose repertoire was as unchanged since that November day as the menu.

Only Sheila was different. That day she had hardly been able to sit still on her stool. She had thrilled inside herself each time she remembered something he had said and had kept throwing smiles at herself into the mirror behind the counter, fascinated with her own bright looks and the perfect way her hair was behaving. She had hardly heard a word of what Dinah and Paddy were saying.

She still did not hear much of what Dinah was saying, but her preoccupation was with worry instead of inward glee. She sat slumped on her stool with her elbows on the counter and her cup in both hands and no longer looked up at her other self in the mirror. She had not even powdered her nose before coming out to lunch. It was no pleasure to look at yourself these days, when your hair was lank and needed a perm which you had not the energy to undertake, when you had a spot on your chin and your skin refused to hold make-up, when your eyes looked tired and the lashes were no longer curly because you could not be bothered to use the little gadget on them. The natural murkiness of her bedroom mirror at Thatcher Street was not improved by the fact that she rarely dusted it, but she hardly looked in it now that she woke so heavy and lingered in bed, dreading the thought of the day ahead, and only being forced out at last by the one unchanging thing in her perplexed existence, the necessity of being at Canning Kyles by half-past seven.

Dinah chatted idly, more from habit than anything else,

undiscouraged by Sheila's monosyllabic answers. She had known for some time that something was wrong with the little Blake bit, but she was not going to interfere before she was invited. She had something on her mind, too: what to give Bill for supper tonight. He always came home starving after his long shift at the works; it would have been the greatest thrill in the world suddenly to slap down a great plate of steak and onions and chips before him as if it were nothing unusual. Tonight she had either got to slap down macaroni cheese, which he would pretend to enjoy, or open the last tin of salmon and have nothing nice for his dinner on Sunday. She sighed and caught Lou as she darted past with a tottering stack of dirty cups.

'Give us another cup of coffee, Lou,' she said. 'How about you, Sheila?'

'What? Oh – I don't mind.'

'Might as well. We've got time. Two then, Louie, with sugar, if you can wangle it.' When the coffee came, Sheila forgot to notice whether it was sweet or not. She had been greedy once; now she simply poured things into herself from habit. She had got to go and see the porter tonight; nothing else mattered to-day but that. Again, even after a week of pinching and scraping, she had got to fob him off with half of what he asked and again he would say that he was not a charity organization and how much longer did she think this could go on? How much longer indeed? What end could there ever be to it until she abandoned the unequal struggle and allowed him to tell Kathleen? From his point of view there was no reason why he should ever stop blackmailing her, and from hers, no reason why she could ever stop paying him. Before her stretched years of poverty and humiliation, with herself moving pathetically through them, a girl who would never be happy again, a figure to bring tears to the eyes.

The youths from the electric light bulb factory had tired at last of 'The Lady in Red'. The music box was dark and mercifully silent for a moment until one of them put in a penny and pressed another button. It leapt into glaring, blaring life with a scooping wail that made Sheila look quickly across at it and then down at the counter to hide the tears that it had shocked to the front of her eyes.

It was the last straw. This was the tune that they had been

playing over and over again that day when she had told Dinah
and Paddy about David.

> My momma done told me,
> When I was in knee pants . . .

It had been identified in her mind ever since with that feeling
of apprehensive exhilaration that was the beginning of love.

> A woman's a thing, that leaves you to sing
> The bloo-ooes . . . in the night.

The merciless drone beat on her ears and brought all her
misery throbbing into her head. Not only the porter and her
present trouble, but all her memories of David – the tune ground
them out with an insistence that seemed bent on reminding her
of what she had lost.

> A woman's a *two . . . time . . . thing.*

He used to sing it. She could have got up and left, but
instead she had to sit on, while the machine plugged misery
into her.

'Anything the matter?' asked Dinah, when she could no
longer ignore the gulpings and sniffs and gropings for a handkerchief that were going on on her left. 'Tell a girl – unless
you'd rather not, of course.'

'Oh, Di –' It didn't need much now to make Sheila release
the whole story. Once started, she began to wonder why she
had never told Dinah before. She was an easy person to un-
burden your soul to. She didn't interrupt, and when she did
say anything, it was always the right thing. She understood.

The machine went on playing. Lou went on darting across in
front of them with trays of food and back again to ring up
change, the girls from the rope factory scraped back their chairs
and clattered out to the accompaniment of mechanical tooth-
sucking from the group by the gramophone, but no one paid
any attention to Sheila and Dinah, sitting engrossed at the
counter.

When Sheila got to the part about the night porter Dinah
stopped her. 'Here, half a minute,' she said, with her eyes
starting from her head. 'That's blackmail.'

'I know,' said Sheila impressively. 'I'm being blackmailed.

I don't know how much longer I can go on, Di. I can't possibly afford it.'

'Don't then. Let him tell your people. They can't kill you.'

'But I *couldn't*. You don't know what they're like. They're not like ordinary people in that way. They'd never get over it.'

'They'd cut you off with a shilling, then, so what? Seems to me they wouldn't be much loss to you.'

'But don't you see? Once, when I still had David, I wouldn't have minded so much their knowing. It would have been terrible of course, even then, but at least I'd have been sort of – sort of proud of being unpopular. But now, they'd probably end up by making me feel ashamed. There'd be all that: "Of course, he's let you down. That's what happens to girls who cheapen themselves," and I wouldn't have a leg to stand on. And I'm not ashamed either. I'd do it again. Isn't it awful, Di? I believe I'd go back to him if he wanted me.'

'You would hell as like,' said Dinah decisively. 'The man's nothing but a pimp if you ask me. You're well rid of him,' she went on, ignoring Sheila's protests. 'But this other fellow, this blackmailing swine of a porter, we've still got him to settle. My God, darling, you do get yourself mixed up with some men! I always said you had an unfortunate upbringing. But I'll fix him. Blackmail, eh? He can't get away with that.'

'But what can you do? It's sweet of you, Dinah, but I wouldn't dream of asking you to lend me any money.'

'Who said anything about money? He's not getting another cent out of you, my girl, and certainly not out of me. No, I'll think of something, don't you worry. Look, we must go back; we're hours late already. You leave it to me, I'll go into a trance over the slipper gears this afternoon and think of something. I'll tell Bill tonight; he'll know what to do. Come on, we've got to run.'

Following Dinah's bare legs across the main road and panting after her down the Estate road, Sheila felt happier than she had been for weeks with the relief of having unloaded her burden. Dinah had said she would fix it, and Dinah always did anything she promised, from getting you half a yard of tape at lunch-time to finding a man who would sell you a wireless set without swindling you. Her confidence began to infect Sheila, who was surprised to hear herself cheeking the grumbling clock-keeper as they skidded into the clockhouse ten minutes late, nearly tore the handle off the clock, and galloped out again past the Ministry of Labour's poster which everyone was always in too much of a hurry to read:

> Time to go? Well, don't *rush* out,
> It's not worth getting knocked about.
> Jams like this just cause delay,
> Shoving simply doesn't pay.

'One thing is quite certain,' said Dinah at six o'clock. 'You're not going back to those rooms tonight.' Sheila had confessed in the milk bar to the shaming gloom of Thatcher Street. 'Sooner you give them up the better, by the sound of it.'

'But I've nowhere else to go! I can't go back to Kathleen, I told you!'

'You're coming back to my place tonight at any rate. Buck up and get your coat on and stop standing there like a half-wit. I want to get home some time before midnight.'

Dinah and Bill's flat was small and hot and crowded with furniture and things that Bill had picked up cheap. He was always coming home with bargains: an electric kettle that didn't fit their voltage, a rug that didn't match the carpet, a book with twenty pages missing from the middle, a cracked casserole that leaked if you put it into the oven. Dinah accepted all these gifts with suitable enthusiasm, found a corner for them and didn't let them trouble her. Tonight he had brought home a patent fire-lighter, which she swore was just the thing.

'I'll find someone to make it work tomorrow,' she said.

'But it worked in the shop.' His nice, pug-jawed face was crestfallen.

'I know, there's not a thing wrong with it. It only wants adjusting.' Dinah forgot all about Sunday's dinner and opened the salmon for supper. Afterwards, Bill got out half a bottle of whisky and the three of them went into a conference about the night porter. Sheila didn't mind Bill knowing; he was only like another bit of Dinah. Why couldn't she and David have been like this? Seeing Dinah and Bill together made their whole relationship, even at its happiest, look like a makeshift. She had thought she was having the best, but it seemed now that she had been nowhere near it. There was a lot more to love

271

than what she had had. Perhaps she hadn't really been in love at all. If not, then she still had something to look forward to. Sitting round the table with Dinah and Bill and listening to them talk, Sheila began to take heart for the future.

At half-past nine they went out, leaving Sheila alone in the flat. She sat for a while in the arm-chair reading the paper and feeling very much at home and then got up and wandered through the three little rooms, trying to find out why it didn't matter that they were cheap and shabby. Presently, as they didn't come back, she put on one of Dinah's nightdresses and made herself up a bed on the sofa as Dinah had told her. It sagged comfortably and the arm rest was low enough not to give you a crick in the neck. It was too short to lie stretched out, so she curled up and put a chair alongside for her knees. Not for anything would she have been back in the great carved bed that humped in the middle like the back of an elephant. There was no cistern above Dinah and Bill's flat and no smell of stale stock pots and washing-up water to come up the stairs from any Greek's kitchen and seep under your door.

She woke when they came back and they sat down on top of her, giggling. Bill was so pleased with himself that he hardly knew what to do. He kept going off into shouts of reminiscent laughter and looking at his hands, punching the fist of one into the palm of the other and admiring them.

Sheila was horrified at first when she understood what they had done. She sat bolt upright, forgetting that the top of Dinah's nightdress was almost non-existent.

'But you'll be had up,' she said. 'He'll tell the police. You can be arrested for that. Oh, Bill, I wish you hadn't. I oughtn't to have told you, Dinah –'

'Don't be crazy,' said Dinah. 'He won't tell. He doesn't know who we are, and even if he did, he wouldn't tell, because he'd be giving himself away.'

'He's in no state to tell anybody anything,' said Bill, going off into another fit of laughter. 'He couldn't take it, could he, Di?'

'He couldn't take it, he couldn't take it!' She bounced joyfully on Sheila's legs. 'Oh, it was heaven, I wouldn't have missed it for anything. His face, Bill, when he realized you weren't joking. Oh, he's yellow as a pig. It was heaven.'

'But supposing he tells Kathleen?' said Sheila. 'What's to stop him telling her now that he knows I'm not going to give him any more money?'

'What's to stop him?' said Dinah and Bill together, and laughed at each other. Bill made boxing passes with his clenched fists. 'Didn't I tell you he couldn't take it?'

After they had gone to bed, Sheila lay on the sofa in the dark, getting used to the idea that she had nothing to worry about. It would be quite odd to wake in the morning and not have that heaviness coming right in on top of your dreams. The door opened and Dinah whispered: 'Are you asleep, Sheila?'

'No.' Sheila sat up and the white figure came up to the sofa.

'Look,' said Dinah, 'I couldn't go to sleep without making sure you were going to do what you promised. You'll turn in those rooms tomorrow, won't you?'

'I've told you, I've nowhere else to go.'

'And I've told you till I'm blue in the face, you're staying here till you find somewhere decent. I know my aunt'll have you as soon as she gets that Civil Servant out of her front room. Anyway, all that's settled. What I really wanted to say is: you know what you said, that you weren't going home for the holiday?'

'I'm not,' said Sheila. 'I couldn't.'

'You could and you are. If you don't, Bill's going straight back to that yellow hound and tell him it's all right for him to spill the beans to Kathleen.'

'But I –' She suddenly couldn't think of any reason why she should not go home. She remembered her mother and father standing by the french windows in the dusk of the loggia, turning their unseen, hurt faces towards her.

'Promise?'

'Well, all right. I might.'

'Good enough.' Dinah got up from the edge of the sofa. Sheila stopped her as she was half-way to the door.

'I say, Di, thanks awfully for helping me. I'm afraid I've been an awful nuisance.' Dinah brushed this off with an exclamation of disgust.

'I must have been awfully silly.'

'Think nothing of it,' said the white shape. 'It's done you a lot of good. You've grown up at last, don't you realize that?'

'Yes, I suppose I have.'

Dinah was now no more than a glimmer in the doorway. 'My God, it was about time,' she said and vanished.

CHAPTER 13

MONTHS ago, looking forward to his week's holiday in September, Edward and Connie had planned to go to his sister's at Wells. There was nothing much to do there and Connie and Edna did not get on very well, but it made a change. However, when the time came, Mr Bell could not spare Connie from the office, so Edward went alone.

He would have loved to spend the week at home among his rabbits, for there was a lot of work to be done. He had recently managed to buy a strip of 'the Ponds', the waste land at the bottom of the garden, to accommodate his growing stud and this week would have been a fine opportunity to take down the garden fence and put the wire round his new property and get some more hutches built. He had some articles to write, too. The editor of *Backyard Breeding* had not only printed the first ones written at Allan Colley's suggestion, but had actually asked for more. It seemed that Edward had struck the right note of chatty information for the amateur fancier. Although he had been contributing quite regularly to the magazine for some time, he had not yet got over the dizzy wonder of seeing his name in print. It was not his own name; he had taken a *nom de plume*, in accordance with the policy of the paper. Remembering the name which he had worn as the hero of his boyhood fancies, he called himself 'Cheviot Freemantle'.

The name leaped out at him from the printed page, as it seemed it must do to everyone within range. On Thursdays, he went about all day with *Backyard Breeding* folded back at his article, reading it ostentatiously in buses and cafés in case someone should look over his shoulder and say, 'Mm, looks interesting. Wonder who Cheviot Freemantle is.'

But neither Connie nor Edna could be expected to accept the excuse that he could not leave his rabbits. It was not even worth hazarding it, so to Wells he went. Ruth Lipmann, whose interest in the stud grew with its growing prosperity, had undertaken to look after the rabbits. When he got home, Edward was going to give her a young quality buck to repay her for her trouble.

Wells was no duller or less dull than it had ever been, but after two days he was already wondering how he was going to last out the rest of the week. His sister Edna was an animated widow who kept a small teashop in a house backing on to the Cathedral green. The rooms above, where she lived with her schoolgirl daughter, and her friend, Miss Pudney, who helped to run the shop, were as bright as herself. She was always going over them with dusters and chamois leathers whenever she had a spare minute. Edward could not remember ever having seen her sit down except to meals, and even then she was jumping up the whole time to tweak a curtain or pull a dead flower out of a vase, or to rush dishes out to soak in the sink the moment they were empty.

Edward always had indigestion when he stayed at Edna's, because almost before you had swallowed your last mouthful, she had cleared the plates and was at the table with a pad and a tin of polish. There was no chance to sit and sip a cup of tea and let your juices work in peace.

All the furniture was so highly polished that things had to stand on little mats to prevent them sliding off, and if you hurried from one room to another, the rugs shot from under your feet and landed you on the base of your spine.

Edna and Miss Pudney were busy in the kitchen and the shop most of the day; Edward's niece, Rosamund, who was studying for a scholarship was usually either at school or doing homework, so Edward was left to occupy himself.

He liked the town, but once you had revisited the Palace and the Cathedral and the Close and had marvelled at the quality of the turf on the green and had sat there for a while to savour the atmosphere of arrested tranquillity, there was not much else to do. A girls' school was evacuated now to the Palace and when you walked round the gardens, you came upon little groups of them studying in niches in the walls. Edward thought he heard some of them laughing at him after he had passed, so he didn't go into the gardens again.

He went for walks on the little hills towards Bath, but on the third day of his visit, it began to rain and went on raining. He took a bus to Weston-super-Mare and walked out to the end of the pier in a drizzle. Guns were firing far out to sea and he leant on the railing with nothing between him and America and fancied himself the Captain of a Destroyer escorting a convoy, with the wet, salt wind beating on his face.

After a time, he got tired of feeling nautical and went back along the pier to look for tea. All the teashops seemed to be shut or full. After queuing for a quarter of an hour for a seat, he shared a table with a woman whose idea of a suitable four o'clock meal was brown Windsor soup followed by prunes and custard. By the time Edward's tea and buns arrived, he had only ten minutes left to catch his bus, so he had to bolt them under the censorious gaze of the woman, who had finished her prunes and was removing bits of skin from behind her teeth with her tongue.

That night, when Edna had finished with the table, Edward got out his notebook and tackled his article on 'How to keep damp out of home-made hutches.'

Rosamund sat opposite him doing her mathematics, surrounded by text-books of which a mere glimpse made Edward's head reel. If she was like that at fourteen, what would she be like by the time she grew up? She was a nice child, though unresponsive to avuncular jocularity. However, Edward persevered with his little jokes, like calling her 'The Brains Trust' and say: 'Good morning. How are the fractions? Not too vulgar, I hope.'

Rosamund's sums seemed to be coming out. Each time she ruled the neat double lines for the answer, she would clear her throat complacently before passing with confidence to the next. Occasionally, she asked politely: 'How are you getting on, Uncle Ted?' and he would say: 'Fine, thank you,' although his article would not get on at all. It would not even get started. He was fretting for his rabbits. He kept thinking of little things which he had left out of Ruth Lipmann's long list of instructions. He kept thinking of his forty square yards of landed property, with its little mounds of rubbish among the tussocky grass. It was such a waste of time to be here when there was so much to be done. If he could have worked on it all this week, he might have got the place straight and some of the rabbits transferred before the end of the holiday. By the time he got back, the evenings would be drawing in; it would take him a long time to get it finished now. He was anxious too about that last litter of Butterfly's that he had left with symptoms of the Snuffles. If only he could be sure that Ruth was keeping them scrupulously isolated. Supposing she were mixing up the feeding bowls. It might be running through the whole stud by the time he got home.

Miss Pudney came up from the kitchen where she and Edna were baking and inquired what he was so studious about, if she might ask. When told, she went into raptures over his cleverness and Edward had to put down his pen and wait until she had finished. She was an eager woman with mild brown eyes and bobbed hair looped across her forehead and secured by a schoolgirl's slide. She had always been interested in the Press, because her uncle had been a printer on a London newspaper. He had once taken her to see the presses – 'Oh, donkey's years ago, when I was only a kiddie,' and ever since then she had been fascinated by journalism. Had Edward read the new series in one of the Sunday papers dealing with the Life after Death? She herself thought it very fine, but would be gratified to have his opinion, as an expert.

Edward shut his notebook, screwed the top on his fountain-pen and was polite to her. Presently Edna came up in her flowered cooking apron and began to plump up cushions and cover the birdcage and generally prepare the room for the night. They all had their Horlicks and a little conversation about the shortage of eggs and cooking fat, and then they went to bed and Miss Pudney played her nightly game of Peep-Bo, by which she contrived to get to the bathroom to brush her teeth without being seen by Edward in her dressing-gown.

In bed, Edward tried once more to get his article going, but it was hopeless. He had even lost track of a humorous phrase he had just coined when Miss Pudney came up from the kitchen. Rather neat, it had been – a parody of the Ministry of Health's poster: 'Coughs and sneezes spread diseases.' What was it? 'Draughts and moisture –' He had thought of a rhyme, but now he could only think of 'posture'. It couldn't be that. 'Draughts and moisture –' Now it had gone, dispelled by the ensuing conversation. The atmosphere here was not conducive to logical thought and he was too restless to concentrate, irritated by the passing of the precious days, with nothing to show for them. What should he do tomorrow? Take a walk, perhaps, if his brogues were dry, go to the cinema, look in the windows of the curio shops, have tea downstairs in the shop, with Miss Pudney in her cretonne overall waiting on him as if he were the guest of honour? Whatever he did would just be to pass the day – wicked when one's free time was so precious.

By the next morning's post came a bulletin from Ruth Lip-mann, which aggravated his homesickness but gave him an idea. He went down to the teashop where Edna, with her head tied in a scarf, was dusting the wheel-back chairs, polishing each spoke separately, and turning them up to wipe under the feet.

An important breeder was coming down from the North, Edward told her, to look at his stud. He would have to go back by the noon train. He pretended to think it a great nuisance, and he could see that Edna was annoyed. She kept giving little jerks of her head as she went on dusting, moving from table to table so that Edward had to follow her round the shop.

Almost the only thing Edna and Connie had in common was that they thought nothing of rabbits. Edna could not see how anything connected with rabbits could be important enough to take Edward away before the supper party she had planned for the last day of his visit. It was not going to be anything much, only Mr and Mrs Tyler from the hotel opposite and Mr Bede from the bank with his daughter, and cold salmon salad and one of Miss Pudney's celebrated apple flans, but it began now to assume tremendous proportions in her mind. It might have been a full-dress reception with Gunter's catering. She passed on to the dresser and began to rub up the dazzling brass candle-sticks, moving her lips, but at last Edward managed to make it all right by explaining that there was quite a lot of money involved in the deal, an excuse which Edna, who after her husband's death had had a brave and bitter struggle against poverty, understood.

She stopped polishing and turning to Edward said: 'Well all right then, if you must you must, but I shall be sorry to lose you. It's been so nice.' She was really very fond of Ted when she stopped to think about it.

278

Edward felt guilty at first in the train going home, but presently he began to plan what he was going to do in the remaining three days.

When he got home, Connie was in the living-room, entertaining, of all people, E. Dexter Bell's sister. Miss Bell was sitting upright but at ease in the most comfortable chair. She never lolled or crossed her legs or leaned against furniture or stood with her weight on one foot. If she wanted to relax, she simply maintained her alert posture and authorized her muscles and nerves to relax, without moving her limbs.

'Whatever are you doing home, Ted?' cried Connie.'I thought you weren't coming back till Sunday.' She was obviously not pleased to see him, but could not show it too bluntly, in view of the company, which affected even her accent and the pitch of her voice. Ordinarily, she would at least have raised her voice at him, and her reproachful: 'I wish you'd have let me know!' would have been: 'You might at least have let me know. But I suppose that's too much to expect. Heaven knows I'm used to your being inconsiderate.'

'I thought you knew I was coming back today,' lied Edward blithely, taking advantage of his reprieve. 'Didn't you get my letter?'

Connie shook her head. 'The posts these days are a disgrace,' said Miss Bell.

'Oh, do excuse me, Miss Bell,' said Connie, recovering herself from the shock of seeing Edward when she thought she was rid of him for another three days. 'I was so surprised to see my husband, I never – This is Miss Bell, Ted, Mr Bell's sister, you know.' Edward shook hands.

'Oh, Miss Bell and I are old friends,' he said, so pleased to be home that he almost believed it.

'Yes, indeed,' said Miss Bell. 'And how are the rabbits, Mr Ledward?'

'They're fine, thank you – at least as far as I know. I'm just going out to see how they've got on while I've been away. If you'll excuse me –' He moved towards the door. 'I'll see you again. You're staying to supper, of course?'

Miss Bell shook her head with a smile that spoke of better plans.

'Miss Bell and I are going to the concert at the Town Hall,' said Connie. 'Dorothy will get you something to eat when she comes in.'

'Oh, well, I hope you enjoy yourselves,' said Edward, and hurried out to the garden, taking off his jacket as he went through the hall. There were still a good two hours' light left.

So it was concerts now, was it? The old girl was coming on in her ideas. Fancy her chumming up with old Bell's sister! Funny taste. Himself, he wouldn't spend half an hour in the woman's company from choice. She always made him feel as if he hadn't shaved.

He stayed out in the garden long after it was too dark to see what he was doing, and coming into the kitchen, happy and hungry, caught Dorothy helping herself to Connie's jam ration and gave her the fright of her life.

On the Monday morning, Canning Kyles, which had been given over for a week to stock-taking, chugged into motion again and the machines hummed as if they had never been silent. In the Inspection Shop, nobody felt like getting down to work at first. They stood about telling each other what they had done, or sat yawning, trying to work up enough energy to get started and thinking that they had forgotten how much they disliked the place. You went on holiday and within a few hours you could hardly believe you had ever been doing anything else but what suited you. After a day or two, you could hardly even visualize the Shop, or the faces of your workmates. Then you came back, expecting it all to seem a little unfamiliar: people would look different, or be saying different things. You found that the place and everyone in it was just the same, deadeningly the same, and when you forced yourself to start work, your fingers moved of their own accord and within a very short time you could not believe that you had ever done anything but sit at a factory bench in a grey overall with the smell of oily metal in your nostrils and creeping into your hair. You had had a holiday – oh, ages ago – but it was as unreal as a dream. This was reality. By lunch-time the holiday might never have been.

Edward, standing at the top of the bench and looking round his girls, tried to imagine what their holidays had been like. He had somehow expected there to be a subtle difference in their looks or behaviour, but there they all were, perched dutifully round the bench as if they had never left it, giving no clue of what they had been up to. It had always fascinated him, the idea of them turning up here day after day, no matter what had happened the night before. Of the private lives of any of them, except Wendy, he knew scarcely anything. He only knew that from six at night until seven-thirty in the morning each was an individual, at whose activities he could only guess, but from seven-thirty until six, each turned herself into a cog, subjugating her hopes and troubles and passions to the machine that drove them while they drove it.

He often stood watching them from the end of the bench and tried to imagine what they were like at home. He fancied all sorts of things about them. He supposed he was what you would call a fanciful man – always had been, from a boy. He was very fond of his girls, even quite fond of Ivy, who disliked him undisguisedly. His responsibility for them made them somehow his. They were his collection, brought together from every possible environment to converge within the limits of his supervision. His Fancy, he sometimes called them to himself. They were his Fancy, as important to him in their way as his rabbits.

His eyes travelled round the bench. Grace, treating her valves with maternal solicitude. Kitty, next to her, back at work at last and looking, if anything, younger than before she had the baby. She was normally plump and her figure had still not yet returned to normal. The skin of her face was healthy and tight almost to bursting point. She was bursting out of her overall, too, as Edward saw when she raised her arms to hold a flame trap to the light. Len had been home on week-end leave for the last part of her holiday. He was very proud of his son and would play with him shyly for as long as Mrs Ferguson allowed. She did not believe in picking babies up too much. 'Let him lay' was a remark which sprang automatically to her lips whenever anyone approached the cot.

She had looked after the baby entirely so that Kitty and Len would be out together all day, and had taken him into her own room at night. Kitty thought it was wonderful to be able to combine being married with living at home. Since the baby's birth, she had relied more and more on her mother. She couldn't think what she would have done without her encyclopædic

281

store of infant knowledge. There was so much *to* a baby; no wonder the mothers at the factory were always asking each other how they managed. Well, they should live at home, like she did. It really worked very well and Len seemed quite happy. He had eaten enormously of her mother's cooking; Kitty on her own could never have fed him like that when he came on leave. Chips and Welsh Rarebit were her only dishes which always succeeded. She would have to learn a lot from her mother before the end of the war.

Edward saw her smile to herself as she remembered how Len had tucked into the steak pudding they had had Sunday night. His leave had really been a great success.

Len had gone back to Wiltshire and Air Force cooking wondering if he were really married. He had a son and a wife, certainly; their photographs were waiting for him above his bunk when he got back to the hut, but although they were inscribed '*Your* loving wife, Kitty', and '*Your* little son, Victor', he had an uncomfortable feeling that they were not his at all.

Next to Kitty was Sheila, a little browner, Edward thought, but you could never tell with the make-up girls used. Where had she been? He imagined her going away with her young man; she was not the sort to spend the holiday quietly at home with her parents.

Then Madeleine, wearing outside her overall the mauve cardigan that signified autumn – who knew what she had been through? Edward always wanted to say something to her, to show that he understood and sympathized. He had prepared countless little speeches, but never got them said.

Next to her, where Paddy used to sit, was Rachel, husky-voiced and full-bosomed, handling gear-wheels fastidiously for fear of breaking her scarlet nails, ready to tremble her ripe lower lip and flood her eyes with tears at the first hint of criticism. Edward allowed his mind to linger on the possibilities of her holiday. You dirty old man, he told himself, and passed across to Freda. Now what on earth did a girl like that do in her spare time? Perhaps she had helped with the harvest. He could imagine her driving a tractor in a man's shirt and breeches, like those pictures of Landgirls you saw in the papers. Freda, who had spent most of her week in lecture halls or the Tatler Cinema, or arguing with her friend who had recently taken up Federal Union, banged away at a crooked bracket, glad on the whole to be back at work.

Dinah. Ah, Dinah – you couldn't even guess what was happening to her life because she always looked happy. Perhaps she always was happy, but that did not give Edward much scope for his fancies. Reenie, next to her – would that girl never learn how to use a pair of pliers? She must have some sort of an existence; even tadpoles did, after all, but for the life of him he could not think what it was.

If he once started to think about Ivy, he could go on for ever. There was no telling what a girl like that might not get up to. He would not be surprised to hear she had committed murder one night and turned up next morning just the same. She always looked shifty; he didn't trust her a yard. The men in the factory had a name for girls like Ivy.

Wendy was back at last. She had only said 'good morning' to him so far and asked politely after his holiday, but although she had not yet mentioned her father, Edward was going to ask after him in a moment. It would not be tactless, because Wendy could not be back to work unless he were better. It was nice to have her sitting there again, sorting the rockers into a pattern on the bench and polishing up the camshaft as diligently as Edna with her brasses. Although she never brought out a comb and mirror as the other girls did, her hair always looked smooth and neat, tucked behind her clean little ears into the slide on the nape of her neck and lying all in one piece on her back, like a pony's tail. Everyone had clean overalls today, but Wendy's was always clean and crisp, even on a Saturday. He noticed for the first time today how she had altered it with buttons and tucks and pleats until it was no longer just an industrial covering but something that fitted becomingly her tiny figure. Clever little thing, he thought admiringly. It was a shame to see her small-boned hands, which were so deft at all the feminine things, getting bruised and stained by the uncongenial metal. His own fingers itched to help hers when he saw them working so conscientiously but so inexpertly. She had never really mastered her job; it was no sort of work for a girl like Wendy.

'For the Lord's sake, Ted,' said Jack Daniels, the other charge hand, coming up behind him. 'Are you deaf, or drunk or what? I've been yelling at you for the last five minutes, and Charlie's been whistling on his fingers, but all you do is stand there with your mouth open and your belly stuck out.'

'Sorry, Jack,' said Edward. 'I was thinking. About that new salvage scheme, you know. What d'you want?'

'Thinking my foot. D'you realize you've passed an engine through, a crash job, without having any of the stuff checked for distortion? The A.I.D. have just found a vane ring that's buckled like an old bicycle wheel and there's hell to pay.'

Edward clapped a hand to his forehead. 'Oh, my God, that was the one we did last thing before the holiday. I was going to have it done when we came back and it went clean out of my head.'

'You've properly boxed it this time, old man. Better go over there and think up an excuse. And look here, snap out of it, for Christ's sake. We've got enough trouble to catch up on the target without you piddling around like somebody's grandmother.'

Edward went sulkily over to where the diabolical Mr Rutherford was calling people to come and see how the vane ring oscillated when he spun it. It made him furious to fall down on the job, because secretly he thought he was rather a good charge hand.

Wendy's father was dead. She had found him already bruised and blue when she went in to wash him one morning. She had never seen a dead person and was surprised to find that she was not afraid at all. She felt sad for him, dying all alone, but not shocked. Indeed, he was far less repugnant to her than he had been when he was alive. As she had the bowl of water with her, she washed his face and hands and combed back his thick white hair, buttoned the neck of his pyjamas, turned the pillow and straightened the sheets before going down to tell her mother.

They had both cried for him gently, and neither of them in the days that followed had ever said by word or look how nice it was to be alone. It was difficult at first to realize that they were alone. His presence had dominated the house too long to desert it all at once, and Mrs Holt wandered about in a lost way, unable to indulge her own inclinations now that she at last had the chance. They were both so used to regulating their meal-times according to his stomach that they were now incapable of regulating them according to their own, so they kept to his time-table. Mrs Holt went on cooking from habit the food he had liked, and the first time they had their bacon fried instead of boiled it seemed quite disloyal.

They still talked quietly and shut doors softly and did not bang the lid of the dustbin. Once, when some boys shouted in the street, Wendy caught herself looking upward quickly, listening for the thump of the stick, with which, since his stroke had robbed him of speech, he had registered disapproval.

But although his spirit kept its eye on them for a long time, loth to leave them to their own devices, it gradually withdrew and they began imperceptibly to realize and enjoy their freedom. A great weight had been lifted from the little house. It even looked different from the outside, Wendy thought, less cowering into the earth. She cleaned the windows and whitened the step, and, hoping her mother would not mind, took down the thick lace curtains which had kept out the light and his fear of people looking in from the street. He had never allowed flowers into the house, saying that they were unhealthy, but after a time she began to bring back little bunches and arrange them in jam jars, since they had never had any vases.

'Oh, how pretty!' her mother had exclaimed, seeing pansies and wallflowers on the table, and then looked guilty for a moment before she remembered that she need not.

Wendy asked Edward where she could buy a window-box and he made her one himself and went with her to the market to buy geranium plants. One Sunday when Connie and Dorothy had taken the baby over to Schoolbred Buildings for the afternoon, Wendy and Mrs Holt went to see his rabbits. They were in ecstasies over them and Wendy displayed a real aptitude, Edward thought, for the fundamental points of breeding, which he explained as they went round. They listened to him enthralled for as long as he chose to hold forth, and it ended by Edward giving Wendy a young doe in kindle and walking home with them carrying a hutch, while Wendy cradled the doe in her arms like a mother with her first baby. They had no garden, but Edward saw the doe comfortably installed in the lean-to coal-shed before going home to Connie and Dorothy, who had seen an accident on the way home, and finding that he did not want to hear the details, hardly spoke a word to him all evening. He was only too pleased, as he wanted to start an article to which the afternoon had inspired him: 'YOUR FIRST DOE. Starting a stud from scratch.'

Wendy had never had a pet of her own. After her father's death, his little dog, Lassie, after waiting to see who was going to give her her food, had attached herself to Wendy, but she was not her pet. Wendy had never liked the pop-eyed little toy with its spindling legs and sycophantic rat's tail. She did not melt towards her with pride and adoration as she did every time she looked at her beloved doe.

It was quite different coming home these days. Even the street looked less shabby as she turned into it, hurrying to get home as she never had before. Then the house, with its green window boxes and a jar of pinks between the blue curtains in the sitting-room window, then opening the door and calling cheerfully to her mother, who had lost the power of calling out long ago, but would hurry into the hall and talk to her there instead of first drawing her into the kitchen and shutting the door; finally hurrying to the coal-shed, with her heart in her mouth in case the babies had already arrived. Edward had said that a first litter was often early. Any day now she might come come and find the hay moving, as he had described. Life was wonderful.

It stopped being wonderful when Mr Holt's sister came up from Newton Abbot to say she was going to turn them out of the house. It was her house, but they had lived in it for thirty years without an inkling of this possibility. But their lease was up at the end of this year, and now that her brother was dead, Mrs Colquhoun did not see why she should renew it for his relict and daughter, whom she had never thought good enough for him. Indeed, it was an excellent opportunity of getting her own back on them after all these years, for she had always maintained that if her brother was queer, it was they who had driven him so.

She was very business-like with them. She came in a black coat and skirt and a fox fur, drank a cup of tea and ate the last of the biscuits, and told them that they had three months in which to find somewhere else to live.

She might as well have said three years. It was not so much

finding somewhere, although that would be hard enough, but finding somewhere with a rent as small as they had always paid for this house. They had been hard up when Mr Holt was alive, but at his death his pension from his old firm had ceased. They now had only Wendy's earnings at Canning Kyles, which fluctuated according to output, and Mrs Holt's Old Age Pension. The mere expense of moving was unthinkable, and even if they found a cheap flat, there would be the furniture to store. They would never manage.

Mrs Holt began to deny herself her mid-morning cup of tea and other things which she loved, saving pennies pathetically in a red tin pillar-box on the mantelpiece. When Wendy began to suspect that she sometimes went without her lunch, she pretended that there was no need to worry. They would manage splendidly; she was on the track of a dear little house out Collis Common way, well within their means. She even emptied the tin pillar-box as a gesture and took her mother to the cinema on what was inside. She was not on the track of a house, Collis Common or any other way, but she had nearly three more months to search, so her mother could be spared for at least that long the dragging worry which now accompanied Wendy everywhere, and even clouded the joy of her doe's long-awaited litter. And if *she* went without her lunch, that was quite a different thing. She had never been a big eater.

She did not tell Edward that anything was wrong and he did not suspect anything. She was always quiet and thin, and when she became a little quieter and a little thinner, it was not very noticeable. In any case, he had a worry of his own. It was not financial: he was better off at the moment than he had ever been. Not only had a year as charge-hand brought him a rise, but his rabbits, which he now felt entitled to advertise as 'The Ledward Strain' were fetching increasingly good prices both for sale and at stud.

'Making quite a name for yourself in the Fancy, you are,' Allan Colley had remarked at a show where a vast grandson of Freda's had caused quite a sensation, and Edward had realized, to his surprise, that this might be so. His ascension in the rabbit world had been so gradual that he had not noticed when he ceased to be a novice and became proficient, when he ceased to be merely proficient and became an expert.

Although Edward did not think of himself in the same breath as Allan Colley, Cheviot Freemantle was an established feature of *Backyard Breeding*, as popular in his way as *Giganta*. People would have written to the editor if his articles had ceased to appear. They liked his practicality and the way his information, however instructive, was always flavoured with homely humour. Husbands bored their wives reading the funny bits out of Cheviot Freemantle to them after supper. The fee for the articles was not staggering, but it was a nice regular little cheque.

It was not money that was on Edward's mind, it was the Collis Park Rabbit Club. Although outwardly prospering, it was as far, even farther than ever, from being the informal, congenial fellowship of his plans. Dissatisfaction was creeping insidiously among its members. Edward was getting stilted letters, resignations were more frequent than applications for membership, people like Mr Marchmont not only cherished sick thoughts, but gave voice to them, and Edward began to notice mutterings in corners at shows and Club meetings. Mr Bell was unperturbed. He was planning to throw the Club open soon to professionals and was not concerned with the antics of the small fry. If they wanted to resign, let 'em. He was after bigger game. Dick Bennett, too, refused to see anything wrong, and at first Edward tried not to let it worry him either, but after the Grand Summer Show on Collis Common in September, he knew that he was justified in worrying.

He had reported the Show in *Backyard Breeding* as 'an all round success with old man Sol for once not failing us, and a gratifyingly high standard obtaining in both Fur and Fancy class. Spectators and exhibitors alike went home with the satisfaction of a day spent under the optimum conditions of weather and good fellowship,' forbearing to mention the all too noticeable discontent among the members at the number of prizes carried off by outside exhibitors.

Mr Marchmont had tackled Edward inside the little Secretary's tent where he sat checking the list of results after the judging was over.

'Look here, Ledward,' Mr Marchmont had said, planting himself in the entrance so that the stuffy little tent rapidly became suffocating, 'it's not good enough. That's all I have to say: it's not good enough.'

'I'm afraid I don't quite understand,' said Edward, who understood only too well. 'Is anything wrong?'

'Everything's wrong,' replied Mr Marchmont, his naturally red complexion deepening to an interesting shade of magenta round the nose. 'Everything's wrong, with this Club and everything about it. In plain English, Ledward, I don't like the way it's run. We're supposed to be an amateur organization – correct me if I'm wrong – but whenever we have a show, you let in every Tom, Dick and Harry of an outsider and professional, and what's the result? The *bona fide* members, the people who after all the Show's supposed to be *for*, are cut right out; they simply don't get a chance. Frankly, Ledward, it's not good enough.'

'Oh, yes, of course,' said Edward tactlessly, 'I wanted to tell you how sorry I was your Havana didn't get more than a third; I personally thought there was no comparison between her and the winning doe. I can't agree with the judge's decision over that.'

'I wasn't speaking about myself,' said Mr Marchmont hastily. 'I was speaking for my fellow Club members. I don't mind telling you there's a great many besides me – Mrs Ledbetter for one, and Mr Simkiss, and Miss Newberry – oh, I could name you a dozen more who are not satisfied with the way things are run. There's a certain element – mind you I'm naming no names, Ledward – I merely say that there's a certain undesirable element that's infecting the whole policy of the Club, and I thought I ought to tell you that unless something's done about it, I, for one, shall resign.' He paused to see whether Edward blanched, and added darkly: 'And I believe I shall not be alone.'

There was no need for him to name names. Edward knew only too well to whom he was referring. Everything that Mr Marchmont said had been an echo of his own thoughts, and yet all he could say was: 'Oh, come now, Mr Marchmont, we mustn't be too hasty. Aren't you perhaps exaggerating just a little? I'm sure I've never noticed any lack of confidence among the Club members. In any case, I'll look into the matter, since you've raised it, and I can promise you that if I find any cause, etc. etc . . . you can rest assured that in the future, etc. etc. . . .' He tried to mollify him, hypocritically, but Mr Marchmont refused to be mollified and with a final: 'I for one shall resign,' made as dignified a withdrawal as was possible with his figure.

What could Edward do? Nobody more than he desired to rid the Club of the 'undesirable element', but how could one get rid of an element that had wormed its way, not only into the Club but into his private life? Even if the Club could carry on without him – and could it? – who had provided the marquees today, for example? – How could he make trouble with a man who had established himself as *persona grata* in his own house, who was honorary godfather to Dorothy's baby, and who furthermore was his own wife's employer? Connie would never forgive him.

He had sounded her once, asking her casually: 'How d'you get on with Bell at the office, Connie?'

'Very well,' she said, surprised. 'Everyone does, I should think – except you. You don't like him, I know.'

'What d'you mean?' said Edward, taken aback. He thought he had disguised this. 'Of course I like him.'

'No.' Connie shook her head with a superior smile. 'Don't think I haven't noticed how funny you are in your manner to him sometimes, even if he's gentleman enough not to remark it. I don't know what he must think of you, when he's always been so friendly. I'm sure I should be ashamed to let a man see I was jealous of him being in a better position.'

'Jealous!' said Edward. 'That's ridiculous. Why should I be jealous of him in Heaven's name? I've told you already, I think he's a grand chap. I've got nothing against him personally; it's just that I don't always agree with some of his ideas in connexion with the Club.'

'Oh, you and that Club!' said Connie disgustedly. 'Your life's ruled by that silly little affair. As to his share in it, from what I hear, though I must say I'm not interested, the Club couldn't carry on without him.'

'Of course he's done an awful lot for us – too much perhaps. You see, Con, it's only meant to be a little Club for amateurs and he's trying to make it too big and take it out of the range of the people for whom it was meant. Some of his ideas are too grand.'

'Well, that's natural, I suppose, a man like him, with his own business. You could hardly expect him to think on the same level as some of the people you've got hold of: railway workers and errand boys and postmen and goodness knows what all.' Her tone included charge-hands in aircraft factories.

'What really worries me,' said Edward, suddenly deciding to lay his cards on the table, 'is that I'm not certain that he's keeping to the rules of the Club. You see, we're all supposed to make a return of our stock eligible for a share of the bran ration.' She was only half listening, but he told her of the suspicions which he had already voiced to Dick. He told her about selling half the young stock for flesh, stressing its patriotic significance, and how suspicious it was that E. Dexter Bell chose to deal with his own butcher rather than the Club's.

As she made no comment, he was emboldened to hazard the suggestion that he had been wanting to make for some time: 'Look here, Con, you've got the opportunity. You're always in and out of his house since you've got so friendly with Miss Bell. Couldn't you possibly do a bit of sleuthing for me? I could tell you some questions to ask, and perhaps you could have a discreet look round the rabbits. He's put me off every time I suggested coming up to see his stud, but you could do it without rousing any suspicion; they know you've got no interest in the Club. Be a sport, Con. If you won't do it for me, you might at least do it for the Government. What do you say?'

As soon as he had said it, he realized what a crashing *faux pas* it was. She had been pressing the baby's clothes, banging away on the ironing board without looking at him as he spoke, and now she set down the iron with a crash on its stand and faced him across the board to give him the full force of her scorn.

She was right. How could he have thought it of her? He must have been mad to suggest it.

'And I warn you, Ted,' she concluded. 'Don't you dare go trying to make trouble with Mr Bell just because you're jealous of him and want to get rid of him so that you can have more importance in your potty little Club. Not that you'd succeed – I never heard of anything more preposterous than accusing him of dishonesty – but if you go making a fool of yourself, what sort of a position d'you think that would put me in? It wouldn't be very nice for me, would it, holding the position I do in his office, while my own husband was scheming behind his back? Whatever Miss Bell would think I simply dare not imagine.'

No, there was nothing he could do. In the matter of E. Dexter Bell his hands were tied.

'What did old Marchmont want?' asked Dick, prising himself into the Secretary's tent and, once inside, filling it as if he were wearing it. 'He went stumping past me muttering like an old bear.'

Edward told him.

'Silly ass,' said Dick. 'He's jealous because he didn't win a prize.'

'Oh, I dare say,' said Edward wearily.

'By the way, Ted, I'm glad you've given up that nonsense you told me once about Edgar fiddling the bran ration and so on. I must say it wasn't like you. You must have been tired or something – needing the holiday.'

'I expect so.' But Edward had not given it up. He was more suspicious than ever and nothing that Dick or Connie or anyone could say could convince him that he was wrong. But what could he do? He had just got to go on treating the man as a friend of the family, while all the time his precious Club was crumbling to atoms before his very eyes.

This was later in the evening, this lugubrious thought, after his third whisky at the Saturday supper dance at the Four in Hand, where Mr Bell was giving a small party to celebrate the Show.

Mr Bell, sweating from a jolly romp in the Palais Glide, brought Connie back to the table. She was flushed and pretending to be all of an unusual dither. He was a terror. He had nearly dragged her off her feet. She declared she was quite winded.

Silly, thought Edward sourly, how could anyone be winded by the Palais Glide?

'Lordy, Lordy,' panted Mr Bell, downing somebody else's glass of whisky, 'that certainly was *hot*. You shouldn't have missed that, Ted. Even old Richard took the floor like a good 'un. Look at him!' Dick came through the crowd with glazed eyes and heaving chest. 'How did you fare, Richard?'

'We had a wonderful romp,' said Miss Bell, answering for him, as he was speechless. Not a hair of her head was disturbed. She had gone through the dance as if it were a minuet, pointing her toe like a dancing mistress when you were supposed to swing one leg in front and bending one knee slightly when it came to kicking out behind.

Mr Bell was in great form. 'She's my lady love –' he kept singing. 'What's the matter with you, Ted, boy? Young chap like you should be out on the floor, and you've hardly danced once all evening. What's the matter with you tonight?'

'Yes, you are a regular sobersides, Mr Ledward,' said Miss Bell, sipping tonic water, with little finger arched.

'What you want's another drink. We all do,' said Mr Bell, clapping his hands. 'Boy! Chota Peg, quickee, quickee.' Many men in that crowd could not get served, but Mr Bell could always get a waiter, even when he called for them like that.

After teasing Edward for a while, they forgot about him, and he sat on, drinking as much whisky as he could get – he never got a chance to stand drinks because he could never get served – and brooding on the Irony of Life.

'Troubles,' said Edward to Wendy in the morning break a week later, 'never come singly.'

'What do you mean?' She lifted her head from her mug of tea. 'You're not in any trouble except this silly business here?' For life at the factory had chosen to go wrong too.

'Oh, no, it's nothing really,' said Edward. 'I was only thinking aloud.'

'Do tell me – unless you'd rather not.'

'No, I want to get this business straightened out first. Time enough then to worry about other things.'

This business had started with the quarterly interview with which Mr Gurley sought to keep up the standard of aero-inspection. One by one he summoned the girls to his office, conducted a post-mortem on their black marks and told them what he thought of their work, and one by one they came out looking tearful, encouraged or defiant, according to what he had told them. He did not just curse them impartially as Jack Daniels did, or appeal to their sense of honour, like Bob Condor. Mr Gurley fancied himself as something of a psychologist and used this opportunity to warn the careless, to bolster up the timid and to take the over-confident down several pegs. Madeleine, for instance, whose space in the black-mark book was always virgin, was told what a grand war effort she was making.

'I wish they were all like you,' said Mr Gurley this time. 'Then we should see results in this section. Still, I suppose we must be thankful for one bright spot; I don't know what we should do without you, Mrs Tennant, I really don't.'

Madeleine fiddled with the belt of her overall. 'You're very kind, Mr Gurley,' she said, 'but I'm afraid I don't do more than do my work as best I can –'

'Ah, that's the point,' he gave her his quick, lively, smile. 'You do your best, but that's more than you can say for all of 'em. Some of these girls' ideas of a day's work is to clock in on time and spend the rest of the day looking decorative.'

'You mustn't be too hard on them,' said Madeleine earnestly. 'After all, most of them are quite unused to factory life. I always feel that it's a little bit easier for me because of what I went through in the last war. I'm an old factory hand, you know, Mr Gurley.'

'Oh, yes, of course, you were in munitions, weren't you?'

'Shell-filling,' said Madeleine, 'at Coventry.' As soon as was politely possible, he cut short the recital of the *camaraderie* and the community singing and the brown overalls. He had all the other girls to see yet.

'Well, I won't keep you from the bench any longer,' he said, getting up from behind his desk. 'I've got no list of crimes to go into with you.' He flipped the black mark book with the back of his hand.

'Oh, but,' said Madeleine masochistically, 'what about that dreadful slip I made on the scavenge pump casing? Surely I got a mark for that?'

'Don't be absurd,' he said, steering her gently but firmly towards the door. 'Nowhere near one. This factory isn't quite inhuman, you know.' He opened the door. 'Right you are then. Send me Miss Dale, would you?'

Reenie had a lot of black marks, but as she did not understand what half of them were for, it was not much use cursing her. One simply had to explain patiently the more elementary points which one had been explaining regularly every three months and hope that she was absorbing something through the open mouth if not through the ears.

He began the interview in his chair, but was soon up and round his desk, walking about as if he could instil some of his own abundant vitality into her. She stood on one spot with her hands hanging uselessly, following his pacing figure with slow eyes without moving her body. The questions with which he tried to poke her intellect bounced off her like bullets off armour plating. However, she seemed a little better this time. She had actually mastered at last the right type of levers to fit with Rotax Magnetos, and he was encouraged to say: 'Let's see, you've been here – a year, isn't it? You should be getting top rate by now, but I can't give it until you learn one of the skilled jobs on the bench. How would you feel about learning the wheelcase, say? We could do with another girl on that.'

'I don't mind,' said Reenie.

'You should be able to manage it. You must have picked up something after all this time by watching the other girls, haven't you?'

Reenie shook her head.

'Well, have a shot at it, at any rate. Your charge-hand'll help you.' Poor old Ledward, it was rather a shame to land him with this, but if he didn't at least give the girl a chance to earn her top rate, he would have the women's Shop Steward on to him again, and he really couldn't be doing with that red-haired Higginson harpy coming in here and blowing off at him as if he were Colonel Blimp and Simon Legree rolled into one.

When he had got rid of Reenie he had a short, man-to-man session with Freda, who admitted to her few mistakes and was damn sorry about them.

'Makes me feel a worm,' she said. 'The least one can do is keep one's end up here, if one can't be shouldering a gun.'

'That's the spirit,' said Mr Gurley. 'You want to feel that every crack you find in that supercharger is a bullet in the body of a Nazi.' He knew this had more effect on Freda than calling them merely Germans. 'Send me in Miss Blake, would you?' he said as she squared her shoulders and went out.

He had had to change his policy towards Sheila recently. She used to be one of the ones who had to be taken down a peg, countering each reminder of a black mark with stubborn hauteur.

'The reduction gear's a tricky job, you know,' he used to say. 'You can't take chances with it,' and she would smile and pretend to be indifferent to his recital of her black marks, implying that she was too good for the reduction gear and the whole place and everyone in it, including himself. He would have to tell her pithily what a little fool she was, gauging results, if she were wearing her hair on top of her head, by the flush on the back of her neck that betrayed her brazen expression. The interview had always ended by her banging the door as she flounced out.

But today she did not bang the door. Today he had no need to go behind her to see how he was doing. He had no need at all to take her down a peg, because she seemed recently to have taken herself down several pegs of her own accord.

He talked to her as if she were grown up, which she seemed to be at last. She had been making a lot of careless mistakes about two months ago, but when he mentioned them she was not up in arms as she once would have been. She actually blushed all over her face instead of only on her neck, and said that she was sorry; she would try to be more careful.

They had quite a pleasant talk about all sorts of things except work. She reminded him very much of his own daughter, who had only just emerged from the stage of thinking her whole family impossible and rushing away from meals to lock herself in her room, and was now a delightful companion, unscarred by the farouche period which had once been his despair. He realized now that all girls had to go through it. He wished he had another daughter; he would have known better how to treat her.

Wendy entered the office stiff with fright and left it scarcely less stiff in spite of his efforts. The little mouse seemed to have something on her mind, but it was more than he could do to make her disclose it. He had a dull session with Grace, during which he sat in his chair and fiddled with a pencil, a fatherly one with Kitty, and a lively one with Dinah, who treated him as an equal and made him laugh. It was not worth while lecturing Dinah about black marks. Any that she did make you felt she was entitled to. Dinah was a law unto herself.

He asked her to send in Rachel. 'Better leave the door open,' said Dinah, 'and call me if you want any help. That girl would rape the recording Angel to get herself off a few days' hell.'

He had no sooner begun: 'That was a pretty good brick you dropped, over the upper vertical shaft,' than Rachel's willing

296

eyes brimmed over and she took a step forward as if she would have cried on his very waistcoat. He kept the desk between them.

'Don't start that yet,' he said tersely. 'I want to talk to you about that overheated spring drive, too. You'd better save a few tears for that.'

'Oh, Mr Gurley,' faltered her luscious, trembling lips, 'you are unkind. I don't know why you should go on at me like this, when I don't make any more mistakes than anyone else. How can you be so unfair?' She rested her inappropriately clean hands on the edge of the desk and leaned towards him so that he should get the benefit of her perfume.

'Don't be silly,' he said. 'If you make mistakes, you've got to be pulled up for them, same as everyone else. You can't get away with murder, you know, just because you're rather attractive.' Damn, damn, damn. He wouldn't have said that if she hadn't been so overpoweringly close. He got up from his chair hastily as her face brightened to a melting smile, and walking towards the bookcase, took out a technical book at random and pretended to look through it while he talked with his back towards her. She had come up behind him. He could feel her radiating sex like a gas-stove radiating heat.

'The three stage variable data boost control,' he read, while she was saying softly: 'What is it about me that you don't like? I can't help feeling miserable when you're so mean to me and I do try so hard.'

'What I don't like about you,' he said, shutting the book with a snap and turning to see her face poised ready to weep or seduce according to what he was going to say. 'What I don't like about you is your damn fool mistakes, that's all. I'm not interested in you as a person, I'm only interested in your work, and I'm telling you here and now, it stinks.'

For the rest of the afternoon Rachel sat at the bench with tears streaming down her face on to the gearwheels, but the only person who paid any attention was Edward, who said: 'If you go on like that, we'll have to send those gears for anti-salt water corrosion treatment.'

Mr Gurley had left Ivy until the last, putting off what he knew was going to be an unpleasant interview. She stood before his desk, not meeting his eye when he spoke, trying to read upside-down what was written against her name in the book on his desk.

He was convinced that her mistakes were the result of neither carelessness nor stupidity. She made them deliberately, it seemed, to get her own back on the unspecified 'they' who embittered her life. Mr Gurley was tired of Ivy and her mistakes. He had tried threats, reasoning, ridicule and once even sympathy, but she had accepted them all with her sideways look as if she had just poisoned your tea, and continued to make the mistakes. The A.I.D. was tired of Ivy, too. They had told Mr Gurley he had got to either pull her up or get rid of her, so he said, without even bothering to discuss her black marks: Ivy, I'm taking you off the sump and putting you back on valves. You can do the valves for both the benches and Winnie and Grace can get on and learn another job.'

'But Mr Gurley,' said Ivy in a voice that began shrill and grew strident. 'You can't do that to me. I was promoted from valves months ago. You can't put me back on a job that gets less money.'

'Can't I?' said Mr Gurley with pleasure. 'That's where you're wrong. I don't know what'll happen about your money; that's not important. What is important is that you do those valves properly. Even you ought to be able to, but if I catch you out on them ' – he jerked his thumb towards the door – 'out on your ear.'

'You can't do this to me,' began Ivy, through lips drawn back to a thin line, but he picked up the telephone and dialled a number, any number. 'Hullo?' he said to the dialling tone. 'That you, Mr Levy? Gurley here. All right, Ivy, that's all.' He waved a hand at her. 'Look, Mr Levy, what I was going to say –'

'Look 'ere, Mr Gurley,' Ivy was saying, 'I don't know who you think I am, but I'd like you to know –'

'It's about those new type coolant pumps,' he went on, pressing the receiver to his ear so that she could not hear the dialling tone. 'We're still getting them through without couplings, you know. What's that? Yes ... yes, I understand, but the point is ...' He talked on without looking up until he heard the vicious slam of the door. Then he hung up the receiver, blew out his cheeks, looked at his watch, and wished

298

that someone would walk in through the door with a tall, bottomless drink in which ice clinked.

It was a disgrace to go back on valves. Everyone knew that. You started on valves when you first came, and soon discovered that once you had mastered the simple technique, it was the easiest and most monotonous job on the bench. You simply tried each valve in the gauge and then turned it round and round under a strong light and a magnifying glass. If it was cracked or damaged, you put it on your left – Unserviceable; if it was pitted where the rocker struck it, you put it on your right – Redundant; if it was neither, you put it back in the box – Serviceable. That was all. Any novice could do valves after a day's tuition, and the most enthusiastic novice would tire of them in a week. Grace had been unlucky; she had been on valves for several months because everyone else refused to do them, but she didn't really mind. It was a nice safe job and it gave her plenty of opportunity to plan her evening chores and how she was going to lay out her points.

When she came out of Mr Gurley's office, Ivy returned to her stool without a word and went on inspecting an oil filter as if nothing had happened. But somebody heard Bob Condor talking to Edward, and the news spread like wildfire round the bench: 'Ivy's been put back on valves!' She pretended not to notice them looking at her and whispering. The girls on the other bench were staring, too, enjoying the smug little thrill of it not having happened to them. Hardly anyone liked Ivy, and what little sympathy was offered, she rebuffed.

'Oh, please don't be sorry for *me*,' she said, shaking Madeleine's hand from her arm. 'I'm sure I don't mind. It'll make quite a change.'

'Poor Ivy, she's taking it very well,' Madeleine said to Dinah, but Dinah and everyone else knew how Ivy felt. Sour at the best of times, she must be fermenting now.

On the following morning she moved her stool round to Grace's corner and started work at once. Grace excitedly joined Dinah on the other side of the bench and approached with awe the subject of slipper gears. Ivy hardly spoke a word all day. When she had finished one set of valves, she took her bulb out of the light, picked up the gauge and her stool and tool box and crossed to the other girls' bench, where she went through their valves in equal silence. When she had finished, she looked round to see whether her own team had started a new engine, and rejoined them aloofly as if they were strangers.

At tea-time she did not get out her magazine as usual and read avidly until the last possible moment. She simply sat puckering her lips to the hot tea, eating nothing, staring into space with eyes that were narrowed to slits of malice.

By the afternoon, having two people's work to do, she was beginning to fall behind, but when some foolhardy person offered to help her, she snapped their head off and went on turning the detested, winking valves round and round under the light, turning her bitterness round and round in her heart.

At half-past five Bob Condor padded up to her. His shoes never had to be re-heeled, because he always walked on the ball of his foot.

'How are you getting on, Mrs Shaunders?'

'All right,' she said without looking up.

He picked up a valve and peered at it suspiciously. 'No mishtakes, I hope. Valves are one of the most important parts of the engine, valves are. You can't afford to let anything through.' Ivy took the valve out of his hand without answering and put it into the gauge. 'I'm afraid I'll have to ask you to stay on and do a little overtime tonight,' he went on. 'There's a stack of valves that were held up last week just come through from the Dishmantling. The engines are being held up for them, so I want to rush them through. There shouldn't be more than a couple of hours' work at the mosht. I'll see the Timekeeper about your overtime money.'

Ivy looked at him as if he smelled. 'I can't stop on,' she said. 'I've made arrangements to go out.'

'I'm afraid I must insist that you do. It's an order, Mrs Shaunders, not a request. I'm sorry to upset your plans, but in wartime work comes before pleasure, you know.'

She gave him another look, and he said: 'You can telephone from my office if you want to let anyone know. That'll be quite all right.'

'You can't make me do overtime,' said Ivy defiantly. 'I'm entitled to go at six o'clock, that's my rights. I'll tell my Shop Steward about this. The Union won't stand for it.'

'You're wrong there,' said Bob. 'The Union is more interested in advancing progresh than hampering it as you seem to think. I've been into the whole question of overtime with them, and I'm glad to say that I have their whole-hearted shupport in any demands I think necessary. And this is necessary.' Necessary was an unwise sibilant for him, but he liked using it.

Edward strolled up with the genial air of a man who sees knocking-off time in sight.

'Anything the matter, Bob?' he asked. 'Don't tell me this girl's made a bloomer. She's been working like a saint all day.'

'Glad to hear it,' said Bob. 'Hope she goes on as she's started. No, the fact is, Ted, I was just telling her she's got to stop on for a while to-night and get those outstanding valves cleared up.'

'Yes, I suppose she'll have to. That all right with you, Ivy?' asked Edward.

'Oh, don't consult me,' she said huffily, shrugging her thin shoulders. '*I've* got no say. It seems it's all the same whether it upsets a person's arrangements or not. I thought I was working in a factory, not a Concentration Camp.' She turned her back on them and began to put valves one after the other into her gauge with angry speed. Bob and Edward looked at each other. Bob looked concerned. It was not correct for people to be rude to him, but Edward smiled tolerantly. 'Difficult girl,' he mouthed.

Bob nodded. 'I'll get the cards ready. She can let me have them tomorrow morning.'

'Bad luck, Ivy,' said Edward to Ivy's hunched back when Bob had gone. 'I know it's annoying when you've counted on getting away. Still, you'll have the satisfaction of knowing you're helping the jolly old war effort. It's an important job, you know.' Fortunately he could not tell from her back what she was thinking about him.

'I tell you what,' he said, enjoying the unselfish impulse that came over him. 'I'll stay on with you and help you out if you like. Two of us ought to be able to get them packed up in no time. What do you say?'

'You can if you like,' she said ungraciously. 'Please yourself. I'm sure I don't trouble one way or the other.'

There was no nightshift in the Inspection Department. It was quite an eerie feeling to be sitting in an island of light at the end bench, while behind you the Shop stretched away into darkness, unfamiliar in the silence that had followed on the mad trampling exodus at six o'clock. Except for the click of the valves as Ivy and he dropped them into the gauges there was only the faint hum from behind the distant doors of the Fitting Shop, and the occasional hiss and gurgle of a relaxing water pipe. Here and there bits of metal unaccountably ticked, like furniture creaking in a slumbering house.

At first, Edward tried to make conversation to Ivy. They might as well have a chat if they were going to be shut up here together for an hour or so, but she was more than unresponsive, she was actively discouraging. He soon gave up the attempt, and worked away in a silence as unbroken as hers, examining each valve with deadly care. He was not going to let anything get by him; it would look too bad – he a charge-hand, slipping up on work that he supervised all day.

Occasionally he looked along the bench at Ivy, isolated from him by the dark space in between their two circles of light, and removed in spirit so much farther than those few yards. It reminded him of those jokes about people being stranded on a desert island for months without introducing themselves.

'How are you getting on?' he asked, his voice breaking the long silence startlingly. They had been working for nearly an hour.

'I've nearly finished,' she said. 'I'm going in a minute.'

'You're nearly – Good God, you've been quick! I've got half a dozen more boxes to do.' They had divided the work up equally between them. 'Hope you've inspected them properly,' he said.

'Of course I have. I don't intend to spend all night here though, even if you do. I've got better things to do.'

Ten minutes later, she slammed the last box on to the pile at her end of the bench and stood up.

'Well, that's that, thank God,' she said. 'I'm off.'

'Don't worry about me,' he said unnecessarily. 'I'll just carry on and get these finished. I don't know how you managed to do yours so quickly. Slow but sure, that's me.' Ivy put on her hat and coat and switched off her lamp, leaving him alone in his little island of light. He heard her feeling her way to the door.

'Well, good night,' she called from the darkness. 'I suppose you'll be here till morning,' and she was gone without a word of thanks, to salvage the remains of her evening's entertainment.

He heard the little door within the double doors click open, saw with surprise that it was only twilight outside the blacked-out Shop, and then he was alone with the long lines of engines crouching behind him. He had to look over his shoulder from time to time because of an absurd fancy that they were creeping up on him.

Knowing that Ivy was furious at being made to work overtime, he had quite expected her to stay out or at least come in late the next morning by way of protest. But when he arrived himself at twenty-past seven, she was already sitting at the bench in her overall, reading as if she had been there for some time.

It was not until that afternoon that the trouble started. Edward was in conference with Freda over a cracked supercharger casing when Bob Condor came up to him, with a fitter from the cylinder section in tow, who clutched a number of valves in his hand like a bunch of metallic flowers.

'Hullo, Bob,' said Edward. 'I want a word with you. We've got a rear half-casing here. It's a moot point whether it's salvageable.'

'And I want a word with you,' said Bob, unusually brusque. 'The blower can wait.' He took Edward over to an empty bench and motioned to the fitter, who laid the valves down with a righteous air.

'What's the trouble?' asked Edward. 'One of my girls been making a fool of herself?' He picked up one of the valves. 'Whee-ee-ew! Is this supposed to be serviceable? Blast that Grace. She's been long enough on the job to know better than to let a thing like that through.'

'No,' said Bob, 'it's not Grace.'

'But Ivy's only been on them since yesterday. Hers wouldn't be through to the next Shop yet. Unless they're what she did last night – they went straight through, didn't they?'

'No,' said Bob, monotonously, 'it's not Ivy.'

'Then why come to me? Jack Daniels is your man.'

'I only wish it were one of the girls,' said Bob, and sighed.

'What are you getting at?' asked Edward cheerfully. 'Why all the mystery?'

For answer Bob held out his hand. One of the Canning Kyles labels lay in the palm and Edward leaned forward and read out: 'Passed O.K. E.L.P. Led – but this is a label I put on Serviceable stuff last night! You surely don't think –'

Bob shook his head. 'I don't know what to think. All I know is that these valves came out of a box with this label on it.'

'There must be some mistake. Joking apart, old man, I'd never let a thing like that through in a million years. I mean, look at it!' He shook the offending valve under Bob's nose. 'Look at it – cracked to blazes, let alone burned on the seating.'

'Yes, and the whole box is almost as bad,' put in the fitter, who was a little man with a crooked white moustache and a jumping face. 'And there's another box as well – two or three of 'em in fact. Inspection! Whoever inspected these didn't know B from a bull's foot, or else they just signed 'em off without giving 'em so much as a glance. Inspection? It's a scandal, that's what it is.'

'That Ivy,' said Edward. 'I'll murder her for this. No wonder she polished them off so quickly.'

'But I've already told you,' said Bob with sad patience, 'they're not Ivy's work. God knows, I only wish they were, but hers are O.K. and all the dud boxes have got your signature on. I simply can't understand it, Ted! I can't understand how you came to –'

'But it's crazy!' Edward was horrified. 'I'd swear on oath I never let stuff like that go through. I was over-careful, if anything. Look here,' he appealed to the fitter. 'There must be some mistake. You've got the labels mixed up or something.' The old man looked jittery enough for anything.

But he shook his veined head. 'The labels are on the boxes just as they came to us. That I do know! You can come into the next Shop and see for yourself if you doubt me. Personally, I don't care 'oo inspected 'em; what I want to know is how I'm expected to set up blocks with stuff like this.' He gathered up the valves and tossed them back on to the bench with a contemptuous jingle.

'That's all right, Carter,' said Bob. 'I'll see you get two or three sherviceable sets through straightaway. You go on back to your section. Thanks for bringing these through.'

When they had got rid of the old man, Bob stood scratching the bald tonsure on the back of his head and looking at Edward as though he were at a loss. This was an eventuality for which he did not know the correct procedure. Edward, equally at a loss, picked up a valve and looked at it from every angle as if he could not believe his eyes.

'I'd have staked my oath,' he said. 'I simply can't understand it.'

'More can I,' said Bob. 'I suppose you rushed the job because you wanted to get off, but if that was the case, why did you offer to stop on and help? It would have been better to have left the things alone than to mess it up like this.'

'I didn't rush,' said Edward. 'I'm sure there's been some muddle. I'm going to get this thing straightened out.'

'They'll all have to be re-inspected, Ted,' said Bob, without listening to him, 'and it's going to look so bad.'

For the rest of that day, Edward argued until words no longer had any meaning, with Bob, with Jack Daniels, with the A.I.D., and with Mr Gurley, on whose desk the valves were displayed like exhibits in Court. 'I'm going to get this thing straightened out if it's the last thing I do,' he declared a dozen times during the next few days. He cross-questioned every labourer, every fitter on the cylinder block section, anyone who could have had contact with those cursed valves. But all his investigations led to the same result. The boxes had reached the old fitter exactly as they had been taken from the floor by the end bench where he had stacked them before he went home on that unfortunate night.

Not only Edward but everyone was anxious for him to find an explanation. They could not believe it of him, but when days passed and still no explanation was found, they had no alternative but to believe it, until in the end he began to believe it of himself. Doubt crept into his mind, as he tried to visualize the valves that had passed before his eyes that night. There had been plenty of dud ones, but surely he had slung them all out. Or had he? Could he have missed them when he was bored and tired and his thoughts were wandering? Perhaps he had had a temporary blackout, like people in the papers who found themselves in the Police Court.

Of course the story got round. Edward was teased about it in a friendly enough way, but he knew that people were asking each other the same question that he was asking himself: What would happen to him?

Nothing happened to him. Long before Edward wearied of his fruitless efforts to find an explanation, the Management dropped the subject as if they had more important things to worry about. But Edward went on worrying. He almost wished something had happened to him. It would have been better to have been sent back to the Fitting Shop in disgrace than to remain a charge-hand, but a charge-hand under a cloud. After all these months, the position that he had worked up for himself in the Inspection Shop was struck from under him. He was no longer the man who had all the salvage schemes at his fingertips, the man who could give you a snap decision about a worn bush as soon as look at you. Even the girls, even his girls whose resentment he had conquered, and whose confidence he had gradually won since those first difficult weeks must have lost faith in him. If their attitude to him remained unchanged, it was only because they were sorry for him. Poor old Ted, they were thinking. Poor sap. He was a mockery of a charge-hand. How could he presume to set himself up to give decisions and correct mistakes if he himself had made a mistake that even Reenie could hardly have committed?

He was left out of all the absorbing little conferences with the A.I.D., when blueprints and schedules were spread on tables and pipes lit and strong men argued for hours over ten-thousandths of an inch on a nut no bigger than a pea. He saw them at it sometimes through the glass window of Mr Gurley's office. Once he would have gone in, and even carried some weight perhaps with his opinion, but now he did not like to intrude. He would always feel an outsider unless he could clear himself and as the days passed, his hopes of clearing himself dwindled and grew faint.

CHAPTER 14

WELL might Edward remark to Wendy that troubles never came singly. He lived on a see-saw of trouble. During the day, the Canning Kyles business took precedence, but in the evenings and at week-ends the worry of the Rabbit Club came uppermost in his mind. Mr Bell was going full steam ahead with his new idea. He had circularized professional studs soliciting membership; he was arranging an auction sale for fanciers, ostensibly in aid of the Red Cross, but more, as far as Edward could see, as a sound commercial enterprise. Edward had put it to him tentatively that many of the Club members besides himself were not in favour of the sale. Mr Marchmont had written twice to say it smelled fishy and Mrs Ledbetter, whom Edward had met outside the Co-operative Stores in the High Street, had said that she could not bring herself to fancy the idea. But Mr Bell laughed at Edward and went ahead, saying it would be a good thing when the Club was purged of some of these dead heads and got in a few sound men who knew what was what. Edward began to feel that he was as much a mockery of a secretary as of a charge-hand.

It was with a heavy heart that he pulled the curtains against a drizzling October evening and sat down to write his article for *Backyard Breeding*. Since everything else was going wrong, he was expecting any day to hear that the editor no longer required weekly articles from him, or even any articles at all. Meanwhile, although he was in no mood for it, 'The Dread Hand of Coccidiosis' had to be ready for the post tomorrow.

He wrote his articles in a school exercise book, typing them out in the lunch-hour next day on the Estimating section's typewriter. He sat down at the table, piling beside him the textbooks from which he cribbed when necessary, opened the exercise book at a clean page and hoped that inspiration would come with writing. But his fountain-pen would hardly write the title. Edward shook it without result, and when he lifted the lever gingerly, the nib only bubbled at him. Tipping back his chair, he reached behind him to open the sideboard cupboard without getting up, but the ink was not in its usual corner with

307

the laundry book. He got up and looked on the mantelpiece, on the bookshelf and on the little table in the window where Connie sometimes wrote long dull letters to her friend who was married to a clergyman in the Isle of Wight. He went into the kitchen, looked on the dresser, under the dresser, in the cupboard, on the window-sill, lifted the lids of saucepans and vegetable dishes, bent to look under the sink where the pail and floor-cloths were kept and knocked his head on the draining board as he straightened up. He was no more successful in the bedroom. Annoyed, he even looked in Connie's dressing-table drawer, which was strictly forbidden, and banged it shut, disgusted by the mess in which she kept it. Lidless boxes of powder, grubby puffs, a hairpin sticking to a pot of Vaseline, bits of cotton wool, a hair-tidy full of old hair, a hair-net entangled in a scurfy brush, a suspender and a pair of dress preservers. Once, long ago when he had been courting Connie, he had thought her the delicate mystery that he thought all women. That was before he shared a bedroom with her.

He looked in the spare room, shrouded once more now that Dorothy and little Donny had gone back to the Buildings; he even looked in the bathroom cupboard where his own and Connie's toothbrush shared a beaker in somehow indecent intimacy. The beaker was scummed with dried toothpaste and he rinsed it under the tap and also cleaned out the basin before going downstairs. Connie had never taken a pride in her house, but she was more cursory than ever now that she had the excuse of being busy all day. Other women managed, he knew; he had heard them at the factory talking about their evening's housework and how they were going to turn out the bedroom on Sunday, but when Connie was not with Miss Bell, she usually spent her evenings reading a book from the library which she had recently joined. He had long ago given up asking her why she never read anything except magazines and a picture daily, and now that she had at last taken to it of her own accord, she seemed to be more conscious of the process of self-improvement than of pleasure in the book. She read with eyebrows slightly raised, lips moving, sitting very upright with a book on a level with her eyes, moistening her finger to turn the pages and clearing her throat decisively at the end of each chapter. When he looked up from his own reading or writing to ask companionably: 'Good book, Con?' she would say: 'Very interesting. You wouldn't enjoy it though; it's not a detective story,' as if he never read anything but that.

He was pleased that she had taken to reading, but he could not help wishing that it were not at the expense of the house. After all, why be married if you had to clean out the bath every time before you used it? It had been better when Dorothy was with them; at least, there had always been food in the house, but now, when he knew Connie was going out with Miss Bell, he always called in at the Lipmann's grocery on the way home. He had been told too often that they were so busy at the office that she had barely had time to pop out for lunch, let alone go hunting round for fish. She collected the rations all right on Saturday afternoons, but she was very good at running out of bread. People ate too much bread, she said. It wasn't good for you. Far better to eat the rye crispbread which she now placed on the table in a toast rack and nibbled at during the meal. Edward missed the fat Coburg loaves from which they used to hack doughy crusts all the way round, leaving the middle for breadcrumbs for treacle tart. They never had treacle tart nowadays. Connie hadn't time to make pastry.

It was not exactly that she was sloppy; indeed, she was more particular than ever about certain things. Milk now came to the table in a jug instead of its own bottle, and sardines never appeared in their tin. You must not help yourself to butter or cheese with your own knife, and since she had found that the Bells used mats on a polished table instead of a cloth, Connie had put away her tablecloths and got out the embroidered set that had been a wedding present. Edward might no longer come to the table in shirt-sleeves and slippers, because it would look so funny if anybody called; nor might he put his feet up on the fireplace when he sat in his arm-chair. She had varnished over the scratches on the paint that he had made over a span of years. Doilies and antimacassars broke out like a pox all over the place, and a little painted lacquer tray stood on the table in the hall for letters and circulars.

Their laundry bills were bigger now, but although she had no time to do any washing for Edward, she was for ever rinsing out and ironing collars and cuffs and little bows to wear at the office. She bought herself a pair of rubber gloves for washing up, but neglected to clean out the oven for so long that Edward had to do it himself one Sunday. She would dust with a feather duster and polish up the letter-box and knocker on the front door, but she never scrubbed floors now nor beat carpets. When Edward suggested mildly that she might give a little attention to the fundamentals of housework instead of only its trimmings, he had got the same reply as when he said that if she did not darn some of his socks soon he would have to go bare-legged: 'You know I'm at business all day. I can't be a slave to the house as I used. Goodness knows you were on at me often enough to take a job, and now that I have, you're still not satisfied, it seems.'

Of course he understood, but it seemed wrong to him that she did not care. Other women cared. Wendy had told him only the other day how she had spent the whole week-end doing what she called 'Autumn cleaning'. Spring cleaning was such fun, she said, that she didn't see why it should only be enjoyed once a year. But when he spoke to Connie about the dust under the bed, she said: 'Well, if you're so particular, I'll have to get a woman in to do the rough. Goodness knows we can afford it, and everybody else does.' But most women in Connie's position didn't. They were not as well off as all that. And most women would have stayed up all night sooner than let another woman rob them of the work that was theirs by right of being married.

And now there was no ink. This must certainly be the worst run house in Collis Park. What was the good of having a vase of artificial flowers on the sideboard when a man could not even fill his pen in his own house? thought Edward, angrily sharpening a pencil on the blunt bread-knife. He pulled out one of the paper carnations and threw it maliciously into the fire.

'Coccidiosis,' he wrote, sitting down slightly relieved, 'is the bugbear of every fancier, be he amateur or professional.' He looked sideways at the open page of the *Encyclopaedia of Rabbit Breeding*.

'It takes two forms,' he went on, adding 'as everyone knows,' in accordance with his policy of keeping himself on a level with his readers so as not to be didactic in his information. 'The bloated or dropsical cases, where the germ has attacked the bowel' – he crossed out 'bowel' and substituted 'colon' – 'are always fatal. Hard though it may be, it is best to kill the rabbit as soon as you detect trouble, knowing that you are cruel only to be kind.'

At the factory today, a man from the cylinder block fitting section had come in with a query about exhaust manifold nuts. The old man had obviously told him about Edward and the valves, for a half smile played about his lips as he watched Edward tackle Reenie, who was responsible for nuts and bolts. It was a silly query, for Edward knew that they pooled the manifold nuts in her Fitting Shop, so it was no tragedy if an engine did go through short, but the man pretended he could not read Reenie's handwriting. Although this was understandable, Edward thought it a trumped-up excuse to come and look at the curio – the charge-hand who did not know a dud valve from a good one. He treated the fitter with dignity and hoped he had not heard Reenie say: 'Oh, don't *nark* me, Ted. You'd better count the nuts yourself if you think I can't add.' He did not want everybody to know that his girls had no respect for him, even if it were true.

Finding that he was staring at the brown velvet curtains, with pencil poised, thinking about Canning Kyles instead of Coccidiosis, Edward shook himself and wrote: 'I was in my rabbitry with a friend the other day, talking shop as fanciers will the world over when they get together, and watching a litter of youngsters in a run, when one young doe left her succulent wild greens, walked a few paces, staggered and fell on her side. She got up, staggered again, and fell again, then got up and continued her repast.

'"I don't like that," said my friend. "Speaking as a poultry man, I've seen many a young fowl behave just like that when the Coccidiosis germ, which has been dormant in the gut, suddenly becomes active and strikes its victim."

'"I hope you're wrong, old man," I said, but I isolated the doe as a precaution, and sure enough she sank, so rapidly that I was obliged in a few days to put an end to her suffering.'

This was not true, but it was always best to illustrate a point from personal experience, to get the human touch.

'Don't blame me for not trying treatment; it would have been useless.' E. Dexter Bell always swore that he could cure intestinal Coccidiosis by a draught of his own invention comprising Permanganate of Potash, but Edward, trying it once as a last resort, had found it useless.

'Ah, you haven't the knack,' said Mr Bell, seeing himself as a kind of Bernadette of Lourdes. 'Don't ask me why, but it never fails with me. Never lost a rabbit yet.'

To get his own back, Edward wrote: 'Some people maintain that with strange alchemies of their own they can arrest this fell disease, but, personally, I don't believe a word of it.'

Feeling better, he wrote on rapidly. 'Now the second form, where the germ only attacks the liver, is quite a different pair of shoes. The rabbit loses flesh and becomes generally unthrifty, but does not necessarily lose his appetite. Tackle him right and he may yet turn out a good rabbit – nay, a prize-winner even. This is what I do.' He looked up again at the brown velvet curtains, seeking to make his treatment pithy. The editor was short of space this week.

Could he be bothered to get up and pull the curtains closer together in case the wardens came? It must be getting on for black-out time. He looked at his watch. Connie had said she would be back for supper, but if she didn't come soon he was going to get himself something to eat and be hanged with waiting. He was tired of coming home hungry and having to wait so long that he had lost his appetite by the time they did sit down. It had happened last week when Mr Bell had been coming to supper to talk over plans for the auction sale. Connie had come home all right in time to cook – oh yes, she could cook for company, if not for her husband, reflected Edward bitterly – but Mr Bell had arrived more than an hour late, sublimely unaware that he had kept them waiting. He had helped himself to the cottage pie with the same sublime unawareness that other people existed besides himself, so it was just as well that Edward was no longer hungry.

His mind wandered still farther away from Coccidiosis and brooded on their conversation after supper. It was a farce to call it discussing plans, when it consisted in Mr Bell laying down the law and overcoming any opposition by the simple expedient of raising his voice. He was going to give the sale great publicity; he was full of plans which seemed to Edward cheap and vulgar. The thing was taking on the nature of a stunt

312

instead of a sincere enterprise to promote rabbit breeding and raise money for the Red Cross.

'I'll have to see that we get a good write-up in the papers,' Mr Bell had said, drawing patterns on the tablecloth.

'I'll give it a good bit of space in *Backyard Breeding*, of course,' said Edward, feeling that here at least was something in which he had the advantage of Mr Bell.

'Do that by all means, my dear chap, but I was thinking of the real thing, papers that people read.'

'But they do read *Backyard Breeding*,' said Edward. 'It's got a circulation of –'

'Oh, yes, yes, a certain class of people do, I don't doubt, but we're aiming at the great general public, not at the poor little sheep who would trot anywhere after somebody that said "rabbits". You've got to learn to broaden your outlook, Ted. I was saying to Connie only today: "Ted's getting narrow-minded," I said. "He wants to go about more and see what's going on in the great world." Didn't I, Connie?' Connie nodded and bit off a thread. Edward had taken the opportunity of asking her to turn a pair of cuffs for him, knowing that she could not refuse with any graciousness in Mr Bell's presence.

When the broad figure had gone paddling off into the night, after standing long on the doorstep and letting a lot of cold air into the house, Edward had said to Connie: 'That chap certainly knows what he wants – and sees that he gets it. I only wish I could think that he were on the right tack.'

'You get on my nerves with all your moping and worrying, really you do,' said Connie, rolling up the shirt with only one cuff done. 'Why don't you leave the arrangements to him without trying to interfere? He knows much more about it than you do. You may know something about aeroplane engines, but that doesn't mean to say you know everything. Just because you're a charge-hand at Kyles, you can't expect to take charge everywhere.' She had gone up to bed, pleased with her pun, and there was Edward's see-saw, tipping him from one of his worries to the other again.

He had not mentioned his trouble at work to Connie. What was the use? She was no more interested in the factory than in rabbits, and even if she did listen, she would not try to understand or take his part. The habit of criticizing everything he did was too strong in her. She always knew he was wrong. If he told her it was quicker to go to Harrow by train, she would take a bus without further inquiry. If he said that he thought the Germans could not make another blitz on London, she would begin to agitate about the condition of their street shelter.

Sitting musing at the table, when he should have been writing his article, he allowed himself to wonder what it would be like to be married to a woman in whom you could confide. How different everything would be now if he could come home and indulge in self-pity and be told how unfair it was, and that of course he was in the right and that the Management ought to be shown up. He remembered how Tom Presser's wife had once come raging up to the factory like a tigress when Tom was being kept on night duty against the doctor's advice.

That was the sort of wife to have. For a long time now, Connie had not even been a wife to him in 'that way'. That bewildering but gratifying period when she had suddenly started being nice to him had not lasted very long. She was back on her own extreme edge of the bed, and it would take a thicker-skinned man than Edward to invite her into the middle.

Things might have been different if they had only had a child. They never would now. The last time he had suggested that Connie might pay another visit to the doctor, she had rounded on him with: 'If you ask me, it's you who ought to see a doctor, not me!' He had not mentioned the subject again.

Because he was feeling particularly low tonight, he allowed himself the forbidden fancy of what his life might have been if he had married someone different. The disturbing part of thinking like this was that, picture her as he might, the woman always insisted on looking like Wendy. If he went on imagining what life might have been like if he had married someone like Wendy, it made him feel embarrassed when he saw her next day.

He recollected himself, and, looking at his watch again, saw that he had not written a word for fifteen minutes. Here, this would never do. 'Snap out of it, Cheviot Freemantle,' he said, and got up briskly to pull the curtains across the window.

Sitting down again, he concentrated on his treatment of biliary Coccidiosis. 'I give no medicine,' he wrote. 'No bread, no bran or oats. I give milk only and any choice tit-bits of green

314

food that the ailing animal will fancy. Just as human invalids must be coaxed to eat, so with the invalid rabbit. Time spent on persuading it to partake of nourishment will not be wasted, believe me.'

He was well into his stride, when he heard Connie's key in the latch and then the thud of her umbrella dropping into the stand. She opened the door, breaking the thread of his thoughts, and he closed the book and stood up. He would finish the article later when she had gone to bed.

'Ah, there you are, Con. I was beginning to wonder what had happened to you. I'm as hungry as a hunter.'

She came into the room taking off her gloves, and then unwound her scarf and began to fold it carefully on the table, smoothing out the creases She looked subtly different tonight, flushed, as if she were excited about something or had been running. When she spoke, she did not meet his eyes. She went over to the mantelpiece and began to fiddle with the things on it, winding up the green glass clock, emptying a clean ashtray into the grate. She seemed to have something on her mind.

'Well,' said Edward, rubbing his hands. 'What's on the menu for tonight? Tell me what you want to have, and I'll get supper, Con, if you're tired.'

'I've got something to tell you, Edward,' she said, turning round to face him, as if she had not heard him.

'Fire away,' he said. 'If it's about that shaving mirror you broke, don't worry, because I've already seen it.'

'How silly you are!' She frowned at him. 'Can't you ever be serious except when you've got some worry about your Rabbit Club? You're glum enough then, goodness knows. In fact, that's why I haven't told you this before, although I've had it in my head for quite a time. You seemed so wrapped in yourself that I didn't think you'd trouble about discussing anything else.'

'Well, let's discuss it now,' said Edward, 'whatever it is, and get it over. I want my supper.'

She came forward and stood her large patent leather handbag on the table, resting her hands on it. 'There's nothing really to discuss now,' she said. 'I've made up my mind.' She went on rapidly, but speaking in that careful new voice of hers which she used not only with the Bells but when she spoke of them. 'You know how interested I am in my work at the estate agency.

I can't think what I should do without it now. Well, it happens that Edgar – Mr Bell has to go to Birmingham for a while to take charge of the branch of the agency there. They've got into difficulties through being under-staffed, and he has to go and straighten things out. Mr Lorrimer will take charge of the London branch; he's a very capable man.'

Edward was not interested in the machinations of Bell, Watson and Lampeter, but he said: 'How does it affect you though? I should have thought they'd need you at the office more than ever. Don't tell me your job's coming to an end; that would be too bad.'

'Oh, goodness no.' She gave a little laugh. 'Quite the reverse. The fact is, Ted, Mr Bell wants me to go up to Birmingham to work for him up there. They're short of staff, and I know his ways, you see.' She gave the little laugh again. 'He says he doesn't know how he would manage without me.'

'But Connie, you can't – I mean, where would you live? Unless you're planning to live with him by any chance?' he joked.

'Really, Ted. His sister's going, too, to keep house for them, and she's very kindly suggested that if I go up there to work, I should live with them as a paying guest.'

'You'd like that, I expect. How long would it be for, then? A week or so, just to help them to get straight, I suppose.'

Connie began to open and shut her fat, shiny bag, making a sharp click every time she snapped the fastener. 'A good deal longer than that, Ted. Mr Bell may take over the Birmingham branch permanently, and they'll let "Uanmee" and settle down up there as soon as they find a suitable house.'

Edward was so overjoyed at the news that Providence was ridding him of E. Dexter Bell that he did not realize at first what Connie was implying. His mind raced ahead. This would put paid to that auction sale, this would settle Mr Marchmont and the other grumblers. Edward would be able to refuse membership to pros, he could be President . . .

'Do you hear what I'm saying, Ted?' asked Connie tartly. 'I try to tell you that I mean to go away from here and you don't seem to trouble at all. I'm very glad I'm sure that it doesn't inconvenience you. That was the only thing that kept me from deciding, but now I see that I needn't have worried.' She took out her handkerchief and dabbed politely at one nostril. Connie never blew her nose, even when she had a cold.

'Well, here's a nice thing,' said Edward easily. 'My own wife walking out on me! This'll make some talk I can tell you.'

His jaw dropped suddenly in the middle of the laugh as he looked at her and realized all at once what she did mean.

'Con,' he said unbelievingly. 'You're joking. You don't honestly mean that you want to go away – apart from work, I mean. Aren't you happy here? I'll admit that we've had our little tiffs and all that sort of thing, but we've rubbed along all right up to now!' He was appalled. She was his wife, bound to him 'till death do us part'. She couldn't be suggesting – 'You can't mean that you want to make a break after all these years!' He leaned forward, trying to fathom her careful face.

'I never said that,' she hedged. 'If you like to take it that way, please yourself. As to being happy – well, if you've been happy, I'm very glad, I'm sure.' She sniffed. Edward wished that they could have both been sitting down. It felt so silly to be standing up like people on their way to somewhere when things were being said that were shattering the whole security of life.

'But I'd no idea! You mean you want to go away for *good*, Connie?' He could not seem to take it in. 'You don't want to come back at all?'

'Oh, don't be so sweeping,' she said irritably. 'Who knows what I'll do? I've merely said I'm going away for a bit and under the circumstances, I think it's the best thing for both of us. There's no need to be so dramatic about it.'

But Edward felt dramatic. He stopped her with a hand on her arm as she picked up her bag and made to go out of the room. 'Look here,' he said tensely. 'Are you trying to tell me you want a divorce, is that it?'

Connie recoiled slightly as she did when anyone called a stomach a belly. 'Divorce is an ugly word,' she said severely, and shaking off his hand, went out to the kitchen before she could be tricked into putting herself into the wrong by revealing her intentions.

He had not given Connie the satisfaction of hearing him say: 'But you can't go. How'll I manage without you?' Whenever she tried to make practical arrangements, he had waved them

317

aside, saying: 'Don't you worry about me. I shall get along famously.' She had suggested that he might like to let the house for a bit and take rooms in the neighbourhood, but he had laughed: 'Whatever for? D'you think I can't manage on my own? And where d'you think I'm going to keep my rabbits if I move out of the house?'

She was gone within a week, still not committing herself about the future. Mr Bell had behaved queerly. He had not come near Edward before he left, although Edward, in his delight at being rid of him, was quite willing to have a farewell party and part on the friendliest possible terms. Mr Bell had even avoided Dick, merely writing him a letter to apologize for leaving them in the lurch, and trusting that Dick would understand that the claims of business, etc. etc.

'What are we going to do?' Dick had kept moaning, when he showed Edward the letter. 'What about the auction? We'll never be able to carry it through on our own.'

'The auction, my dear Dick,' said Edward happily, 'is off – nah poo – down the drain.' He turned both thumbs towards the ground.

'But the Club! However are we going to carry it on without him? Looks as though we shall have to dissolve it, Ted,' said Dick, sticking out his underlip and staring dolefully at the floor.

'Dissolve it!' cried Edward, as hearty as E. Dexter Bell had ever been, giving Dick a clap across the shoulders that made him stagger and cough. 'You crazy fool. We're going to run it now as we never could before. We're going ahead with it in our own way. Listen, I've got plans for a bright little show . . .' But Dick had shaken his head and repeated: 'I don't like it, Ted. I don't like it.' So Edward had left him alone to recover from the blow of losing Edgar. He would come to presently. Dick needed time to cope with new situations.

Connie's family did not seem to realize that anything was wrong between her and Edward. They had accepted the explanation that she was going away on essential work, and rubbed into their neighbours at Schoolbred Buildings how important she was. Mrs Munroe had assured Edward that he would never manage. Mr Munroe had suggested that he might come and live with them at the Buildings, but had been sat on at once for his tactlessness. The flat was full enough already what with

Dorothy and the baby, even if Mrs Munroe had wanted Edward there. She was not prepared to help him in any way except to impress on him how much he would miss Connie.

Connie herself, just before she left, had wavered in the hall with the taxi ticking outside the gate. 'I'm sure I do hope you won't miss me too much,' she had said, longing for him to admit that he would. But he was not going to. He had covered up the awkwardness of her departure by giving her a hearty kiss and telling her that she would miss her train if she didn't get a move on. He waved her off from the gate and saw the corner of Mrs Dowlinson's front window curtain drop guiltily as he turned to go indoors and put the kettle on for his tea.

Connie had found a sloppy old woman who came in when she felt inclined and did a little short-sighted housework, and sometimes prepared something to eat. He hardly ever saw her, for she had always gone by the time he got home from work, and she communicated with him by a system of illiterate notes which she left in unexpected places all over the house.

'Did I do write to buy vim,' he found on the back of a coal bill lying in the bath. 'took 2 loaves from bker to last you sunday. Collifiour cheese is in ov.'

On Thursday there was always a note on his pillow or impaled on a stair rod or even curling up and browning on top of the boiler, to say: 'Don't forget to leve mony same place. You o me for:' —Here followed a list of sundries that she had been moved to buy in his interest.

He lived picnic fashion, using the same plate and knife and fork each time, eating in the kitchen, on the floor in front of the living-room fire, or even in bed if he felt like it. He was in his arm-chair one evening, with his shoes off and his feet up on the side of the fireplace, a cup of tea on the arm of the chair and the pot in the fender, a plate of bread and cheese and pickles in his lap. The old woman had not been in for the last three days. She seemed to have forgotten about him, but as he did not know where she lived, nor for certain whether her name was Mrs Whitten or Mrs Whiffen, he could not get hold of her.

The front door bell sounded unusually loud in the empty house. Dick probably. Grunting, Edward put the plate on the floor, heaved himself out of the chair and padded out to the front door in his stockinged feet.

An unknown woman in a three-cornered hat stood in the moonlight, looking out to the street. Unknown at least, until she turned round and he saw with surprise that invaluable Club member, Mrs Ledbetter.

'Glorious moon,' she said briskly. 'May I come in, Mr Ledward?'

She sat opposite him in Connie's chair, drinking tea, the tight skirt of her costume drawn up by the spread of her seated hips and her sturdy legs planted apart so that he had an occasional embarrassing glimpse of her bloomers, and told him an amazing story. She related it in her deep, matter-of-fact voice, her strong man's face unmoved, only the peak of her tricorne jerking forward every now and then to emphasize a point.

'If I did wrong, Mr Ledward, I can only say I'm sorry. I did what I thought right, and in view of what I discovered, I think I was justified. But if you're angry at my interfering, please say so.' She waited calmly for him to speak.

'Angry!' cried Edward. 'Why, I'm so pleased, I – I don't know what to say.' He spread his hands helplessly. 'You've done what I've been longing to do for months. I'd been convinced for ages that Bell wasn't playing the game.'

'Then why didn't you do something about it, if one may ask?'

'I couldn't. My wife works in his office, you see. He was quite a family friend, although I personally couldn't stand the sight of him. I simply couldn't make trouble, though goodness knows what it cost me to have to sit back and see him having his own way with the Club, and all of you getting dissatisfied – and I must say I don't blame you. But it's all right now, you know. He's gone, left the district – probably for good. Did you know?'

'Did I know? That's a good one!' She laughed resoundingly, slapping her hands on her thighs. 'Why it was I who made him go, Mr Ledward.'

'Oh, no, he had to go up to Birmingham on business, my wife told me.'

'Aha, that's the official excuse he gave, no doubt, to save his face, but the truth of the matter is after I'd done my detective work and confronted him with the proof of his dishonesty, he ran from me like a scalded cat. I made him. I gave him the alternative of clearing out or letting me set the B.R.C. on to him. The police even might have taken it up after I discovered that business about the Egg Club.'

'Egg Club?' asked Edward, bewildered.

'Oh, I didn't tell you. In addition to swindling over the bran ration and the flesh stock, he'd been getting people to give him their egg coupons to buy rations for his hens in return for giving them eggs when the hens started to lay.'

'But that's perfectly legal, isn't it? A lot of people do that.'

'Yes, but our friend Bell didn't have any hens! Not – one – hen.' She spaced the words out, accompanying each by a jerk of the tricorne. 'He would have been bound to have been rumbled sooner or later. I can't think how he was stupid enough to embark on such a thing. He was a very petty criminal, I'm afraid, Mr Ledward.' She washed her hands of him, and stood up. 'Well, I must be on my way now. I just thought I'd better come and confess to you what I'd done.'

'No, don't go yet, Mrs Ledbetter. I feel I haven't thanked you properly for all you've done.'

'It's Mr Ledbetter you ought to thank really,' she said. 'After all, it was he who had to force an entrance to the place and get me all the facts. I only put two and two together.'

'Jolly sporting of him,' said Edward.

'He didn't want to do it, I can tell you, but it was that or nothing. I couldn't go myself, you see, because Mr Bell knew me, but he never recognized my husband, although he's been at all the shows.' Of course he wouldn't. Insignificant Mr Ledbetter with his narrow, sloping shoulders was always occupied in the background at shows, washing up behind the refreshment counter, or labelling travelling boxes in a corner well out of sight.

Edward could not help smiling when he thought of him pretending to be a big stock breeder from Ireland and being shown round the stud at 'Uanmee' with all respect and flattery. What a fool old Bell must have felt afterwards! It was a joyous thought.

'Well,' said Mrs Ledbetter, moving towards the door. 'Give my regards to your wife. I'm sorry to have missed her. I don't think we've ever met.'

'No, she didn't – she doesn't come to the shows,' said Edward. 'She's away now, as a matter of fact.'

'Yes, I can see that.' Mrs Ledbetter looked round the untidy room, littered with traces of purely masculine occupation. Edward blushed and found himself telling her: 'As a matter of fact, she's gone up to Birmingham to work for Bell in his office. His sister's up there, you know, and she lives with them.'

Mrs Ledbetter was horrified. 'You don't mean to say that you've let her go up there with those horrible people? The sister's no better – I've seen her. Wouldn't trust her a yard. And that unpleasant man – no more than a common criminal! I don't know how you can have a moment's peace, Mr Ledward. I suppose you'll send for her though, now that you've heard what I told you tonight.'

Edward shrugged his shoulders. 'Wouldn't be much good, I'm afraid.' Somehow, he felt that he could confide in Mrs Ledbetter. 'She's a very independent character. Goes her own way, you know.'

'Yes, but she wouldn't want to stay up there once you'd told her.' Mrs Ledbetter had come back into the room, intrigued by Edward's domestic affairs.

'She wouldn't probably take it from me. She likes being up there. I had a letter from her only the other day, full of it. She seems to get on very well with the Bells and their friends.' Connie had written to him after three weeks, not from compunction, but to be sure he understood the high standard under which she was now living. There were dinner-parties; she had been to a civic function; the Bells were very well connected in Birmingham. She did not omit to mention that Miss Bell kept two maids, a sleeping-in cook and a daily, and she also alluded to hot lobster and mushrooms casually as if it were an everyday occurrence. It was all so different, she said. Quite a change. She said nothing at all about coming home.

'Yes, but you'll be glad to get her back, all the same, I dare say,' probed Mrs Ledbetter, watching him closely.

'I don't worry really. Connie can look after herself pretty well.'

'We must meet when she comes back. Perhaps you'd both come round to supper at the Hollies?'

'That's very kind of you. She won't be back just yet, though, I'm afraid.' Breaking down under her searching gaze, he suddenly said: 'I don't know why I should tell you, for I'm sure it can't interest you, but between you and me, she's been glad of the excuse to get away. We – we didn't get on too famously. Nothing serious, but you know how it is. Little things mount up. It was my fault entirely. I should have been able to make her happy, but evidently I didn't, and so –' he shrugged his shoulders. 'She decided to make a break.'

'Hm – hm.' The tricorne nodded. 'She did, did she? From my experience, Mr Ledward, it's the woman who makes or ruins a marriage, not the man. I don't think you should blame yourself.'

'If she never comes back,' said Edward, 'I shall always feel that it's my fault.'

'By the sound of it,' said Mrs Ledbetter, dogmatically, 'it wouldn't be the end of the world for you if she didn't. Am I right, or am I perhaps speaking out of turn?'

Edward gave her a nervous grin and then hung his head and said sheepishly, drawing his toe along the pattern of the carpet: 'I believe you are right, Mrs Ledbetter. It sounds terrible to say, but I'm happier without her than I ever was when she was at home.' He looked up to see whether she was scandalized, but she was grinning now.

'*I* thought so!' she said triumphantly, and having got to the bottom of things was ready now to take herself off. When she picked up her bag from the hall table, she saw the clear space it had made in the dust there.

'My goodness, Mr Ledward,' she said, 'you may be enjoying your bachelor freedom, but you can't live like this, you know. Haven't you anyone to do for you?' Edward told her about Mrs Whitten or Whiffen.

'Far too unreliable,' said Mrs Ledbetter, blowing dust off her bag. 'And what about your food? Does this woman cook for you?'

'Sometimes.'

'And other times?'

'Oh, I manage all right. I throw something together for myself. I usually have my main meal in the middle of the day, you know, so that I don't need much at night.'

'You need more than bread and cheese,' said Mrs Ledbetter, who had missed nothing in the living-room.

'I'm all right, really. It's very nice of you to bother, but –'

323

'And I'm going on bothering,' said Mrs Ledbetter. Now that the Bell business was finished with, she needed a new campaign. 'The first thing is, why do you stay on here? A man by himself doesn't want to be burdened with a house like this. Why not look for a flat, or I could find you some nice, homey rooms. I know my way about this district. I'd soon find you somewhere.'

Edward shook his head. 'No, I must stay here because of the rabbits, thanks all the same. I've got a couple of score now. I need all my garden space and more.'

'Yes, of course.' She understood this at once. 'Well, the thing then is to find you a good reliable little woman to come in by the day and look after you. I shall start right away in the morning making inquiries.'

'Please don't bother,' said Edward, but she did not even hear him. She looked round the hall, her mind busy with plans. 'You ought to get a better curtain on this door, then you could have more light in the hall. This is like a mausoleum.'

'I know,' said Edward, 'but it's always been like that.'

'The more I think of it,' she said suddenly, 'the more pleased I am with myself for having killed two birds with one stone.'

'I beg your pardon?'

'It was I who got rid of the Bell creature, wasn't it? And if he hadn't gone your wife wouldn't have gone either, would she? Think that over, Mr Ledward. You may think me interfering now, but I believe you'll come to thank me in the end. Good night.' Opening the door, before he could get to it, she was away down the path in the moonlight, squat and earthbound, quite the wrong shape for a fairy godmother.

Mrs Ledbetter, however, was cheated of her fun. Three days after their conversation, while she was still only on the distant scent of a good, reliable little woman, Edward suddenly forestalled her by finding not only one, but two good little women all by himself.

Wendy was at the end of her tether. In three weeks' time, Mrs Colquhoun would be turning them out and she still had not found anywhere to live. She was dreading to see her mother's face when she told her. If she did not find anywhere – and why should she now after two months of searching? – she had no idea what they were going to do. She saw them sleeping in the Tube, or in a street shelter. Perhaps they would have to go to the workhouse? What did people do?

Edward, coming back early from the canteen at lunch-time, found her hunched on her stool in the dark, deserted Shop, crying in quiet despair. There was nobody about, so he put his arms round her, gingerly at first and then tightening them as she made no resistance but turned and clung to him, burying her head on his chest.

She was lovely to hold. He had not embraced any woman but Connie for ten years, and never in his life one as fragile as this. She felt almost breakable. She smelled of apples and he was dying to kiss her thin white neck, wilting only an inch from his cheek. She was still crying, and when he bent his head, trembling, and just brushed her neck with his lips, he was not sure whether she felt it.

After she had told him, still with her face hidden, he had not at first dared to voice the thought, the wonderful thought that flashed across his brain like a light. It would be impossible. Things like that just didn't happen.

Only when she had sat up and apologized and was blowing her nose with a little snuffle, so exactly like that little grey doe, he said with his heart in his mouth, looking away from her out into the Shop, where stray lights were going on as people trickled back from lunch: 'Why don't you and your mother come and live with me for a bit? I'm all alone in the house. My wife's away – there's plenty of room.'

He did not have to explain about Connie because Wendy never tried to find out. She accepted the fact that Connie had gone away without curiosity, as naturally as she accepted his offer. When the light over the bench went on he saw that crying did not make her face ugly and blotchy. Her nose was not even red. She looked at him out of tired, wet eyes and simply said: 'Oh, Edward, *yes.*'

Was it only a month ago that Edward had sat trying to write about Coccidiosis and known that everything in his life was going wrong? The very day after Wendy arrived, bringing her mother along with the rest of her luggage, the shadow that lay over Edward at the factory was miraculously lifted. Ivy's husband arrived, truculent and not quite sober, to say that his wife wasn't coming in no more. She was fed up, that was what it was, and as far as she was concerned, they knew what they could do with their factory; she was going for a AT. She wasn't going to stop on and be suspicioned by everybody. She didn't fancy working in a place where people looked at a person as if they thought she had come in early and changed over the labels on the boxes of valves. An interesting possibility which Mr Gurley had not considered before, but now realized on further reflection to be the right one.

With the clearing of his name, Edward also discovered that it hardly needed clearing. Most people had forgotten the incident long ago. They had thought nothing of it at the time, they said, and Edward began to wonder whether the contumely in which he had thought himself held had not been mostly in his imagination.

'Just look what happens,' he said to Wendy in the garden that night. 'The day after you come to live with me, that business with the valves is cleared up at last and Ledward Julie has a first litter of six. You bring me luck, that's what it is.'

'Do I really?' she said seriously. The kitchen door opened and a bar of light slanted across the garden.

'Oh, mother, the blackout!' cried Wendy, starting forward, and obediently the kitchen light went off.

'Are you coming in to supper?' Mrs Holt's voice wavered and cracked when she tried to raise it.

'Rather.' Edward took Wendy's arm and moved with her towards the house. 'What's on the menu?'

'Fish,' said the voice. 'How do you want it done?'

'How do you usually have it?'

'We always used to have it boiled or steamed when father was alive,' said Wendy. Boiled or steamed: that was how Connie had always wanted it. He had not had a bit of fried fish in his own house for ten years.

'Do as you always do, of course,' he said, wanting them to feel they were at home.

'Well,' said Wendy tentatively, 'Mother and I really like it fried.'

Edward was so happy in his present life that he did not look far into the future. It was up to Connie to decide what she was going to do, and at the moment she showed no signs of wanting to come back. Her only communication in three months had been a postcard with a view of the Railway Hotel on one side and a request for her winter dressing-gown on the other.

Wendy, although she was equally happy, worried quite a lot. She had no idea what the situation was between Edward and his wife, and as he never mentioned it, she could not possibly ask. What worried her most of all was that she had decided that she was fonder of Edward than was right. Sometimes, as she lay in the double bed listening to the snufflings that came from the curled-up ball that was her mother, she found herself imagining wonderful things about the two of them, and had to make herself break off and think about something prosaic like tomorrow's supper.

Since that time when she had felt him kiss her neck in the dark Inspection Shop, he had never given her more than brotherly gestures of affection, but she knew that he was as happy in her company as she was in his. What was going to happen if his wife came home and she and her mother had to go away? She wished she could ask him.

When Connie did come home, Wendy was alone in the house. It was Sunday morning and Edward had taken Mrs Holt to Kew Gardens, while Wendy, in one of her old grey factory overalls and a sacking apron, did out her kitchen. The bell rang while she was scrubbing the floor and she got up, pink, wrinkled marks on her knees and clambered over the kitchen table which she had put outside in the passage, drying her hands on her apron as she went to the door.

Connie's eyebrows, which were plucked now and lengthened with a pencil, went up. This was not the woman she had found to clean for Edward.

'Is Mr Ledward in?' she asked, her eyes busy.

'I'm sorry,' said Wendy, 'he's out for the morning. Did you want to leave a message for him?' She thought it must be someone from the Club, and when Connie said: 'I am Mrs Ledward,' and stepped firmly into the hall, Wendy stood back against the wall with a sinking heart and could find nothing to say except 'Oh.'

Connie's eyebrows went higher and higher as she discovered who Wendy was, and that she and her mother were living in the house, although she kept saying: 'I see,' and 'naturally', as though she were not surprised at all.

In the sitting-room, her eyes travelled round, noting changes, dwelling on the row of plants on the window-sill and the picture of carthorses looking over a stable door, which Wendy had hung over the mantelpiece.

'Did you mean to – I mean, are you – will you be staying here tonight?' faltered Wendy. She would have to start packing at once and take her mother away as soon as she got back. She was too agitated to begin to think of where they would go.

'Good Heavens, no,' said Connie. 'I have to get back to Birmingham tonight. My friend had to come down on business, so I took the opportunity to come and collect one or two things I'd left here. What have you done with my green clock?'

'Oh, I'm sorry.' Wendy made a dive for the sideboard cupboard. 'I put it away because it loses so. It was always making us late for work.'

'I've never known that clock to lose,' said Connie. She took it from her and wound it, putting it on the table, where it ticked loudly in the silence between them.

'Please say when you want to come back,' said Wendy desperately at last, 'and my mother and I'll leave at once. We only came here, you see, because we were turned out of our house and couldn't find anywhere else.'

'I wouldn't hear of you going,' said Connie. 'I'm sure it's been very nice for my husband having someone to look after him. He could never have managed on his own.'

'Yes, but if you want to come back –'

'Oh, please don't think I want to come back,' said Connie with a little laugh, picking up a photograph of a rabbit with a silver cup and putting it down again as if it were no more than could be expected. 'There's far too much work for me to do up in Birmingham. I don't know what my friends would say, I'm sure, if I talked about leaving. And as far as I'm concerned, you're welcome to live in this house. I never did like it. It simply makes work and nothing to show for it. Now, if you don't mind, I'll go and look out the things I want. I haven't too much time.

I left a lot of winter things in a trunk in the cupboard under the stairs. I suppose it's still there?'

'Oh, yes,' said Wendy, thankful that it was. 'I'll just move the kitchen table for you. I stood it out there while I'm doing the floor. It's an awkward floor to do, isn't it, with all those corners?'

Connie had scrubbed it so seldom that she hardly knew. She looked at her smooth, secretary's hands with their oval nails and thought with satisfaction of the detached house on the out-skirts of Birmingham, which had a refrigerator and a gas boiler in the kitchen, which she hardly ever entered except on the maid's day out.

'But you mean she's not coming back at *all*?' Edward kept asking. 'I can't think why she hasn't written before and told me so.'

'Well, she didn't say exactly, but I don't think –'

'Why didn't you ask her what her plans were? I would like to have things straight, I must say.'

'I didn't like to. I wanted to, but – oh, Ted, it was so em-barrassing, her coming and finding me here, and in that awful old overall. I hardly knew what to say. I felt – I felt quite guilty.'

'You are a ninny.' Edward laughed at her, but he knew that power of Connie's of making you feel guilty. He went on chop-ping parsley for the sauce that Wendy was making. 'Only, if she's *not* coming back,' he began thoughtfully.

'She's not,' said Wendy quickly. 'I'm sure she's not. I didn't need to ask her, really, because I felt so sure from the way she spoke. I'm so sorry, Ted. It's not very nice for you.'

'Not nice!' He straightened up, holding the chopper like a weapon. 'Don't you see that if she stays away three years, that's desertion, legally, and you and I could – well, I hardly like to ask you, because I don't suppose you've ever thought about it, but would you consider it, Wendy, dear? Would you think about marrying me?'

'Yes I'll think about it,' said Wendy, who for several hours had been thinking of nothing else.

MORE ABOUT PENGUINS
AND PELICANS

For further information about books available from Penguins please write to Dept EP, Penguin Books Ltd, Harmondsworth, Middlesex, UB7 0DA.

In the U.S.A.: For a complete list of books available from Penguins in the United States write to Dept CS, Penguin Books, 625 Madison Avenue, New York, New York 10022.

In Canada: For a complete list of books available from Penguins in Canada write to Penguin Books Canada Ltd, 2801 John Street, Markham, Ontario L3R 1B4.

In Australia: For a complete list of books available from Penguins in Australia write to the Marketing Department, Penguin Books Australia Ltd, P.O. Box 257, Ringwood, Victoria 3134.

In New Zealand: For a complete list of books available from Penguins in New Zealand write to the Marketing Department, Penguin Books (N.Z.) Ltd, P.O. Box 4019, Auckland 10.

ORIGINAL SINS
Lisa Alther

'Triumphantly surpasses her splendid novel, *Kinflicks*' – *Cosmopolitan*

When Americans believed in God, Fidelity and the Flag Lisa Alther's five 'heroes' were childhood friends in small-town Tennessee. In this triumphant successor to *Kinflicks* she cuts their various careers through the sixties and seventies – back to nature, on to New York, into Civil Rights, women's liberation, the sexual revolution – and gives us a novel that is gutsy, funny, stylish ... a slice of American life you've never tasted before.

A WOMAN'S AGE
Rachel Billington

Stepping into the world of country houses and nannies at the turn of the century, we follow the life of Violet Hesketh, from childhood, through two world wars, the roaring twenties, the depression, through years of social and political upheaval, to the fulfilment of her ambitions, as a leading public figure and politician in the seventies.

'A remarkable history of women over three-quarters of a century' – *Financial Times*

THE MIDDLE GROUND
Margaret Drabble

Clever, impetuous, successful, Kate is at a crossroads, ready to defy fate. Suddenly in her forties, lapped by the affection of her children and her friends, she is forced to make a reconnaissance over the middle ground of her life.

'[Margaret Drabble] is becoming the chronicler of contemporary Britain, the novelist people will turn to a hundred years from now to find out how things were, the person who will have done for late twentieth-century London what Dickens did for Victorian London' – *The New York Times*

Monica Dickens
in Penguins

AN OPEN BOOK

Monica Dickens's light-hearted and honest autobiography takes us from her childhood in the upstairs, downstairs world of the twenties through her celebrated exploits as cook-general, nurse, munitions worker, provincial newspaper reporter, and, finally, bestselling novelist, wife and mother.

Charles Dickens's great-granddaughter shows here that she has inherited his humour and humanity, as well as his zest for everything that life has to offer.

'A rare slice of social history and also a warm self-portrait' – Peter Grosvenor in the *Daily Express*

'Lively, entertaining and gently self-mocking' – P. D. James in *The Times Literary Supplement*

'Entertaining, often touching, always humorous and, best of all, extremely readable' – Margaret Forster in the *Evening Standard*

Monica Dickens
in Penguins

'A novelist who has all the airs and graces a reader can wish. She can tell a story, she is funny, observant, tender, interested in the people she describes. She can etch a character in a single sentence' – John Betjeman in the *Daily Herald*

'In the very short list of the lighter novelists who are also true literary artists' – J. B. Priestley in the *Bookman*

'Perhaps the best woman novelist in Britain' – *Evening News*

'She presents a hilarious variety of character types ... with the brilliant but pitiless verve that is particularly her own' – Pamela Hansford Johnson